**SLOW DANCING
THROUGH TIME**

SLOW DANCING THROUGH TIME

STORIES BY

GARDNER DOZOIS

IN COLLABORATION WITH

JACK DANN, MICHAEL SWANWICK,
SUSAN CASPER & JACK C. HALDEMAN II

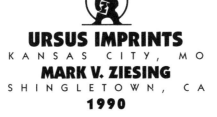

URSUS IMPRINTS
KANSAS CITY, MO
MARK V. ZIESING
SHINGLETOWN, CA
1990

Copyright acknowledgements are continued on page 252, which constitutes an extension of this copyright page.

Library of Congress Catalog Number: 90-71159
ISBN - Trade Edition: 0-942681-03-7   Signed, Limited Edition: 0-942681-04-5

FIRST EDITION
10 9 8 7 6 5 4 3 2 1

Ursus Imprints, 5539 Jackson, Kansas City, MO 64130

CONTENTS

for
Virginia Kidd

WRITE LIKE DOZOIS? I CAN'T EVEN SAY HIS NAME

MICHAEL BISHOP

Over the twenty years that Gardner and I have known each other, we've met in person less than half a dozen times — at a convention in Philadelphia, at a Nebula Awards banquet in New York City, at a booksellers convention in New Orleans, at the World Science Fiction Convention in Atlanta. Four meetings? I *believe* that's all, but memory is always suspect, and I sometimes fear that I wouldn't be able to pick mine out of a "Dragnet"-style lineup even if the other memories up there beside it belonged to, say, Jack Dann, Jay Haldeman, Michael Swanwick, and Susan Casper.

This is what I do remember: around the late 1960s/early 1970s, I read every number of three original SF anthology series: *Orbit* edited by Damon Knight, *New Dimensions* edited by Robert Silverberg, and *Universe* edited by Terry Carr. I was trying to write and sell stories of my own, and the stories in these volumes, especially by such writers as R. A. Lafferty, Kate Wilhelm, Gene Wolfe, Joanna Russ, Edgar Pangborn, and Silverberg himself, struck me as the best of that period's cutting-edge work — stuff I hoped to emulate and, as unlikely as it obviously was, even to surpass. My excuse for thinking that I had a shot at competing with these fine writers — in these prestigious, hard-to-crack anthologies — was that I was young yet, twenty-five, twenty-six, a virtual babe at my brand-new IBM Selectric. Just wait until I got cranked up. I'd overtake the leprechaunish Lafferty, the elegant Ms. Wilhelm, the subtle Wolfe, the sneakily profound Russ, the lyrical Pangborn, and even that prolific but literate Silverberg fellow in, hey, a year or two, tops. And then the SF world would know that a new Zelazny, a new Delany, a new whoever-was-hot-this-week had ridden into town to gun down yesterday's tomorrows.

Problem was, some upstart with a hard-to-say last name and an image-packed, rhythmic prose style had beat me to the draw and was filling up major portions of *Orbit, New Dimensions,* and *Universe* —not to mention other magazines and anthologies—with ambitious, gripping, imaginative, *successful* stories that I could read only with jealous awe. His stories had enigmatic, creep-under-your-skin titles— "Where No Sun Shines," "A Dream at Noonday," "The Last Day of July," "A Special Kind of Morning"—and, damn it all to Philadelphia and back, they actually conjured the kinds of stunning SF-grounded effects I hoped my unwritten stories would one day pull off. But this guy—a long-haired hippie-ish ex-soldier, to paint a rough portrait from some of what Silverberg said about him in his various introductions—was already doing what I still only hoped to do. Worse, it seemed that this infuriating Doh-ZOYS was—damn it all to Alpha Centauri and back—younger than I was, maybe by as much as two years.

AARRRGGH!!!

How did I first make contact with this DUZ-wheeze person? If I remember correctly (and I may not), it was Gardner (thank God his first name wasn't Aloysius or Heneage or Vyvyan) who contacted me. In the late 1960s/early 1970s, he was working, or had worked, as a slush-pile reader for Ejler Jakobsson at *Galaxy* and *If* magazines, and my first sale of a science fiction story was to *Galaxy* with a Bradburyesque little piece titled "Piñon Fall." At the time, I thought that Mr. Jakobsson had discovered my story in his morning's mail, read it with both alacrity and appreciation, and set it aside for six months to allow his admiration to cool. (No, no, no—I figured that the post office had lost my manuscript in the mails.) Actually—or, a bit closer to "actually"—Gardner, according to a letter written in 1970 or 1971, had found "Piñon Fall" in *Galaxy's* slush pile, had liked it well enough to tell Mr. Jakobsson, and had urged him to buy it. The sale took place, and my story appeared in *Galaxy's* October-November 1978 issue, along with the third part of Robert A. Heinlein's *I Will Fear No Evil* and a Silverberg novella called "The World Outside."

So, in a very real way, I owe my first legitimate SF sale to this Duh-ZOID person. With that sale as a credit, I was able to persuade other editors—Edward L. Ferman, David Gerrold, Damon Knight, and, eventually, even Robert Silverberg—to pay me real money (two to five cents a word) for the stories rattling out of my Selectric. In fact, it was Gardner, telling me that he had found "Piñon Fall" among *Galaxy's* unsolicited submissions, who urged me to try to enhance my earnings, my visibility, and my reputation as an up-and-comer by submitting material to the hardcover anthologies then enjoying both a gratifying popularity and a degree of prestige unknown at the digest-sized magazines. ''If,'' wrote Gardner, ''you have something available, you ought to send it to *New Dimensions*.'' He listed reasons, all of which struck me as convincingly astute, and I wrote back to thank him but also to point out that I had only a story or two to my credit and didn't have anything else ''lying around'' for *New Dimensions* or *Orbit* or *Quark*. I was in awe of this Dō-ZWAH fellow (roughly, the correct pronunciation), but I would have never told him so, for my immature competitiveness kept me from viewing anyone younger than myself as a mentor, that person's demonstrable talents be damned. I just couldn't imagine having new stories always at hand, the way this guy apparently did.

Later, I learned that Gardner wasn't as prolific as I had first thought him to be. He worked hard over each of his stories, with the patience and precision of a lapidary, and the style in which he couched his gnomic musings about fate, man's inhumanity to man, and the alien strangeness of life in this universe often verged on the achingly beautiful. It still does, but, briefly at least, he was the object of a couple of bad raps, namely, that his work was pessimistic and/or defeatist, that he was a writer more interested in fine writing than in substance, and that the most likely result of reading his stuff — for those who care mostly for story, with little attention to or concern for style — was the cultivation of an ulcerous depression.

Balderdash, every charge. Gardner always puts his style at the service of content. Early stories like ''Chains of the Sea,'' ''The Visible Man,'' and ''A Special Kind of Morning,'' as well as such fine later stories as ''Dinner Party,'' ''The Peacemaker,'' ''Morning Child'' (the latter two are Nebula Award winners), and ''Solace'' disclose a writer with an insightful sense of what our humanity often demands of or takes from us. Further, Gardner has a compassion big enough to redeem his put-upon and/or wrung-out characters from the snares that they have fallen into or laid for themselves — even when that redemption is philosophical rather than physical. Maybe, in fact, especially then.

But *Slow Dancing* is a collection of collaborations, not of solo stories, so let me add here that the Gardner Dozois who shows up in these collaborations has an antic streak that isn't always visible in his solo work. That's not to say that you won't recognize the ''serious'' Dozois (familiar to us from *The Visible Man* and the four other noncollaborative stories just listed) from ''Touring,'' ''Down

Among the Dead Men,'' ''Executive Clemency,'' and the psychological horror tales ''Playing the Game'' and ''The Clowns,'' but that
at least a bit of the madcap Gardner Dozois, known for years to
convention-goers, crops up conspicuously, and hilariously, in the
stories ''A Change in the Weather,'' ''Afternoon at Schrafft's,''
''Golden Apples of the Sun,'' ''The Stray,'' ''Send No Money,'' and
(maybe idiosyncratically, my favorite of the collection) the at-once
funny and touching ''Slow Dancing with Jesus.''

(By the way, about this last story, Gardner writes, ''I alone am
responsible for the appalling joke at the story's end.'' I may be a
little weird, but I don't see the story's final line—at least on one
level—as either appalling or laughable. It is, I suppose, but it also
isn't. As a result, ''Slow Dancing with Jesus'' harbors resonances
that hoist it out of the territory of clever commercial writing into
the heady vicinity of—hush, now—art. And it may even be why this
volume uses the title of my favorite of Gardner's collaborative efforts
as its title piece, sort of.)

Okay, so you get Gardner being madcap, antic, cutuppish, and
downright laugh-out-loud funny in some of these stories (along with
his fine collaborators, of course). What else do you get? To my mind,
maybe the most obvious thing you get—and why not, given the
diverse hands that brought these stories into existence?—is *variety*.
You get horror (''Down Among the Dead Men,'' ''Touring,'' ''The
Clowns,'' etc.), science fiction (''Executive Clemency,'' ''The Gods
of Mars,'' ''Time Bride,'' ''Snow Job,'' etc.), and fantasy (''Slow
Dancing with Jesus,'' ''Afternoon at Schrafft's,'' ''A Change in the
Weather,'' ''Golden Apples of the Sun,'' ''The Stray,'' etc.). And
it's interesting to note, too, that many of the stories I've arbitrarily
plunked into one category—horror, science fiction, or fantasy—
actually cross genres, sometimes repeatedly. Far more important
to Gardner and his collaborators than into which bin to place one
of their productions were the lovable mongrel demands of an individual tale's own internal logic. Thus, ''Playing the Game'' is both
horror and SF, ''Time Bride'' both humor and smoothly didactic SF,
''Touring'' both wish-fulfillment fantasy and an unsettling kind of
existential horror. And so on.

Suffice it to say that this is a wide-ranging, entertaining, colorful,
and unpredictable collection of stories, well worth both your time
and your money.

I'm sorry—truly sorry—that there's no story here with a byline
citing Michael Bishop as a collaborator of Gardner's. Once upon a
time, I made a half-hearted attempt at a collaboration when Gardner

sent me the opening of a long SF story and gently suggested that I ponder the material to see if I could add to and maybe even resolve the conflicts already set forth—but I stuck, and never got unstuck, and finally Gardner opted to pass the material along to George R. R. Martin. That was a wise decision, even if he and George haven't yet finished the story either, but I remain jealous of all the good souls—Jack, Jay, Michael, and Susan—who have collaborated successfully with Gardner.

I hope that one day, if only for a wisecracking short-short, I can join their company and experience myself the exhilaration of working with Gardner, of bouncing ideas off his bizarrely flexible brain, and of hitting again and again those high-paying slick markets that so often featured his and his collaborators' cunningly hewn stories—tales of mystery, imagination, and *joie de vivre*.

I'm not sure I know how to pronounce *joie de vivre*, but I know it when I encounter it, and Gardner's undoubtedly got it. Over the past few years, incidentally, I *have* learned how to pronounce his lovely last name.

(To reiterate: Dō-ZWAH, Dō-ZWAH, Dō-ZWAH.)

And I keep hoping that some small relaxation of his editorial duties—he does a bang-up job at *Isaac Asimov's Science Fiction Magazine,* assembles a respected annual best-of-the-year anthology, and edits a series of entertaining theme anthologies with Jack Dann—will give him more writing time of his own. In the meantime, we have this handsome collection, and I'm damned grateful to the folks at Ursus Imprints that we do.

February 26-27, 1990
Pine Mountain, Georgia

HOW DID THEY *DO* THAT?

PAT CADIGAN

Immediately, I understood there was Chemistry at work, definitely the capital-C variety. This is the kind you feel when it all works, everything's in synch, in phase — so much so that even the conflicting forces make it all come out right. For a result like that, you need the right combination of people to strike a spark — or maybe it's more like a quark. Then just stand back and watch what happens. You're going to get either some great stories or some great parties. And if you're enormously lucky, both.

So how did they do it?

Further on, you can read the individual accounts of how the stories came about, from Susan's perspective, and Michael's, and Jack Dann's, and Jack Haldeman's. You'll be entertained and amused and you'll learn a few things about some special people who found a way around what I think of as the writer's Privacy Fence. Not all writers can do that and of those who can, not all of them can do it well — and of that minority, almost none can do it with more than two. But here we have some stories with *three* names on them. So how did they *do* it?

It drove me crazy. I wanted to know. I pored over the accounts, looking for the key phrase (or phrases) that would give me the royal road into the process and enable me to divine what was at work here.

My first thought, after all this reading and re-reading, was that I was sorry I hadn't been there. I mean, talk about a writer's idea of a good time —! And . . . well . . . that's about it, really. Sounds like everyone involved was having a good time, and that wasn't exactly a revelation to me. Even though I wasn't around for the collaborating, I've been at a few of the parties.

Only once, however, have I seen all the people in this book in one place at one time. That was in Boston, at the 1989 World Science Fiction Convention. I gather that doesn't happen very often, probably less often than the Worldcon, which is annual.

Most often, I see Gardner and Susan together, but they're married, so that figures. And I suppose it also figures that two writers under the same roof would think of collaborating. The thing is, Gardner and Susan were together for a number of years before Susan's first published work came out, a nasty story having to do with Jack the Ripper and video games called "Springfingered Jack." Then there was "Mama," the kind of horror story anyone who's ever had a mother can relate to; and "The Cleaning Lady," about the woman who breaks into people's houses and *cleans* them; and "Under Her Skin," about the fat vampire—not an obese vampire, but a vampire that makes Weight Watchers obsolete (I didn't make this up; Susan did); and "A Child of Darkness," about a vampire wannabe.

Where Gardner writes mostly science fiction, Susan has gone her own way in horror, speaking in her own voice and doing just fine. I know her work well, but I cannot point to any part of the stories she has had a hand in and say, *There she is—she starts here and leaves off here and comes back again over here.* And yet there in "Send No Money," I hear her. In the blend of "The Clowns," a three-way collaboration, I pick up on her presence and I know that without her, it wouldn't have been the same. How did they *do* that?

Besides Gardner and Susan, only Michael Swanwick also lives in Philadelphia. (Philadelphia is also home to Tess Kissinger, the only person I know of who went to the prom with Jesus. Interesting town.) Author of *In the Drift* and *Vacuum Flowers*, as well as numerous acclaimed short stories like Nebula-nominee "The Feast of St. Janis" and Hugo-nominee "The Edge of the World," Michael is also a fine writer on his own. When I first met him, I thought he would probably have been at home in Monty Python. That kind of humor, by turns goofy and sophisticated, always springing from the unexpected, delivered in a voice that I think of as the sound of merry. I am privileged to own—no, sorry, *my son* owns and I am privileged to borrow (once in a while) a rare cassette recording of the funniest children's story ever, *The Two Buildings Do Lunch,* as performed and interpreted by the authors, Michael and his son Sean. I picture Marianne Porter (wife and mother, respectively) listening to this with a smile identical to my own.

This is the same guy who collaborated on "Snow Job," a story I could see belonging to either him or Gardner—and as Gardner

explains elsewhere, it was more collaboration by surprise than de-
sign. Okay—but how to account for the seamlessness of "Touring"?
If you don't know which part is Michael's, you'll never figure it out.
But you can hear him, loud and clear. How did they *do* that?

Jack Dann lives in upstate New York with his wife Jeanne Van
Buren Dann and son Jody, and if you don't know that he, too, is
another major individual author on his own, you must have just fallen
off the turnip truck yesterday. My initial impression was that Jack
and Gardner had known each other forever, circularly—i.e., they
never actually met for the first time, they'd just always known each
other. Put them together for any length of time and they start sounding like each other. Okay, *I* think they start sounding like each other.
They also get *really silly.* Jack Dann, author of *Junction* and *The
Man Who Melted,* "The Dybbuk Dolls" and "Camps," *giggling?*
Meeting my husband for the first time and ruffling his hair and pinch-
ing his cheek? (Hell, *I* didn't do that the first time *I* met Arnie.) Jack
Dann, distinguished author, extrovert, and party man.

And not just collaborative writer, but editor, too—*Future Power,
MagiCats!, DogTales! Mermaids!* with Gardner, *In the Field of Fire*
with Jeanne, as well as editing alone: *Wandering Stars* and *More
Wandering Stars.*

If I were to put my finger over the byline of "Down Among the
Dead Men," (for one example) this could be either Gardner's alone
or Jack's alone—but if I didn't know for sure, I could not attribute
it to only one or the other by guessing. I hear them both. Granted,
I'm the one who thinks they sound alike, but I meant their speaking
voices. Their writing voices are quite individual, but here they blend,
and boy, does it work. Just like in "Time Bride" and "Slow Dancing
with Jesus" (which also may give you some idea of how funny it
can get at those parties). How did they *do* that?

Jack C. Haldeman is funny, too, another fine author in his own
right, with over forty short stories and three novels to his credit.
He shares with Jack Dann the distinction of being a genuine Jack—
i.e., not a John calling himself Jack but bearing it as his real first
name. I first met him and his wife Vol in New Orleans a couple of
years ago, long after I heard Gardner read "Executive Clemency"
at a convention. Already familiar with Jack's humor in stories like
"Wet Behind the Ears" and "My Crazy Father Who Scares All
Women Away," the story made me blink. It still does. There are
things about the story that are Gardner, but Jack is also unmistakably

and equally present—once again, the voices merge and harmonize without undercutting each other, resulting in a very different story than either of them would have written alone. How did they *do* that?

Well, yes, I did mention Chemistry, didn't I? You could just say Chemistry and leave it at that . . . and I'm afraid that's exactly what you'd have to do. That kind of Chemistry you can't cultivate artificially or bring out by decree or demand. It just happens between people, between writers. *Among* writers, for God's sake. So here they are, in twos and threes, all of them with Gardner in common— and now that I think of it, that's just like all those great parties I've been to. Which means, I guess, that no matter how they did it, we're all going to have a good time here, and that's what really counts.

COLLABORATING

GARDNER DOZOIS

We started writing these collaborative stories at a time when I had been in a creative slump for a couple of years, and, looking at them from the narrowest and most selfish perspective possible, they were invaluable to *me* because they helped to jump-start my creativity, shake me out of a dry spell, and launch me into a high-production period in which I completed, in addition to these collaborations, quite a few stories of my own.

Of course, they were valuable for a lot more than that. For one thing, they made us all a fair amount of money, and got us, as authors, some worthwhile exposure in prestige markets where we had previously been little known. For another thing, we ended up with a bunch of stories that none of us would ever have written on our own, and most of them were, at the least, worth the writing. (I know that I am leaving us wide-open to some sneering hostile critic here, but I *do* think that the collaborative stories were worth writing, and, for what *it's* worth, the public response to them has been pretty good as well — many of them have been reprinted and anthologized, a few have shown up on award ballots, some have been picked up by Best of the Year anthologies, and so forth. My *mother* liked them, or no doubt would have *said* so anyway if she'd ever read any of them. So there.)

For yet another thing, I think that doing them taught us all quite a bit about the craft of writing, about our own strengths and weaknesses as writers, and, ideally, how to *combine* those strengths to create a synergistic effect that sometimes enabled us to accomplish things beyond the ability of any one of us alone.

For me, these collaborations are inextricably bound up with workshopping, and in a sense arose out of the workshopping process itself. Workshop bashing is a popular sport, with some curmudgeon always willing to pop up and blame the decline and moral decay of science fiction as a genre on the advent of workshopping—and it is true that the big formalized teaching workshops like Clarion have their drawbacks (they also have their *good* points, however, something the curmudgeons are never willing to admit). . . . Nevertheless, working SF writers have been getting together to analyze and critique each others' work—take each others' stories apart to see why they're not working right—since before there was such a thing as SF as a formalized genre; Lovecraft and Bloch and Leiber did it—by mail—in the '30s; the Futurians—Kornbluth, Pohl, Knight, Blish, etc.—did it in the '50s, and writers have been doing it ever since. I suspect that they will keep on workshopping too, despite the curmudgeons, since if you can find some people who really know how to workshop—a big "if," admittedly—and who are temperamentally suited to survive the process with their egos reasonably intact, and if those workshoppers are willing to stick to practical nuts-and-bolts criticism rather than spouting ideological party lines or wandering away into the airy realms of obtuse aesthetic theorizing (the two biggest workshop-killers), then workshopping can be a highly valuable tool, not only for fixing flaws in specific stories, but also for learning something about writing as a craft.

I had belonged to one such workshop—the Guilford Workshop—in the early '70s. Perhaps not coincidentally, it was after that workshop had dissolved, and I no longer had any outside inputs on my work, that I slowly drifted into a long dry spell. I'm sure that it was not at all coincidental that my creative juices started to flow again after I got into the habit of having frequent informal workshop sessions with Jack Dann and Michael Swanwick, and, later, after she herself had started to write, with Susan Casper.

These sessions started sometime in 1977, and increased in frequency throughout 1978 and 1979. I was not producing much fiction myself at that point, but Jack was working on a novel he wanted advice on, and Michael was working on the early stories with which he would soon launch his writing career and wanted advice on *them* . . . and so, even though I had nothing of my own to place upon the sacrificial altar (which is considered bad form, usually), we began workshopping; at first, I worked with them individually, and then, after one memorable drunken evening, we all started workshopping together. And at some point in late 1979 or early 1980, we slid from these workshopping sessions to the idea of working on stories together, a transition so natural, gradual, and imperceptible that we almost didn't notice it. Before we quite realized what was happening, we were actually *writing* collaborative stories, in various combinations, and then we started *selling* them.

And so, we kept on doing it.

Perhaps because the collaborations evolved organically from the workshopping experience, we instinctively stumbled upon what I consider to be one of the secrets of successful collaboration, *especially* of *three-way* collaborations, which are as rare as hen's teeth: somebody must do a final unifying and homogenizing draft of the story, smoothing out differences in style, and that somebody must have the authority to decide what goes into the finished draft and what must come out, especially if there are alternate versions or drafts of the same section by different hands. With most of these stories, the person who did that final draft was me, perhaps because of my long experience as a story doctor, perhaps because Jack and Michael had already become inured in the workshop to having me inflict such advice upon them and the habit had been formed. At any rate, nobody ever complained about it, nor was it something that was ever discussed or questioned or formalized — it just worked out that way, an unspoken assumption. Perhaps because the collaborations grew out of workshopping sessions, where we were all used to commenting upon each other's work, regarding a bit of prose as something to be reshaped and changed in the crucible, mutable, improve-uponable, ''in progress,'' we never had any major ego clashes over these stories — although many another collaborative team has foundered on the shoals of Injured Vanity — and those minor ego problems and clashes of creative vision we did have were fleeting and easily worked out.

We just *wrote* the stories, without intellectualizing the collaborative process much, each writer contributing what they could, one set of hands picking up what another set had put down, all of us concentrating on ways to get the *story* down on paper however we could, by hook or crook, whatever worked, changing things around, discarding what didn't work, working things *out* . . . and it wasn't until much later when editors began to marvel that three such different writers could possibly work well-enough together to produce a viable three-way collaboration without murdering each other, that it even occurred to us that we might be doing something unusual.

A word on marketing is perhaps in order, before we get to the stories themselves. These collaborations were all strange stuff, pretty offbeat, occasionally bizarre, and were all pretty much beyond

3

the pale as far as the traditional digest SF-magazine world of the late '70s and early '80s was concerned. Instead—again, without conscious design or even thinking about it much—we ended up selling most of them outside the strict genre boundaries of the time. Kathy Green at *Penthouse* bought several of them, as did Ellen Datlow at *Omni,* and Alice K. Turner at *Playboy.* One of them appeared in *Oui,* another appeared in *The Twilight Zone Magazine,* and yet another appeared in, of all places, *High Times.* Later, we sold one to *Amazing* and then one to *Isaac Asimov's Science Fiction Magazine*—under Shawna McCarthy at this point, when the magazine had started loosening-up—and later still a few of these stories were reprinted in the *Magazine of Fantasy and Science Fiction* and in *Isaac Asimov's Science Fiction Magazine,* but their *initial* acceptance was with the so-called "slick magazine" market; only retroactively did they penetrate the genre market. The funny thing about all this is that there were only a handful of SF writers in those days who were appearing with any regularity in all of the "Big Three" slick markets (*Playboy, Penthouse,* and *Omni*): Robert Silverberg, Thomas M. Disch, Harlan Ellison, and *us.* There were writers working in the genre market who had far bigger reputations than Jack or Michael or I, but somehow we were selling to those markets—the top-paying fiction markets in the country—and they weren't; I suspect that's at least partially because they weren't bothering to submit to those markets, something that doesn't seem to have changed much subsequently.

Once again, we'd done something right—mostly by accident, as usual.

(From here on in, my comments will appear *after* the stories, since I intend to give too much away in them about some of the stories for them to function well as headnotes. Somewhere in this book, scattered throughout at the whim of the publisher, you'll also find general comments by Jack, Michael, Susan, and Jay Haldeman.)

∎
∎
∎
∎
∎

Touring

GARDNER DOZOIS, JACK DANN, & MICHAEL SWANWICK

The four-seater Beechcraft Bonanza dropped from a gray sky to the cheerless winter runways of Fargo Airport. Tires touched pavement, screeched, and the single-engine plane taxied to a halt. It was seven o'clock in the morning, February 3, 1959.

Buddy Holly duckwalked down the wing and hopped to the ground. It had been a long and grueling flight; his bones ached, his eyes were gritty behind the large, plastic-framed glasses, and he felt stale and curiously depressed. Overnight bag in one hand, laundry sack in the other, he stood beside Ritchie Valens for a moment, looking for their contact. White steam curled from their nostrils. Brown grass poked out of an old layer of snow beside the runway. Somewhere a dog barked, flat and far away.

Behind the hurricane fence edging the field, a stocky man waved both hands overhead. Valens nodded, and Holly hefted his bags. Behind them, J. P. Richardson grunted as he leaped down from the plane.

They walked towards the man across the tarmac, their feet crunching over patches of dirty ice.

"Jack Blemings," the man rasped as he came up to meet them. "I manage the dancehall and the hotel in Moorhead." Thin mustache, thin lips, cheeks going to jowl—Holly had met this man a thousand times before: the stogie in his mouth was inevitable; the sporty plaid hat nearly so. Blemings stuck out a hand and Holly shuffled his bags awkwardly, trying to free his own hand. "Real pleased to meet you, Buddy," Blemings said. His hand was soggy and boneless. "Real pleased to meet a real artist."

He gestured them into a showroom-new '59 Cadillac. It dipped on its springs as Richardson gingerly collapsed into the back seat. Starting the engine, Blemings leaned over the seat for more introductions. Richardson was blowing his nose, but hastily transferred the silk handkerchief into his other hand so that they could shake. His delighted-to-meet-you expression lasted as long as the handshake, then the animation went out of him, and his face slumped back into lines of dull fatigue.

The Cadillac jerked into motion with an ostentatious squeal of rubber. Once across the Red River, which still ran steaming with gunmetal pre-dawn mist, they were out of North Dakota and into Moorhead, Minnesota. The streets of Moorhead were empty — not so much as a garbage truck out yet. "Sleepy little burg," Valens commented. No one responded. They pulled up to an undistinguished six-story brick hotel in the heart of town.

The hotel lobby was cavernous and gloomy, inhabited only by a few tired-looking potted rubber plants. As they walked past a grouping of battered arm-chairs and sagging sofas toward the shadowy information desk in the back, dust puffed at their feet from the faded gray carpet. An unmoving ceiling fan threw thin-armed shadows around the room, and everything smelled of old cigar butts and dead flies and trapped sunshine.

The front desk was as deserted as the rest of the lobby. Blemings slammed the bell angrily until a balding, bored-looking man appeared from the back, moving as though he were swimming through syrup. As the desk clerk doled out room keys, still moving like a somnambulist, Blemings took the cigar out of his mouth and said, "I spoke with your road manager, must've been right after you guys left the Surf Ballroom. Needed his okay for two acts I'm adding to the show." He paused. "S'awright with you, hey?"

Holly shrugged. "It's your show," he said.

Holly unlaced one shoe, let it drop heavily to the floor. His back ached, and the long, sleepless flight had made his suit rumpled and sour-smelling. One last chore and he could sleep: he picked up the bedside telephone and dialed the hotel operator for an outside line, so that he could call his wife Maria in New York and tell her that he had arrived safely.

The phone was dead; the switchboard must be closed down. He sighed and bent over to pick up his shoe again.

Eight or nine men were standing around the lobby when Holly stepped out of the elevator, husky fellows, Southern boys by the look of them. Two were at the front desk, making demands of the clerk, who responded by spreading his arms wide and rolling his eyes upward.

Waiting his turn for service, Holly leaned back against the counter, glanced about. He froze in disbelief. Against all logic, all possibility, Elvis Presley himself was standing not six yards away on the gray carpet. For an instant Holly struggled with amazement. Then a second glance told him the truth.

Last year Elvis had been drafted into the army, depriving his fans of his presence, and creating a ready market for those who could imitate him. A legion of Presley impersonators had crowded into the welcoming spotlights of stages across the country, trying vainly to fill the gap left by the King of Rock and Roll.

This man, though—he stood out. At first glance, he *was* Elvis. An instant later you saw that he was twenty years too old and as much as forty pounds overweight. There were dissolute lines under his eyes, and a weary, dissipated expression on his face. The rigors of being on the road had undone his ducktail, so that his hair was an untidy mess, hanging down over his forehead, and curling over his ears. He wore a sequined shirt, now wrinkled and sweaty, and a suede jacket.

Holly went over to introduce himself. "Hi," he said, "I guess you're playing tonight's show."

The man ignored his outthrust hand. Dark, haunted eyes bored into Holly's. "I don't know what kind of game you're playing, son," he said. A soft Tennessee accent underlaid his words. "But I'm packing a piece and I know how to use it." His hand darted inside his jacket, emerged holding an ugly-looking .38.

Involuntarily Holly sucked in his breath. He slowly raised his hands shoulder-high, and backed away. "Hey, it's okay," he said. "I was just trying to be friendly." The man's eyes followed his retreat suspiciously, and he didn't reholster the gun until Holly was back at the front desk.

The desk clerk was free now. Holly slid three bills across the counter, said, "Change please." From the corner of his eye, he saw the imitation Elvis getting into the elevator, surrounded by his entourage. They were solicitous, almost subservient. One patted the man's back as he shakily recounted his close call. *Poor old man,* Holly thought pityingly. The man was really cracking under the pressures of the road. He'd be lucky to last out the tour.

In the wooden booth across the lobby, Holly dumped his change on the ledge below the phone. He dialed the operator for long distance.

The earpiece buzzed, made clicking noises. Then it filled with harsh, actinic static, and the clicking grew faster and louder. Holly jiggled the receiver, racked the phone angrily.

Another flood of musicians and crew coursed through the lobby. Stepping from the booth, ruefully glancing back at the phone, he collided with a small woman in a full-length mink. "Oof," she said, then reached out and gave him a squeeze to show there were no hard feelings. A mobile, hoydenish face grinned up at him.

"Hey, Sport," she said brightly. "I *love* that bow-tie. and those glasses—! Jesus, you look just like Buddy Holly!"

"I know," he said wryly. But she was gone. He trudged back to the elevators. Then something caught his eye, and he swung about, openly staring.

Was that a *man* she was talking to? My God, he had hair down to his shoulders!

Trying not to stare at his amazing apparition, he stepped into the elevator. Back in his room, he stopped only long enough to pick up his bag of laundry before heading out again. He was going to have to go outside the hotel to find a working phone anyway; he might as well fight down his weariness, hunt up a laundromat, and get his laundry done.

The lobby was empty when he returned through it, and he couldn't even find the desk clerk to ask where the nearest laundromat was. Muttering under his breath, Holly trudged out of the hotel.

Outside, the sun was shining brilliantly but without warmth from out of a hard, high blue sky. There was still no traffic, no one about on the street, and Holly walked along through an early morning silence broken only by the squeaking of his sneakers, past closed-up shops and shuttered brownstone houses. He found a laundromat after a few more blocks, and although it was open, there was no one in there either, not even the inevitable elderly Negro attendant. The rows of unused washing machines glinted dully in the dim light cast by a flyspecked bulb. Shrugging, he dumped his clothes into a machine. The change machine didn't work, of course, but you got used to dealing with things like that on the road, and he'd brought a handkerchief full of change with him. He got the machine going, and then went out to look for a phone.

The streets were still empty, and after a few more blocks it began to get on his nerves. He'd been in hick towns before—had grown up in one—but this was the sleepiest, *deadest* damn town he'd ever seen. There was still no traffic, although there were plenty of cars parked by the curbs, and he hadn't seen another person since leaving the hotel. There weren't even any *pigeons*, for goodness sake!

There was a five-and-dime on the corner, its doors standing open. Holly poked his head inside. The lights were on, but there were no customers, no floorwalkers, no salesgirls behind the counters. True, small-town people weren't as suspicious as folk from the bigger cities—but still, this *was* a business, and it looked as if anyone could just walk in here and walk off with any of the unguarded merchandise. It was gloomy and close in the empty store, and the air was filled with dust. Holly backed out of the doorway, somehow not wanting to explore the depths of the store for the sales personnel who *must* be in there somewhere.

A slight wind had come up now, and it flicked grit against his face and blew bits of scrap paper down the empty street.

He found a phone on the next corner, hunted through his handkerchief for a dime while the wind snatched at the edges of the fabric. The phone buzzed and clicked at him again, and this time there was the faint high wailing of wind in the wires, an eerie, desolate sound that always made him think of ghosts wandering alone through the darkness. The next phone he found was also dead, and the next.

Uneasily, he picked up his laundry and headed back to the hotel.

The desk clerk was spreading his hands wide in a gesture of helpless abnegation of responsibility when the fat Southerner in the sequined shirt leaned forward, poked a hard finger into the clerk's chest, and said softly, "You know who I am, son?"

"Why, of course I do, Mr. Presley," the clerk said nervously. "Yessir, of course I do, sir."

"You say you know who I am, son," Elvis said in a cottony voice that slowly mounted in volume. "If you know who I am, then you *know* why I don't have to stay in a goddamned flophouse like this! Isn't that right? Would you give your mother a room like that, you know goddamned well you wouldn't. Just what are you people thinking of? I'm *Elvis Presley*, and you'd give me a room like that!"

Elvis was bellowing now, his face grown red and mottled, his

9

features assuming that look of sulky, sneering meanness that had thrilled millions. His eyes were hard and bright as glass. As the frightened clerk shrank back, his hands held up now as much in terror as in supplication, Elvis suddenly began to change. He looked at the clerk sadly, as if pitying him, and said, "Son, do you know who I am?"

"Yessir," whispered the clerk.

"Then can't you see it?" asked Elvis.

"See what, sir?"

"That I'm *chosen!* Are you an atheist, are you a goddamned atheist?" Elvis pounded on the desk and barked, "I'm the star, I've been given that, and you can't soil it, you atheist bastard! You *sonovabitch!*" Now that was the worst thing he could call anyone, and he never, almost never used it, for his mother, may she rest in peace, was holy. *She* had believed in him, had told him that the Lord had chosen *him,* that as long as he sang and believed, the Lord would take care of him. Like this? Is this the way He was going to take care of me?

"*I'm* the star, and I could *buy* this hotel out of my spare change! Buy it, you hear that?" And even as he spoke, the incongruity of the whole situation hit him, really hit him hard for the first time. It was as though his mind had suddenly cleared after a long, foggy daze, as if the scales had fallen from his eyes.

Elvis stopped shouting and stumbled back from the desk, frightened now, fears and suspicions flooding in on him like the sea. What was he doing *here?* Dammit, he was the King! He'd made his comeback, and he'd played to capacity crowds at the biggest concert halls in the country. And now he couldn't even remember how he'd gotten here—he'd been at Graceland, and then everything had gotten all foggy and confused, and the next thing he knew he was climbing out of the bus in front of this hotel with the roadies and the rest of the band. Even if he'd agreed to play this one-horse town, it would have to have been for charity. That's it, it had to be for charity. But then where were the reporters, the TV crews? His coming here would be the biggest damn thing that had ever happened in Moorhead, Minnesota. Why weren't there any screaming crowds being held back by police?

"What in hell's going on here?" Elvis shouted. He snatched out his revolver, and gestured to his two bodyguards to close up on either side of him. His gaze darted wildly about the lobby as he tried to look into every corner at once. "Keep your eyes open! There's something funny—"

At that moment, Jack Blemings stepped out of his office, shut the door smoothly behind him, and sauntered across the musty old carpet toward them. "Something wrong here, Mr. Presley?" he drawled.

"Damn *right* there is," Elvis raged, taking a couple of steps toward Blemings and brandishing his gun. "You know how many *years* it's been since I played a tank town like this? I don't know what in hell the Colonel was thinking of to send me down here. I—"

Smiling blandly and ignoring the gun, Blemings reached out and touched Elvis on the chest.

Elvis shuddered and took a lurching step backward, his eyes glazing over. He shook his head, looked foggily around the lobby, glanced down at the gun in his hand as though noticing it for the first time, then holstered it absent-mindedly. "Time's the show tonight?" he mumbled.

"About eight, Mr. Presley," Blemings answered, smiling. "You've got plenty of time to relax before then."

Elvis looked around the lobby again, running a hand through his greased-back hair. "Anything to do around here?" he asked, a hint of the old sneer returning.

"We got a real nice bar right over there the other side of the lobby," Blemings said.

"I don't drink," Elvis said sullenly.

"Well, then," Blemings added brightly, "we got some real nice pinball machines in that bar too."

Shaking his head, Elvis turned and moved away across the lobby, taking his entourage with him.

Blemings went back to his office.

J. P. Richardson had unpacked the scotch and was going for ice when he saw the whore. There was no mistaking what she was. She was dressed in garish gypsy clothes with ungodly amounts of jewelry about her neck and wrists. Beneath a light blouse her breasts swayed freely—she wasn't even wearing a bra. He didn't have to be told how she had earned the mink coat draped over one arm.

"Hey, little sister," Richardson said softly. He was still wearing the white suit that was his onstage trademark, his "Big Bopper" outfit. He looked good in it, and knew it. "Are you available?"

"You talking to me, honey?" She spoke defiantly, almost jeeringly, but something in her stance, her bold stare, told him she was ready for almost anything. He discreetly slid a twenty from a jacket pocket, smiled and nodded.

"I'd like to make an appointment," he said, slipping the folded bill into her hand. "That is, if you *are* available now."

She stared from him to the bill and back, a look of utter disbelief on her face. Then, suddenly, she grinned. "Why, 'course I'm available, sugar. What's your room number? Gimme ten minutes to stash my coat and I'll be right there."

"Room four-eleven." Richardson watched her flounce down the hall, and, despite some embarrassment, was pleased. There was a certain tawdry charm to her. Probably ruts like a mink, he told himself. He went back to his room to wait.

The woman went straight to the hotel bar, slapped the bill down, and shouted, "Hey, kids, pony up! The drinks are on Janis!"

There was a vague stirring, and two or three lackluster men eddied toward the bar.

Janis looked about, saw that the place was almost empty. A single drunk sat wall-eyed at a table, holding onto its edges with clenched hands to keep from falling over. To the rear, almost lost in gloom, a big stud was playing pinball. Two unfriendly types, who looked like bodyguards, stood nearby, protecting him from the empty tables. Otherwise — nothing. "Shoulda taken the fat dude up on his offer," she grumbled. "There's nothing happening *here*." Then, to the bartender, "Make mine a whiskey sour."

She took a gulp of her drink, feeling sorry for herself. The clatter of pinball bells ceased briefly as the stud lost his ball. He slammed the side of the machine viciously with one hand. She swiveled on her stool to look at him.

"Damn," she said to the bartender. "You know, from this angle that dude looks just like *Elvis*."

Buddy Holly finished adjusting his bow-tie, reached for a comb, then stopped in mid-motion. He stared about the tiny dressing room, with its cracked mirror and bare light bulbs, and asked himself, *How did I get here?*

It was no idle, existential question. He really did not know. The last thing he remembered was entering his hotel room and collapsing on the bed. Then — here. There was nothing in between.

A rap at the door. Blemings stuck his head in, the stench of his cigar permeating the room. "Everything okay in here?"

"Well," Holly began. But he went no further. What could he say? "How long before I go on?"

"Plenty of time. You might want to catch the opener, though—good act. On in ten."

"Thanks."

Blemings left, not quite shutting the door behind him. Holly studied his face in the mirror. It looked haggard and unresponsive. He flashed a toothy smile, but did not feel it. God, he was tired. Being on the road was going to kill him. There had to be a way off the treadmill.

The woman from the hotel leaned into his room. "Hey, Ace—you seen that Blemings motherfucker anywhere?"

Holly's jaw dropped. To hear that kind of language from a woman—from a *white* woman. "He just went by," he said weakly.

"Shit!" She was gone.

Her footsteps echoed in the hallway, were swallowed up by silence. And that was *wrong*. There should be the murmur and nervous bustle of acts preparing to go on, last-minute errands being run, equipment being tested. Holly peered into the corridor—empty.

To one side, the hall dead-ended into a metal door with a red EXIT sign overhead. Holly went the other way, toward the stage.

Just as he reached the wings, the audience burst into prolonged, almost frenzied applause. The Elvis impersonator was striding on-stage. It was a great crowd.

But the wings were empty. No stagehands or go-fers, no idlers, nobody preparing for the next set.

"Elvis" spread his legs wide and crouched low, his thick lips curling in a sensual sneer. He was wearing a gold lamé jumpsuit, white scarf about his neck. He moved his guitar loosely, adjusting the strap, then gave his band the downbeat.

> Well it's one for the money
> Two for the show
> Three to get ready
> Now go cat go!

And he was off and running into a brilliant rendition of "Blue Suede Shoes." Not an easy song to do because the lyrics were laughable. It relied entirely on the music, and it took a real entertainer to make it work.

This guy had it all, though. The jumps, gyrations, and forward thrusts of the groin were stock stuff—but somehow he made them look right. He played the audience, too, and his control was perfect. Holly could see shadowy shapes beyond the glare of the footlights, moving in a more than sexual frenzy, was astonished by their rapturous screams. All this in the first minutes of the set.

He's good, Holly marveled. Why was he wasting that kind of talent on a novelty act? There was a tug at his arm, and he shrugged it off.

The tug came again. "Hey, man," somebody said, and he turned to find himself again facing the woman. Their eyes met and her expression changed oddly, becoming a mixture of bewilderment and outright fear. "Jesus God," she said in awe. "You *are* Buddy Holly!"

"You've already told me that," he said, irritated. He wanted to watch the man on stage—who *was* he, anyway?—not be distracted by this foul-mouthed and probably not very clean woman.

"No, I mean it—you're *really* Buddy Holly. And that dude on stage—" she pointed—"he's Elvis Presley."

"It's a good act," Holly admitted. "But it wouldn't fool my grandmother. That good ol' boy's forty if he's a day."

"Look," she said. "I'm Janis Joplin. I guess that don't mean nothing to *you,* but—Hey, lemme show ya something." She tried to tug him away from the stage.

"I want to see the man's act," he said mildly.

"It won't take a minute, man. And it's important, I swear it. It's— you just gotta see it, is all."

There was no denying her. She led him away, down the corridor to the metal door with its red EXIT sign, and threw it open. "Look!"

He squinted into a dull winter evening. Across a still, car-choked parking lot was a row of faded brick buildings. A featureless gray sky overhung all. "There used ta be a lot more out here," Janis babbled. "All the rest of the town. It all went away. Can you dig it, man? It just all—went away."

Holly shivered. This woman was crazy! "Look, Miss Joplin," he began. Then the buildings winked out of existence.

He blinked. The buildings had not faded away—they had simply ceased to be. As crisply and sharply as if somebody had flipped a switch. He opened his mouth, shut it again.

Janis was talking quietly, fervently. "I don't know what it is, man, but something *very weird* is going down here." Everything beyond the parking lot was a smooth even gray. Janis started to speak again, stopped, moistened her hips. She looked suddenly hesitant and oddly embarrassed. "I mean, like, I don't know how to break this to ya, Buddy, but you're *dead.* You bought it in a plane crash way back in '59."

"This *is* '59," Holly said absently, looking out across the parking lot, still dazed, her words not really sinking in. As he watched, the cars snapped out of existence row by row, starting with the furthest row, working inward to the nearest. Only the asphalt lot itself remained, and a few bits of litter lying between the painted slots. Holly's groin tightened, and, as fear broke through astonishment, he registered Janis's words and felt rage grow alongside fear.

"No, honey," Janis was saying, "I hate to tell ya, but this is 1970." She paused, looking uncertain. "Or maybe not. Ol' Elvis looks a deal older than I remember him being. We must be in the future or something, huh? Some kinda sci-fi trip like that, like on *Star Trek?* You think maybe we—"

But Holly had swung around ferociously, cutting her off. "*Stop it!*" he said. "I don't know what's going on, what kind of trick you people are trying to play on me, or how you're doing all these things, but I'm not going to put up with any more of—"

Janis put her hand on Holly's shoulder; it felt hot and small and firm, like a child's hand. "Hey, listen," Janis said quietly, cutting him off. "I know this is hard for you to accept, and it *is* pretty heavy stuff . . . but Buddy, you're *dead.* I mean, really you are. . . . It was about ten years ago, you were on tour, right? And your plane *crashed,* spread you *all* over some farmer's field. It was in all the goddamm papers, you and Ritchie Valens, and . . ." She paused, startled, and then grinned. "And that fat dude at the hotel, that must've been the *Big Bopper.* Wow! Man, if I'd known *that* I might've taken him up on it. You were all on your way to some diddlyshit hick town like . . ." She stopped, and when she started to speak again, she had gone pale. ". . . like Moorhead, Minnesota. Oh Christ, I think it *was* Moorhead. Oh boy, is that spooky. . . ." She fell silent again.

Holly sighed. His anger had collapsed, leaving him hollow and confused and tired. He blinked away a memory that wasn't a memory of torn-up black ground and twisted shards of metal. "I don't *feel* dead," he said. His stomach hurt.

"You don't *look* dead, either," Janis reassured him. "But honey, I mean, you really *were.*"

They stood staring out across the now-vacant parking lot, a cold, cinder-smelling wind tugging at their clothes and hair. At last, Janis said, her brassy voice gone curiously shy, "You got real famous, ya know, after . . . afterwards. You even influenced, like, the *Beatles.* . . . Shit, I forgot—I guess you don't even know who they *are,* do you?" She paused uncomfortably, then said, "Anyway, honey, you got real famous."

"That's nice," Holly said dully.

The parking lot disappeared. Holly gasped and flinched back. Everything was gone. Three concrete steps with an iron pipe railing led down from the door into a vast, unmoving nothingness.

"What a trip," Janis muttered. "What a trip. . . ."

They stared at the oozing gray nothingness until it seemed to Holly that it was creeping closer, and then, shuddering, he slammed the door shut.

Holly found himself walking down the corridor, going noplace in particular, his flesh still crawling. Janis tagged along after him, talking anxiously. "Ya know, I can't even really remember how I got to this burg. I was in L.A. the last I remember, but then everything gets all foggy. I thought it was the booze, but now I dunno."

"Maybe you're dead too," Holly said, almost absent-mindedly.

Janis paled, but a strange kind of excitement shot through her face, under the fear, and she began to talk faster and faster. "Yeah, honey, maybe I am. I thought of that too, man, once I saw you. Maybe whoever's behind all this are *magicians,* man, black magicians, and they conjured us all *up.*" She laughed a slightly hysterical laugh. "And you wanna know another weird thing? I can't find any of my sidemen here, or the roadies, or *anybody,* ya know? Valens and the Bopper don't seem to be here either. All of 'em were at the hotel, but backstage here it's just you and me and Elvis, and that motherfucker Blemings. It's like *they're* not really interested in the rest of them, right? They were just window dressing, man, but now they don't need 'em anymore, and so they sent them *back.* We're the headline acts, sweetie. Everybody else *they* vanished, just like they vanished the fucking parking lot, right? Right?"

"I don't know," Holly said. He needed time to think. Time alone.

"Or, hey—how about this? Maybe you're *not* dead. Maybe we got nabbed by flying saucers, and these aliens faked our deaths, right? Snatched you out of your plane, maybe. And they put us together here—wherever here is—not because they dig Rock—shit, they probably can't even *understand* it—but to study us and all that kinda shit. Or maybe it *is* 1959, maybe we got kidnapped by some time-traveller who's a big Rock freak. Or maybe it's a million years in the future, and they've got us all *taped,* see? And they want to hear us, so they put on the tape and we *think* we're here, only we're not. It's all a recording. Hey?"

"I don't *know.*"

Blemings came walking down the corridor, cigar trailing a thin plume of smoke behind him. "Janis, honey! I been beating the bushes for you, sweetie-pie. You're on in two."

"Listen, motherfuck," Janis said angrily. "I want a few answers from you!" Blemings reached out and touched her hand. Her eyes went blank and she meekly allowed him to lead her away.

"A real trouper, hey?" Blemings said cheerfully.

"Hey!" Holly said. But they were already gone.

Elvis laid down his guitar, whipped the scarf from his neck, and mopped his brow with it. He kissed the scarf and threw it into the crowd. The screams reached crescendo pitch as the little girls fought over its possession. With a jaunty wave of one hand, he walked offstage.

In the wings, he doubled over, breathing heavily. Sweat ran out of every pore in his body. He reached out a hand and no one put a towel in it. He looked up angrily.

The wings were empty, save for a kid in big glasses. Elvis gestured weakly toward a nearby piece of terrycloth. "Towel," he gasped, and the kid fetched it.

Toweling off his face, Elvis threw back his head, began to catch his breath. He let the cloth slip to his shoulders, and for the first time got a good look at the kid standing before him. "You're Buddy Holly," he said. He was proud of how calmly it came out.

"A lot of people have told me that today," Holly said.

The crowd roared, breaking off their conversation. They turned to look. Janis was dancing onstage from the opposite side. Shadowy musicians to the rear were laying down a hot, bluesy beat. She grabbed the microphone, laughed into it.

"Well! Ain't this a kick in the ass? Yeah. Real nice, real nice." There were anxious lines about her eyes, but most of the audience wouldn't be able to see that. "Ya know, I been thinking a lot about life lately. 'Deed I have. And I been thinkin' how it's like one a dem ole-time blues songs. Ya know? I mean, it *hurts* so bad and it feels so *good!*" The crowd screamed approval. The band kept laying down the rhythm. "So I got a song here that kind of proves my point."

She swung an arm up and then down, giving the band the beat, and launched into "Heart and Soul."

"Well?" Elvis said. "Give me the message."

Holly was staring at the woman onstage. "I never heard anyone sing like that before," he murmured. Then, "I'm sorry—I don't know what you mean, Mr. Presley."

"Call me Elvis," he said automatically. He felt disappointed. There had been odd signs and omens, and now the spirits of departed Rock stars were appearing before him—there really ought to be a message. But it was clear the kid was telling the truth; he looked scared and confused.

Elvis turned on a winning smile, and impulsively plucked a ring

17

from one of his fingers. It was a good ring; lots of diamonds and rubies. He thrust it into Holly's hands. "Here, take this. I don't want the goddamned thing anymore, anyway."

Holly squinted at the ring quizzically. "Well, put it on," Elvis snapped. When Holly had complied, he said, "Maybe you'd better tell me what you *do* know."

Holly told his story. "I understand now," Elvis said. "We're caught in a snare and delusion of Satan."

"You think so?" Holly looked doubtful.

"Squat down." Elvis hunkered down on the floor, and after an instant's hesitation, Holly followed suit. "I've got powers," Elvis explained. "The power to heal—stuff like that. Now me and my momma, we were always close. Real close. So she'll be able to help us, if we ask her."

"Your mother?"

"She's in Heaven," Elvis said matter-of-factly.

"Oh," Holly said weakly.

"Now join hands, and concentrate real *hard*."

Holly felt embarrassed and uncomfortable. As a good Baptist, which he certainly tried to be, the idea of a backstage séance seemed blasphemous. But Elvis, whether he was the real item or not, scared him. Elvis's eyes were screwed shut and he was saying, "Momma. Can you hear me, momma?" over and over in a fanatic drone.

The séance seemed to go on for hours, Holly suffering through it in mute misery, listening as well as he could to Janis, as she sung her way through number after amazing number. And finally, she was taking her last bows, crowing "Thank you, thank you," at the crowd.

There was a cough at his shoulder, and a familiar stench of tobacco. Holly looked up. "You're on," Blemings said. He touched Holly's shoulder.

Without transition, Holly found himself onstage. The audience was noisy and enthusiastic, a good bunch. A glance to the rear, and he saw that the backup musicians were not his regular sidemen. They stood in shadow, and he could not see their faces.

But the applause was long and loud and it crept up under his skin and into his veins, and he knew he had to play *something*. "Peggy Sue," he called to the musicians, hoping they knew the number. When he started playing his guitar, they were right with him. Tight. It was a helluva good backup band; their playing had bone and sinew to it. The audience was on its feet now, bouncing to the beat.

He gave them "Rave On," "Maybe Baby," "Words of Love," and "That'll be the Day," and the audience yelped and howled like wild beasts, but when he called out "Not Fade Away" to the musicians, the crowd quieted, and he felt a special, higher tension come into the hall. The band did a good, strong intro, and he began singing.

I wanna tell you how it's gonna be
You're gonna give your love to me

He had never felt the music take hold of him this immediately, this strongly, and he felt a surge of exhilaration that seemed to instantly communicate itself to the audience, and be reflected back at him redoubled, bringing them all up to a deliriously high level of intensity. Never had he performed better. He glanced offstage, saw that Janis was swaying to the beat, slapping a hand against her thigh. Even Elvis was following the music, caught up in it, grinning broadly and clapping his ring-studded hands.

For love is love and not fade away.

Somewhere to the rear, one of the ghostly backup musicians was blowing blues harmonica, as good as any he'd ever heard.

There was a flash of scarlet, and Janis had run onstage. She grabbed a free mike, and joined him in the chorus. When they reached the second verse, they turned to face each other and began trading off lines. Janis sang:

My love's bigger than a Cadillac

and he responded. His voice was flat next to hers. He couldn't give the words the emotional twist she could, but their voices synched, they meshed, they worked together perfectly.

When the musical break came, somebody threw Janis a tambourine, so she could stay onstage, and she nabbed it out of the air. Somebody else kicked a bottle of Southern Comfort across the stage, and she stopped it with her foot, lifted it, downed a big slug. Holly was leaping into the air, doing splits, using every trick of an old rocker's repertoire, and miraculously he felt he could keep on doing so forever, could stretch the break out to infinity if he tried.

Janis beckoned widely toward the wings. "Come on out," she cried into the microphone. "Come on."

To a rolling avalanche of applause, Elvis strode onstage. He grabbed a guitar and strapped it on, taking a stance beside Holly. "You don't mind?" he mumbled.

Holly grinned.

They went into the third verse in unison. Standing between the other two, Holly felt alive and holy and—better than either alive or holy — *right*. They were his brother and sister. They were in tune; he could not have sworn which body was his.

Well, love is love and not fade away

Elvis was wearing another scarf. He whipped it off, mopped his brow, and went to the footlights to dangle it into the crowd. Then he retreated as fast as if he'd been bitten by a snake.

Holly saw Elvis talking to Janis, frantically waving an arm at the crowd beyond the footlights. She ignored him, shrugging off his words. Holly squinted, could not make out a thing in the gloom.

Curious, he duckwalked to the edge of the stage, peered beyond.

Half the audience was gone. As he watched, the twenty people furthest from the stage snapped out of existence. Then another twenty. And another.

The crowd noise continued undiminished, the clapping and whooping and whistling, but the audience was *gone* now — except for Blemings, who sat alone in the exact center of the empty theater. He was smiling faintly at them, a smile that could have meant anything, and, as Holly watched, he began softly, politely, to applaud.

Holly retreated backstage, pale, still playing automatically. Only Janis was singing now.

Not fade away

Holly glanced back at the musicians, saw first one, then another, cease to exist. Unreality was closing in on them. He stared into Elvis's face, and for an instant saw mirrored there the fear he felt.

Then Elvis threw back his head and laughed, and was singing into his mike again. Holly gawked at him in disbelief.

But the *music* was right, and the *music* was good, and while all the rest — audience, applause, someplace to go when the show was over — was nice, it wasn't necessary. Holly glanced both ways, and saw that he was not the only one to understand this. He rejoined the chorus.

Janis was squeezing the microphone tight, singing, when the last sideman blinked out. The only backup now came from Holly's guitar — Elvis had discarded his. She knew it was only a matter of minutes before the nothingness reached them, but it didn't really matter. *The music's all that matters,* she thought. *It's all that made any of it tolerable, anyway.* She sang.

Not fade away

Elvis snapped out. She and Holly kept on singing.

20   *If anyone out there is listening,* she thought. *If you can read my*

mind, or some futuristic bullshit like that—I just want you to know that I'd do this again anytime. You want me, you got me.

Holly disappeared. Janis realized that she had only seconds to go herself, and she put everything she had into the last repetition of the line. She wailed out her soul, and a little bit more. *Let it echo after I'm gone,* she thought. *Let it hang on thin air.* And as the last fractional breath of music left her mouth, she felt something seize her, prepare to turn her off.

                   Not fade away

It had been a good session.

A F T E R W O R D   T O
TOURING

This was the first of the collaborations, and, as I've mentioned, an important story for me, since it was the first story I'd worked on in a couple of years.

I wasn't keeping up my work calendar at that point, so the exact date of this story's origin is lost in the mists of time. My own guess is that we started work on it one weekend in the spring or summer of 1979 when Jack was down for a visit. I know that a complete draft of it was finished in time for it to be submitted for scrutiny at the first formal workshop we held—a full-dress affair, with several other writers in attendance, as opposed to our regular sessions, which consisted of Jack and Michael and me sitting around somewhere with a bottle of wine—the first Philford Workshop, held over the weekend of April 11-13, 1980, at Michael and Marianne's house. (A few years later, the weekend of May 16-18, 1986, we held the second Philford Workshop at my new apartment on Spruce Street; so far no third.) And I know that I read the final draft of the story to a convention crowd in Austin, Texas, on October 4, 1980, when I was down there doing a Guest Of Honor stint at Armadillocon, but whether the story had been initially completed in late 1979 or early 1980, I can no longer recall.

Michael's recollection is that Jack and I had come up with the idea for this story on our own the night before, and that when Michael came over to my place for a visit the next day, we cut him in on the story because we knew that he'd just written a story featuring Janis Joplin and another featuring Buddy Holly, and we were too lazy to duplicate his research. My own recollection is that Michael had actually *been* there the night before, when Jack and I came up with the idea for this story during a brainstorming session, and that we cut him in on the *spot,* because we were too lazy to duplicate his research, and so on. (Actually — he says piously — I did end up duplicating much of Michael's research anyway in the course of writing the story, and even ended up correcting him on a point of Buddy Holly Trivia. For Elvis Trivia we depended on Jack, who is a much bigger Elvis fan than either Michael or myself.)

I'm pretty sure that it was Jack who first said that it would have been neat if Buddy Holly, Janis Joplin, and Elvis had ever gotten a chance to perform together. As soon as he said this, the basic plot of the story blossomed in my mind in an instant, and a few moments later we were hammering out details of the storyline. I conceived of it from the start as a *Twilight Zone* episode — I still think that it would have made a good one — and that's the way we wrote it; if you like, you can visualize the ghost of Rod Serling looming up solemnly at the end to wrap things up before the commercial.

Our original plan, I think, was that each of us would take one character and write about that character throughout — I was assigned to do Buddy Holly, Michael got Janis Joplin, and Jack, of course, got Elvis — but this quickly proved to be unworkable, and we all ended up writing scenes for each other's characters: Michael, for instance, writing the very funny scene where Elvis coerces Buddy Holly into praying to Momma with him, and I contributing a long scene where Janis raps semi-hysterically about just what might be happening to them all. After we gave up on the initial plan, my memory is that Michael wrote the first complete draft of the story, incorporating most of the pages we'd produced under the abortive one-character-per-writer plan, Jack then did another draft, and I then did a final unifying draft, adding several new scenes and interjecting new material throughout. I think that the first scene I worked on was the scene where Buddy Holly goes to the laundromat — I have a clear memory of sitting on the white marble steps of an old brownstone building at 40th and Walnut, writing furiously in longhand in a three-ring notebook, while Jack and Michael and Susan were in the Fun Arcade next door playing pinball; perhaps this was the same weekend.

"Touring" sold to *Penthouse.* Kathy Green squashed our original plan to publish the story under the collective pseudonym of "Phil Ford" — get it? hyuck hyuck — and insisted that we use our real names on it instead, although beforehand *everyone* had assured us that no magazine would be willing to list three authors for one story, and that we would have no choice but to use a collective pseudonym.

This turned out not to be true—in fact, nobody ever gave us the slightest bit of trouble about listing three authors for one story, and so "Phil Ford" went early and unmourned to an unmarked grave.

This was one of the most popular of the collaborations, and, I think, one of the best. It has been reprinted a number of times, including an appearance in Karl Edward Wagner's *The Year's Best Horror Stories*, where one critic later judged it to have been the single best story ever published in the series. Not too shabby.

The ods of Mars

GARDNER DOZOIS, JACK DANN, & MICHAEL SWANWICK

They were outside, unlashing the Mars lander, when the storm blew up.

With Johnboy and Woody crowded against his shoulders, Thomas snipped the last lashing. In careful cadence, the others straightened, lifting the ends free of the lander. At Thomas's command, they let go. The metal lashing soared away, flashing in the harsh sunlight, twisting like a wounded snake, dwindling as it fell below and behind their orbit. The lander floated free, tied to the *Plowshare* by a single, slim umbilicus. Johnboy wrapped a spanner around a hex-bolt over the top strut of a landing leg and gave it a spin. Like a slow, graceful spider leg, it unfolded away from the lander's body. He slapped his spanner down on the next bolt and yanked. But he hadn't braced himself properly, and his feet went out from under him in a slow somersault. He spun away, laughing, to the end of his umbilicus. The spanner went skimming back toward the *Plowshare*, struck its metal skin, and sailed off into space.

"You meatballs!" Thomas shouted over the open intercom. The radio was sharp and peppery with sun static, but he could hear Woody and Johnboy laughing. "Cut it out! No skylarking! Let's get this done."

"Everything okay out there?" asked Commander Redenbaugh,

from inside the *Plowshare*. The commander's voice had a slight edge to it, and Thomas grimaced. The last time the three of them had gone out on EVA, practicing this very maneuver, Johnboy had started to horse around and had accidentally sent a dropped lugnut smashing through the source-crystal housing, destroying the laser link to Earth. And hadn't the commander gotten on their asses about *that*; NASA had been really pissed, too—with the laser link gone, they would have to depend solely on the radio, which was vulnerable to static in an active sun year like this.

It was hard to blame the others too much for cutting up a little on EVA, after long, claustrophobic months of being jammed together in the *Plowshare*, but the responsibility for things going smoothly was his. Out here, *he* was supposed to be in command. That made him feel lonely and isolated, but after all, it was what he had sweated and strived for since the earliest days of flight training. The landing party was his command, his chance for glory, and he wasn't going to let anybody or anything ruin it.

"Everything's okay, Commander," Thomas said. "We've got the lander unshipped, and we're almost ready to go. I estimate about twenty minutes to separation." He spoke in the calm, matter-of-fact voice that tradition demanded, but inside he felt the excitement building again and hoped his pulse rate wasn't climbing too noticeably on the readouts. In only a few minutes, they were going to be making the first manned landing on Mars! Within the hour, he'd be down there, where he'd dreamed of being ever since he was a boy. On *Mars*.

And *he* would be in command. *How about that, Pop,* Thomas thought, with a flash of irony. *That good enough for you? Finally?*

Johnboy had pulled himself back to the *Plowshare*.

"Okay, then," Thomas said dryly. "If you're ready, let's get back to work. You and Woody get that junk out of the lander. I'll stay out here and mind the store."

"Yes, *sir*, sir," Johnboy said with amiable irony, and Thomas sighed. Johnboy was okay but a bit of a flake—you had to sit on him a little from time to time. Woody and Johnboy began pulling boxes out of the lander; it had been used as storage space for supplies they'd need on the return voyage, to save room in *Plowshare*. There were jokes cracked about how they ought to let some of the crates of flash-frozen glop that NASA straight-facedly called food escape into space, but at last, burdened with boxes, the two space-suited figures lumbered to the air lock and disappeared inside.

26   Thomas was alone, floating in space.

You really *were* alone out here, too, with nothing but the gaping immensity of the universe surrounding you on all sides. It was a little scary, but at the same time something to savor after long months of being packed into the *Plowshare* with three other men. There was precious little privacy aboard ship — out here, alone, there was nothing *but* privacy. Just you, the stars, the void . . . and, of course, Mars.

Thomas relaxed at the end of his tether, floating comfortably, and watched as Mars, immense and ruddy, turned below him like some huge, slow-spinning, rusty-red top. Mars! Lazily, he let his eyes trace the familiar landmarks. The ancient dead-river valley of Kasei Vallis, impact craters puckering its floor . . . the reddish brown and gray of haze and frost in Noctis Labyrinthus, the Labyrinth of Night . . . the immense scar of the Vallis Marineris, greatest of canyons, stretching two-thirds of the way around the equator . . . the great volcanic constructs in Tharsis . . . and there, the Chryse Basin, where soon they would be walking.

Mars was as familiar to him as the streets of his hometown — *more* so, since his family had spent so much time moving from place to place when he was a kid. Mars had stayed a constant, though. Throughout his boyhood, he had been obsessed with space and with Mars in particular . . . as if he'd somehow always known that one day he'd be here, hanging disembodied like some ancient god over the slowly spinning red planet below. In high school he had done a paper on Martian plate tectonics. When he was only a gangly grade-school kid, ten or eleven, maybe, he had memorized every available map of Mars, learned every crater and valley and mountain range.

Drowsily, his thoughts drifted even further back, to that day in the attic of the old house in Wrightstown, near McGuire Air Force Base — the sound of jets taking off mingling with the lazy Saturday afternoon sounds of kids playing baseball and yelling, dogs barking, lawn mowers whirring, the rusty smell of pollen coming in the window on the mild, spring air — when he'd discovered an old, dog-eared copy of Edgar Rice Burroughs's *A Princess of Mars*.

He'd stayed up there for hours reading it while the day passed unnoticed around him, until the light got so bad that he couldn't see the type anymore. And that night he'd surreptitiously read it in bed, under the covers with a pencil flashlight, until he'd finally fallen asleep, his dreams reeling with giant, four-armed green men, thoats, zitidars, long-sword-swinging heroes, and beautiful princesses . . . the Twin Cities of Helium . . . the dead sea bottoms lit by the 27 opalescent light of the two hurtling moons . . . the nomad caverns of the Tharks, the barbaric riders draped with glittering jewels and rich riding silks. For an instant, staring down at Mars, he felt a childish disappointment that all of that really wasn't waiting down there for him after all, and then he smiled wryly at himself. Never doubt that those childhood dreams had power—after all, one way or another, they'd *gotten* him here, hadn't they?

Right at that moment the sandstorm began to blow up.

It blew up from the hard-pan deserts and plains and as Thomas watched in dismay, began to creep slowly across the planet like a tarp being pulled over a work site. Down there, winds moving at hundreds of kilometers per hour were racing across the Martian surface, filling the sky with churning, yellow-white clouds of sand. A curtain storm.

"You see that, Thomas?" the commander's voice asked in Thomas's ears.

"Yeah," Thomas said glumly. "I see it."

"Looks like a bad one."

Even as they watched, the storm slowly and relentlessly blotted out the entire visible surface of the planet. The lesser features went first, the scarps and rills and stone fields, then the greater ones. The polar caps went. Finally even the top of Olympus Mons—the tallest mountain in the solar system—disappeared.

"Well, that's it," the commander said sadly. "Socked in. No landing today."

"Son of a *bitch!*" Thomas exploded, feeling his stomach twist with disappointment and sudden rage. He'd been so *close.* . . .

"Watch your language, Thomas," the commander warned. "This is an open channel." Meaning that we mustn't shock the Vast Listening Audience Back Home. Oh, horrors, certainly *not.*

"If it'd just waited a couple more hours, we would have been able to get *down* there—"

"You ought to be glad it didn't," the commander said mildly. "Then you'd have been sitting on your hands down there with all that sand piling up around your ears. The wind can hit one hundred forty miles an hour during one of those storms. *I'd* hate to have to try to sit one out on the ground. Relax, Thomas. We've got plenty of time. As soon as the weather clears, you'll go down. It can't last forever."

Five weeks later, the storm finally died.

Those were hard weeks for Thomas, who was as full of useless energy as a caged tiger. He had become overaware of his surroundings, of the pervasive, sour human smell, of the faintly metallic taste of the air. It was like living in a jungle-gym factory, all twisting pipes and narrow, cluttered passages, enclosed by metal walls that were never out of sight. For the first time during the long months of the mission, he began to feel seriously claustrophobic.

But the real enemy was time. Thomas was acutely aware that the inexorable clock of celestial mechanics was ticking relentlessly away . . . that soon the optimal launch window for the return journey to Earth would open and that they *must* shape for Earth then or never get home at all. Whether the storm had lifted yet or not, whether they had landed on Mars or not, whether Thomas had finally gotten a chance to show off his own particular righteous stuff or *not*, when the launch window opened, they had to go.

They had less than a week left in Mars orbit now, and still the sandstorm raged.

The waiting got on everyone's nerves. Thomas found Johnboy's manic energy particularly hard to take. Increasingly, he found himself snapping at Johnboy during meals and "happy hour," until eventually the commander had to take him aside and tell him to loosen up. Thomas muttered something apologetic, and the commander studied him shrewdly and said, "Plenty of time left, old buddy. Don't worry. We'll get you down there yet!" The two men found themselves grinning at each other. Commander Redenbaugh was a good officer, a quiet, pragmatic New Englander who seemed to become ever more phlegmatic and unflappable as the tension mounted and everyone else's nerves frayed. Johnboy habitually called him Captain Ahab. The commander seemed rather to enjoy the nickname, which was one of the few things that suggested that there might actually be a sense of humor lurking somewhere behind his deadpan facade.

The commander gave Thomas's arm an encouraging squeeze, then launched himself toward the communications console. Thomas watched him go, biting back a sudden bitter surge of words that he knew he'd never say . . . not up here, anyway, where the walls literally had ears. Ever since *Skylab*, astronauts had flown with the tacit knowledge that everything they said in the ship was being eavesdropped on and evaluated by NASA. Probably before the day was out somebody back in Houston would be making a black mark next to his name in a psychological-fitness dossier, just because he'd let the waiting get on his nerves to the point where the commander had had to speak to him about it. But damn it, it was *easier* for the rest—they didn't have the responsibility of being NASA's token Nigger in the Sky, with all the white folks back home waiting and watching to see how you were going to fuck up. He'd felt like a third wheel on the way out here — Woody and the commander could easily fly the ship themselves and even take care of most of the routine schedule of experiments — but the landing party was supposed to be *his* command, his chance to finally do something other than be the obligatory black face in the NASA photos of Our Brave Astronauts. He remembered his demanding, domineering, hard-driving father saying to him hundreds of times in his adolescent years, "It's a white man's world out there. If you're going to make it, you got to show that you're *better* than any of them. You got to force yourself down their throats, *make* them need you. You got to be twice as good as any of them . . ."*Yeah, Pop,* Thomas thought, *you bet, Pop* . . . thinking, as he always did, of the one and only time he'd ever seen his father stinking, slobbering, falling-down drunk, the night the old man had been passed over for promotion to brigadier general for the third time, forcing him into mandatory retirement. *First they got to give you the chance, Pop,* he thought, remembering, again as he always did, a cartoon by Ron Cobb that he had seen when he was a kid and that had haunted him ever since: a cartoon showing black men in space suits on the moon — sweeping up around the Apollo 58 campsite.

"We're losing Houston again," Woody said. "I jes cain't keep the signal." He turned a dial, and the voice of Mission Control came into the cabin, chopped up and nearly obliterated by a hissing static that sounded like dozens of eggs frying in a huge iron skillet.". . . read? . . . not read you . . . *Plowshare* . . . losing . . ." Sunspot activity had been unusually high for weeks, and just a few hours before. NASA had warned them about an enormous solar flare that was about to folld half the solar system with radio noise. Even as they listened, the voice was completely drowned out by static; the hissing noise kept getting louder and louder. "Weh-ayl," Woody said glumly, "that does it. That solar flare's screwing *every*thing up. If we still had the laser link"—here he flashed a sour look at Johnboy, who had the grace to look embarrassed—"we'd be okay, I guess, but with*out* it . . . weh-ayl, shit, it could be days before reception clears up. *Weeks,* maybe."

Irritably, Woody flipped a switch, and the hissing static noise stopped. All four men were silent for a moment, feeling their suddenly increased isolation. For months, their only remaining contact with Earth had been a faint voice on the radio, and now, abruptly, even that link was severed. It made them feel lonelier than ever and somehow farther away from home.

Thomas turned away from the communications console and

automatically glanced out the big observation window at Mars. It took him a while to notice that there was something different about the view. Then he realized that the uniform, dirty yellow-white cloud cover was breaking up and becoming streaky, turning the planet into a giant, mottled Easter egg, allowing tantalizing glimpses of the surface. "Hey!" Thomas said, and at the same time Johnboy crowed. "Well, *well*, lookie there! Guess who's back, boys!"

They all crowded around the observation window, eagerly jostling one another.

As they watched, the storm died all at once, with the suddenness of a conjuring trick, and the surface was visible again. Johnboy let out an ear-splitting rebel yell. Everyone cheered. They were all laughing and joking and slapping one another's shoulders, and then, one by one, they fell silent.

Something was wrong. Thomas could feel the short hairs prickling erect along his back and arms, feel the muscles of his gut tightening. Something was *wrong*. What was it? What . . . ? He heard the commander gasp, and at the same time realization broke through into his conscious mind, and he felt the blood draining from his face.

Woody was the first to speak.

"But . . ." Woody said, in a puzzled, almost petulant voice, like a bewildered child. "But . . . *that's not Mars*."

The air is thin on Mars. So thin it won't hold up dust in suspension unless the wind is traveling at enormous speeds. When the wind dies, the dust falls like pebbles, fast and all at once.

After five weeks of storm, the wind died. The dust fell.

Revealing entirely the wrong planet.

The surface was still predominantly a muddy reddish orange, but now there were large mottled patches of green and grayish ocher. The surface seemed softer now, smoother, with much less rugged relief. It took a moment to realize why. The craters—so very like those on the moon both in shape and distribution—were gone, and so were most of the mountains, the scarps and rills, the giant volcanic constructs. In their place were dozens of fine, perfectly straight blue lines. They were bordered by bands of green and extended across the entire planet in an elaborate crisscrossing pattern, from polar icecap to polar icecap.

"I cain't *find* anything," Woody was saying exasperatedly. "What *happened* to everything? I cain't even see Olympus Mons, for Christ-sake! The biggest fucking volcano in the solar system! Where is it? And what the fuck are those lines?"

31

Again Thomas felt an incredible burst of realization well up inside him. He gaped at the planet below, unable to speak, unable to answer, but Johnboy did it for him.

Johnboy had been leaning close to the window, his jaw slack with amazement, but now an odd, dreamy look was stealing over his face, and when he spoke, it was in a matter-of-fact, almost languid voice. "They're canals," he said.

"Canals, my ass!" the commander barked, losing control of his temper for the first time on the mission. "There aren't any canals on Mars! That idea went out with Schiaparelli and Lowell."

Johnboy shrugged. "Then what are *those?*" he asked mildly, jerking his thumb toward the planet, and Thomas felt a chill feather up along his spine.

A quick visual search turned up no recognizable surface features, none of the landmarks familiar to them all from the *Mariner* 9 and Viking orbiter photomaps — although Johnboy annoyed the commander by pointing out that the major named canals that Percival Lowell had described and mapped in the nineteenth century — Strymon, Charontis, Erebus, Orcus, Dis — *were* there, just as Lowell had said that they were.

"It's *got* to be the sandstorm that did it," Thomas said, grasping desperately for some kind of rational explanation. "The wind moving the sand around from one place to another, maybe, covering up one set of surface features while at the same time exposing *another* set. . . ."

He faltered to a stop, seeing the holes in that argument even as Johnboy snorted and said. "Real good, sport, *real* good. But Olympus Mons just isn't *there*, a mountain three times higher than Mount Everest! Even if you could cover it up with sand, then what you'd have would be a fucking *sand dune* three times higher than Everest . . . but there don't seem to be any big mountains down there at all anymore."

"I know what happened," Woody said before Thomas could reply.

His voice sounded so strange that they all turned to look at him. He had been scanning the surface with the small optical telescope for the Mars-Sat experiments, but now he was leaning on the telescope mounting and staring at them instead. His eyes were feverish and unfocused and bright and seemed to have sunken into his head. He was trembling slightly, and his face had become waxen and pale.

He's scared, Thomas realized, *he's just plain scared right out of his skull. . . .*

"This has all happened before," Woody said hoarsely.

"What in the world are you talking about?" Thomas asked.

"Haven't you read your history?" Woody asked. He was a reticent man, slow-voiced and deliberate, like most computer hackers, but now the words rushed from his mouth in a steadily-accelerating stream, almost tumbling over one another in their anxiety to get out. His voice was higher than usual, and it held the ragged overtones of hysteria in it. "The *Mariner* 9 mission, the robot probe. Back in 1971. Remember? Jes as the probe reached Mars orbit, before it could start sending back any photos, a great big curtain storm came up, jes like this one. Great *big* bastard. Covered *everything*. Socked the whole planet in for weeks. No surface visibility at all. Had the scientists back home pulling their hair out. But when the storm finally did lift, and the photos did start coming in, everybody was jes flatout *amazed*. None of the Lowellian features, no canals, *nothing*—jes craters and rills and volcanoes, all the stuff we expected to see *this* time around." He gave a shaky laugh.

"So everybody jes shrugged and said Lowell had been wrong— poor visibility, selector bias, he jes *thought* he'd seen canals. Connected up existing surface features with imaginary lines, maybe. He'd seen what he wanted to see." Woody paused, licking at his lips, and then began talking faster and shriller than ever. "But that wasn't *true*, was it? We *know* better, don't we, boys? We can see the proof right out that window! My crazy ol' uncle Barry, *he* had the right of it from the start, and everybody else was *wrong*. He tole me what happened, but I was jes too dumb to believe him! It was the *space* people, the UFO people! The Martians! *They* saw the probe coming, and they whomped that storm up, to keep us from seeing the surface, and then they changed everything. Under the cover of the sandstorm, they changed the whole damn planet to fool us, to keep us from finding out *they* were there! This *proves* it! They changed it *back!* They're out there right *now*, the flying saucer people! They're *out* there—"

"Bullshit!" the commander said. His voice was harsh and loud and cracked like a whip, but it was the unprecedented use of obscenity that startled them more than anything else. They turned to look at him, where he floated near the command console. Even Woody, who had just seemed on the verge of a breakdown, gasped and fell silent.

When he was sure he had everyone's attention, the commander smiled coldly and said, "While you were all going through your little psychodrama, I've been doing a little elementary checking. Here's the telemetry data, and you know what? *Everything* shows up the same as it did before the sandstorm. Exactly . . . the . . . same. Deep radar, infrared, everything." He tapped the command console. "It's just the same as it ever was; no breathable air, low atmospheric pressure, subzero temperatures, nothing but sand and a bunch of goddamn rusty-red rocks. No vegetation, no surface water, *no canals.*" He switched the view from the ship's exterior cameras onto the cabin monitor, and there for everyone to see was the familiar Mars of the Mariner and Viking probes: rocky, rugged, cratered, lifeless. No green oases. No canals.

Everyone was silent, mesmerized by the two contradictory images.

"I don't know what's causing this strange visual hallucination we're all seeing," the commander said, gesturing at the window and speaking slowly and deliberately. "But I do know that it *is* a hallucination. It doesn't show up on the cameras, it doesn't show up in the telemetry. It's just not real."

They adjourned the argument to the bar. Doofus the Moose — an orange inflatable toy out of Johnboy's personal kit — smiled benignly down on them as they sipped from bags of reconstituted citrus juice (NASA did not believe that they could be trusted with a ration of alcohol, and the hip flask Woody had smuggled aboard had been polished off long before) and went around and around the issue without reaching any kind of consensus. The "explanations" became more and more farfetched, until at last the commander uttered the classic phrase *mass hypnosis*, causing Johnboy to start whooping in derision.

There was a long, humming silence. Then Johnboy, his mood altering, said very quietly. "It doesn't matter anyway. We're never going to find out anything more about what's happening from up here." He looked soberly around at the others. "There's really only one decision we've got to make: Do we go on down, or not? Do we land?"

Even the commander was startled. "After all this — you still want to land?"

Johnboy shrugged. "Why not? It's what we came all the way out here for, isn't it?"

"It's too dangerous. We don't even know what's happening here."

"I thought it was only mass hypnosis," Johnboy said slyly.

"I think it is," the commander said stoutly, unperturbed by Johnboy's sarcasm. "But even if it is, we still don't know *why* we're having these hallucinations, do we? It could be a sign of organic deterioration or dysfunction of some sort, caused by who *knows* what. Maybe there's some kind of intense electromagnetic field out there that we haven't detected that's disrupting the electrical pathways of our nervous systems: maybe there's an unforeseen flaw in the recycling system that's causing some kind of toxic buildup that affects brain chemistry. . . . The point is, we're not *functioning* right; we're seeing things that aren't there!"

"None of that stuff matters," Johnboy said. He leaned forward, speaking now with great urgency and passion. No one had ever seen him so serious or so ferociously intent. "We have to land. Whatever the risk. It was hard enough funding *this* mission. If we fuck up out here, there may never be another one. NASA itself might not survive." He stared around at his crewmates. "How do *you* think it's going to look, Woody? We run into the greatest mystery the human race has ever encountered, and we immediately go scurrying home with our tails tucked between our legs without even investigating it? That sound good to you?"

Woody grunted and shook his head. "Sure doesn't, ol' buddy," he said. He glanced around the table and then coolly said, "Let's get on *down* there." Now that he was apparently no longer envisioning the imminent arrival of UFO-riding astronaut mutilators, Woody seemed determined to be as cool and unflappable and ultramacho as possible, as if to prove that he hadn't really been frightened after all.

There was another silence, and slowly Thomas became aware that everyone else was staring at him.

It all came down to him now. The deciding vote would be *his*. Thomas locked eyes with Johnboy, and Johnboy stared back at him with unwavering intensity. The question didn't even need to be voiced; it hung in the air between them and charged the lingering silence with tension. Thomas moved uneasily under the weight of all those watching eyes. How *did* he feel? He didn't really know — strange, that was about the closest he could come to it . . . hung up between fear and some other slowly stirring emotion he couldn't identify and didn't really want to think about. But there was one thing he suddenly was certain about: They weren't going to abandon *his* part of the mission, not after he'd come this far! Certainly he was never going to get another chance to get into the history books. Probably that was Johnboy's real motive, too, above and beyond the jazz about the survival of NASA. Johnboy was a cool enough head to realize that if they came home without landing, they'd be laughing stocks, wimps instead of heroes, and somebody *else* on some future mission would get all the glory. Johnboy's ego was much too big to allow him to take a chance on *that*. And he was right! Thomas had even more reason to be afraid of being passed over, passed by: When you were black, opportunities like this certainly didn't knock more than once.

"We've still got almost three days until the launch window opens." Thomas said, speaking slowly and deliberately. "I think we should make maximum use of that time by going down there and finding out as much as we can." He raised his eyes and stared directly at the commander. "I say we *land*."

Commander Redenbaugh insisted on referring the issue to Houston for a final decision, but after several hours of trying, it became clear that he was not going to be able to get through to Earth. For once, the buck wa refusing to be passed.

The commander sighed and ran his fingers wearily through his hair. He felt old and tired and ineffectual. He knew what Houston would probably have said, anyway. With the exception of the commander himself (who had been too well-known *not* to be chosen), de facto policy for this mission had been to select unmarried men with no close personal or family ties back home. That alone spoke volumes. They were *supposed* to be taking risks out here. That was what they were here for. It was part of their job.

At dawn over Chryse, they went down.

As commander of the landing party, Thomas was first out of the lander. Awkward in his suit, he climbed backward out of the hatch and down the exterior ladder. He caught reeling flashes of the Martian sky, and it was orange, as it should be. His first, instinctive reaction was relief, followed by an intense stab of perverse disappointment, which surprised him. As he hung from the ladder, one foot almost touching the ground, he paused to reel off the words that some P.R. man at NASA had composed for the occasion: "In the name of all humanity, we dedicate the planet of war to peace. May God grant us this." He put his foot down, then looked down from the ladder, twisting around to get a look at the spot he was standing on.

"Jesus *Christ*," he muttered reverently. Orange sky or not, there were *plants* of some kind growing here. He was standing almost knee-deep in them, a close-knit, springy mat of grayish-ocher vegetation. He knelt down and gingerly touched it.

"It looks like some kind of moss," he reported. "It's pliant and giving to the touch, springs slowly back up again. I can break it off in my hand."

The transmission from the *Plowshare* crackled and buzzed with static. "Thomas," said the commander's voice in his ear, "what are you *talking* about? Are you okay?"

Thomas straightened up and took his first long, slow look around. The ocher-colored moss stretched out to the orange horizon in all directions, covering both the flat plains immediately around them and a range of gently rolling hills in the middle distance to the north. Here and there the moss was punctuated by light clusters of spiny, misshapen shrubs, usually brown or glossy black or muddy purple, and even occasionally by a lone tree. The trees were crimson, about ten feet high; the trunks glistened with the color of fresh, wet blood, and their flat, glassy leaves glittered like sheets of amethyst. Thomas dubbed them flametrees.

The lander was resting only several hundred yards away from a canal.

It was wide, the canal; and its still, perfectly clear waters reflected the sky as dark as wine, as red as blood. Small yellow flowers trailed delicate tentacles into the water from the edging walls, which were old and crumbling and carved with strange geometrical patterns of swirls and curlicues that might, just possibly, be runes.

It can't possibly be real, Thomas thought dazedly.

Johnboy and Woody were clambering down the ladder, clumsy and troll-like in their hulking suits, and Thomas moved over to make room for them.

"Mother dog!" Woody breathed, looking around him, the wonder clear in his voice. "This is really something, ain't it?" He laid a gloved hand on Thomas's shoulder. "*This* is what we saw from up there."

"But it's impossible," Thomas said.

Woody shrugged. "If it's a hallucination, then it's sure as hell a *beautiful* one."

Johnboy had walked on ahead without a word, until he was several yards away from the ship; now he came to a stop and stood staring out across the moss-covered plain to the distant hills. "It's like being born again," he whispered.

The commander cut in again, his voice popping and crackling with static. "Report in! What's going *on* down there?"

Thomas shook his head. "Commander, I wish I knew."

He unlashed the exterior camera from the lander, set it up on its tripod, removed the lens cover. "Tell me what you see."

"I see sand, dust, rocks . . . what else do you *expect* me to see?"

"No canals?" Thomas asked sadly. "No trees? No moss?"

"Christ, you're hallucinating again, aren't you?" the commander said. "This is what I was afraid of. All of you, listen to me! Listen good! There aren't any goddamn *canals* down there. Maybe there's water down a few dozen meters as permafrost. But the surface is as dry as the moon."

"But there's some sort of moss growing all over the place," Thomas said. "Kind of grayish-ocher color, about a foot and a half high. There's clumps of bushes. There's even *trees* of some kind. Can't you see any of that?"

"You're hallucinating," the commander said. "Believe me, the camera shows nothing but sand and rock down there. You're standing in a goddamn lunar desert and babbling to me about trees, for Christ's sake! That's enough for me. I want everybody back up here, right *now*. I shouldn't have let you talk me into this in the first place. We'll let Houston unravel all this. It's no longer our problem. Woody, come back here! Stick together, dammit!"

Johnboy was still standing where he had stopped, as if entranced, but Woody was wandering toward the canal, poking around, exploring.

"Listen up!" the commander said. "I want everybody back in the lander, right now. I'm going to get you out of there before somebody gets hurt. Everybody back *now*. That's an order! That's a direct order!"

Woody turned reluctantly and began bounding slowly toward the lander, pausing every few yards to look back over his shoulder at the canal.

Thomas sighed, not sure whether he was relieved to be getting out of here or heartbroken to be going so soon.

"Okay, Commander," Thomas said. "We read you. We're coming up. Right away." He took a few light, buoyant steps forward—fighting a tendency to bounce kangaroolike off the ground—and tapped Johnboy gently on the arm. "Come on. We've got to go back up."

Johnboy turned slowly around. "Do we?" he said. "Do we *really*?"

"Orders," Thomas said uneasily, feeling something begin to stir and turn over ponderously in the deep backwaters of his own soul. "I don't want to go yet, either, but the commander's right. If we're hallucinating . . ."

"Don't give me that shit!" Johnboy said passionately. "Hallucinating, my ass! You *touched* the moss, didn't you? You *felt* it. This isn't a hallucination, or mass hypnosis, or any of that other crap. This is a *world*, a new world, and it's *ours*!"

"Johnboy, get in the lander right now!" the commander broke in. "That's an order!"

"Fuck you, Ahab!" Johnboy said. "And fuck your orders, too!"

Thomas was shocked—and at the same time felt a stab of glee at the insubordination, an emotion that surprised him and that he hurried uneasily to deny, saying, "You're out of line, Johnboy. I want you to listen to me, now—"

"No, you listen to *me*," Johnboy said fiercely. "Look around you! I know you've read Burroughs. You *know* where you are! A dead sea bottom, covered with ocher-colored moss. Rolling hills. A *canal*."

"Those are the very reasons why it can't be real," Thomas said uneasily.

"It's real if we *want* it to be real," Johnboy said. "It's here *because* of us. It's made *for* us. It's made *out* of us."

"Stop gabbing and get in the lander!" the commander shouted. "Move! Get you asses in gear!"

Woody had come up to join them. "Maybe we'd better—" he started to say, but Johnboy cut in with:

"Listen to me! I knew what was happening the moment I looked out and saw the Mars of Schiaparelli and Lowell, the *old* Mars. Woody, you said that Lowell saw what he wanted to see. That's *right*, but in a different way than you meant it. You know, other contemporary astronomers looked at Mars at the same time as Lowell, with the same kind of instruments, and saw no canals at all. You ever hear of consensual reality? Because Lowell wanted to see it, it existed for him! Just as it exists for us—because we want it to exist! We don't have to accept the gray reality of Ahab here and all the other gray little men back at NASA. They *want* it to be rocks and dust and dead, drab desert; they *like* it that way—"

"For God's sake!" the commander said. "Somebody get that nut in the lander!"

"—but *we* don't like it! Deep down inside of us—Thomas. Woody— we don't *believe* in that Mars. We believe in this one—the *real* one. That's why it's here for us! That's why it's the way it is—it's made of our dreams. Who know what's over those hills: bonewhite faërie cities? four-armed green men? beautiful princesses? the Twin Cities of Helium? There could be *anything* out there!"

"Thomas!" the commander snapped. "Get Johnboy in the lander *now*. Use force if necessary, but *get him in there*. Johnboy! You're emotionally unstable. I want you to consider yourself under house arrest!"

"I've been under house arrest all my life," Johnboy said. "Now I'm *free.*"

Moving deliberately, he reached up and unsnapped his helmet.

Thomas started forward with an inarticulate cry of horror, trying to stop him, but it was too late. Johnboy had his helmet completely off now and was shaking his head to free his shaggy, blond hair, which rippled slightly in the breeze. He took a deep breath, another, and then grinned at Thomas. "The air smells *great,*" he said. "And, my God, is it clean!"

"Johnboy?" Thomas said hesitantly. "Are you *okay?*"

"Christ!" the commander was muttering. "Christ! Oh my God! Oh my sweet God!"

"I'm fine," Johnboy said. "In fact, I'm *terrific.*" He smiled brilliantly at them, then sniffed at the inside of his helmet and made a face. "Phew! Smells like an armpit in there!" He started to strip off his suit.

"Thomas, Woody," the commander said leadenly. "Put Johnboy's body into the lander, and then get in there yourselves, fast, before we lose somebody else."

"But . . ." Thomas said, "there's nothing wrong with Johnboy. We're *talking* to him."

"God damn it, *look at your med readouts.*"

Thomas glanced at the chinstrap readout board, which was reflected into a tiny square on the right side of his faceplate. There was a tiny red light flashing on Johnboy's readout. "Christ!" Thomas whispered.

"He's *dead,* Thomas, he's *dead.* I can see his body. He fell over like he'd been poleaxed right after he opened his helmet and hemorrhaged his lungs out into the sand. *Listen* to me! Johnboy's *dead—*anything else is a hallucination!"

Johnboy grinned at them, kicking free of his suit. "I may be dead, kids," he told them quizzically, "but let me tell *you,* dead or not, I feel one-hundred-percent better now that I'm out of that crummy suit, believe it. The air's a little bit cool, but it feels *wonderful.*" He raised his arms and stretched lazily, like a cat.

"Johnboy—?" Woody said, tentatively.

"*Listen,*" the commander raged. "You're hallucinating! You're talking to yourselves! Get in the lander! That's an *order.*"

"Yes, *sir,* sir." Johnboy said mockingly, sketching a salute at the sky. "Are you actually going to *listen* to that asshole?" He stepped forward and took each of them by the arm and shook them angrily. "Do I *feel* dead to you, schmucks?"

Thomas *felt* the fingers close over his arm, and an odd, deep thrill shot through him — part incredulity, part supernatural dread, part a sudden, strange exhilaration. "I can *feel* him," Woody was saying wonderingly, patting Johnboy with his gloved hands. "He's solid. He's *there*. I'll be a son of a *bitch* —"

"Be one?" Johnboy said, grinning. "Ol' buddy, you already *are* one."

Woody laughed. "No hallucination's *that* corny," Woody said to Thomas. "He's real, all right."

"But the readout —" Thomas began.

"Obviously wrong. There's got to be some kind of mistake —" Woody started to unfasten his helmet.

"No!" the commander screamed, and at the same time Thomas darted forward shouting, "Woody! Stop!" and tried to grab him, but Woody twisted aside and bounded limberly away, out of reach.

Cautiously, Woody took his helmet off. He sniffed suspiciously, his lean, leathery face stiff with tension, then he relaxed, and then he began to smile. "Hoo*ie*," he said in awe.

"Get his helmet back on, quick!" the commander was shouting. But Woody's medical readout was already flashing orange, and even as the commander spoke, it turned red.

"Too late!" the commander moaned. "Oh God, too *late*. . . ."

Woody looked into his helmet at his own flashing readout. His face registered surprise for an instant, and then he began to laugh. "Weh-ayl," Woody drawled, "now that I'm officially a corpse, I guess I don't need *this* anymore." He threw his helmet aside; it bounced and rolled over the spongy mass. "Thomas," Woody said, "*you* do what you want, but I've been locked up in a smelly ol' tin can for months, and what *I'm* going to do is *wash my face* in some honest-to-God, unrecycled water!" He grinned at Thomas and began walking away toward the canal. "I might even take me a *swim*."

"Thomas . . ." the commander said brokenly. "Don't worry about the bodies. Don't worry about *anything* else. Just get in the lander. As soon as you're inside I'm going to trigger the launch sequence."

Johnboy was staring at him quizzically, compassionately — waiting.

"Johnboy . . ." Thomas said, "Johnboy, how can I tell which is real?"

"You *choose* what's real," Johnboy said quietly. "We all do."

"*Listen* to me. Thomas," the commander pleaded; there was an edge of panic in his voice. "You're talking to yourself again. What-ever you think you're seeing, or hearing, or even *touching*, it just *isn't real*. There can be tactile hallucinations, too, you know. It's not *real*."

"Old Ahab up there has made his choice, too," Johnboy said. "For him, in his own conceptual universe, Woody and I *are* dead. And that's real, too—for *him*. But you don't have to choose that reality. You can choose *this* one."

"I don't know," Thomas mumbled, "I just don't *know*. . . ."

Woody hit the water in an explosion of foam. He swam a few strokes, whooping, then turned to float on his back. "C'mon in, you guys!" he shouted.

Johnboy smiled, then turned to bring his face close to Thomas's helmet, peering in through the faceplate. Johnboy was still wearing that strange, dreamy look, so unlike his usual animated expression, and his eyes were clear and compassionate and calm. "It calls for an act of faith, Thomas. Maybe that's how every world begins." He grinned at Thomas. "Meanwhile, I think I'm going to take a swim, too." He strolled off toward the canal, bouncing a little at each step.

Thomas stood unmoving, the two red lights flashing on his chin-strap readout.

"They're both going swimming now," Thomas said dully.

"Thomas! Can you hear me, Thomas?"

"I hear you," Thomas mumbled.

They were having *fun* in their new world—he could see that. The kind of fun that kids had . . . that every child took for granted. The joy of discovery, of everything being *new* . . . the joy that seemed to get lost in the gray shuffle to adulthood, given up bit by incremental bit. . . .

"You're just going to have to trust me, Thomas. *Trust me*. Take my word for it that I know what I'm talking about. You're going to have to take that on faith. Now *listen* to me: No matter what you think is going on down there, *don't take your helmet off.*"

His father used to lecture him in that same tone of voice, demanding, domineering . . . and at the same time condescending. Scornful. Daddy knows best. Listen to me, boy, I *know* what I'm talking about! Do what I *tell* you to do!

"Do you hear me? Do *not* take your helmet off! Under any circumstances at all. That's an *order*."

Thomas nodded, before he could stop himself. Here he was, good boy little Tommy, standing on the fringes again, taking orders, doing what he was told. Getting passed over *again*. And for what?

Something flew by in the distance, headed toward the hills.

It looked to be about the size of a large bird, but like a dragonfly, it had six long, filmy gossamer wings, which it swirled around in a complexly interweaving pattern, as if it were rowing itself through the air.

"Get to the lander, Thomas, and close the hatch."

Never did have any fun. Have to be twice as good as *any* of them, have to bust your goddamn ass—

"That's a direct order, Thomas!"

You've got to make the bastards respect you, you've got to *earn* their respect. His father had said that a million times. And how little time it had taken him to waste away and die, once he'd stopped trying, once he realized that you can't earn what people aren't willing to sell.

A red and yellow lizard ran over his boot, as quick and silent as a tickle. It had six legs.

One by one, he began to undog the latches of his helmet.

"No! Listen to me! If you take off your helmet, you'll *die*. Don't do it! For God's sake, don't do it!"

The last latch. It was sticky, but he tugged at it purposefully.

"You're killing yourself! Stop it! *Please. Stop!* You *goddamn stupid nigger! Stop—*"

Thomas smiled, oddly enough feeling closer to the commander in that moment than he ever had before. "Too late," he said cheerfully.

Thomas twisted his helmet a quarter turn and lifted it off his head.

When the third red light winked on, Commander Redenbaugh slumped against the board and started to cry. He wept openly and loudly, for they had been good men, and he had failed all of them, even Thomas, the best and steadiest of the lot. He hadn't been able to save a goddamned one of them!

At last he was able to pull himself together. He forced himself to look again at the monitor, which showed three space-suited bodies sprawled out lifelessly on the rusty-red sand.

He folded his hands, bent his head, and prayed for the souls of his dead companions. Then he switched the monitor off.

It was time to make plans. Since the *Plowshare* would be carrying a much lighter-than-anticipated return cargo, he had enough excess fuel to allow him to leave a bit early, if he wanted to, and he *did* want to. He began to punch figures into the computer, smiling bitterly at the irony. Yesterday he had been regretting that they had so little time left in Mars orbit. Now, suddenly, he was in a hurry to get home . . . but no matter how many corners he shaved, he'd still be several long, grueling months in transit—with quite probably a court-martial waiting for him when he got back.

For an instant, even the commander's spirit quailed at the thought of that dreadful return journey. But he soon got himself under control again. It would be a difficult and unpleasant trip, right enough, but a determined man could always manage to do what needed to be done.

Even if he had to do it alone.

When the *Plowshare*'s plasma drive was switched on, it created a daytime star in the Martian sky. It was like a shooting star in reverse, starting out at its brightest and dimming rapidly as it moved up and away.

Thomas saw it leave. He was leaning against his makeshift spear—flametree wood, with a fire-hardened tip—and watching Johnboy preparing to skin the dead hyena-leopard, when he chanced to glance up. "Look," he said.

Johnboy followed Thomas's eyes and saw it, too. He smiled sardonically and lifted the animal's limp paw, making it wave bye-bye. "So long, Ahab," Johnboy said. "Good luck." He went back to skinning the beast. The hyena-leopard—a little bit larger than a wildcat, six-legged, saber-tusked, its fur a muddy purple with rusty-orange spots—had attacked without warning and fought savagely; it had taken all three of them to kill it.

Woody looked up from where he was lashing a makeshift flametree-wood raft together with lengths of wiring from the lander, "I'm sure he'll make it okay," Woody said quietly.

Thomas sighed. "Yeah," he said, and then, more briskly, "Let me give you a hand with that raft. If we snap it up, we ought to be ready to leave by morning."

Last night, climbing the highest of the rolling hills to the north, they had seen the lights of a distant city, glinting silver and yellow and orange on the far horizon, gleaming far away across the black midnight expanse of the dead sea bottom like an ornate and intricate piece of jewelry set against ink-black velvet.

Thomas was still not sure if he hoped there would be aristocratic red men there, and giant four-armed green Tharks, and beautiful Martian princesses. . . .

THE GODS OF MARS

This story started, as many of these stories did, during an informal workshopping/brainstorming session at my apartment. As I recall, Jack was down on a visit, Michael had come over, and we were sitting around in my "backyard," which was a rectangular slab of concrete surrounded by a head-high wooden fence, because it was too hot in my apartment to use it for anything other than perhaps drying meat into beef jerky. It was dusk, and this was July of 1982 — July 20th, I think. We'd been trying to come up with new ideas for collaborative stories, and this was one of the plot-ideas I threw out to them from my story-idea notebook, where it had been sleeping since 1971, when I'd read an account of the *Mariner* 9 mission. As Woody says in the story, a duststorm had hidden the entire planet just before *Mariner* 9 could begin taking the first closeup photos of Mars; when the storm lifted, and the photos were taken, the Mars that they showed was totally unlike the Mars that everyone had expected to see — no canals, none of the classic Lowellian features at all. And so, I immediately thought, what if the Lowellian features had really *been* there after all, but, under cover of the sandstorm, Somebody had *changed* it all before we could get photos of it, changed it to the now-familiar Mars of the Mariner and Viking photos? And then suppose, just before the first manned expedition gets there, it gets changed *back*, so that the Mars the astronauts land on is the Mars of Burroughs and Lowell, not the Mars of *Mariner* 9?

This idea seemed to appeal to everyone, and we spent the rest of the evening talking about the story, working out the details of the plot. The story seemed to call for a high-tech opening sequence, with a NASA mission orbiting Mars, and since we considered Michael to be our High-Tech Expert (he, after all, had actually written stories with *spaceships* in them, which was considerably more than Jack or I had ever done), he was tapped to take first crack at a draft of the story. By the weekend of Jack's wedding to Jeanne Van Buren, the weekend of January 1, 1983, Michael had produced a draft which took the story up to the initial landing sequence, and brought the draft with him to the wedding; at some decent interval after the wedding (the next day, I think), we had a quick story conference, and decided that Jack, as our Phenomenology Expert, should take it from there—which he did, roughing it out to a point just before the actual ending.

Michael may have taken a crack at another draft at this point, I'm not sure. At any rate, my work calendar shows that I started work on it myself on March 5, 1983, worked on it pretty intensively during the middle of April, and finished the story on April 20, 1983. I added an ending, and did an extensive coordinating and homogenizing draft, going back through the story from the beginning, adding new sections and injecting new material interstitially into existing sections throughout. It seems to me that my biggest contribution to the story was in deepening and intensifying the characterization of Thomas throughout, giving him a more complex personal background that increased his psychological motivation to actually do what he later does; in the process, I got to work in mention of an old Ron Cobb cartoon that I had been impressed by years before.

Shockingly, neither Jack nor Michael had ever read any of Edgar Rice Burroughs's Martian novels—so all the Barsoom Nostalgia here was supplied by me.

Our working title for this was "Sex Kings of Mars." (It's a *joke*, son.) We sent it out under the title "Storm Warning," which Ellen Datlow talked us into changing to "The Gods of Mars." We also did a cut at Ellen's prompting, eliminating a couple of thousand words from the manuscript. Michael and I worked on making the cuts in a couple of sessions at the end of July and the beginning of August. The story was published in *Omni,* and showed up on that year's final Nebula ballot, much to the disgust of Sue Denim in *Cheap Truth.*

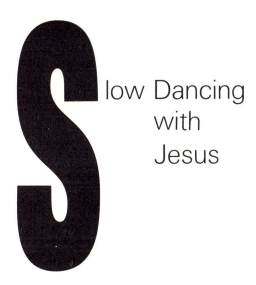

Slow Dancing with Jesus

GARDNER DOZOIS & JACK DANN

Jesus Christ appeared at Tess Kimbrough's door dressed in a white tuxedo with a blue cummerbund and matching bow-tie. His chestnut-brown hair was parted in the middle and fell down past his shoulders, and his beard and mustache were close-cropped and neatly combed.

Tess's mother answered the door. "Come right inside, Tess will be down in a jiffy." She led Jesus into the front room. "Tess," she called. "Your date is here."

Upstairs, Tess checked the bobby pins that held her French Twist together, and smoothed imaginary wrinkles out of her dress. It was the emerald green one, with dyed-green shoes to match, that her urbane and sophisticated mother had helped her pick out, and she was somewhat nervous about it, but then she was so nervous anyway that her teeth were chattering. She told her image in the mirror that this was going to be the most perfect night of her life, but the image in the mirror didn't look convinced. She practiced breathing evenly for a moment, flaring her nostrils. Then she walked down the stairs to meet Jesus, remembering not to look at her feet, and trying to maintain good posture.

Jesus stood up as she entered the room and presented her with a corsage, a small orchid on a wristlet. She thanked him, kissed her

47

mother good-bye, promised that she'd be back at a reasonable hour, and then she was sitting beside Jesus in the leatherette seat of his Thunderbird convertible. Jesus refrained from laying rubber in front of Tess's house, as most kids would have done; instead he shifted smoothly and skillfully through the gears. Tess momentarily forgot about being nervous as the wind rushed by against her face and she thought that she was actually—right now—going to the prom.

"How are you doing?" Jesus asked. "Do you want a cap or something so the wind won't mess your hair?"

"No, thanks," Tess said shyly. She was almost afraid to look at him, and kept stealing sidelong glances at him when she thought his attention was elsewhere.

"You nervous?"

Tess glanced at him again. "You mean, about the prom?"

"Uh, huh," Jesus said, executing a high-speed turn with an easy, expert grace. The buildings were going by very fast now.

"Yeah . . . I guess so."

"Don't be," Jesus said, and winked.

Tess felt herself blushing, but before she could think of something to say, Jesus was bringing the car to a smooth stop in the lower parking lot of the high school. A kid whose Vaseline-smeared hair was combed back into a duck's tail opened the door for Tess, and then slid into the driver's seat when Jesus got out. Jesus gave him a five-dollar tip.

"Jeez, thanks," the boy said.

Cinders crunched under their feet as they crossed the parking lot toward the open fire door of the gym, which was now framed by paper lanterns that glowed in soft pastel colors. Tess walked hesitantly and slowly now that they were really here, already beginning to feel the first sick flutterings of panic. Most of the kids didn't like her—she had long ago been classified as uncool, and, worse, a "brain"—and she didn't see any reason why they'd start to like her now. . . .

But then Jesus was surrendering their tickets at the door, and it was too late to flee.

Inside the gym, the bleachers had been pulled back from the dance floor, and the basketball nets had been folded up. Paper streamers hung from rafters and waterpipes, herds of slowly jostling balloons bumped gently against the ceiling, and crêpe-paper roses were everywhere. The band—five sullen young men in dark red jackets that had "The Teen-Tones" written on them in sequins—had set up in the free-throw zone and were aggressively but unskillfully playing "Yakety Yak." Kids in greasy pompadours, crewcuts, and elephant trunks milled listlessly around the dance floor, looking stiff and uncomfortable in their rented suits. Only a few couples were dancing, and they jerked and twitched in lethargic slow-motion, like people slowly drowning on the bottom of the sea.

Most of the girls were still standing by the refreshment tables on the other side of the room, where the punch bowls were, and Tess made her way toward them, feeling her stomach slowly knot with dread. Already she could see some of the kids smirking at her and whispering, and she heard a girl say loudly "Just look at that *dress!* What a nerd." One of the class clowns made a yipping, doggy noise as she passed, and someone else broke up into high-pitched asthmatic laughter. Blindly, she kept walking. As she came up to the group around the punch bowls, her friend Carol gave her an unenthusiastic smile and said "Hey, lookin' good" in an insincere voice. Vinnie, Carol's bulletheaded boyfriend, made a snorting sound of derision. "I just don't understand why you have anything to do with that dog," he said to Carol, not even making a pretense of caring whether Tess could hear him or not. Carol looked embarrassed; she glanced at Tess, smiled weakly, and then looked uneasily away — she genuinely liked Tess, and sometimes hung out with her after school (in the classic teen configuration, encountered everywhere, of one pretty girl and one "dog" doing things together), but as a captain of cheerleaders she had her own status to worry about, and under the circumstances she'd lose face with the cool kids if she stuck up too vigorously for Tess. "I mean, *look* at her," Vinnie complained, still speaking to Carol as if Tess wasn't there. "She's *so* uncool, you know?"

Tess stood frozen, flushing, smiling a frozen smile, feeling herself go hot and freezing cold by turns. Should she pretend that she hadn't heard? What else *could* she do? The clown had drifted over, and was making yipping noises again. . . .

Jesus had been a few steps behind her coming through the crowd, but now he stepped up beside her and took her arm, and all the other kids suddenly fell silent. "Leave her alone," Jesus said. His voice was rich, strong, resonant, and it rang like a mellow iron bell in the big empty hall. "She's here with *me*." Vinnie's mouth dropped open, and Carol gasped. All the kids were gaping at them, their faces soft with awe. Tess was intensely aware of Jesus' strong warm fingers on the bare flesh of her arm. Jesus seemed to have grown larger, to have become huge and puissant, a giant, and his rugged, handsome face had become stern and commanding. He radiated strength and warmth and authority, and an almost tangible light — a clear and terrible light that seemed to reveal every zit and pimple and blackhead in the sallow, shallow faces of her tormentors, each slack mouth and weak chin and watery eye, a light that dwindled them to a petty and insignificant group of grimy children. "She's here with me," Jesus repeated, and then he smiled, suavely, jauntily, almost rakishly, and winked. "And if I say she's cool, believe it, she's cool."

Then, before anyone could speak, Jesus had taken Tess's hand and led her onto the dance floor, and they were dancing, slow dancing, while the band played "A Million to One." She had never been able to dance before, but now she danced with effortless skill, swirling around and around the floor, following Jesus' lead, moving with beauty and flowing silken grace, shreads of torn paper roses whispering around her feet. One by one the other couples stopped dancing and stood silently to watch them, until they were surrounded by a ring of pale, gaping, awed faces, small as thumbnails and distant as stars, and they drifted and danced within that watching ring as the band played "Goodnight, My Love" and "Twilight Time" and "It's All in the Game," moving through the night together like silk and fire and warm spring rain.

After the dance, Jesus drove her home and kissed her goodnight at her door, gently but with authority, and with just the slightest sweet hint of tongue.

Tess let herself in and went upstairs to her room, moving quietly so that her mother wouldn't realize that she was back. She switched on a soft light and stared at herself in the mirror; her flesh was tingling, and she was sure that she must be glowing in the darkness like freshly-hammered steel, but her face looked the same as always, except perhaps for the expression around the eyes. She sat down at her night-table and took her diary out from the locked, secret drawer. She sat there silently for a long while, near the open window, feeling the warm night breeze caress her face and smelling the heavy sweet perfume of the mimosa trees outside. A dog was barking out there somewhere, far away, at long intervals, and cars whined by on the highway, leaving a vibrant silence in their wake. At last she opened her diary, and in a bold neat hand wrote

Dear Diary,
Tonight I met — Him. . . .

SLOW DANCING WITH JESUS

My friend Tess Kissinger has the most wonderful dreams.

Get her to tell you the dream she had about the diner on Jupiter, or the one about the centaur in the driveway, or the one about the inflatable bull, or the one about how the aliens land and insist that we change the way we've been spelling the word "Mexico." Or any of a dozen others. Tess has one of the most fertile imaginations of anyone I know, and it works all the time — even when she's asleep.

At some point in 1981, she told me about a dream she'd had years before, in high school — about how Jesus was taking her to her school prom, much to the amazement and consternation of the snooty cool kids, who disliked her because she was "uncool" and "a brain."

I thought this was wonderful. I saw fictional possibilities in it at once, and suggested that she should write it up into a story. But although Tess is a highly-skilled graphic artist and illustrator, she was uncertain at that point of her ability as a writer — she later wrote and illustrated several marvelously imaginative and funny children's books, none of which, puzzlingly, have sold to anyone as yet — and this lack of confidence made her shrug this suggestion off. On a couple of later occasions, I nagged her again about writing the story, without result, and even once — Michael is my witness here — hinted gently that I would be willing to work on it with her as a collaboration, but that suggestion bounced off her too; she just wasn't taking the idea that *she* could write a story seriously enough to actually try to *do* so, often a problem with beginning writers.

Then Jack came down for a visit, and on the night of March 1, 1982, Jack and Susan and I went out to dinner in Chinatown with Tess and her boyfriend, artist Bob Walters. Toward the end of dinner, at my prompting, Tess related her Jesus At The Prom dream.

Jack's eyes bugged out. "Wow!" he said. "What a great idea for a *story*! Hey!" He lunged at Tess across the pineapple chunks and shattered fortune cookies. "Hey! Can *we* write that? It'll make a *great* story. Can we *write* it? Can we?" Tess blinked at him, startled and bemused. "Well, yeah, I guess so," she said dazedly. "Yeah, sure. Go ahead."

We paid up, and Jack hurried us out of the restaurant at record speed, afire with enthusiasm. In the cab on the way home, the thought of the subtle technical difficulties that would have to be overcome to actually get the story effectively down on paper daunted me, and I began to get cold feet, but Jack was made of sterner stuff— a writer of intense energy and fierce ambition, he would fearlessly attack *any* project, no matter how technically difficult the material was, or how great the creative challenges to be overcome; who else would calmly sit down and start writing a 1,000-page historical fantasy novel about Leonardo Da Vinci?

So when we got home, Jack rushed to the typewriter, sat down, and at once began working furiously on the story. By the time he left, a day or so later, he'd carried the story through the opening scenes to the scene where Jesus and Tess arrive at the parking lot outside the building where the prom is being held. I started work on the story on March 8th. I carried the storyline through to the end, then went back and did a light unifying draft on Jack's opening sequences. The story was finished on March 10, 1982.

In some ways, I think that this was the most technically difficult to write of any of the collaborations, because the mood that needed to be maintained throughout the story if it was going to work at all was so fragile that one false step, one sour note, one wrongly-executed sentence, would shatter it, and ruin the spell we were attempting to weave around the reader. It was a story full of potentially-fatal pitfalls. I didn't want it to be just a sacrilegious joke, like a Monty Python routine—I wanted it to be simultaneously funny and sad, bittersweet and strange and driftingly wistful, arising as it had from a young girl's longing dreams. It called for the creation of a special and very fragile mood, and to maintain that mood it was necessary to tiptoe through the writing of the story as carefully as a soldier negotiating a minefield. I was even very careful in my selection of the songs the characters dance to, for instance, and the order in which they are played, and listened to them all—and others—many times before making up my mind. The flower symbology is also carefully worked out. The physical details of the prom setting are

an amalgamation of details from proms that Jack, Tess, Susan, and

I had been to at one time or another when we were in school. Much of Jesus' dialogue at the prom is verbatim from Tess's dream, including Jesus' great line, "She's here with me. And if I say she's cool, she's cool." I alone am responsible for the appalling joke at the story's end.

Everyone — including my agent — told us that we would never sell this story. To some obscure little literary magazine, maybe, but never to a commercial market. Certainly we would never sell it to the slicks. It broke every rule for selling to the slicks — it had a female protagonist, it was about grungy high-school kids instead of affluent Brand-Name-product-consuming yuppies, it was blasphemous, it was short, it was *weird*.

It sold on the second attempt, to *Penthouse,* and I really must salute Kathy Green for her courage in buying it, especially at a time when Christian Fundamentalist TV evangelists and Moral Majority-ites were howling to have *Penthouse* and *Playboy* driven off the newsstands altogether, and the government seemed all too eager to cooperate. I'm not sure where we *would* have sold it if Kathy had turned it down; certainly not inside the genre, not at the time, anyway. *Penthouse* also had enough guts to publish my even riskier solo story "Disciples," and I think that this willingness to take a chance with "dangerous" material is something to keep in mind when people say — as I've heard self-proclaimed liberals say, with a sniff of pious, prudish disapproval — that it wouldn't bother *them* at all if the men's magazines *were* banned from publication . . . and that, of course, is just the way we lose our freedom, step by step.

After the check came in, Jack and I took Tess and Bob out to dinner at my favorite Hungarian restaurant, *Dave Shore's* (now defunct, alas). It was a good meal, but Tess still looked a bit bemused, and I think that she was thinking that she *should* have written the story herself after all.

Maybe the *next* time she'll listen to me. After all, she still has plenty of dreams left. . . .

IT DOESN'T GET ANY BETTER

MICHAEL SWANWICK

There we were: Gardner Dozois and myself in the back of a rented Japanese subcompact, and Jack and Jeanne Dann in the front, Jack driving. Gardner and I sat stiffly in that way you do when you're crammed into far too small a space with someone you like, but have no aspirations for physical intimacy with. It was a drearily overcast day and we were all on our way to a small science fiction convention in midstate New York. We'd been on the turnpike for hours, and still had a long way to go. We had the windows rolled up and the air conditioning straining against the muggy heat, and Jack and Jeanne were arguing because Jack insisted on smoking a cigar anyway. Meanwhile, because it was the first day of the hunting season, cars kept passing us on either side, with large dead animals tied to their hoods, blood oozing from stiffened mouths and nostrils.

Suddenly Jack interrupted himself to throw an arm over the top of the seat, lean back and, grinning around his cigar, expansively observe, ''You know—it doesn't get any better than this!''

''It *doesn't?*'' I said, horrified.

What would we do without our friends? Life would be a lot grayer without them. That goes double if you happen to be a writer. Because writing is for the most part deadly dull work, and when my wife, Marianne, comes home of an evening to ask how the day went, there isn't much to say. ''Three pages,'' or maybe even, ''Five pages,'' and that's about it. It's different with collaborations. Gardner and Jack are larger-than-life characters, full of wild ideas and loud notions and a rowdy sense of fun. You hang around with these guys and you have to be able to give and take with the best of 'em. You learn things, some of which change your thinking forever. You come away with stories to tell.

There's a serious side to collaboration, artistic depth and insight, challenge, and that shock of delight when exactly the right phrasing has been applied to our thought by someone else. I'm not going to discuss that. Right now I want to tell a few, just the merest fraction, of the funny things that happened to me on the way to this book. Because literature, as Ezra Pound observed, we have with us always. But good stories are rare.

I want it down on record that the dreadful pun contained in the title ''Golden Apples of the Sun'' was my own. I don't make all that many dreadful puns, and when I manage to come up with one that makes Gardner Dozois himself wince with disgust and admiration, I demand full credit.

The story itself began during a late-night creative session with the boys. These sessions have been an irregular tradition over the years. I'll get a phone call from Gardner saying Jack has just breezed into town, and everyone is going out to Chinatown for dinner, do I want to come along? When we finally get back to Gardner-and-Susan's digs, we'll go into a jumbled confusion of creative endeavor, casual insults, and joking wordplay. Great things have come out of these evenings, both high and low art, grandiose projects that collapsed in daylight, and stories that went on to place on the Nebula ballot. Novels are plotted and critiqued, stories begun, and straight-faced lies told. This is Literature with the hooves and horns attached.

On this particular evening, an old friend and former Philadelphian, Don Keller, had just recently visited his old stomping grounds with daughter Deirdre and wife Tatiana. Gardner and I were quoting various things that Tatiana had said, without bothering to explain exactly who she was. ''Who's Tatiana?'' Jack asked. Gardner continued expounding on Tatiana's observations. ''Who's Tatiana?'' Jack insisted. I went into the possible application of Tatiana's thoughts to one of our prospective stories. ''Who's Tatiana?'' Jack asked for the fifth time.

Gardner, who had somehow confused the name with Titania, jokingly said, ''She's the Queen of the Fairies.''

Trying to be helpful, I added, ''She's also Don Keller's wife.''

''Jeez,'' Jack said. ''That's a bit of a comedown, isn't it?''

''I used ta be da Queen a da Fairies,'' Gardner said, ''and now I'm selling computers in Poith Amboy.''

We were off and running.

Later, we sold the story to *Penthouse*. The editors there didn't like our title and with exquisite good taste changed it to "Virgin Territory." They also thought that ten thousand words was a trifle long, and wanted us to cut it. By five thousand.

Gardner and I got together and did the dirty deed over one long, hideous day. We began by cutting scenes. Then we went through the manuscript and out paragraphs. Then sentences. Then words. Then we changed every "can not" to "can't." Then we began rephrasing things, from three words down to two words, from seven to six. By the eighth time through the story, Gardner had lost not only the willingness to make the required cuts, but much of his will to live. The manuscript was drenched with blood. But I needed the money. I was ruthless. We cut it down to four thousand nine hundred and ninety nine words. Exactly.

In a weird way, though, that was a good experience. I learned a lot, cutting that piece down in such a way as to retain its coherence as a story despite being compressed far below its natural length. And it's an experience I could only have had on a collaborative work. Because I would never cut down a solo work like that, no more than would Gardner or Jack. The secret, should you ever find yourself in a similar situation, is to tell yourself that you're not cutting your own words, but theirs.

"Afternoon at Schrafft's" was, I am proud to say, all my fault.

Jack and Jeanne were in town, so Marianne and I invited them, Gardner, and Susan to dinner. After cocktails, wine, and dinner (in honor of Jack, Marianne created Metaphysically Referential Chicken, a boned chicken stuffed with vegetables, served whole and then sliced like a loaf of bread), we retired to the library for conversation and brandy.

"Let's write a story," I said.

Jack, always easily misled, agreed at once. Gardner, however, disapproved of the project on principle. He felt strongly that we shouldn't write a story without some idea to base it on.

"My idea is that it should be *very short*," I said with drunken cunning, "because our attention spans aren't terribly long at the moment."

Gardner remained unconvinced, so Jack and I started without him. I proposed that the story should include a wizard, a cat, and a dinosaur so we could sell reprints to each of three anthologies Jack and Gardner were planning. Jack contributed the observation that he'd always wanted to set a story in Schrafft's. It was enough.

(I should interpose here that we did later sell reprint rights to *one* of the anthologies—*Magicats!* by name—and that My Pals paid me all of nine dollars for my share. It happened that the Virginia Kidd Agency sent me its payment on the same check as the payment *Penthouse* made for one third of another collaborative story. For a long time I stood unmoving, staring at the amazingly lopsided figure of eleven hundred and nine dollars. "This is a funny way to make a living," I told Marianne.)

So Jack and I started the story. Gardner *wanted* to stay out of it, *wanted* to have nothing to do with a story so cynically begun, *wanted* to stay morally aloof from the whole wretched mess. But he couldn't resist making a comment here, offering an idea there, and soon we were all enthusiastically working out the plot. I took notes and a week later typed up the first draft.

"Afternoon at Schrafft's" is a pleasant little soufflé of a story, but it will always have a special place in my heart because it gave me that evening: laughing, joking, slinging ideas about, drinking and arguing in the library, all six of us (because of course we took Marianne's, Jeanne's, and Susan's comments and ideas and incorporated them into our story, without offering them credit or recompense, according to the iron law of literature: that anything said in front of writers is Their Property), building a story out of nothing, jiggering the plot, playing a game that only true writers can. Making stone soup.

It didn't always work out so well for me.

I am thinking of course of another wonderfully crowded evening when Jack came to town. We three sat around Gardner's kitchen table, working on a dozen projects all at once. Jack had a novel nearly completed, and wanted Gardner's advice on rewriting major portions as stand-alone stories. The two of them had the usual round of anthologies to put together. We all three were eager to plot a batch more collaborations. And Gardner had a new typewriter.

This was a major event in Gardner's life. Before this he had written virtually every story he had ever sold on a battered old Royal, and he was not perfectly assured that he *could* write on another typewriter. There was something wrong with the platen of the Royal, so that the line of print did not go straight across the page but up and down in a sinuous flow, as if the prose were the surface of the ocean, endlessly rocking. Nor was it a regular flow; at the crest of its wave, a word from one line might bump against a word from the line above that was hitting the bottom of its trough. Gardner wrote on onionskin paper (he denies this, however), and the gray quality of the print leads me to suspect he had a lucky ribbon as well, perhaps given to him at birth, which he could never bring himself to change.

The overall affect of a classic Dozois manuscript was a worrying sense of impending seasickness. It is a measure of the high regard with which he was held in the field that editors were actually *eager* to see his stories.

The new typewriter, however, wrote straight across the page in clear black letters. The keys didn't stick, either, the way a proper typewriter's should. Gardner was dubious about the whole affair. Periodically throughout the evening, one of us would wander over to the machine and type out a sentence or two, sometimes a paragraph, to try out the action.

At one point when Jack and Gardner were plotting hot and heavy some story or novel or anthology that did not involve me, I sat down at the typewriter. There was a sheet of paper in it on which Jack had written an opening sentence about an old man sitting on a park bench. This was for a story Jack wanted to work up about a man growing young again. He was so excited about the idea that he could not manage to explain to us what it was. ''I think this could be really sensitive,'' he'd say. ''Yes, but what's it *about?*'' Gardner would ask, exasperated. ''I picture it as a kind of life-affirming exploration into death as a metaphor for failure.''

In reaction to Jack's elaborate artistic theorizing (Jack is hands down the intellectual of the group, the kind of guy who reads Faulkner in the original Greek), and in that heightened kind of silliness that comes late in an evening of creative endeavor, I pecked out a couple of lines about dinosaurs lumbering by and pterodactyls nipping at bits of trash in the gutter.

''What's he doing?'' Jack asked. He looked at what I'd written. ''My God! He's writing our story for us! This is terrific! This is exactly the way I pictured it!''

''No it's not,'' I said. ''I'm making fun of you.''

''This could be very sensitive!''

''It's a *joke,* Jack.''

Eventually, I left. I came back the next day to find they'd taken my paragraph and expanded it into a short-short entitled ''A Change in the Weather.'' It was a light, charming little nothing, and Gardner and Jack offered to put my name on it and cut me in for a third of the take as my reward for kicking off the whole thing.

But I, as a serious *littérateur,* wanted no part of it. Anyway, I reasoned, how much money were they going to get for that thing?

A lot, as it turned out. About a month later Gardner called me up to break the news gently. "You stupid putz!" he said. "We just sold that story to *Playboy!*"

In the long run the lesson I learned then (something about professionalism, I think, or maybe about respecting one's own work; I forget exactly) may well have been worth the money it cost me. But I think back every now and then to that little story and I regret not the money itself, but the fact that had I kept my big mouth shut, I could now legitimately brag that I had once been paid (I worked it out) thirty dollars a word.

Finally, there was the time I dropped by Gardner's old apartment on Quince Street. This was midway in his evolution from poverty to bourgeois affluence, and while the apartment lacked the dismaying squalor of his old place on South Street, it had a certain funky, cluttered charm to it yet. "Let me finish writing something," he said, "I'll be done in a minute."

So I sat on the edge of a gutsprung sofa, while Gardner typed a final half page, added it to a pile on the table alongside his typewriter, and evened up the edges to make a neat manuscript.

"So what's up?" I asked.

"Congratulations, Michael." He handed me the manuscript. "You've just completed a story."

Of course I thought he was joking. It had been a while since our last collaboration, and we had no projects going, no irons in the fire, not even an unfinished work gathering dust in the corner. But to my absolute, slackjawed astonishment, he was right. There in my hands was a complete, polished collaborative story, and it was half mine. It was called "Snow Job."

To explain, I must go back a year to an abortive attempt I had made at a first novel. It was going to be about con men (I read everything I can on confidence games, and do my best to apply it to my work) jumping between parallel universes, and I had written an entire first chapter before realizing it was not to be and going on to other things. Now, long assured that the novel was dead, Gardner had removed the first and last pages from my chapter, and substituted his own beginning and end.

Which, I must emphasize, had nothing at all to do with my old plot. Gone were the parallel universes, gone the sinister otherworldly villains, gone all the clanking huggermugger that had soured me on the project in the first place. In their place was a light and sprightly tale about coke-dealing time-travellers. And yet it had all been written so skillfully that I defy anyone to determine where Gardner's prose leaves off and mine begins.

"We've got to do more collaborations like this!" I said.

Beaming with justifiable satisfaction, Gardner shook his head. "Sorry, only one to a customer."

I'm not exactly Pangloss reincarnate, and I'd certainly think long and hard before voicing the proposition that ours is the best of all possible worlds. But let's be honest. A universe where smack dab out of nowhere and for no discernible good reason at all, a man can find himself suddenly given a complete story, suitable for publication and payment, with absolutely no effort on his own part, and that story co-written with as fine a writer and stylist as Gardner Dozois. . . . Well, I hate to admit it, but Jack may be right. It *doesn't* get any better than this.

■
■
■
■
■

Executive Clemency

GARDNER DOZOIS & JACK C. HALDEMAN II

The President of the United States sat very still in his overstuffed chair on the third floor and watched early morning sunlight sweep in a slow line across the faded rug.

He couldn't remember getting out of bed or sitting down in the chair. He could dimly recall that he had been sitting there for a long time, watching the slow advent of dawn, but he was only just beginning to become fully aware of himself and his surroundings.

Only his eyes moved, yellow and wet, as the world seeped in.

This happened to him almost every morning now. Every morning he would return slowly to his body as if from an immense distance, from across appalling gulfs of time and space, to find himself sitting in the chair, or standing next to the window, or, more rarely, propped up in the corner against the wall. Sometimes he'd be in the middle of dressing when awareness returned, and he'd awake to find himself tying a shoelace or buttoning his pants. Sometimes, like this morning, he'd just be sitting and staring. Other times he would awaken to the sound of his own voice, loud and cold in the bare wooden room, saying some strange and important things that he could never quite catch. If he could only hear the words he said at such times, just once, he knew that it would change everything, that he would understand everything. But he could never hear them.

He didn't move. When the lines of sunlight reached the chair, it would be time to go downstairs. Not before, no matter how late it sometimes made him as the sunlight changed with the seasons, no matter if he sometimes missed breakfast or, on cloudy winter days, didn't move at all until Mrs. Hamlin came upstairs to chase him out. It was one of the rituals with which he tried to hold his life together.

The east-facing window was washed over with pale, fragile blue, and the slow-moving patch of direct sunlight was a raw, hot gold. Dust motes danced in the beam. Except for those dust motes, everything was stillness and suspension. Except for his own spidery breathing, everything was profoundly silent. The room smelled of dust and heat and old wood. It was the best part of the day. Naturally it couldn't last.

Very far away, floating on the edge of hearing, there came the mellow, mossy bronze voice of a bell, ringing in the village of Fairfield behind the ridge, and at that precise moment, as though the faint tintinnabulation were its cue, the house itself began to speak. It was a rambling wooden house, more than a hundred years old, and it talked to itself at dawn and dusk, creaking, groaning, whispering, muttering like a crotchety old eccentric as its wooden bones expanded with the sun or contracted with the frost. This petulant, arthritic monologue ran on for a few minutes, and then the tenants themselves joined in, one by one: Seth in the bathroom early, spluttering as he washed up; Mr. Thompkins, clearing his throat interminably in the room below, coughing and hacking and spitting as though he were drowning in a sea of phlegm; Sadie's baby, crying in a vain attempt to wake her sluggard mother; Mrs. Hamlin, slamming the kitchen door; Mr. Samuels's loud nasal voice in the courtyard outside.

The sunlight swept across his chair.

The President of the United States stirred and sighed, lifting his arms and setting them down again, stamping his feet to restore circulation. Creakily he got up. He stood for a moment, blinking in the sudden warmth, willing life back into his bones. His arms were gnarled and thin, covered, like his chest, with fine white hair that polarized in the sunlight. He rubbed his hands over his arms to smooth out gooseflesh, pinched the bridge of his nose, and stepped across to the gable window for a look outside. It seemed wrong somehow to see the neat, tree-lined streets of Northview, the old wooden houses, the tiled roofs, the lines of smoke going up black and fine from mortar-chinked chimneys. It seemed especially wrong that there were no automobiles in the streets, no roar and clatter of traffic, no reek of gasoline, no airplanes in the sky—

He turned away from the window. For a moment everything was sick and wrong, and he blinked at the homey, familiar room as though he'd never seen it before, as though it were an unutterably alien place. Everything became hot and tight and terrifying, closing *down* on him. *What's happening?* he asked himself blindly. He leaned against a crossbeam, dazed and baffled, until the distant sound of Mrs. Hamlin's voice—she was scolding Tessie in the kitchen, and the ruckus rose all the way up through three floors of pine and plaster and fine old penny nails—woke him again to his surroundings, with something like pleasure, with something like pain.

Jamie, they called him. Crazy Jamie.

Shaking his head and muttering to himself, Jamie collected his robe and his shaving kit and walked down the narrow, peeling corridor to the small upstairs bedroom. The polished hardwood floor was cold under his feet.

The bathroom was cold, too. It was only the beginning of July, but already the weather was starting to turn nippy late at night and early in the morning. It got colder every year, seemed like. Maybe the glaciers were coming back, as some folks said. Or maybe it was just that he himself was worn a little thinner every year, a little closer to the ultimate cold of the grave. Grunting, he wedged himself into the narrow space between the sink and the downslant of the roof, bumping his head, as usual, against the latch of the skylight window. There was just enough room for him if he stood hunch-shouldered with the toilet bumping up against his thigh. The toilet was an old porcelain monstrosity, worn smooth as glass, that gurgled constantly and comfortably and emitted a mellow breath of earth. It was almost company. The yard boy had already brought up a big basin of "hot" water, although by now, after three or four other people had already used it, it was gray and cold; after the last person used it, it would be dumped down the toilet to help flush out the system. He opened his shaving kit and took out a shapeless cake of lye soap, a worn hand towel, a straight razor.

The mirror above the sink was cracked and tarnished—no help for it, nobody made mirrors anymore. It seemed an appropriate background for the reflection of his face, which was also, in its way, tarnished and dusty and cracked with age. He didn't know how old he was; that was one of the many things Doc Norton had warned him not to think about, so long ago. He couldn't even remember how long he'd been living here in Northview. Ten years? Fifteen?

He studied himself in the mirror, the blotched, earth-colored skin, the eyes sunk deep under a shelf of brow, the network of fine wrinkles. A well-preserved seventy? Memory was dim; the years were misty and fell away before he could number them. He shied away from trying to remember. Didn't matter.

He covered the face with lathered soap.

By the time he finished dressing the other tenants had already gone downstairs. He could hear them talking down there, muffled and distant, like water bugs whispering at the mossy bottom of a deep old well. Cautiously Jamie went back into the hall. The wood floors and paneling up here were not as nicely finished as those in the rest of the house. He thought of all the hidden splinters in all that wood, waiting to catch his flesh. He descended the stairs. The banister swayed as he clutched it, groaning softly to remind him that it, too, was old.

As he came into the dining room, conversation died. The other tenants looked up at him, looked away again. People fiddled with their tableware, adjusted their napkins, pulled their chairs closer to the table or pushed them farther away. Someone coughed self-consciously.

He crossed the room to his chair and stood behind it.

"Morning, Jamie," Mrs. Hamlin said crossly.

"Ma'm," he replied politely, trying to ignore her grumpiness. He was late again.

He sat down. Mrs. Hamlin stared at him disapprovingly, shook her head, and then turned her attention pointedly back to her plate. As if this were a signal, conversation started up again, gradually swelling to its normal level. The awkward moment passed. Jamie concentrated on filling his plate, intercepting the big platters of country ham and eggs and corn bread as they passed up and down the table. It was always like this at meals: the embarrassed pauses, the uneasy sidelong glances, the faces that tried to be friendly but could not entirely conceal distaste. Crazy Jamie, Crazy Jamie. Conversation flowed in ripples around him, never involving him, although the others would smile dutifully at him if he caught their eyes, and occasionally Seth or Tom would nod at him with tolerably unforced cordiality. This morning it wasn't enough. He wanted to talk, too, for the first time in months. He wasn't a child, he was a man, an old man! He paid less attention to his food and began to strain to hear what was being said, looking for a chance to get into the conversation.

Finally the chance came. Seth asked Mr. Samuels a question. It was a point of fact, not opinion, and Jamie knew the answer.

"Yes," Jamie said, "at one time New York City did indeed have a larger population than Augusta."

Abruptly everyone stopped talking. Mr. Samuels's lips closed up tight, and he grimaced as though he had tasted something foul. Seth shook his head wearily, looking sad and disappointed. Jamie lowered his head to avoid Seth's eyes. He could sense Mrs. Hamlin swelling and glowering beside him, but he wouldn't look at her, either.

Damn it, that wasn't what he'd meant to say! They hadn't been talking about that at all. He'd said the wrong thing.

He'd done it again.

People were talking about him around the table, he knew, but he could no longer understand them. He could still hear their voices, but the words had been leached away, and all that remained was noise and hissing static. He concentrated on buttering a slice of corn bread, trying to hang on to that simple mechanical act while the world pulled away from him in all directions, retreating to the very edge of his perception, like a tide that has gone miles out from the beach.

When the world tide came back in, he found himself outside on the porch — the veranda, some of the older folks still called it — with Mrs. Hamlin fussing at him, straightening his clothes, patting his wiry white hair into place, getting him ready to be sent off to work. She was still annoyed with him, but it had no real bite to it, and the exasperated fondness underneath kept showing through even as she scolded him. "You go straight to work now, you hear? No dawdling and mooning around." He nodded his head sheepishly. She was a tall, aristocratic lady with a beak nose, a lined, craggy face, and a tight bun of snowy white hair. She was actually a year or two younger than he was, but he thought of her as much, much older. "And mind you come right straight back here after work, too. To-night's the big Fourthday dinner, and you've got to help in the kitchen, hear? Jamie, are you listening to me?"

He ducked his head and said "Yes'm," his feet already fidgeting to be gone.

Mrs. Hamlin gave him a little push, saying, "Shoo now!" and then, her grim face softening, adding, "Try to be a good boy." He scooted across the veranda and out into the raw, hot brightness of the morning.

He shuffled along, head down, still infused with dull embarrassment from the scolding he'd received. Mr. Samuels went cantering by him, up on his big roan horse, carbine sheathed in a saddle holster, horseshoes ringing against the pavement; off to patrol with the Outriders for the day. Mr. Samuels waved at him as he passed, looking enormously tall and important and adult up on the high saddle, and

65

Jamie answered with the shy, wide, loose-lipped grin that sometimes seemed vacuous even to him. He ducked his head again when Mr. Samuels was out of sight and frowned at the dusty tops of his shoes. The sun was up above the trees and the rooftops now, and it was getting warm.

The five-story brick school building was the tallest building in Northview — now that the bank had burned down — and it cast a cool, blue shadow across his path as he turned onto Main Street. It was still used as a school in the winter and on summer afternoons after the children had come back from the fields, but it was also filled with stockpiles of vital supplies so that it could be used as a stronghold in case of a siege — something that had happened only once, fifteen years ago, when a strong raiding party had come up out of the south. Two fifty-caliber machine guns — salvaged from an Army jeep that had been abandoned on the old state highway a few weeks after the War — were mounted on top of the school's roof, where their field of fire would cover most of the town. They had not been fired in earnest for years, but they were protected from the weather and kept in good repair, and a sentry was still posted up there at all times, although by now the sentry was likely to smuggle a girl up to the roof with him on warm summer nights. Times had become more settled, almost sleepy now. Similarly, the Outriders who patrolled Northview's farthest borders and watched over the flocks and the outlying farms had been reduced from thirty to ten, and it had been three or four years since they'd had a skirmish with anyone; the flow of hungry refugees and marauders and aimless migrants had mostly stopped by now — dead, or else they'd found a place of their own. These days the Outriders were more concerned with animals. The black bears and grizzlies were back in the mountains and the nearby hills, and for the past four or five years there had been wolves again, coming back from who-knew-where, increasing steadily in numbers and becoming more of a threat as the winters hardened. Visitors down from Jackman Station, in Maine, brought a story that a mountain lion had recently been sighted on the slopes of White Cap, in the unsettled country "north of the Moosehead," although before the War there couldn't have been any pumas left closer than Colorado or British Columbia. It had taken only twenty years.

There was a strange wagon in front of the old warehouse that was now the Outriders' station, a rig Jamie had never been before. It was an ordinary enough wagon, but it was *painted.* It was painted in mad streaks and strips and random patchwork splotches of a dozen different colors — deep royal blue, vivid yellow, scarlet, purple, earth-brown, light forest-green, black, burnt orange—as if a hundred children from prewar days had been at it with finger paint. To Jamie's eyes, accustomed to the dull and faded tones of Northview's weather-beaten old buildings, the streaks of color were so brilliant that they seemed to vibrate and stand out in raised contrast from the wagon's surface. He was not used to seeing bright colors anymore, except those in the natural world around him, and this paint was *fresh*, something he also hadn't seen in more years than he could remember. Even the big horse, which stood patiently in the wagon's traces—and which now rolled an incurious eye up at Jamie and blew out its lips with a blubbery snorting sound—even the *horse* was painted, blue on one side, bright green on the other, with orange streaks up its flanks.

Jamie goggled at all this, wondering if it could possibly be real or if it was one of "effects"—hallucinations, as even *he* understood—that he sometimes got during particularly bad "spells." After a moment or two—during which the wagon didn't shimmer or fade around the edges at all—he widened his attention enough to notice the signs: big hand-painted signs hung on either side of a kind of sandwich-board framework that was braced upright in the wagon bed. At the top each sign read MOHAWK CONFEDERACY in bright red paint, and then, underneath that, came a long list of words, each word painted in a different color:

HAND-LOADED AMMUNITION
PAINT
FALSE TEETH
EYEGLASSES—GROUND TO PRESCRIPTION
LAMP OIL
PAINLESS DENTISTRY
UNTAINTED SEED FOR WHEAT, CORN, MELONS
FLAX CLOTH
WINDOW GLASS
MEDICINES & LINIMENT
CONDOMS
IRON FARM TOOLS
UNTAINTED LIVESTOCK
NAILS
MUSICAL INSTRUMENTS
MARIJUANA
WHISKY
SOAP
PRINTING DONE
!ALL MADE IN MOHAWK!

Jamie was puzzling out some of the harder words when the door to the Outriders' station opened and Mr. Stover came hurriedly down the stairs. "What're you doing here, Jamie?" he asked. "What're you hanging around here for?"

Jamie gaped at him, trying to find the words to describe the wonderful new wagon, and how strange it made him feel, but the effort was too great, and the words slipped away. "Going to Mr. Hardy's store," he said at last. "Just going to sweep up at Mr. Hardy's store."

Mr. Stover glanced nervously back up at the door of the Outriders' station, fingered his chin for a moment while he made up his mind, and then said, "Never mind that today, Jamie. Never mind about the store today. You just go on back home now."

"But—" Jamie said, bewildered. "But—I sweep up every day!"

"Not today," Mr. Stover said sharply. "You go on home, you hear me? Go on, git!"

"Mrs. Hamlin's going to be awful mad." Jamie said sadly, resignedly.

"You tell Edna I said for you to go home. And you stay inside, too, Jamie. You stay out of sight, hear? We've got an important visitor here in Northview today, and it'd never do to have him run into *you*."

Jamie nodded his head in acceptance of this. He wasn't so dumb that he didn't know what the unvoiced part of the sentence was: run into *you*, the half-wit, the crazy person, the nut. He'd heard it often enough. He knew he was crazy. He knew that he was an embarrassment. He knew that he had to stay inside, away from visitors, lest he embarrass Mrs. Hamlin and all his friends.

Crazy Jamie.

Slowly he turned and shuffled away, back the way he had come.

The sun beat down on the back of his head now, and sweat gathered in the wrinkled hollows beneath his eyes.

Crazy Jamie.

At the corner, bathed in the shadow cast by the big oak at the edge of the schoolyard, he turned and looked back.

A group of men had come out of the Outriders' station and were now walking slowly in the direction of Mr. Hardy's store, talking as they went. There was Mr. Jameson, Mr. Galli, Mr. Stover, Mr. Ashley, and, in the middle of them, talking animatedly and waving his arms, the visitor, the stranger—a big, florid-faced man with a shock of unruly blond hair that shone like beaten gold in the sunlight.

Watching him, the visitor—now clapping a hand on Mr. Galli's shoulder, Mr. Galli shrinking away—Jamie felt a chill, that unreasoning and unreasoned fear of strangers, of everything from outside Northview's narrow boundaries, that had affected him ever since he could remember, and suddenly his delight in the wonderful wagon was tarnished, diminished, because he realized that it, too, must come from outside.

He headed for home, walking a little faster now, as if chivied along by some old cold wind that didn't quite reach the sunlit world.

That night was the Fourthday feast — "Independence Day," some of the old folks still called it — and for Jamie, who was helping in the kitchen as usual, the early part of the evening was a blur of work as they sweated to prepare the meal: roast turkey, ham, wild pigeon, trout, baked raccoon, sweet potatoes, corn, pearl onions, berry soup, homemade bread, blackberries, plums, and a dozen other things.

That was all as usual; he expected and accepted that. What was not usual — and what he did not expect — was that he would not be allowed to eat with the rest when the feast was served. Instead, Tessie set a plate out for him in the kitchen, saying, not unkindly, "Now, Jamie, mind you stay here. They've got a guest out there this year, that loud-mouthed Mr. Brodey, and Mrs. Hamlin, she says you got to eat in the kitchen and keep out of sight. Now don't you mind, honey. I'll fix you up a plate real nice, just the same stuff you'd get out there."

And then, after a few moments of somewhat embarrassed bustling, she was gone.

Jamie sat alone in the empty kitchen.

His plate was filled to overflowing with food, and he'd even been given a glass of dandelion wine, a rare treat, but somehow he wasn't hungry anymore.

He sat listening to the wind tug at the old house, creaking the rafters, making the wood groan. When the wind died, he could hear them talking out there in the big dining room, the voices just too faint for him to make out the words.

An unfamiliar anger began to rise in him. "Crazy Jamie," he said aloud, his voice sounding flat and dull to his own ears. It wasn't fair. He glanced out the window, to where the sun had almost set in a welter of sullen purple clouds. Suddenly he slashed out at the glass of wine, sending it spinning to the floor. It wasn't fair! He was an adult, wasn't he? Why did he have to sit back here by himself like a naughty child? Even if — In spite of — He was —

Somehow he found himself on his feet. He *deserved* to eat with the others, didn't he? He was as good as anybody else, wasn't he? In fact — In *fact* —

The corridor. He seemed to float along it in spite of his stumbling, 69 hesitant feet. The voices got louder, and just at the point where they resolved into words he stopped, standing unnoticed in the shadows behind the dining-room archway, hanging onto the door-jamb, torn between rage and fear and a curious, empty yearning.

"Sooner or later you'll find that you have to incorporate with the Confederacy," Mr. Brodey, the stranger, was saying. The other faces around the big dining-room table were cool and reserved. "The kind of inter-village barter economy you've got up here just can't hold up forever, you know, even though it's really a kind of communal socialism—"

"Are you sayin' we're *communists* up heah?" Mr. Samuels said, outraged, but before Brodey could reply (if he intended to), Jamie strode to the table, pulled out an empty chair—his own habitual seat—and sat down. All faces turned to him, startled, and conversation stopped.

Jamie stared back at them. To walk to the table had taken the last of his will; things were closing down on him again, his vision was swimming, and he began to lose touch with his body, as if his mind were floating slowly up and away from it, like a balloon held by the thinnest sort of tether. Sweat broke out on his forehead, and he opened his mouth, panting like a dog. Through a sliding, shifting confusion, he heard Mrs. Hamlin start to say, "Jamie! I thought I told you—" at the same time that Mr. Ashley was saying to Mr. Brodey, "Don't let him bother you none. He's just the local half-wit. We'll send him back to the kitchen," and Brodey was smiling in tolerant, condescending amusement, and something about Brodey's thin, contemptuous smile, something about the circle of staring faces, *something* wrenched words up out of Jamie, sending them suddenly flying out of his mouth. He hurled the familiar words out at the pale staring faces as he had so many times before, rattling their teeth with them, shaking them to their bones. He didn't know what the words meant anymore, but they were the old strong words, the right words, and he heard his voice fill with iron. He spoke the words until there were no more words to speak, and then he stopped.

A deathly hush had fallen over the room. Mr. Brodey was staring at him, and Jamie saw his face run through a quick gamut of expressions: from irritation to startled speculation to dawning astonishment. Brodey's jaw went slack, and he gasped—a little startled grunt, as if he had been punched in the stomach—and the color went swiftly out of his face. "My God!" he said. "Oh, my God!"

For Jamie, it was as if the world were draining away again, everything pulling back until he could just barely touch reality with his fingertips, and the room shimmered and buzzed as he struggled to hold on to even that much control. All the faces had gone blank, wiped clean of individuality, and he could no longer tell which of the featureless pink ovoids was the sweating, earnest, astounded face of Mr. Brodey. He got clumsily to his feet, driving his leaden body by an act of conscious will, as though it were some ill-made clockwork golem. He flailed his arms for balance, knocked his chair over with a clatter, and stood swaying before them, smelling the sour reek of his own sweat. "I'm sorry," he blurted. "I'm sorry, Mrs. Hamlin. I didn't *mean* to—"

The silence went on a moment longer, and then, above the mounting waves of buzzing nausea and unreality, he heard Mrs. Hamlin say, "That's all right, child. We know you didn't mean any harm. Go on upstairs now, Jamie. Go on." Her voice sounded dry and flat and tired.

Blindly Jamie spun and stumbled for the stairs, all the inchoate demons of memory snapping at his heels like years.

Downstairs, Mr. Brodey was still saying, "Oh, my God!" He hardly noticed that the dinner party was being dissolved around him or that Mrs. Hamlin was hustling him out onto the porch "for a word in private." When she finally had him alone out there, the cool evening breeze slapping at his face through the wire mesh of the enclosed porch, he shook himself out of his daze and turned slowly to face her where she stood hunched and patient in the dappled shadows. "It's *him*," he said, still more awe than accusation in his voice. "Son of a *bitch*. It really is him, isn't it?"

"Who, Mr. Brodey?"

"Don't play games with me," Brodey said harshly. "I've seen the old pictures. The half-wit, he really was—"

"*Is*."

"—the President of the United States." Brodey stared at her. "He may be crazy, but not because he thinks he's the President—he *is* the President. James W. McNaughton. He *is* McNaughton, isn't he?"

"Yes."

"My God! Think of it. The very last President."

"The *incumbent* President," Mrs. Hamlin said softly.

They stared at each other through the soft evening shadows.

"And it's not a surprise to you, either, is it?" Anger was beginning to replace disbelief in Brodey's voice. "You've known it all along, haven't you? All of you have known. You all knew from the start that he was President McNaughton?"

"Yes."

"My God!" Brodey said, giving an entirely new reading to the phrase, disgust and edgy anger instead of awe. He opened his mouth, closed it, and began turning red.

"He came here almost twenty years ago, Mr. Brodey," Mrs. Hamlin said, speaking calmly, reminiscently. "Perhaps two months after the War. The Outriders found him collapsed in a field out by the edge of town. He was nearly dead. Don't ask me how he got there. Maybe there was some sort of hidden bunker way back up there in the hills, maybe his plane crashed nearby, maybe he walked all the way up here from what's left of Washington—I don't know. Jamie himself doesn't know. His memory was almost gone; shock, I guess, and exposure. All he remembered, basically, was that he was the President, and even that was dim and misty, like something you might remember out of a bad dream, the kind that fades away and comes back sometimes, late at night. And life's been like a half-dream for him ever since, poor soul. He never did get quite right in the head again."

"And you gave him shelter?" Brodey said, his voice becoming shrill with indignation. "You took him in? That butcher?"

"Watch your mouth, son. You're speaking about the President."

"God damn it, woman. Don't you know— *he caused the War?*"

After a smothering moment of silence, Mrs. Hamlin said mildly, "That's your opinion, Mr. Brodey, not mine."

"How can you deny it? The 'One Life' Ultimatum? The 'preventative strikes' on Mexico and Panama? It was within hours of the raid on Monterrey that the bombs started falling."

"He didn't have any other *choice!* The Indonesians had pushed him—"

"That's crap, and you know it!" Brodey was shouting now. "They taught us all about it down in Mohawk; they made *damn* sure we knew the name of the man who destroyed the world, you can bet on that! Christ, everybody knew *then* that he was unfit for office, just a bombastic backwoods senator on a hate crusade, a cracker-barrel warmonger. Everybody *said* that he'd cause the War if he got into the White House—and he did! By God, he did! That pathetic half-wit in there. *He* did it!"

Mrs. Hamlin sighed and folded her arms across her middle, hugging herself as if in pain. She seemed to grow smaller and older, more withered and gnarled. "I don't know, son," she said wearily, after a heavy pause. "Maybe you're right, maybe you're wrong. Maybe *he* was wrong. I don't know. All that seemed so important then. Now I can hardly remember what the issues were, what it was all *about*. It doesn't seem to matter much anymore, somehow."

"How can you *say* that?" Brodey wiped at his face—he was sweating profusely and looking very earnest now, bewilderment leaching away some of the anger. "How can you let that . . . that man . . . *him*—how can you let *him* live here, under your roof? How can you stand to let him live at all, let alone cook for him, do his washing. My God!"

"His memory was gone, Mr. Brodey. His *mind* was gone. Can you understand that? Old Doc Norton, rest his soul, spent months just trying to get Jamie to the point where he could walk around by himself without anybody to watch him too close. He had to be taught how to feed himself, how to dress himself, how to go to the bathroom —like a child. At first there was some even right here in Northview that felt the way you do, Mr. Brodey, and there's still some as can't be comfortable around Jamie, but one by one they came to understand, and they made their peace with him. Whatever he was or wasn't, he's just like a little child now—sick, old, frightened child who doesn't really understand what's happening to him, most of the time. Mr. Brodey, you can't hate a little child for something he can't even remember he's done."

Brodey spun around, as though to stalk back into the house, and then spun violently back. "He should be dead!" Brodey shouted. His fists were clenched now, and the muscles in his neck were corded. "At the very *least*, he should be dead! Billions of lives on that man's hands! *Billions*. And *you*, you people, you not only let him live, you make excuses for him! For *him!*" He stopped, groping for words to express the enormity of his outrage. "It's like . . . like making excuses for the Devil himself!"

Mrs. Hamlin stirred and came forward, stepping out of the porch shadows and into the moonlight, drawing her shawl more tightly around her, as though against a chill, although the night was still mild. She stared eye to eye with Brodey for several moments, while the country silence gathered deeply around them, broken only by crickets and the hoarse sound of Brodey's impassioned breathing. Then she said, "I thought I owed it to you, Mr. Brodey, to try to explain a few things. But I don't know if I can. Things have changed enough by now, steadied down enough, that maybe you younger people find it hard to understand, but those of us who lived through the War, we all had to do things we didn't want to do. Right there where you're standing. Mr. Brodey, right here on this porch, I shot a marauder down, shot him dead with my husband's old pistol, with

Mr. Hamlin himself laying stiff in the parlor not ten feet away, taken by the Lumpy Plague. And I've done worse things than that, too, in my time. I reckon we all have, all the survivors. And just maybe it's no different with that poor old man sitting in there."

Brodey regained control of himself. His jaw was clenched, and the muscles around his mouth stood out in taut little bands, but his breathing had evened, and his face was tight and cold. He had banked his anger down into a smoldering, manageable flame, and now for the first time he seemed dangerous. Ignoring—or seeming to ignore—Mrs. Hamlin's speech, he said conversationally, "Do you know that we curse by him down in Mohawk? His name is a curse to us. Can *you* understand *that?* We burn him in effigy on his birthday, in the town squares, and over the years it's become quite a little ceremony. He must atone, Mrs. Hamlin. He must be made to pay for what he's done. We don't suffer monsters to live, down in Mohawk."

"Ayuh," Mrs. Hamlin said sourly, "you do a lot of damnfool, jackass things down there, don't you?" Mrs. Hamlin tossed her head back, silver hair glinting in the silver light, and seemed to grow taller again. There was a hard light in her eyes now, and a hard new edge in her voice. "Atone, is it now, you jackass? As if you're some big pious kind of churchman, some damn kind of saint, you red-faced, loud-mouthed man. You with your damnfool flag and damnfool Mohawk Confederacy. Well, let me tell *you*, mister, this isn't any Mohawk Confederacy here, never has been, never will be: This is Northview, sovereign state of Vermont, *United States of America.* Do you hear me, mister? This here is the United States of America, and that poor fool in there—why, he's the *President* of the United States of America, even if sometimes he can't cut his meat up proper. Maybe he was a fool, maybe he was wrong long ago, maybe he's crazy now, but he's still the *President.*" Eyes snapping, she jabbed a finger at Brodey. "As long as this town stands, then there's still an America, and that old man will be President as long as there are still *Americans* alive to serve him. We take care of our own, Mr. Brodey; *we take care of our own.*"

A shadow materialized at Brodey's elbow and spoke with Seth's voice. "Edna?"

Brodey turned his head to glance at Seth. When he turned back to face Mrs. Hamlin, there was a gun in her hand, a big, old-fashioned revolver that looked too huge for the small, blue-veined hand that held it.

"You can't be serious," Brodey whispered.

"You need any help, Edna?" the shadow said. "I brought some of the boys."

"No, thank you, Seth." The barrel of the revolver was as unwavering as her gaze. "There's some things a person's got to do for herself." Then she cocked the hammer back.

The President of the United States didn't notice the shot. Alone in the small upstairs bathroom, he avoided the eyes of the tarnished reflection in the mirror and compulsively washed his hands.

EXECUTIVE CLEMENCY

As I mentioned, I was once a member of the now-defunct Guilford Writers Workshop. This was a group of—at the time—Young Turks— oh God, can this really have been almost *twenty years ago?* Jesus!— who met pretty frequently for workshopping sessions throughout the early '70s, the sessions starting, at a guess, sometime in late 1970 and running through 1974. The Workshop was held at Jack (Jay) Haldeman's rambling old house in the pretty Guilford section of Baltimore. Charter members included Jay, his brother Joe Haldeman, Jack Dann, George Alec Effinger, Ted White, and me, although writers such as Bob Thurston, Tom Monteleone, Jean Sullivan, William Nabors, Ev Leif, and others attended one session or another over the years.

At one Guilford—I think that it was in late 1973—Jay put an unfinished manuscript fragment into the workshop to be critiqued. Sardonically titled, for convenience's sake, "One of Our President's Brain Cells is Missing," the fragment consisted of an early version of the opening scene of the present story, with a man who is referred to as the President of the United States waking up in the attic of an old boardinghouse, going downstairs to where the other boarding-house residents are having breakfast, and humiliating himself by breaking into the conversation with an answer to a question that hadn't really been asked, about how at one time New York City did indeed have a larger population than Augusta (although I think it was Albany in Jay's draft). There the fragment ended.

After the fragment was workshopped, somewhat inconclusively (since the workshop process really doesn't work that well with in-complete story fragments or chunks taken out of unfinished novels-in-progress), I got to talking to Jay about it. There was something about the atmosphere of the fragment that fascinated me, and brought up all sorts of questions. The bigger-than-New-York-City answer seemed to indicate that this was an After-the-Bomb scenario, but that didn't quite fit with the shabby boardinghouse ambience, and if this was the President, why did everybody treat him like a half-witted servant? Did he just *think* he was the President? And so on. Jay said that he had no idea; he was completely stalled on the story, and had no idea where it was going. I continued to pester him with questions, and with suggestions about where I thought the story should go, and then Jay made a big mistake: he smiled affably at me and said, "Well, why don't *you* finish the story, then? We can do it as a collaboration." I agreed enthusiastically, and left Baltimore a couple of days later with the fragment tucked safely into my bag.

Time passed. A *lot* of time . . . during which Jay no doubt gave up all hope of ever hearing anything about his story again.

Then one day, sometime in late 1979 or early 1980, I was browsing through some old files, and happened to pick up the fragment again. I'd just finished working on "Touring," and was feeling confident and full of creative energy for the first time in quite a while — I looked at the fragment again, and this time, I suddenly knew what to do with it. I'd been thinking about it all this time as being about a man who thinks that he's the President of the United States, a poor soul with delusions of grandeur; all at once, I saw that the story ought to be about a poor soul in mean circumstances who really *is* the President of the United States, and, once I saw that, everything else fell instantly into place.

I sat down at once, on my back stoop, and began working on the story in longhand in a three-ring notebook, starting with the scene where Jamie goes out and sees the strange wagon in front of the Outriders' station. In a couple of days, I'd finished the rest of the story, and then went back and worked on the opening scene, smoothing it out so that it would be a better stylistic match with the rest of the text, fluffing it out some, and inserting a few more introspective passages for Jamie. I was interested to see that by the time I'd finished the story, the figure of the President, who had started out as a typical Liberal Bugbear — we'd both been thinking of him as a kind of gloating, mean-spirited caricature of Nixon, down on his luck at last — had become a pitiable, sympathetic character who even had a good deal of his own odd sort of dignity; stories often know what you should do with them, and insist that you do it, even when *you* don't.

So then I wrote to Jay and told him the glad news—I had indeed finished the story, and it had taken me *only six years!* Or maybe *seven;* I'd lost track. Boy, talk about cost efficiency! Wasn't he *lucky?* I'd actually finished it before the Twentieth Century ran out.

The story sold to *Omni,* and remains one of my favorites.

Oh, yeah—I changed the title, too.

■
■
■
■
■

Afternoon at Schrafft's

GARDNER DOZOIS, JACK DANN, & MICHAEL SWANWICK

The wizard sat alone at a table in Schrafft's, eating a tuna sandwich on rye. He finished off the last bite of his sandwich, sat back, and licked a spot of mayonnaise off his thumb. There was an ozone crackle in the air, and his familiar, a large brindle cat, materialized in the chair opposite him.

The cat coldly eyed the wizard's empty plate. "And where, may I ask, is my share?" he demanded.

The wizard coughed in embarrassment.

"You mean you didn't even leave me a crumb, is that it?"

The wizard shrugged and looked uncomfortable. "There's still a pickle left," he suggested.

The cat was not mollified.

"Or some chips. Have some potato chips."

"Feh," sneered the cat. "Potato chips I didn't want. What I *wanted* was a piece of your sandwich, Mister Inconsiderate."

"Listen, aggravation I don't need from you. Don't make such a big deal—it's only a *tunafish sandwich*. So who cares!"

"So who *cares?*" the cat spat. "So I care, that's who. Listen, it's not just the sandwich. It's everything! It's your *attitude.*"

"Don't talk to *me* about *my* attitude—"

"Somebody should. You think you're *so* hot. Mister Big Deal! The big-time Wizard!" The cat sneered at him. "Hah! You need me more than I need you, believe me, Mister Oh-I'm-So-Wonderful!"

"Don't make me laugh," the wizard said.

"You couldn't get along without me, and you know it!"

"I'm laughing," the wizard said. "It's such a funny joke you're making, look at me, I'm laughing. Hah. Hah. Hah."

The cat fluffed itself up, enraged. "Without me, you couldn't even get through the day. What an ingrate! You refuse to admit just how much you really need me. Why, without me, you couldn't even—" The cat paused, casting about for an example, and his gaze fell on the check. "Without me, you couldn't even pay the *check*."

"Oh yeah?"

"Yeah. Even something as simple as *that*, you couldn't do it by yourself. You couldn't handle it."

"*Sure* I could. Don't get too big for your britches. Stuff like this I was handling before *you* were even weaned, bubbie, let *alone* housebroken. So don't puff yourself up."

The cat sneered at him again. "Okay, so go ahead! Show me! Do it!"

"Do what?" said the wizard, after a pause, a trace of uneasiness coming into his voice.

"Pay the check. Take care of it yourself."

"All right," the wizard said. "All right, then, I will!"

"So go ahead, already. I'm watching. This ought to be good." The cat smiled nastily and faded away, slowly disappearing line by line—the Cheshire cat was one of his heroes, and this was a favorite trick, although for originality's sake he left his nose behind instead of his grin. The nose hung inscrutably in mid-air, like a small black-rubber UFO. Occasionally it would give a sardonic twitch.

The wizard sighed, and sat staring morosely down at the check. Then, knowing in advance that it would be useless, he pulled out his battered old change purse and peered inside: nothing, except for some lint, the tiny polished skull of a bat, and a ticket stub from the 1876 Centennial Exposition. The wizard never carried money—ordinarily, he'd have just told the cat to conjure up whatever funds were necessary, an exercise so simple and trivial that it was beneath his dignity as a Mage even to consider bothering with it himself. That was what familiars were *for*, to have tasks like that delegated to them. Now, though. . . .

"Well?" the cat's voice drawled. "So, I'm waiting. . . ."

"All right, all right, big shot," the wizard said. "I can handle this, don't worry yourself."

"I'm not worried—I'm *waiting*."

"All right already." Mumbling to himself, the wizard began to work out the elements of the spell. It was a very *small* magic, after all. Still. . . . He hesitated, drumming his fingers on the table. . . . Still, he hadn't had to do anything like this for himself for years, and his memory wasn't what it used to be. . . . Better ease his hand in slowly, try a still smaller magic first. Practice. Let's see now. . . . He muttered a few words in a hissing sibilant tongue, sketched a close pattern in the air, and then rested his forefinger on the rim of his empty coffee cup. The cup filled with coffee, as though his finger was a spigot. He grunted in satisfaction, and then took a sip of his coffee. It was weak and yellow, and tasted faintly of turpentine. So far, so good, he thought. . . .

Across the table, the nose sniffed disdainfully.

The wizard ignored it. *Now* for the real thing. He loosened his tie and white starched collar and drew the pentagram of harmony, the *Sephiroth*, using salt from the shaker, which was also the secret symbol for the fifth element of the pentagram, the *akasha*, or ether. He made do with a glass of water, catsup, mustard, and toothpicks to represent the four elements and the worlds of Emanation, Creation, Formation, and Action. He felt cheap and vulgar using such substitutes, but what else could he do?

Now . . . he thought, that *is* the pentagram of harmony . . . isn't it? For an instant he was uncertain. Well, it's close enough. . . .

He tugged back his cuffs, leaving his wrists free to make the proper passes over the pentagram. Now . . . what was the spell to make money? It was either the first or the second Enochian Key . . . *that* much he did remember. It must be the second Key, and that went . . . *"Piamoel od Vaoan!"* No, no, that wasn't it. Was it *"Giras ta nazodapesad Roray I?"* That *must* be it.

The wizard said the words and softly clapped his hands together . . . and nothing seemed to happen.

For an instant there was no noise, not even a breath. It was as if he was hovering, disembodied, between the worlds of Emanation.

There was a slow shift in his equilibrium, like a wheel revolving ponderously in darkness.

But magic doesn't just disappear, he told himself querulously—it has to go *somewhere*.

As if from the other side of the world, the wizard heard the soft voice of his familiar, so faint and far away that he could barely make it out. What was it saying?

"Putz," the cat whispered, "you used the Pentagram of Chaos, the *Qliphoth*."

And suddenly, as if he really had been turned upside-down for a while, the wizard felt everything right itself. He was sitting at a table in Schrafft's, and there was the usual din of people talking and shouting and pushing and complaining.

But something was odd, something was wrong. Even as he watched, the table splintered and flew to flinders before him, and his chair creaked and groaned and swayed like a high-masted ship in a strong wind, and then broke, dumping him heavily to the floor. The room shook, and the floor cracked and starred beneath him.

What was wrong? What aethers and spheres had he roiled and foiled with his misspoken magicks? Why did he feel so *strange?* Then he saw himself in the goldflecked smoked-glass mirrors that lined the room between rococo plaster pillars, and the reflection told him the terrible truth. He had turned himself into some kind of giant lizard. A dinosaur. Actually, as dinosaurs go, he was rather small. He weighed about eight hundred pounds and was eleven feet long—a Pachycephalosaurus, a horn-headed, pig-snouted herbivore that was in its prime in the Upper Cretaceous. But for Schrafft's, at lunch-time—big enough. He clicked his stubby tusks and tried to say "Gevalt!" as he shook his head ruefully. Before he could stop the motion, his head smashed into the wooden booth partition, causing it to shudder and crack.

Across from him, two eyes appeared, floating to either side of the hovering black nose. Slowly, solemnly, one eye winked. Then— slowly and very sinisterly—eyes and nose faded away and were gone.

That was a bad sign, the wizard thought. He huddled glumly against the wall. Maybe nobody will notice, he thought. His tail twitched nervously, splintering the booth behind him. The occupants of the booth leaped up, screaming, and fled the restaurant in terror. Out-of-towners, the wizard thought. Everyone else was eating and talking as usual, paying no attention, although the waiter *was* eyeing him somewhat sourly.

As he maneuvered clumsily away from the wall, pieces of wood crunching underfoot, the waiter came up to him and stood there making little *tsk*ing noises of disapproval. "Look, mister," the waiter said. "You're going to have to pay up and go. You're creating a disturbance—" The wizard opened his mouth to utter a mild remon-strance, but what came out instead was a thunderous roaring belch, grindingly deep and loud enough to rattle your bones, the sort of noise that might be produced by having someone stand on the bass keys of a giant Wurlitzer. Even the wizard could smell the fermenting, rotting-egg, bubbling-prehistoric-swamp stink of sulphur that his belch had released, and he winced in embarrassment. "I'm sorry," the wizard said, enunciating with difficulty through the huge, sloppy mouth. "It's the tunafish. I know I shouldn't eat it, it always gives me gas, but —" But the waiter no longer seemed to be listening — he had gone pale, and now he turned abruptly around without a word and walked away, ignoring as he passed the querulous demands for coffee refills from the people two tables away, marching in a straight line through the restaurant and right out into the street.

The wizard sighed, a gusty, twanging noise like a cello being squeezed flat in a wine-press. Time — and *past* time — to work an obviation spell. So, then. Forgetting that he was a dinosaur, the wizard hurriedly tried to redraw the pentagram, but he couldn't pick up the salt, which was in a small pile around the broken glass shaker. And everything else he would need for the spell was buried under the debris of the table.

"Not doing so hot now, Mister Big Shot, are you?" a voice said, rather smugly.

"Alright, alright, give me a minute, will you?" said the wizard, a difficult thing to say when your voice croaked like a gigantic frog's — it was hard to be a dinosaur and talk. But the wizard sill had his pride. "You don't make soup in a second," he said. Then he began thinking feverishly. He didn't really *need* the elements and representations of the four worlds and the pentagram of Kabbalistic squares, not for an obviation spell, although, of course, things would be much more elegant *with* them. But. He *could* work the obviation spell by words alone — *if* he could remember the words. He needed something from the Eighteenth Path, that which connects *Binah* and *Geburah*, the House of Influence. Let's see, he thought. "*E pluribus unum.*" No, no. . . . Could it be "*Micaoli beranusaji UK?*" No, that was a pharmacological spell. . . . But, yes, of *course*, this was it, and he began to chant "*Tstske, tstskeleh, tchotchike, tchotchkeleh, trayf, Qu-a-a-on!*"

That should do it.

But nothing happened. Again! The wizard tried to frown, but hadn't the face for it. "Nothing happened," he complained.

The cat's head materialized in midair. "That's what *you* think. As a matter of fact, all the quiches at Maxim's just turned into frogs. Great big ones," he added maliciously. "Great big green *slimy* ones."

The wizard dipped his great head humbly. "All right," he grumbled.

"Enough is enough. I give up. I admit defeat. I was wrong. From now on, I promise, I'll save you a bite of every sandwich I ever order."

The cat appeared fully for a moment, swishing its tail thoughtfully back and forth. "You do know, don't you, that I prefer the part in the middle, without the crust . . . ?"

"I'll never give you the crust, always from the middle—"

The waiter had come back into the restaurant, towing a policeman behind him and was now pointing an indignant finger toward the wizard. The policeman began to slouch slowly toward them, looking bored and sullen and mean.

"I mean, it's not really the sandwich, you know," the cat said.

"I know, I know," the wizard mumbled.

"I get insecure too, like everyone else. I need to know that I'm wanted. It's the *thought* that counts, knowing that you're thinking about me, that you want me around—"

"All right, all right!" the wizard snapped irritably. Then he sighed again, and (with what would have been a gesture of final surrender if he'd had hands to spread) said "So, okay, I want you around." He softened, and said almost shyly, "I *do*, you know." "I know," the cat said. They stared at each other with affection for a moment, and then the cat said, "For making money, it's the new moon blessing, '*Steyohn, v's-keyah-lahnough*—'"

"Money I don't need anymore," the wizard said grumpily. "Money it's gone beyond. Straighten out all of *this*—" gesturing with his pig-like snout at his—feh!—scaly green body.

"Not to worry. The *proper* obviation spell is that one you worked out during the Council of Trent, remember?"

The cat hissed out the words. Once again the wheel rotated slowly in darkness.

And then, the wizard was sitting on the floor, in possession of his own spindly limbs again. Arthritically, he levered himself to his feet.

The cat watched him get up, saying smugly, "And as a bonus, I even put money in your purse, not bad, huh? I told—" And then the cat fell silent, staring off beyond the wizard's shoulder. The wizard looked around.

Everyone else in Schrafft's had turned into dinosaurs.

All around them were dinosaurs, dinosaurs in every possible variety, dinosaurs great and small, four-footed and two-footed, horned and scaled and armor-plated, striped and speckled and piebald, all busily eating lunch, hissing and grunting and belching and slurping, huge jaws chewing noisily, great fangs flashing and clashing, razor-sharp talons clicking on tile. The din was horrendous. The policeman had turned into some sort of giant spiky armadillo, and was contentedly munching up the baseboard. In one corner, two nattily-pinstriped allosaurs were fighting over the check, tearing huge bloody pieces out of each other. It was impossible to recognize the waiter.

The cat stared at the wizard.

The wizard stared at the cat.

The cat shrugged.

After a moment, the wizard shrugged too.

They both sighed.

"Lunch tomorrow?" the wizard asked, and the cat said, "Suits me."

Behind them, one of the triceratops finished off its second egg cream, and made a rattling noise with the straw.

The wizard left the money for the check near the cash register, and added a substantial tip.

They went out of the restaurant together, out into the watery city sunshine, and strolled away down the busy street through the fine mild airs of spring.

A F T E R W O R D   T O
AFTERNOON AT SCHRAFFT'S

Somewhere in this book, Michael refers to "Afternoon at Schrafft's" as a "pleasant little soufflé of a story," and tells the story of its eccentric origin. There really is little left for me to add.

Michael was undoubtedly the godparent of this particular story, practically forcing it into existence by sheer effort of will, tirelessly bullying and cajoling us into starting to plot it at his famous party, when our resistance was at low ebb, due to a superabundance of alcohol in the blood. All this took place on February 28, 1982. Michael also took first draft on this, I believe, then Jack, then me. In spite of all the back-and-forth, we worked quickly, and the story was finished, according to a note on my calendar, on March 30, 1982. I had worked on it just after finishing work on my story "Morning Child," just before starting work on "Dinner Party," and *while* I was working on our story "Slow Dancing With Jesus." As I said, this was a high-production period for me.

All of the spells and the Kabbalist magical lore here were provided solely by Jack — so argue with *him* if you think they're wrong. When I write a story with Jack that contains comic Yiddish-*shtick* dialogue, people usually assume that Jack writes all of those parts, but, in fact, both here and in "Time Bride," I wrote much of it myself — which just goes to show that it's dangerous to make assumptions about who contributed what to collaborations. The image of the nose hanging in the air like a black rubber UFO was Michael's, I think. And Bob Walters, our Friendly Neighborhood Dinosaur Expert, supplied the Pachycephalosaurus.

As anyone who has worked with me will testify, I attach a great deal of importance to the last lines of stories, and I have been known to agonize for weeks to come up with just the right last line. (It's my own opinion that even a story that is otherwise in every way good *except* for the last line can lose 30-40% of the impact it would have had, if it had a good last line.) For this particular story, I came up with *three* possible last lines, and, unable to decide between them, used them all, in sequence. I'd done the same thing once before, in my solo story "The Storm."

The story was published in *Amazing*, March 1984.

We've tried to sell this story as a children's book, but no one seems interested, just as no one is interested in Michael's own brilliant series of children's stories about The Two Buildings (starting with that classic, *The Two Buildings Do Lunch*), or in Tess Kissinger's work, or in several other pieces I can think of. Of course, since I once heard a major children's book editor say, during a speech, that "children, of course, must under no circumstances be exposed to fantasy," I suppose that I really shouldn't be surprised.

A Change in the Weather

GARDNER DOZOIS & JACK DANN

It looked like rain again, but Michael went for his walk anyway.

The park was shiny and empty, nothing more than a cement square defined by four metal benches. Piles of rain-soaked garbage were slowly dissolving into the cement.

Pterodactyls picked their way through the gutter, their legs lifting storklike as they daintily nipped at random pieces of refuse.

Muttering, the old man shooed a pterodactyl from his favorite bench, which was still damp from the afternoon rain, sat down, and tried to read his newspaper. But at once his bench was surrounded by the scavengers: they half-flapped their metallic-looking wings, tilted the heads at the ends of their snakelike necks to look at him with oily green eyes, uttered plaintive, begging little cries, and finally plucked at his clothes with their beaks, hoping to find crusts of bread or popcorn. At last, exasperatedly, he got suddenly to his feet — the pterodactyls skittering back away from him, croaking in alarm — and tried to scare them off by throwing his newspaper at them. They ate it, and looked to him hopefully for more. It began to rain, drizzling down out of the the gray sky.

Disgustedly, he made his way across the park, being jostled and almost knocked over by a hustling herd of small two-legged dromaei-saurs who were headed for the hot-dog concession on Sixteenth Street. The rain was soaking in through his clothes now, and in spite of the warmth of the evening he was beginning to get chilly. He hoped the weather wasn't going to turn nippy; heating oil was getting really expensive, and his social security check was late again. An ankylosaur stopped in front of him, grunting and slurping as it chewed up old Coke bottles and beer cans from a cement trash-barrel. He whacked it with his cane, impatiently, and it slowly moved out of his way, belching with a sound like a length of anchor chain being dropped through a hole.

There were brontosaurs lumbering along Broadway, as usual taking up the center of the street, with more agile herds of honking, duckbilled hadrosaurs dodging in and out of the lanes between them, and an occasional carnosaur stumping along by the curb, shaking its great head back and forth and hissing to itself in the back of its throat. It used to be, a person could get a bus here, and without even needing a transfer get within a block of the house, but now, with all the competition for road space, they ran slowly if they ran at all—another good example of how the world was going to hell. He dodged between a brachiosaur and a slow-moving stegosaurus, crossed Broadway, and turned down toward Avenue A.

The triceratops were butting their heads together on Avenue A; they came together with a crash like locomotives colliding that boomed from the building fronts and rattled windows all up and down the street. Nobody in the neighborhood would get much sleep tonight. Michael fought his way up the steps of his tenement brown-stone, crawling over the dimetrodons lounging on the stoop. Across the street, he could see the mailman trying to kick an iguanodon awake so that he could get past it into another brownstone's vesti-bule. No wonder his checks were late.

Upstairs, his wife put his plate in front of him without a word, and he stopped only to take off his wet jacket before sitting down to eat. Tuna casserole again, he noticed without enthusiasm. They ate in gloomy silence until the room was suddenly lit up by a sizzling bolt of lightning, followed by a terrific clap of thunder. As the echoes of the thunder died, over even the sound of the now torrential rain, they could hear a swelling cacophony of banging and thudding and shrieking and crashing.

"Goddamn," Michael's wife said, "it's doing it again!"

The old man got up and looked out of the window, out over a panorama of weed-and-trash choked tenement backyards. It was literally raining dinosaurs out there—as he watched they fell out of the sky by the thousands, twisting and scrambling in the air, bouncing from the pavement like hail, flopping and bellowing in the street.

"Well," the old man said glumly, pulling the curtain closed and turning back from the window, "at least it's stopped raining cats and dogs."

A CHANGE IN THE WEATHER

There's probably not much that really needs to be said about this little piece of fluff. Michael's anecdote about its origin is fundamentally accurate. If I hadn't wanted to type something—anything—to test my new typewriter ribbon, and if we hadn't all been drunk at the time, and at that stage in the festivities when you'll laugh at *anything*, it never would have been written.

My agent, Virginia Kidd, wisely persuaded us to change its title from "Fortean Phenomenon"—my choice—to the more evocative "A Change in the Weather," and we sold it first crack out of the box to the highest-paying fiction market in America, for a larger word-rate than any of us had ever even dreamed of before.

What else can you possibly say?

Time Bride

GARDNER DOZOIS & JACK DANN

The man-who-wasn't-there first spoke to Marcy when she was eight years old.

She had gone out to play with her friends Shelley Mitnich and Michelle Liebman, a rare time out from under the eyes of her strict and over-protective parents, and in later years she would come to remember that long late-summer afternoon as an idyll of freedom and happiness, in many ways the last real moments of her childhood.

The sky was high and blue and cloudless, the sun warm without being blisteringly hot, the breezes balmy, and as they played time seemed to stretch out, slow down, and then stop altogether, hanging suspended like honey melting on the tongue. They played Mother May I, halfball, Chinese jump rope, and giant steps. They played jacks—onesies, twosies, threesies, sweepsies, and squeezesies. They played hid-and-go-seek. They played Red Light Green Light, and Red Rover, and Teakettle Hot Teakettle Cold. They played double-dutch. They played Mimsy, chanting

a mimsy, a *clapsie*
I *whirl* my hands to *bapsie*
my *right* hand
my *left* hand
high as the *sky*

low as the *sea*
touch my *knee*
touch my *heel*
touch my *toe*
and under we *go!*

while they went through a complicated routine of throwing a ball up and clapping before catching it, throwing a ball up and whirling their hands and touching their shoulders (*bapsie*) before catching it, and so forth, until at last they threw the ball under their legs on the final word, their faces as grimly intent and serious as the faces of druids performing holy mysteries at the summer solstice. And when Shelley got mad and went home because she got stuck on the Qs while playing A My Name Is Alice, and Marcy *hadn't* —coming right out with "Q my name is Queenie, my husband's name is Quintin, we come from Queensbury where we sell *quilts,*" cool as could be, making it look infuriatingly easy—Michelle and Marcy kept right on playing, playing hop-scotch, playing dolls, playing Movie Star, in which Michelle pretended to be Nick Charles and Marcy got to be Nora and walk a pillow named Asta on a leash. And when Michelle had to go in because it was time for her dumb piano lesson, Marcy kept on playing by herself, not wanting the afternoon to end, reluctant to go back to the gloomy old house where there was nothing to do but watch television or sit in her room and play pretend games, which weren't any fun because she felt *locked up* in that house.

Marcy ran through the scrub lots behind the houses, swishing through the waist-high tangles of grass and wild wheat and weeds, pretending to be a horse. Usually when she played horses it was with Michelle and yucky old Shelley—Marcy's name was *Lightning,* and she was a beautiful black horse with a white mane and white tail, and Michelle was Star, and Shelley was Blaze—and she hadn't been sure that she would like playing horses all by herself, with nobody to run from forest fires with or chase rustlers with, but she found that she *did* like it. Running alone and free, the wind streaming her hair out behind her, the sky seeming to whirl dizzily around her as she ran, running so fast that she thought that she could run right off the edge of the world, so far and fast that no one could ever catch her again—yes, she liked it very much, perhaps more than she had ever liked anything up to that moment.

She ran through the scrub lots and the patches of trash woods— pines and aspens growing like weeds—and down through the sunlit meadow to the river.

There she paused to catch her breath, teetering dramatically on the riverbank with her arms stretched out to either side. This time of year, the river ran nearly dry—just the barest trickle of water, perhaps an inch deep, worming its way through a dry bed littered with thousands of rocks of all sizes and shapes, from tiny rounded pebbles to boulders the size of automobiles—but Marcy pretended that she was about to fall in and maybe drown, so that Mommy would be sorry, or maybe she'd have to swim like *anything* to escape, or maybe a mermaid would save her and take her to a magic cave. . . . She whirled around and around on the riverbank, her arms still outstretched to either side. She was one of those classically beautiful children who look like Dresden china figurines, with wide liquid eyes and pale blemishless skin and finely chiseled features, an adult face done in miniature. She was wearing a new blue dress trimmed with eyelet lace, and her hair shone like beaten gold as she spun in the sunlight.

She whirled until she was too dizzy to stand, and then she sat down with a plop in the mud of the riverbank, which was still soggy from the morning's rain. She was dismayed for a second, realizing what she'd done; then she smiled, and began to pat her hands in the mud with a kind of studied perversity.

"You shouldn't play in the mud," an adult voice said sternly.

She flinched and looked up—expecting to see one of the neighbors, or perhaps a workman from the new house they were putting up on the far side of the meadow.

No one was there.

"You're getting your dress all muddy that way," the voice complained, "and I can just imagine how much your mother must have had to pay for it, too. Have some consideration for others!"

Marcy stood up slowly, feeling gooseflesh prickle along her arms. Again, no one was there. Carefully, she looked all around her, but there was no place for anyone to hide—the grass was too short here, and the nearest clump of trees was a hundred yards away—so she didn't see how anyone could be playing a trick on her.

She stood there silently, frowning, trying to figure it out, still composed but beginning to be a little scared. The wind ruffled her hair and fluttered the lace on her muddy dress.

"You're the one," the voice said gloatingly. It seemed to emanate from the thin air right beside her, loud and unmistakable. "I knew it as soon as I saw you. Yes, you're the right one—you'll do very nicely indeed, I can tell. Boy, am I going to get my money's worth out of this. Every cent—it's worth it."

The voice sounded smug, pleased-with-itself, somewhat pompous. Like the voice of one of those sanctimonious and not-terribly-bright adults who would always insist on telling her stories with a moral or giving her Words To Live By, the kind of adults who would show slides of their vacation trip, or pinch her cheeks and tell her how big she was getting, like her Uncle Irving, who always stunk up the house with cigar smoke and whose droning-voiced company was more annoying than the nickel he invariably gave her was worth. A *schlimazel,* as her father would say, a *schlimazel's* voice, coming at her out of the empty August sky.

"Are you a ghost?" she asked politely, more intrigued than frightened now.

The voice chuckled. "No, I'm not a ghost."

"Are you invisible, then, like on TV?"

"Well . . ." the voice said, "I guess I'm not really *there* at all, the way you mean it, although I can see you and talk to you whenever I want, little Marcia."

Marcy shook her head. In spite of him saying that he wasn't a ghost, she pictured him as one, as a little-man-who-wasn't-there, like in the poem Mommy had read her, and for a long time that would be the way she would think of him. "How did you know my name?" she asked.

The man-who-wasn't-there chuckled smugly again. "I know lots of things, Marcia, and I can find out nearly anything I want to know. My name is Arnold Waxman, and someday I'm going to marry you."

"No you're *not.*" she said, startled.

"Oh yes I am. I'm going to be your husband, little Marcia, you'll see. With my guidance you're going to grow up to be a perfect young lady, the perfect bride, and when the time is right, you'll marry me."

"Oh no I *won't,*" she said, more vehemently, feeling tears start in her eyes. "I won't, I *won't.* You're a liar, a yucky old *liar.*"

"Have some respect!" the man-who-wasn't-there said sharply. "Is this a way to talk to your future husband?"

But Marcy was already running, whizzing suddenly away like a stone shot out of a sling, up the slope, across the meadow, past the foundations for the new house. Not until she reached the first line of trees, the riverbank far behind her, did she whirl and yell back "I'm not going to marry you, you dumb old ghost! I'm not!"

"Oh, I think you will," said a voice beside her, from the thin and empty summer air.

96 Barry Meisner, Marcy's father, was putting on his *tallis* and *t'fillen,*

preparing to pray, when a voice spoke to him out of the ceiling: "Mr. Meisner? I have a proposition to make to you."

"What?" Mr. Meisner said, turning around, as if the voice might have emanated out of the red leather bar across the room. He cautiously walked over to the bar and looked behind it, but found nothing but his collection of vintage wines, a towel that had fallen to the floor, and a bottlecap that the maid had overlooked.

"So now you're hearing things," Mr. Meisner mumbled, scolding himself.

"Mr. Meisner," said the voice clearly, "please, just listen to me for a moment, and I'll explain everything."

"Oh, my God!" Mr. Meisner said, now looking straight up at the ceiling light which spotlit the bar and the ivory collection which filled the narrow mirrored shelves on the wall behind it. Mr. Meisner, a successful businessman who attributed his success to a personal God who took a particular interest in *him*, Mr. Meisner suddenly began to shake. "Oh, my *God*. I always *knew* you were real. I'm your son, Barry," and he raised his arms before him and intoned the *Shema*: "Hear Oh Israel, the—"

"*Please*, Mr. Meisner," said the voice, "I am most certainly *not* God. Now if you'll just listen—"

Mr. Meisner lowered his arms reluctantly. "You're not God?"

"Absolutely not."

"Then who are you, *what* are you?" Mr. Meisner looked this way and that. "Come out! Show yourself!"

"I can't show myself, Mr. Meisner, because I'm from the future."

"The future!"

"That's right," said the voice, sounding somewhat smug.

Mr. Meisner squinted suspiciously up at the ceiling. "So, you're from the future, huh? You have a time machine, maybe, like in the movies? So, you want to talk to a person, why don't you step out and say hello, instead of doing tricks like a ventriloquist with the ceiling?"

"Mr. Meisner," the voice said, and you could almost hear the sigh behind the words, "there is no such thing as a time machine. Not the kind that you're talking about, anyway. It's quite impossible for anybody to *physically* travel through time. Or so the scientists tell me—I must admit that I don't really understand it myself. But the point is that I *can't* step out and shake hands with you, because I'm not really *there*, not physically. You understand? Now what I *do* have is a device that lets me *see* through time, and enables me to speak to you, and hear what you have to say in return. And let me tell *you*, Mr. Meisner, it's expensive. The timescopes were developed only a little while ago (from my point of view, of course), and you wouldn't *believe* how much it's costing me to talk to you right now."

"Long distance calls are always expensive," Mr. Meisner said blandly; he had regained some of his composure, and he wasn't about to let a voice from the ceiling think that it could impress him by bragging about its money. He idly fingered the loose leather strap of the *t'fillen* while he looked thoughtfully upward. "So, then, Mr. Voice—" he said at last.

"Mr. Meisner, *please*. I'm not a voice, I'm a person just like you, and I have a name. My name is Arnold Waxman."

Mr. Meisner blinked. "So, then, Mr. . . . . Waxman," he began again. "So you're up there in the future, and you're calling me, and it's costing you a million dollars a minute, or whatever they use for money in the future, and any time now the operator is going to break in and start yelling you should put another dime in the slot. . . ." He paused. "So what do you want? Why are you bothering *me?*"

"I'd like to speak to you about your daughter, Marcy."

"What about my daughter?" demanded Mr. Meisner, startled again.

"I would like your permission to marry her."

"Marry her? Are you a pervert, is that it?" Mr. Meisner began shaking with anger and fear. No one was going to marry his daughter. She wasn't even *bat mitzvahed* yet. Suddenly he stopped, and buried his face in his hands. "I *am* hearing things," Mr. Meisner said flatly, satisfied that he had finally had a breakdown. "*Now* let my wife deny that I've been working too hard."

A sigh filled the room. "Mr. Meisner, you're not crazy. You're living in the Twentieth Century, please try to act like a civilized man, not some superstitious aborigine."

"*You* should talk about civilized! My daughter is *eight years old*. Is this what they do in the future, marry eight-year-old girls?" A thought struck him and he began to panic. "Where is she? Oh my God, is she alright? What—"

"Calm yourself, Mr. Meisner," Arnold said. "Your daughter is fine; in fact, she's on her way home right now."

"She better be okay," Mr. Meisner said ominously.

"Please let me explain, Mr. Meisner. I don't want to marry Marcy *now*. I want to marry her in the future, ten years from now, when she's eighteen. That is, I believe, an acceptable age. And I am, as I believe I've already mentioned, a very rich man. A very respectable man. She could do far worse, believe me."

Mr. Meisner shook his head dubiously. "I should arrange a marriage like my Grandmother who lived in a *shtetl*?"

"I think you will find that the old ways contained much wisdom."

"Are you Jewish?" Mr. Meisner asked suspiciously.

"Of course I'm Jewish. Would I want to marry your daughter if I wasn't?"

"We're not Orthodox," said Mr. Meisner.

"Neither am I," Arnold said.

"No — come back in ten years when you're real and we can talk again. Until then, you're a figment of my imagination."

"You know perfectly well that I'm real, Mr. Meisner," Arnold said angrily, "and in ten years it will be too late for Marcy."

"What do you mean?"

"Mr. Meisner, do you have any idea what's going *on* up here in the future?"

Mr. Meisner shrugged. "I should know the future? I have enough trouble with the present."

"Well, let me tell *you*, you think it's bad down there *now*, you just wait until you see the future! It's a zoo. A jungle. The complete breakdown of all moral values. Kids running wild. Lewdness. Indecency. Do you want to live to see the day when your daughter is *schtupping* every boy she passes on the street?"

"Don't you dare talk like that about my daughter!"

"Mr. Meisner, without my guidance, *she'll marry a goy!*"

There was a heavy silence. "That's a lie," Mr. Meisner said at last, but he said it without much conviction. He paused again, then sighed. "So if I make an arrangement with you, how will that change what happens to my Marcy?"

"I'll look after her. I'll help her through the pitfalls of life. I'll make sure she grows up *right*."

"I can do that myself, thank you," said Mr. Meisner.

"Ah, but you can't watch over her *all* the time, can you?" Arnold said triumphantly. "In fact, just today I caught her rolling in the mud, deliberately getting her dress dirty, and I sent her straight home. Can *you* know what other trouble she'll get into when your back is turned? Can you guard her from every bad influence she'll run into outside the home, point out every mistake to her as she makes it, help her to resist every temptation she'll ever run into, anywhere? I can do all that."

"But . . ." said Mr. Meisner, rather dazedly, "why are you willing to wait ten years for my daughter?"

"So that I can make absolutely *sure* that she's the kind of woman

I want to marry." Arnold sighed. "I've been disappointed twice before, Mr. Meisner, with fiancées who were girls from good families, supposedly well brought up . . . and yet, underneath it all, it turned out that they were really . . . sluts. They had been *spoiled,* in spite of their good backgrounds, in spite of all their parents could do. Somewhere along the line, Mr. Meisner, *somewhere,* at some time, the germ of corruption had worked its way in." He paused broodingly, and then, his voice quickening with enthusiasm, said, "But *this* way, using the timescope, I can actually help to mold Marcy into the type of girl she should be, I can personally supervise every detail. . . ."

The study door opened, and Marcy was standing there, looking flushed and rather flustered, her dress splattered with mud. "Daddy —" she began breathlessly.

"There! See!" Arnold said smugly. "*There* she is, and she's perfectly all right. And look, there's the mud, just like I told you. . . ."

Marcy gasped and flinched, and fell back a step, her eyes widening. Her face filled with fright, and, after a moment, with guilt.

Her father was staring at her oddly. "Go upstairs now, Marcy," he said at last. "We'll talk about what you did to your dress later on."

"But *Daddy* . . ."

"Go upstairs now," Mr. Meisner said curtly, "I'm very busy."

As the door was swinging shut, he turned his face back up to the ceiling and said, "Now, then, Mr. Waxman —"

Marcy stood outside the door of her father's study for a long time, listening to the voices rising and falling within, and then, troubled, she went slowly upstairs to her room.

That night, as she was getting ready to turn out her light and go to sleep, the voice spoke to her again. She shrieked and jumped into bed and pulled the covers up over her head. She lay there quivering, somehow shocked that the voice could follow her even into her very own room. The voice droned on for what seemed like an eternity while she hugged the covers tighter and tried not to listen, telling her stupid stories about how wonderful their lives together would be, the wonderful things they would do, how they would live in a castle. . . .

Later, after her room had become quiet again, she cautiously poked one eye and her nose out from under the blanket, looked warily around, and then snaked her hand over to turn out the light, hoping that *he* wouldn't be able to find her in the dark.

They were lies, she told herself as she stared up at the shadowy ceiling of her room, all the things he'd said, all lies. None of that was going to happen. Marcy already had her life planned anyway: she was going to live in the Congo and be like Wonder Woman who never had to marry anybody, even though everybody was in love with her because she saved people's lives all the time and was beautiful.

There would be no room in such a plan for *Arnold*.

The next day, at dinner, Marcy's mother said, "But Marcy, this *is* for your own good." She and Mr. Meisner and Marcy were seated at the kitchen table. "Arnold sounds like a very nice man, and Mommie and Daddy and Arnold are going to make sure that you have a wonderful life and have everything you want."

"I don't want everything I want," Marcy whined. "Not if I have to listen to that dumb old Arnold all the time. I won't, I won't, I *won't*."

"Now that certainly isn't the way a young lady speaks to her parents." Arnold's voice seemed to be coming from the radar range under the Colonial-style kitchen cabinets. "Little Marcia, do you —"

"Don't call me 'Little Marcia.' My name is Marcy, and I'm not little."

"Very well," said Arnold. "Marcy, do you remember the Ten Commandments?"

Marcy looked down at her bowl of strawberry ice cream, and then carefully mashed the artificially colored mounds flat with the back of her teaspoon.

"Well, *do* you remember the Ten Commandments?" Mrs. Meisner asked. Mrs. Meisner had once been beautiful, but she had allowed herself to gain weight, which clouded the once-strong features of her face. But she still had beautiful pale skin and eyes as pale blue as Marcy's. She wore her thick, dyed red hair shoulder-length, but it was sprayed so heavily that it shone as if it were shellacked. "Marcy, stop playing with your ice cream and answer Arnold. And be polite!"

"I know you're not supposed to steal or kill anybody or eat lobster," Marcy said sullenly.

"But you *are* supposed to respect your parents . . . and your elders." Now Arnold's stern voice seemed to be coming from somewhere above the table. "'Honor thy father and mother,'" the voice intoned ominously.

"Not if they try to make me marry a stupid old voice!" Marcy said, and she ran out of the kitchen, through the red-carpeted hallway, and up the stairs to her bedroom.

"I think you owe your parents an apology," the voice said to Marcy, who was lying on her bed, her arms extended as if she were flying or perhaps floating.

Marcy stuck her tongue out at the ceiling, which was where she thought Arnold might be.

"I think a spanking would be in order unless you apologize to your parents this very moment," Arnold said.

"Who's going to spank me?" Marcy asked petulantly. "You?"

"I think your father is very capable of taking care of that."

"Well, he's *never* spanked me ever, so shut up and go away."

Five minutes later, Marcy received her first spanking from her father.

The first few weeks under the new regime weren't *too* bad, although Arnold was an awful pest, and nagged her a lot, particularly when her parents weren't around. By now, everybody was talking about the Voices from the future — more than thirty different cases had been reported from all over the globe, the contacts initiated for a bewildering variety of reasons, most of them amazingly frivolous — but Arnold at first was reasonably discreet about lecturing her in front of other people, and only Marcy's parents knew about him.

All that ended, along with the last shreds of her old life, one night, perhaps a month later, when Marcy was having dinner at Shelley Mitnich's house.

"Are you *sure* your parents won't mind if you eat this?" Mrs. Mitnich asked Marcy as she served a platter filled with lobster tails. She also placed a little bowl of melted butter between Marcy and Shelley.

"No, they don't mind," March said. "We can't eat it at home, but I'm allowed to have it in restaurants or at my friends', like here." Lobster was Marcy's favorite food.

Mr. Mitnich mumbled something Marcy couldn't hear, and Mrs. Mitnich gave him a nasty look.

"Well, I know your parents aren't Orthodox," Mrs. Mitnich said; but before Marcy could put a piece of the pink meat into her mouth, a voice said, "Put that fork down this very instant!"

"Shut up, Arnold!" Marcy shouted. Her face turned red, and she looked around the dining room, as if Arnold would suddenly appear in the flesh to mortify her.

"You know better than to eat *traif*," Arnold said.

With shocked expressions on their faces, Shelley and her parents looked around the room and then at Marcy.

"I can eat whatever I want," Marcy whined. "My parents let me eat whatever I want when I'm out . . . and it's none of your business, you goddamn *geek!*"

"Little girls with breeding do not use such language," Arnold said.

"Who the hell are you?" Mr. Mitnich asked as he stood up and waved his hands over the table where the voice seemed to be coming from, as if he could brush it away like a spiderweb. "I've heard all about weirdos like you." Then he leaned over toward Marcy and asked, "Honey, when did this weirdo from the future start bothering you?"

"I *beg* your pardon, sir," said the voice, which seemed to be coming from the far side of the room now.

"Shut up, you," Mr. Mitnich said to the wall, and then he turned toward Marcy again. "Do your parents know about this pervert?"

"They most certainly do, sir," Arnold said smugly. "I've arranged to marry Marcy when she's of age. I'm simply trying to save her from *your* daughter's fate. If that's being a pervert, then so be it."

"And just what *is* my daughter's fate?" Mr. Mitnich asked, looking at the wall.

"I'd rather not say."

Mr. Mitnich was livid. "Get out of here, you! Oh . . . and Marcy . . . I don't think you should be playing with Shelley anymore. Your parents should be ashamed of themselves. Bringing such filth into their own home . . . and ours."

"You just wait and see what happens to *your* daughter," Arnold said nastily. "Boy! You should only be so lucky to have someone like me to look after her!"

Mr. Mitnich threw his coffee cup at the ceiling.

Then Marcy was outside, trudging along toward her house as the bitter tears runneled her cheeks, and Arnold was telling her that she didn't need friends like that anyway, because after all, she had *him.*

After that, the word got out and Marcy became a minor celebrity for a while, even appearing on a television news program. This was small comfort to Marcy, though—Arnold became more and more strict as time went by, reprimanding her constantly in front of the other kids, snapping at children and adults who he thought were "bad influences," until eventually no one would play with her at all. She had lost all her friends, and even her teachers tended to leave her alone, tucking her away in back of the class where they could safely ignore her.

Arnold was with her nearly all the time now, and Marcy soon learned that it was nearly impossible to hide from him. When she hid under the azalea bush in the backyard and "touched herself," Arnold was suddenly there too, thundering wrath from out of the cloudy sky, loudly telling her parents about the disgusting thing their daughter had been doing, and Marcy had to promise never to do it again, and cried herself to sleep from the shame of it every night for a week. When Marcy stole a chocolate-covered cherry from her mother's candy box, Arnold was there. When Marcy wiped her nose on the sleeve of her new jacket, Arnold was there. When Marcy tried to hide her report card, Arnold was there. When Marcy let Diane Berkowitz talk her into trying a cigarette, Arnold was there.

He came to her every day and lectured her about morality and sin and perversion. He loved to talk about etiquette and deportment, and he made her read thick musty books to "expand her horizons."

He told her in secret that her parents weren't very smart or, for that matter, very well educated.

He told her that he was her only friend.

He told her that she was very lucky to have him, for he was her salvation.

Soon after Marcy's fifteenth birthday, someone finally invented the timescope, belatedly justifying the prophecy of its existence. The inventor had been prompted by hints and "pointers" from the future, but with the exception of a few nitpicking scientists, no one seemed particularly disturbed by the hair-raising tangle of paradoxes this implied. Within a year, timescopes were for sale on the commercial market, although they were indeed very expensive to own and operate.

Soon after Marcy's sixteenth birthday, Shelley Mitnich got pregnant, and by a *shvartzer* yet: Arnold crowed about that for months, and his stock with Mr. Meisner became unassailably high.

Soon after Marcy's seventeenth birthday, she tried talking to her mother about Arnold. Marcy still didn't see any way out of marrying Arnold if her parents said that she had to—although if she'd been a few years older, or less dominated by her parents and Arnold, or if her counselor at school had been sympathetic enough to really open up to, or if she'd had any real friends with whom to talk things over, she might have seen several other options—and the prospect terrified her. Mrs. Meisner put down the *Soap Opera Digest* and listened patiently to her daughter, but her tired fat face was unsympathetic. "You don't love him," Mrs. Meisner said. She made a rotating motion with her hand and said, "So? You can't learn to love a rich man just as easily as a poor one?"

Marcy's eighteenth birthday was approaching. She lay unsleeping in the close darkness of her room, night after night, listening to the buzzing and clicking of the street lamp outside her window, watching the glow of car headlights sweep across the ceiling in oscillating waves, like phosphorescent surf breaking on a black midnight beach.

In the mornings, the face that looked back at her from her mirror was haggard and pale. She began to grow gaunt, the flesh pulling back tightly over her cheekbones, her eyes becoming hollowed and darkly bruised. She had almost stopped eating. During the day she would pace constantly, like a caged animal, unable to stand still, awash with a sick, directionless energy that left her headachy and nauseous. At night she would lie rigid and unmoving in her bed, still as a statue, the blankets pulled up to her neck, taut with dread and anticipation of the voice that might speak to her from the darkness at any moment, without warning, the voice and the watching presence she could never escape. . . .

On the third such night, lying tensely in darkness and watching leaf-shadows shake and reticulate across the walls, she made her decision.

Slowly, cautiously, she pushed the blankets aside and got out of bed. She groped across the room to the dresser, not daring to turn on the light, finding her things by touch. Since puberty, since her body hair had begun to grow and her breasts had started to bloom, she had kept her room totally dark at night, unable to bear the thought of *him* staring at her while she undressed; she had taken to dressing under the sheet in the morning, hurrying through baths and showers as quickly as she could, certain that he was staring at her nakedness whenever he got the chance, convinced that she could feel his eyes crawling over her whenever she was obliged to take off the swaddling, smothering, all-concealing clothes she had come to prefer. Tucked away under the shapeless, tent-like dresses, though, she still kept a pair of jeans and a dark blue cardigan sweater, perhaps unconsciously saved for an emergency like this. She fumbled her way into the clothes, hesitating after every movement, trying to inch her dresser drawer open soundlessly and freezing for a long terrified moment when it emitted a loud raucous squeak, glancing compulsively upward at the milky ceiling (where *he* lived, or so the child in the back of her mind still believed), more than half-expecting to hear his voice any second, asking her in that snide and chilly tone just *what* in the world she thought she was *doing*. But by the time she had tied the last lace on her sneakers, crouching in the deep shadow of the chiffonier, she had begun to feel a little more confident — she had been quiet and unrebellious for a long time now, she hadn't tried to sneak out of her room at night for *years*, and even *he* couldn't watch her *all* the time, every moment. He had to sleep *sometime*, after all.

Maybe it was going to work.

No longer moving with quite the same exaggerated stealth, Marcy slid her window open and climbed out onto the slanting second-story roof. Surely if *he* were watching, he would say something *now* . . . but then she was outside, feeling the slippery tile under her feet, seeing the fat pale moon overhead through a scrim of silhouetted branches, and still the alarm hadn't come. She walked surefootedly along the roof to the big elm that grew at the corner of the house, leaped across to it, and shimmied down it to the ground in a shower of brittle leaves and displaced twigs, and only when she was standing on the ground, her feet planted firmly in the damp grass, only then did she sway and become dizzy. . . .

The bus into the center of town stopped right across from her house, but she caught it a few blocks down, just to be safe. She held her breath until the bus doors sighed shut behind her, and then she slumped into a seat, and was taken by a fit of convulsive shivering. She had to wrap her hands around the edge of the seat in front of her and squeeze it until her knuckles whitened before the shivering stopped, and when it had, and she was calmer, she was content to just sit for a moment and watch the pastel lights of the city ticking by outside the window. But she mustn't allow herself to be lulled. She mustn't allow herself to think that she was safe, not yet. She had worked it all out a dozen times. There was no sense in just running away — sooner or later, Arnold would find out where she had gone, track her down no matter where she went, and then her parents would just come and get her, or send the cops to pick her up. And the next time they'd watch her more closely, make it far more difficult for her to get away. No, it was now or never; she must use this opportunity *now*, while she had the chance, and there was only one thing she could think of to do with the stolen time that *might* be effective enough to break her free of Arnold.

She had become uneasy again, thinking about it. How much time *did* she have? Maybe a few hours . . . at the most. . . . Possibly as little as a half an hour, twenty minutes, maybe *less*. Sooner or later, the alarm would sound. . . . She felt the tension building up inside her again, like a hand rhythmically squeezing her guts, and she began to look anxiously around her at the people getting on and off the bus. She had not worked out the logistical details, the practical details, of her plan—she had vaguely imagined going to a bar, or a nightclub (but what if they wouldn't let her in?), or maybe to a bowling alley, or a restaurant, or . . . but she didn't have *time* for all that! Any minute now, the alarm was going to come, she *knew* it. She was running out of *time*. . . . And now the bus was emptying out, there were fewer and fewer people getting on. . . .

There was a man sitting a few seats away, reading a magazine. *You're it,* she thought. *You'll have to be it.* Gritting her teeth, she somehow forced herself to stand up, take a swaying step down the aisle toward him. He was probably a goy, but he was clean-looking anyway, his hair a bit longer than she liked it (and—ugh!—a mustache), dressed in slacks and a workshirt and an Eisenhower jacket, hushpuppies, plastic eyeglasses. . . . She took another step toward him, feeling her legs turning to rubber, her knees buckling, the fluttery panic coming up inside her.

At least he was *old*—he must be twenty-one, maybe even twenty-two. An older man, that should make it easier. . . .

The bus accelerated with a jolt, and Marcy took the next few steps in a stumbling half-run, almost falling, sprawling into the seat next to the man and then lurching against him as the bus took a sharp curve, knocking the magazine out of his hands. He stared at her, startled, and Marcy drew herself up and said "Hi!" brightly, showing all of her teeth to him in what was supposed to be a smile. He kept staring at her, blankly, and so she leaned in until their faces were nearly touching, and said "Hiiiii there," making her voice low and drawly, fanning her eyelashes, trying desperately to remember what the vamps on television did. He blinked, and then said "Uh . . . hi."

There was a long silence then, and they stared at each other through it while the bus bounced and swayed around them.

My God, my god, *say* something.

What?

"You know," she said, her voice harsh with tension, so that she had to swallow and start speaking again, "you know, you're a very good-looking man."

"I *am?*" he said, gaping at her.

"Yes, you're a very attractive guy." She looked up sidelong at him, up from under her eyelashes. "I mean—really you are. You know, 107 *really.*" She batted her eyelashes at him again. "What's your name, anyway? Mine's Marcy."

"Uh . . . Alan," he said. He was beginning to smile in a sort of tentatively-fatuous way, although he still looked puzzled. "My name's Alan."

She leaned in even closer, until she could feel his breath on her face. It smelled faintly of pepperoni, faintly of mouthwash. She fixed him with a long, smolderingly-significant look, then said, "Hi, Alan," in a breathless whisper.

"Hi . . . um, Marcy . . ." he said. He still looked nervous, glancing around to see if anyone else was watching him. She took his arm, and he jumped a little. She could feel herself blushing, but she couldn't stop now. "I was sitting over there watching you," she said, "and I said to myself, you can't let a guy this gorgeous get away without even saying *hello* or something, you know? No matter *how* forward he thinks you are. . . . I mean, I'd like to get to know you better, Alan. Would *you* like to get to know *me* better, too? Would you?"

Alan licked nervously at his lips. "Why sure. We could go out. . . . We could, uhhh, go to the movies or something, I guess, or go get a coke. . . ."

Too long! This was all taking too long!

She gritted her teeth, and put her hand in his lap.

He goggled at her, and through buzzing waves of embarrassment she was surprised to see that he was blushing too, blushing red as a beet.

"Jesus Christ . . ." he whispered.

No turning back now. "I . . . I want to be alone with you," Marcy said, her voice wavering, forcing herself to keep her hand there. "Don't you have someplace we can go?"

"Yeah," he said in a strangled voice, "we can go to my place. . . ."

They got off a few stops later, and walked down half-lit streets to Alan's apartment. Marcy was hanging on to Alan's arm as though he might float up and away into the evening sky if she didn't guy him down, and he was walking so quickly that he was dragging her along, her feet almost not touching the sidewalk. He was chattering nervously, talking a mile a minute, but she hadn't heard a word he'd said. She could feel the tension building higher and tighter inside her, she could almost *smell* it, a scorched smell like insulation burning. She was almost out of time—she knew it, she *knew* it. Dammit, hurry *up.*

Alan's apartment was a fifth-floor walk-up in a battered old brownstone building that had seen better centuries, let alone better years. There was a shag couch, a bookcase made of boards and bricks, a coffee table, empty wine bottles with candles melted into them, a lamp with a red light bulb in it, rock posters on the walls. He took her coat and threw it over a chair, and then turned to her, rubbing his hands on his hips, looking uncertain again. "Ah, would you like a drink, or . . ."

"Don't talk." She slid into his arms. "I . . . I *need* you, Alan," she said huskily, remembering lines from a romance novel, too young to realize that he was young enough not to giggle. "Take me, take me *now!*"

Then—thank God! at last!—he was kissing her, while she tried not to fidget with impatience. After a moment's reluctance, she opened her lips and let him put his tongue in her mouth; she could feel it wandering clumsily around in there, bumping into her teeth, wagging back and forth like some kind of spongy organic windshield-wiper. His tongue felt huge and bloated in her mouth, and it made her feel a little ill, but he was making a sort of low moaning noise while he was kissing her, so apparently she was on the right track.

After a moment, he began fumbling with the buttons on her cardigan sweater, so clumsily that she had to help him, her own fingers shaking with nervousness. Then he was easing her blouse off. It felt odd to be standing in a strange room, in front of a stranger, in her brassiere, but she didn't have time to worry about it. It *couldn't* be much longer before they caught up with her. . . . Somehow he had figured out how to get the hooks undone. He tugged her brassiere off, and ran his hands over her breasts. She still felt nothing but anxiety, but the room was chilly, and if he took the hardening of her nipples as a sign of passion, well, all the better. . . .

He leaned down and put his mouth to her breast, his tongue encircling the nipple, and that *was* pleasurable in a low-key way, as if there were a mild electric current shooting through her, but she didn't have *time* for all these frills. "Hurry *up*," she snarled, tugging clumsily at his belt, breaking a fingernail, finally getting his pants open.

Alan would have been gratified to know that to her his penis looked enormous—a terrifying purplish spear of flesh, a foot long at least.

He threw her down on the couch, and they wrestled inconclusively together for a while—she staring up at the waterpocked ceiling with dread, and thinking hurry *up*, hurry *up*, hurry *up*, banging her chin on his shoulder for emphasis—but of course he was too nervous, and he went soft. He smiled weakly at her and said something apologetic, but she ignored all that and reached for him determinedly. His penis felt warm and dry and rubbery under her hands. She was blushing furiously now, blushing to her hair-roots, but she worked grimly away at him, telling herself that it was not that much different from milking a cow, something she'd done one summer at 4H Camp.

He rolled onto her again, hovered fumblingly above her, poised, and at that moment a loud furious voice said "You *slut!!*"

Alan jerked and gasped, startled, and began to pull away, but Marcy growled "Oh, no, you don't!"—not yet! not after all that trouble!—and grabbed him back down. "Whore!" Arnold was screaming, "Filthy strumpet!" and Alan was saying "What?! What?!" in a kind of wild dazed panic, but she kept rubbing herself up against him, hugging him with her arms and legs, saying "Don't worry about that! Don't pay any attention!" until at last he gave a convulsive shudder and lunged forward. She felt a sharp, tearing pain, and then he was gasping stertorously next to her ear as Arnold screamed and raved and gibbered incoherently from the ceiling. After a few moments Arnold's voice fell silent, and she smiled.

At last Alan moaned and collapsed crushingly on top of her. She lay unprotestingly under his weight, not even caring if she'd gotten pregnant.

Free of him at last, she thought.

Alan sat up, still bewildered.

"You can put your pants on now," she said dryly.

A few minutes later, her father began to pound at the door.

There was the expected scene. Screaming, slapping, crying, hysteria. "You're not my daughter—you're no daughter of mine." Slut. Whore. Etcetera. Marcy remained dry-eyed and unmoved through it all. Alan cowered in a corner, wrapped in a sheet, looking tousled and terrified, occasionally opening his mouth to speak, only to shut it again when one of Marcy's parents advanced shrieking upon him. Her parents swore that they would press charges against Alan— especially if (God forbid) she was pregnant—and hurled sulfurous threats involving jail and lawyers back at him as they left, but eventually they would give up on the idea of prosecution, fearing more scandal. Fortunately, Marcy was *not* pregnant. She said goodbye politely to Alan—he gaped at her, still looking bewildered, still wrapped in a sheet, and said nothing—and calmly followed her sputtering parents out of his apartment. She never saw him again. She packed a bag, took the money she had been saving, and moved out of her parents' house that very night. She never saw them again, either.

She stayed that night in a Holiday Inn, and spent the next few weeks in an inexpensive boardinghouse. She got a job at a five-and-dime, later worked as a counter-girl in a second-rate greasy spoon. After a couple of months, she landed a better job in the accounting department of a moderate-sized engineering firm, and was able to afford a small apartment of her own in a shabby-genteel neighborhood on the far side of town.

For the first few weeks she stayed in her apartment every night, scared and lonely, still more than half-expecting to hear Arnold's voice at any second. Then she went into what she herself would later refer to as her "slut phase," haunting bars and discos, dragging a different man home with her nearly every night. Some of these men were much more attractive and skillful than Alan, but she felt nothing with any of them, no pleasure, not even the mild tingle she had felt during the tussle in Alan's apartment. She tried getting drunk, and stoned, let lovers ply her with cocaine and buzzing electric novelties and mildly kinky sexual variations, but nothing worked. After a few months of this, she got tipsy after work and let one of the salesgirls coax her into bed—but sex was just as unexciting with Sally as it had been with the faceless parade of male pickups. No matter how desperately she tried to be abandoned and wild, it seemed that she could not make herself stop *listening* for Arnold's disapproving voice, listening for it and dreading it with some deep and unreasoned part of her mind, and for her sex remained only a mildly unpleasant form of exercise, like being forced to do a hundred sit-ups or jumping jacks in a row.

She got another, and better, job, with a larger engineering firm, and stopped dating at all. She worked with impressive efficiency and a total concentration that brought her rapid promotions; after a while she was doing very well financially, and she moved into a much better apartment in a quiet residential high-rise whose other occupants were almost all over fifty years of age. She was generally popular with her co-workers, although she only occasionally joined them on Bowling Night or went with them on their expeditions to movies or restaurants or bars, and never showed the slightest hint of romantic interest in anyone, not even engaging in the harmless "social flirting" that went on almost constantly in the office. Those few who resented her reserve sometimes called her "Little Mary

Sunshine" or "The Nun," but most of her colleagues appreciated her even-tempered disposition and her calm unflappable efficiency, and the speculation that she "just didn't go out much" because she was still recovering from an unhappy love affair soon became an unquestioned part of office mythology—some people could even tell you all about the guy and why they'd broken up (in one version he'd turned out to be married; in another, he'd died slowly and dramatically of cancer).

A few of the more perceptive of her friends noticed that occasionally, right in the middle of things—while she was chatting over morning coffee, or discussing an audit with a section head, or telling the latest Polack joke in a bar during Happy Hour—Marcy would suddenly fall completely silent and freeze motionless for a heartbeat or two, as if she had abruptly and magically been turned to stone. None of them noticed, however, that at such times her eyes would invariably and almost imperceptibly flick upwards, as if she had suddenly sensed someone looking over her shoulder.

Marcy only ever actually saw Arnold in the flesh once, and that was years after she had left home, at a party.

It was a reception given for the opening of the new wing of the Museum, and Marcy was sipping pale sherry and talking to Joanne Korman when she heard an unmistakable voice, a voice that she hadn't actually *heard* since she was eighteen, although it had often whispered through her dreams at night. She turned around, and there was Arnold, eating cucumber sandwiches and blathering pompously about something or other to a Museum staffer. Arnold turned out to be a short, potbellied man with a large nose and a receding chin, impeccably groomed—his hair was slick and shiny and combed into photographically exact furrows—and expensively, if somewhat conservatively, dressed. He held his cucumber sandwich as if he was a praying mantis, holding it up near his chin with both hands and turning it around and around and around before taking a small surgical bite out of it. His eyes were small, humorless, and opaque, and he never seemed to blink. Marcy watched him in fascination. It was so strange to see Arnold's lips move and hear that familiar voice—sanctimonious, self-righteous, self-satisfied—issue from them instead of from the empty air. . . .

Arnold felt her watching him, and looked up. They stared at each other for a moment across the crowded room. There was no doubt that he recognized her. She saw his lips purse up tight, as if he had tasted something foul, and then he sneered at her, his face haughty and smugly contemptuous. Slowly, deliberately, disdainfully, he turned his back on her.

Marcy could never remember how she got back to her apartment that night.

She woke from abstraction, hours later, to find herself sitting at her kitchen counter, her mind full of circular, tail-swallowing thoughts about rope, and razor blades, and a long slow fall into dark water.

With an immense effort of will, she wrenched her mind out of this downward spiral, and forced herself to think about Arnold for the first time in a very long time, really *think* about him, and the more she thought about him the more her hands began to shake, until the coffee cup she was clutching (the cup she couldn't remember filling) cracked and clattered and spilled.

He was so *smug*. That was what was not to be borne — after everything that he'd done to her, *he* still considered himself to be the injured party! He was so goddamned sleek and smug and self-satisfied, it made her feel dizzy with hate just to think of it. Undoubtedly he was smirking at himself in the mirror right now and telling himself how *right* he had been about her, how he had tried and *tried* to help her lead a decent life, but she just wouldn't *listen,* how she had proved herself unworthy of him. . . .

She couldn't stand to think of it.

He had won! In spite of everything, he had *won.* He had shamed and warped and twisted her, tormented her for a decade, ruined her childhood, blighted her life, and then he had simply turned and walked away, congratulating himself that all his worst expectations had come true.

And she had let him get *away* with it. That was the worst thing of all, the most unbearable part. She had let him get away scot-free. . . .

She spent the long, sleepless night pacing restlessly up and down the length of her apartment, seeming with every step she took to hear Arnold's gloating voice saying "every cent — it's worth it," repeating obsessively to the rhythmic clicking of her heels, "every cent — it's worth it, every cent — it's worth it, every cent — it's worth it," until long before dawn she had decided that somehow — *any*how — she would have to make him *pay,* pay more than he had ever been willing to spend.

Early the next day, she went shopping.

Later that night, long after the technicians had left, she sat in her darkened living room before the newly installed console and ran her fingers caressingly over the switches and keyboards. She had been practicing for hours, and now she thought that she'd gotten the hang of it. She touched the keyboard, and the viewscreen lit up with a misty collage of moving images. She punched in the co-ordinates, and then used the fine-tuning to hunt around until she found a place where the young Arnold Waxman—pimply-faced and fat, just barely post-pubescent—was standing alone in his bathroom at night. His pants were down around his knees, and he had a *Playboy* gatefold in one hand. He had a stupid, preoccupied look on his face, and there was a strand of saliva glistening in the corner of his half-opened mouth.

Marcy leaned forward and touched the *Transmit* button. "Arnold!" she said sternly, watching him jump and gasp, "Arnold, you mustn't *do* that!"

Then, slowly, she smiled.

TIME BRIDE

I can't pinpoint exactly what the specific trigger for this story was, but no doubt I was thinking at some point about the moderately large body of stories in which someone invents a device to let you see into the past, and it probably occurred to me that there were areas of human life that usually *weren't* spied upon by time-peering future scientists in those stories, and that the potentials there for abuse — and thus, for interesting fictional conflicts — were fairly large. At any rate, the plot of this story was sketched out pretty completely in my story-idea notebook, pretty close to the way it actually came out, and sat there for a couple of years in that form, only — "only" — needing to be translated into an actual *story:* to have characters invented for it to fit it, and then to have those characters *live* through the plot in narrative.

This was one of the story ideas Jack and I talked over during a brainstorming session at my place early in 1981. According to my calendar, I didn't do much more extensive work on it after that until the week of November 9th of that year — I think Jack had been working on it off and on in the meantime — and it was finished on January 22, 1982. It's my memory that Jack started working on the middle sections of the story — starting with Mr. Meisner's first talk with Arnold — while I was simultaneously working on the opening section (after first grilling Susan intensively on games young girls play, stealing large portions of her childhood) and later, the long bus ride / seduction scene. Later, Jack and I bounced drafts of the closing scene, the coda, back and forth, and then I did a homogenizing and unifying draft, adding some new material throughout to smooth things out. Later still, at the end of November, we did a rewrite for Shawna McCarthy, working mostly on the coda. (The story as it appears here *is* somewhat different than the *IAsfm* version — Shawna let us get away with a fair amount of Smut for a digest magazine . . . but not as much as was *in* the story in the first place.)

This is usually considered to be a comic story, and there are some pretty good laughs here, but the understory is pretty grim. Marcy perpetuates what has been called the Chain of Blows by taking her revenge on Arnold. What goes around, comes around, as they say — and every parent must come to terms with the instinct to dish out to their own children the mistreatment (in all its forms) that they themselves were given. The story would have been Karmically more wholesome if Marcy had *broken* the Chain of Blows, set out to heal Arnold rather than warping him as he had warped her — but it would have been less convincing as something the character would really do, and considerably less powerful as a story. Thus the fiction writer's dilemma. Usually, story values win over Political Correctness, and they did here.

▪
▪
▪
▪
▪

GUILFORD GAFIA REVISITED

JACK C. HALDEMAN II

It was a strange old house, even for Baltimore, which has its fair share of them. It came fully equipped with its own pickled brain in the root cellar. My keen biologist's training told me it was a shark's brain floating in a mason jar filled with formaldehyde. I moved it to the fireplace mantel. A third-floor bathroom had been converted into a bedroom by simply pulling out all the fixtures. It had not been painted or papered in fifty years because it was occupied by the Blind Aunt. In the attic I found three packs of WWII cigarettes hidden under a board. Several smoked butts sat in a carefully arranged circle in an old jar lid. I felt a pang of sympathy for the returning serviceman forced to crouch in the attic to smoke, perhaps by the Blind Aunt. The walls of the old coal bin were still standing in the basement, covered with hand-scrawled notations such as *two tons #2, December 3, 1932*. Clearly this house was destined to be a focal point for writers; stories leaped from every wall.

In the early '70s Gardner and my brother Joe dropped by on their way back from one of Damon Knight's Milford writers conferences. They were all charged up by the experience of workshopping their manuscripts with other writers. The problem was that the Milfords were held only once a year. Since I had just started selling stories, we decided to form our own workshop, mostly with writers in the early stages of their careers. We called it the Guilford Science Fiction Writers Conference after the neighborhood I lived in. The Guilford Gafia was born.

Who to invite? We had lots of bedrooms to fill. Joe had a friend down in Florida named Bill Nabors. There was a fellow named Jack Dann who I'd just met at a convention. He was jumping up and down on a bed at the time, but I understood he could write a good sentence or two. There was a new writer named George Alec Effinger someone had heard of. Ted White lived nearby, as did Tom Monteleone. These eventually formed the nucleus of the Guilford, with occasional appearances by others, including Bob Thurston.

It was a heady time to be writing science fiction. Something called the New Wave was surfacing in England. The drug culture and counter-culture were influencing some literary stylists. Hard science fiction was getting harder. There were lots of SF magazines that needed to be filled every month, and we were the Young Turks who were going to do it while all those old farts out there ground out the same old novels.

The conferences lasted for several days and we held them two or three times a year. We would wander around the sprawling house reading copies of each others' manuscripts and taking notes. Then we'd spend two days workshopping each manuscript in turn. As in the Milfords, we would sit in a circle and the criticism would start with the person to the left of the author. He would talk as long as he wanted and then the person to his left would comment. The author could not interrupt the criticism except to answer a direct question. He got his say at the end.

The system worked well, primarily because all the participants were published writers. The few times we had unpublished writers there it didn't do as well. Face-to-face criticism by your peers—in particular by writers you respect—is strong stuff. You may think you've got a gem, but if one by one they trash it for the same reasons, perhaps you ought to reconsider. I know, because it happened to me a couple of times. It's incredibly painful to sit through a session like that.

It was a tremendous learning experience, and compressed about ten years of trial and error into a couple of years for me. There were some marvelous highlights.

I remember reading Effinger's first story and it just blew me away. I didn't realize you could do that kind of writing within a science fiction framework. It literally opened doors to a whole new way of writing for me. If *The Last Dangerous Visions* ever sees print, check the story out. It's fantastic.

Joe workshopped ''Hero,'' the novella that became part of *The Forever War.* I remember sitting on the side porch next to the keg of beer, thinking it was great stuff. History shows us the novel went on to win the Nebula, Hugo, and Ditmar awards. It probably *was* great stuff.

But it wasn't all hard work around the beer keg. Down the street from our house was an anarchist bar where we let off steam. The bartender/owner had a habit of cleaning out the till on Friday and going off on a three-day toot, so the hired help never had any change. Sometimes if he was mad enough at the owner, he'd just give the beer away.

Sometimes they'd run out of beer and just collect everybody's money until they had enough for a six-pack. Then they'd send The Hawk two doors down to the liquor store to buy some. The Hawk lived in the bar and once a week moved a broom around the floor.

They were always losing their liquor license because the owner had a habit of writing bad checks. Until he could clear up the mis-understanding, he developed an interim solution. You brought your own beer and wine, which he would store in his fridge. When you wanted one, you'd buy it from him. It made perfect sense at the time.

One favorite Guilford activity was to play "Name That Song" in the bar. It seems that one day the owner got yet another brainstorm and went out and bought a used jukebox. He then proceeded to move all the records from the leased jukebox into his personal one. He figured that way he got all the money, and he could put the records back before they came to collect. Wrong. One day we went in and all the records were back in the leased jukebox and the fridge had a couple of new bullet holes in it. Then complications arose. He'd put all the records back in random order and none of them matched the labels. So we'd punch a number and yell it out. When it started playing he'd jot it down in a notebook. This logical solution failed miserably in practice, due to the fact that he was almost always too drunk to write anything down. The Guilford Gafia solved this problem for him by removing all the record titles from their holders and making up strange science-fictional names for songs.

The bar was a perfect mirror for the craziness of the conference. Even the non-drinkers among us took to hanging out there. After I moved to Florida and the conferences stopped, it turned into a waterbed store.

But what about "Executive Clemency"? I'm getting there.

The Guilford became inbred, which was both good and bad. We reinforced the kind of writing we liked, but we all did it differently. With certain exceptions, we started typecasting ourselves.

Joe was considered the hard SF writer of the bunch. George Effinger had a wry humor, with a bent toward the occasional spec-tacular literary device. ("Too literary by half" became a catch phrase that was aimed at all of us at one time or another. "Turgid prose" 119 and "dense" became others.) Bill Nabors had a vivid imagination and a very distinct style. Jack Dann was sharp and to the point, sometimes creeping toward the New Wave. Ted White's writing was casual, as he was spending most of his time editing *Amazing* and *Fantastic*. (He bought several stories from the conference, often on the spot, and had a special Guilford issue of *Fantastic*.) Ted also won the Name The Brain contest, but the libel laws keep me from revealing the name in print.

But Gardner? He excelled in his criticism of the manuscripts, going straight to the faults of any flawed story, no matter how complex. It was marvelous to observe (unless it was your story he was dissecting), and I thought at the time he'd make a great editor. Again, I was proven right. His prose style in that period was very descriptive. I loved reading it, being led along as he built image upon image.

Although we preferred completed manuscripts for the workshop, we would accept fragments, and Gardner often brought them along as works-in-progress. Since Gardner's writing had a leisurely pace, some of them were quite long. We'd kid him about his 50,000-word fragments. Sometimes I'd realize that there had been no action to speak of in the last five pages, but the description was so well done I hadn't noticed. Even as long as they were, when I tried to find possible places to cut I was never successful. The words were too good, and too interlocked, to remove.

"Executive Clemency" began as a joke I played on Gardner. I wrote a three-page fragment in which absolutely nothing happened. The entire storyline consisted of an ex-president watching the sun's shadow creep across the floor. For added excitement, I had him shave and go down to eat. It seemed to be a perfect Gardner Dozois story and I slipped the pastiche in the stack of manuscripts, not figuring it would be workshopped.

He loved it. Of course he did, it sounded just like he'd written it himself. How could he fail to like it? So we decided to collaborate. We worked out the storyline together and I kept it to do the first draft. A week or two later I sent what I had to Gardner, figuring it was about halfway through. I enclosed notes on the ending and waited to see what happened.

Nothing happened. A few months passed and I asked him about it. He said he was working on it. A year passed, then two. I moved from Baltimore to Florida. Every time I saw Gardner I'd ask him about it and he'd always say he was working on it. Once I dropped by his house in Philadelphia and sure enough, there it was, buried on his table and I could see he *had* been working on it. Another year passed. A couple more. About seven years after I sent the first draft up to him, he called to say he'd finished it. As an afterthought, he added that he hoped I didn't mind that he'd sold it to *Omni*. The highest-paying science fiction market? No, I didn't mind. But I would like to see it. He mailed me a copy and it was just the way I'd hoped it would be, a finely-crafted story.

Since that time, I've been involved in several other collaborations, and they all worked out differently. I did a parody of Jack Dann that turned out to be a collaboration called "Limits" (*Fantastic*). I did the same thing with George Effinger that became the short story "The Terrible Thing They Did to Old McBundy's Son" (*Night Cry*). Joe and I wrote the novel *Starschool* by alternating sections. Bill Nabors and I did three books working together all the time, sharing the same keyboard. Jack and I are working on the novel *High Steel* both together and apart. The most enjoyable collaboration I've done was with my wife Vol. It was an "adult" sf novel (*The Ice World Connection* by "John Cleve"), and people had to jump into bed every five pages or less. The research was most entertaining. We worked with the typewriter on a Lazy Susan between us and sent the chapters off to Andy Offutt for the final draft as soon as they were finished. My most recent collaboration was with Harry Harrison, called *Bill the Galactic Hero on the Planet of Slime Zombies.* In that novel I did the first draft and sent it off to Harry for final revision.

None of the other collaborations, even the novels, took near the time that "Executive Clemency" took. Before it was published, we'd all moved from the "New Writers" panels to the "Old Fart" panels. But I think it's a fine story, thanks to Gardner, and well worth the wait.

Snow Job

GARDNER DOZOIS & MICHAEL SWANWICK

Have you ever toured the Harding Dam in Boulder, Colorado? Have you ever caught that old Errol Flynn movie about the life of Lord Bolingbroke, the man who restored the Stuarts to the British throne and overran half of France but who "couldn't conquer the Queen he didn't dare to love," a real classic, also starring Basil Rathbone and Olivia de Havilland? Have you?

Of course you haven't — which shows what a difference a single line of coke can make.

If it weren't for the coke, the blow-off wouldn't have come hot, and things would have been very, very different.

Just how different, you don't realize. You *can't* realize, in fact. But take my word for it, baby — *I can.*

One little mistake. . . .

I was running, faster than I had ever run in my life, and as I ran those words kept ringing through my head, louder than the pounding of my heart or the breath rasping in my throat: *one little mistake . . .* that was what the losers always said, the gonifs stupid enough to get *caught,* that was what they'd whine as the handcuffs closed over their wrists and the Boys in Blue dragged them away . . . *it's not fair, just one little mistake . . . it's not* fair. . . . But I wasn't a loser, I was tough and smart, I wasn't like *them.* . . .

One little mistake. . . .

I was running through the warehouse district and the cops were right behind me, and not all that far behind me either, in *hot pursuit* as they say on TV, following the trail of blood I was laying down drop by drop. I could hear their footsteps clattering in staccato non-rhythm back there, harbingers of more *hot pursuit* to come. And they were going to catch me this time. This time they were going to get me — the certainty of that sat in a cold lump in my stomach, and made my legs feel cold and slow, so slow. I'd made my one little mistake, and now I was going to pay for it; boy, was I going to pay, my whole *life* was going down the toilet and *it wasn't fair.* . . .

I choked back a laugh that sounded more like a sob.

Behind me, the footsteps were abruptly halved. Tiny hairs crackled on the nape of my neck. I knew without looking that one of the cops was falling into the regulation crouch while his buddy ran far and to the side. Now he would be holding his gun two-handed and leveling it at me. I tried to zig-zag, do some broken-field running, but let's face it, fear drives you *forward*, not to the side. Maybe my path wobbled a bit; you couldn't really call it evasive action.

I *felt* the bullet sizzle by, inches from my head, an instantaneous fraction of a second before I heard it. The time lag would have been subliminal to anyone who wasn't hyper on adrenalin and fear. There was a *ping* as the bullet ricochetted off a brick wall far down the street, and I went into panic mode, pure scrambling terror. Otherwise I'd have know better than to duck into a side alley without checking for exits first.

It was a cul-de-sac.

Belgian block paving stone, a few ripe heaps of garbage, a rusted automobile muffler or three. And dead ahead, the blank back wall of a warehouse. No doors, no windows, no exits.

I skidded to a stop, and gaped idiotically.

What now, wiseass?

The cops rounded the corner behind me.

Galvanized, like a corpse jolted into motion by electrodes, I started running again, blindly, straight at the wall.

There was no place to *go.* . . .

An hour before, I had been trying to sell four kilos of lactose for a hundred thousand dollars. Listen — I had a hell of a nut. My overhead included rent and furnishings for the Big Store (actually the second floor of an old warehouse converted into a loft apartment), a thousand each for the shills, ten percent of the take for the manager, and thirty-five percent for the roper. These things add up.

Stringy — the mark — was a joy to burn, though. He was a pimp and I never *have* liked those suckers. Cheap and lazy grifters, the batch of them.

"It's been stepped on *once*," I said. "Very lightly. And that's only because I prefer it that way. Know what I mean?"

Stringy nodded sagely. The roper, James Whittcombe Harris — better known in some circles as Jimmy the Wit — grinned a trifle too eagerly. In the background half a dozen post-hippie types wandered about, putting Grateful Dead albums on the sound system, rolling joints, discussing the Cosmic All, and doing all those beautiful things that made the '60s die so hard. "I know what you mean, Brother Man," Stringy said meaningfully. Jimmy the Wit snickered in anticipation.

"Jerry's got the best stuff on the Coast," Jimmy the Wit said. "He smuggles it in himself."

"That so?"

I smiled modestly. "I had help. But I'll admit to being pleased with this particular scam. We set up a front office — religious wholesalers — with calling cards, stationery, the whole riff. And we brought the load in inside of a batch of wooden madonnas. You should have seen the things! The absolute, and I mean *ne plus ultra* worst examples of native folk art these tired old eyes have ever seen. The cheeks were painted orange." I shuddered theatrically.

"When we uncrated the things — man, you should've been there! We took a hatchet and split them up the crotch, and all this wonderful white powder tumbled out of the stomachs."

We shared appreciative laughter. Somewhere in the background, a shill put on the *Sgt. Pepper* album. Somebody else lit a stick of patchouli incense.

Sheila chose that moment to send up the steerer. Good timing is what makes a manager, and Sheila was the best. The steerer was a blue jeans and Pink Floyd teeshirt type. He tapped me on the shoulder, said, "Hey Jerry, I'm cutting out now."

"Yeah, well. That's cool, man." I threw Stringy a raised eyebrow, a sort of lookit-the-jerks-I-gotta-put-up-with look. Easing him carefully onto my side. Blue Jeans shifted uncomfortably.

"Uh. You promised to deal me a couple a keys."

"Oh. Right." I called over my shoulder, "Hey, Sheila, honey, bring me the basket, willya?" Then I looked at the steerer as if he were something unpleasant. "That's sixty gee," I said doubtfully.

"Got it right here." He pulled out a wad of money that was eye-popping if you didn't know that all the middle bills were ones. I negligently accepted it, and traded it to Sheila for a large Andean wicker hamper she fetched from the dark recesses of the loft.

If Sheila had no talent at all, I'd still stick her in the background during a play. She stands six-three and weighs about half what you'd swear was humanly possible. She always, even indoors at midnight, wears sunglasses. Creepy. Most people make her out to be a junkie.

"Thanks, sweet." I stuck the top of the hamper under my arm. "Count the money and put it somewhere willya?" She riffled through it, said, "Sixty," in a startlingly deep voice and faded back into obscurity.

I rummaged through the hamper, came up with two brown bags. Then I weighed them judiciously, one in each hand, and dropped one back in. The other I opened to reveal a zip-lock plastic bag crammed to the gills with white powder.

"You want a taste?" My voice said he didn't.

"Naw, I'm on the air in an hour. No time to get wasted."

"Ciao, then." Meaning: Get lost.

"Ciao."

The steerer left, taking his midnight-doper pallor with him. I was playing Stringy against a roomful of *very pale* honkies. The only dark face in the joint was his. Which helped put him on the defensive, raised the fear of appearing to be . . . *not cool* . . . in front of *all these white folk.*

At the same time, I was busily snubbing them *all*, and yet being very warm toward him. Treating him as a fellow sophisticate. Getting him to *identify* with me. It helps create trust.

"Hey, I like your basket, man."

"Yeah?" My voice was pleased. "I got it in S.A. Be going back there as soon as I unload the last—" I glanced in the basket "— *eight* keys. If you like, I could mail you a couple."

"You do that. How much'd you say they cost?"

"Empty or full?" We all three laughed at this. "No, seriously, I'd be glad to. No charge."

Stringy was pleased. "What can I say? I like your *style*, too."

"Hey, man," Jimmy interjected. "How about that *blow*, huh? I got me plans for a very heav-ee date!" Nobody laughed.

"Sure, sure," I said distastefully. He scrabbled inside his pockets for his wad. "No hurry," I said. He thrust it at my face, and I let

it fall into my lap.

"Fifty thousand," he said. "That's two keys for me, 'cause I'm going in with my brother here."

Jimmy the Wit can be a very likeable guy. And when Stringy met him, that's what he was. But once the mark has been roped in, a major part of the roper's job is transferring the mark's respect from himself to the insideman. He quietly makes himself unpleasant, and fosters the feeling in the mark that the roper is not really *deserving* of the great deal that is going down. Not at all a cool person like the insideman. So the mark's loyalties shift. Then, when the blow-off comes, the moment in which the mark is separated from his money and from the insideman, the mark has no desire whatever to stay in the presence of the roper. There is a clean, quiet parting of the ways.

I looked down at the money, picked it up, let it drop. "I really shouldn't be doing this," I said sadly. "I half-promised a friend that I'd hold out six keys for him."

Jimmy the Wit looked stricken. Stringy didn't say anything, but his face got very still, and there was a hungry look in his eyes.

Figure it this way: Coke sells for maybe a hundred dollars a gram. At that rate, Stringy's four keys would be worth four-hundred thousand dollars at what the police call "street prices." Now admittedly Stringy is not going to be selling his coke in four thousand single-gram transactions, so he's not going to get anywhere near that much for it. Still, I've strongly implied that the stuff is at least eighty percent pure. Which means that he can step on it lightly and get another key. Or he can step on it *heavy* and practically double the weight. Which he was likely to do, since his customers were all inner-city and doubtless had never had pure *anything* in their lives. There's profit in the business, never doubt it.

"Hey, look, man," Jimmy whined. "You *promised*."

"I didn't say I wouldn't do it," I said, annoyed. "It's just—" I called over my shoulder, "Hey, Sheila!" She materialized by my side.

"Yes?" she said in that unsettlingly deep voice.

"How long do you think it'll take Deke to come up with the money?"

"Two weeks."

"That long?" I asked.

"Easily." She paused, then added, "You know how he is."

I sighed, and dismissed her with a wave of my hand. Thought for a moment. "What the hell. I'll give him a good deal on the next batch."

Everyone relaxed. Stringy let out a deep breath, the first real indication he'd given as to how deeply hooked he was. Smiles all around.

I sorted through the hamper, carefully choosing six bags, and laying them on the coffee table we were seated around. They made an impressive pile.

I took up a coke mirror from the edge of the table, and wiped it clean against my sleeve. Popping open a bag at random, I spooned out a small mound of lactose. Enough for three generous snorts. Following which, I began chopping it up with a gold-plated razorblade. Ritual is very important in these matters. Stringy and Jimmy the Wit were hanging onto my every move.

"Hey." I paused midway through the chopping. "I've got an idea." I put the blade down and reached for a small brass box. "As long as we're doing this, I want you guys to sample something. It's kind of special." I looked at Stringy as I said this, implying that the offer was really — secretly — for him.

I opened the box and carefully lifted out the Rock.

Stringy's eyes grew large and liquid, as I lifted the Rock up before me, holding it as though it were the Eucharist.

He was staring at a single crystal of cocaine, net weight over one full ounce. It's an extremely rare and valuable commodity. Not for the price it would bring (two thousand dollars "street prices"), but for the status. I paid dearly for that crystal; a *lot* more than two thousand. But the effect was worth it. Stringy positively lusted after it. He was hooked.

Gingerly, delicately, I shaved three more lines from the Rock, and set it back in its box. I resumed chopping, keeping the mound of lactose and the mound of coke carefully separate. "Some jerk offered me twenty thousand for this the other day," I said. "I told him to go fuck himself. He had no appreciation of the beauty of it. This is pure magic, friends. And you can't buy magic, you know what I mean?"

Stringy nodded in a worldly fashion. I finished chopping, and began to lay out the lines with wide sweeps of the razorblade. I'd separate the mounds into three lines each, then merge two and divide them again. I shifted minute quantities back and forth, evening up the amounts. My hand flew gracefully over the mirror, shifting the lines to and fro like a circus grifter shuffling walnut shells under one of which resides a small green pea. Pretty soon you had to be paying very close attention to know which line came from which mound.

Sheila's voice broke in suddenly. "Mind if I borrow the Rock?" I grunted assent without looking up. She faded back into the gloom, taking box and Rock with her. Stringy swiveled to watch it go. He'd have been less than human if he hadn't.

I took advantage of his distraction to shift two or three of the lines. After a bit more fussing, I presented the mirror. On it were two groups of three lines each.

"There," I said. "This—" I tapped the razorblade next to the first group "—is from the stuff you're buying. And this—" tapping next to the second group "—is from the Rock. I suggest you try the merchandise first, so that you can judge it without synergistic effects." Everyone seemed amenable to the notion.

I looked down at the money Jimmy the Wit had dumped in my lap. "Damn, Jimmy, these are all old bills. Either of you guys got—"

Stringy pulled out a leather bill-holder from inside his jacket, and suavely slid out a single crisp and spotless thousand-dollar bill from what was obviously a matched set of one hundred. My expression communicated approval, and he happily rolled it into a snorter.

I held the mirror up to Stringy, and with a gracious smile he did up the first line, half in one nostril and half in the other. Jimmy the Wit was all impatience, and as soon as Stringy had half-shut his eyes and leaned back his head in appreciation, Jimmy snatched the rolled-up bill from his hands. He leaned far forward and did up his line in a single snort. I followed suit. Then all three of us let out small laughs of appreciation.

"Ve-ry niiiiice!" Stringy said. "In fact—" he handed the leather billfold with its hundred-grand cargo to me with a flourish "—I'd go so far as to say 'Keep the billfold.'"

"Sheila," I said quietly. She was there. I handed her Jimmy's wad and Stringy's money. She riffled through Jimmy's first.

"Fifty," she said. Then she riffled through Stringy's money, every bit as quickly, but with a great deal more care.

"Ninety-nine." She faded far back. To the kitchen, in fact, where there was a switch to a signal light in the next building.

"Well," I said. "That was pleasant." I was playing with the empty billfold, admiring it absently. "What say we do up the rest?" No argument.

Of course, Jimmy and I had snorted up lactose while Stringy was inhaling pure Peruvian toot. When I juggled the lines, I laid out the blow in the first, fourth, and sixth places. Which meant that Stringy, being first to sample each group, snorted up powder from the Rock. It also meant that the last line—ostensibly for me—was also real coke. And there's where I made my one little mistake.

The play as written was that in handling the mirror I would bumble and spill the last line all across the rug. What *happened* was that I got greedy. Coke'll do that to you.

I did up the line.

It was just as the rush was hitting me that Sheila's signal was answered. There was a vicious pounding on the door, and then a *crash* as the whole damn thing came splintering off its hinges. Men in blue uniforms, carrying guns, spilled into the room. "Awright, nobody move!" one of them yelled.

I was riding on a great wave of clean energy when it happened, and it threw off my timing. I lurched forward a split-second late, and then everything happened at once.

Stringy jumped to his feet, looking wildly for an exit.

I fell across the coffee table, scattering bags of white powder with gleeful abandon.

One of the shills screamed. Another shouted, "Let's get OUTTA here!" "Blue Jay Way" was playing in the background.

Clouds of white rose from the table as zip-lock bags burst open. There was a gunshot.

Jimmy the Wit grabbed Stringy by the arm and pointed toward a rear window, which led to a fire escape.

The shills ran about frantically.

And Sheila turned the lights out, plunging the room into darkness.

For the next three minutes, we all acted out our parts. Then, when she was certain that Jimmy the Wit had led Stringy safely out of the neighborhood, Sheila turned the lights on again.

Everyone stopped what they were doing. The "police" holstered their guns. The shills straightened up their clothes. And I swiped at the lactose powder on my knees.

Then they all lined up to get paid.

"Good show," I told Sheila, as we left. "Damned good."

"Yeah. Drop you someplace?"

"Naw. I feel like taking a stroll."

When she was gone, I murmured "Damned good" to myself again, and started walking. I was feeling fine. There was a time when they said there were only three Big Cons: the Wire, the Rag, and the Pay-off. The Rock was my own invention, and I was extremely pleased with how well it was working out.

So I strolled along, whistling, following the path I knew Jimmy the Wit would lead the pimp along. This was the final part of my job, to make sure the button hadn't come hot, that the roper had gotten away from the mark clean, and without attracting any attention from the police. But it was pure routine, for I knew, deep in my bones, that the button hadn't come hot. I could feel it.

So I was stunned when I rounded a corner and saw Jimmy the Wit and Stringy in the arms of the Law. There were five cops around a stricken-looking Jimmy and an extremely pissed Stringy.

That's when I realized what a mistake it had been to do up that single, innocuous line of coke. Because Stringy was looking mad because the cops were *laughing* at him. After all, he was holding a hundred-gee bagful of what they had just spot-analyzed as milk sugar.

I realized all in a flash that I was in big trouble. A fraction of a second too late in scattering the bags. Stringy had been able to shove one of them under his arm before fleeing. If I'd been on cue, when the cops nabbed him for suspicious running — which *is* a crime in some of our larger metropoli — we'd have *still* gotten away clean. He'd have never realized that he'd been burned.

Even at that, if Jimmy the Wit had been looking my way when I rounded the corner, he'd have managed to distract Stringy while I eased out of sight. But there's just no arguing with a losing streak. Stringy lashed an indignant finger at me and yelled, "There he is! He's the burn artist that ripped me off!"

I bolted. Behind me, one of the police yelled, "Stop or I'll shoot!" and there was the sharp sound of a bullet hitting the edge of the building inches to my side. A fragment of brick went flying, and cut an evil gash in my upper arm. The pain struck me with all the force of a fist in the ribs.

I stumbled and fell to my knees, recovered, stood, and ran.

The cops ran after me.

They chased me through the warehouse district and into a cul-de-sac.

No place to *go* —

The smooth wall of the warehouse loomed up in front of me, and it might just as well have been Mount Everest.

Dead end, you dumb schmuck, I shrieked silently at myself, *dead end!* My mind gave up at that point, but my legs had developed a will of their own; they wanted to run, so run they did — I imagined them whirring around in huge blurred circles like the legs of cartoon characters, biting into the dirt, sending me sizzling forward like a rocket. *Feets, don't fail me now!*

I hurtled toward the wall. Even if I'd wanted to, I couldn't have stopped in time.

Behind me, I could hear an ominous double click as one of the cops cocked his gun for another shot.

Some distanced part of my mind made me put my hands up in front of me at the last moment to absorb some of the impact.

There was no impact.

I went right through the wall.

There was no impact, but there *was* sudden darkness. The world disappeared. I think I screamed. For a moment or two all was madness and confusion, and then, without having broken stride, I began to lose momentum, my running steps coming slower and slower, as through I were in a film that was being shifted into slow motion, as though I were trying to run through molasses. The resistance I was moving against increased, and just at the point where all my forward momentum had been spilled and I was slooooowing to a stop, there was a slight tugging sensation, like a soap bubble popping, light burst upon me, and I could see again.

I was standing in a room.

Someone's living room, it looked like — an antiquarian's perhaps, a man of quiet tastes and substantial means. There was a Bokhara carpet in scarlet and brown. A large, glassed-in bookcase filled with thick and dusty leather-bound volumes. A browning world-globe on a gleaming brass stand. A highboy with decanters and cut-glass goblets arranged on it. In the middle of everything, about ten feet away from me, was a massive mahogany desk, obviously an antique, with charts carelessly scattered across it and, behind the desk, a tall-backed overstuffed chair — of the type you see in movies that take place in British clubs — with someone sitting in it.

The walls and ceiling of the room were featureless and gray, although it was hard to tell what they were made of — they seemed *oily* somehow, as if there was a faint film over them that would occasionally, almost subliminally, shimmer. There were no doors or windows that I could see. The quickest of head-turns told me that another blank wall was only a step or two behind me. There was no sign of, or sound from, the police, who should also have been only a step or two behind me.

I thought my disorientation was complete until I took a closer look at the man in the chair and saw that it was Stringy.

"Jerry, my man!" Stringy said jovially. "You have been a *baaad* boy."

He smiled at me over a brandy snifter half-filled with some amber-colored fluid.

For the first time in my life, I was at a loss for words.

I opened my mouth, closed it again, like a fish breathing water. My thoughts scurried in a dozen different directions at once. The first thought was that I was dead or in a coma—one of those god-damn cops had shot me, blown me away, and somewhere back there—wherever "There" was; wherever *here* was—I was lying dead or dying in the street, crazed thoughts whirling through my cooling mind like the goosed scurryings of autumn leaves in the wind. Or, less dramatically, I had somehow hallucinated everything that had happened since snorting up that fateful line of coke. *The little boy fell out of bed and woke up. It had all been a dream!*

Screw that. A con man doesn't last long once he starts conning himself; an ability to face reality is *de rigeur* in this trade. I could feel the sweat cooling under my arms, could smell the sour reek of my own fear. The cut on my upper arm throbbed. I had a *bitch* of a headache. No, whatever was happening—it was real.

I didn't like the way Stringy was looking at me.

"You burned me, Jerry," he said. "Jerry—you shouldn't have burned me." He sounded regretful, almost wistful.

Then, slowly, he smiled.

My balls started to retract.

"Hey, man," I said, licking at my lips. "I didn't— I don't know what's—"

"Oh, cut it out," Stringy said impatiently. "Don't bother working your way through Injured Innocence, tape 5-A. You burned me, and I *know* you burned me, and you are going to pay for it, never doubt it." He smiled his glacial sliver of a smile again, thin enough to slice bread, and for the first time in years I began to regret that it wasn't my style to carry a piece. Was *Stringy* packing a gun or a knife? Macho Man is not my style either—I'll run, given a choice—but the thought flickered through my mind that I'd better jump him quick, before he pulled some kind of weapon; even if I couldn't overpower him, maybe I could go over or around or through him and find some way *out* of here—

I spread my hands wide in a weakly conciliatory gesture, at the same time kicking out with my legs and hurling myself at Stringy, thinking *punch him in the throat, people don't expect that. . . .*

Stringy touched something on the desktop, almost negligently, and I stopped.

I just *stopped*, like a fly trapped in amber.

If I'd needed something to confirm that something very weird was going down here, that would have been plenty.

My body was no longer obeying me from the neck down but, oddly, I felt my nerves steady and my panic fade—there are times when things get so bad that it seems you've got little left to lose, and *that* is the time, as all high rollers know, to put your whole bankroll down and pick up those dice and go for broke.

"You've made your point, Stringy," I said in a calm, considering voice. Then I smiled. "*Okay*, then," I said brightly. "Let's talk!"

Stringy stared at me poker-faced for a couple of beats, and then he snorted derisively, and then he laughed. "You know, Jerry," he said, "you're really pretty good."

"Thanks," I said dryly.

"You had *me* fooled, you know," Stringy said, smiling. "And I don't fool easily. I really thought that you were going to come across with all that great snow, I really did. And that setup! Your staging and your timing were superb, you know, quite first-rate, really. You had me going in just the direction you wanted me to go, steered neatly right down the chute. If I hadn't managed to pick up that bag in the confusion, I'd never have known that you were burning me—I would have just shrugged my shoulders and chalked it all up to fate, to the influence of some evil star. I really would have. You are a very subtle man, Jerry."

He was still wearing his Superfly pimpsuit, but his voice had changed—it was cultured now, urbane, almost an octave higher, and although he still employed the occasional smattering of street slang, whatever the unfamiliar accent behind his words *was*, it certainly *wasn't* Pore Black Child from 131st and Lenox. Even his skin—it was different now; there were coppery highlights I'd never seen before, as if he were some refinement of racial type that simply *did not exist*. I was beginning to realize that whoever—or whatever—else Stringy was, he was also a bit of a con man himself.

"You're an alien, aren't you?" I asked suddenly. "From a flying saucer, right? Galactic Federation? The whole bit?" And with any luck a Prime Directive—don't hurt the poor backward natives. Please God?

He curled his lip in scorn. "Shit no."

"What *are* you, then?"

He propped his feet up on the desk, leaned back, put his hands behind his head. "Time-traveller."

I gaped at him. "You're . . . a *time-traveller*?"

"Got it in one, sport," he said languidly.

"If you're a time-traveller — *then why the fuck were you trying to score cocaine from me?*"

"Why not?" he said. He had closed his eyes.

"*Why,* for bleeding Christ's sake?"

He opened his eyes. "Well, I don't know what you do with *yours,* but what I do with *mine* is to stick it right up my nose an snuffle it *up,* snuffleuffle*upagus* until it's all gone. Yum. Gives you a hell of a nice rush. Helps pass the time while you're on your way to the Paleolithic, or *whenever.* Makes a long boring trip through the eons just *fly* by. Other time-travellers may be into speed or reds or synapse-snappers or floaters, but among the elite of the Time Corps, such as myself, coke is *the* drug of choice, no others need *apply.* . . ."

"That's not what I meant, damnit! Why come to *me* for it, why go to all that trouble, sneaking around in back alleys, spending all that money? If you can really travel in time, why not just go back to, say, pre-Conquest Peru, and gather up a sackful for *nothing?* Or if that's too much trouble, why not just go back to the turn of the century when it was still legal and buy all you want, with nobody giving a damn? Or . . ."

Stringy aimed a finger at me like a gun, and made a shooting motion, and I'm ashamed to admit that I flinched — who knew what he could or couldn't do with that finger? Nothing happened, though, except that he made a pow! noise with his lips, and then said, "Right on! You've put your finger right on the veritable *crux* of the problem, sport. Why not indeed?" He winked, laced his hands behind his head again. "The *problem,* my old, is that the authorities are almost as stuffy in *my* time as they were in *yours,* in spite of all the years gone by. Particularly the Powers That Be in the Time Corps, my bosses — they want us to flit soberly through the centuries on our appointed rounds, primly protecting the One and Proper Chain of Events and fighting off paradoxes. They do *not* want us, while we're engaged in protecting and preserving Order by, say, keeping the bad guys from helping the Persians to win at Marathon, they do *not* want us at that particular moment to go sneaking off behind some scrubby Grecian bush and blow our brains right out of the top of our skulls with a big snootful of toot. They frown on that. They are, as I say, stuffy."

He stretched, and ran his fingers back through his afro. "To forestall your next question: no, of course my bosses can't watch all of time and space, but they don't *have* to — they *can* watch the monitors in the control complex that show where and when our timecraft are going. So if we're supposed to be in, say, 1956 Iowa, and we stop off in pre-Conquest Peru instead to grab us a sackful of crystal, why, that'll show up on the *monitors*, right, and we're in big trouble. No, what's been happening instead is that we've been doing a lot of work the last few subjective years more or less in this location and in this part of the century, and it's *so* much easier, when we're scheduled to be in 1982 Philadelphia or whenever *anyway*—when our car is already parked, so to speak, and the monitors off—to just whomp up some money, whatever amount is necessary, and take a few minutes off and go hunt up a native source. To take our bucket to the well, so to speak."

"I see," I said weakly.

"Except," Stringy said, sitting up slowly and deliberately and putting his feet back on the ground and his hands flat on the desk in front of him, "*except*, Jerry, what do you think happened? We went to the well with our bucket this time, and the well was *dry*, Jerry." That flat, evil light was back in his eyes again. "No snow in our forecast, Jerry old bean. And do you know *why*? Because you *burned* us, Jerry. . . ."

"If you can do all that stuff," I said, fighting to control the fear that wanted my voice to break and whine, "why don't you just go back to the start of all this and find yourself another source. Just never come to see me in the first place." *Why me, Lord? Let this cup pass from me. . . .*

Stringy shook his head. "Might create a paradox-loop, and that'd show up on the monitors. I came close *enough* to looping when I shook off the fuzz and came angling back to snatch you way from the long arm of the Law. Although—" he smiled thinly "—I would've loved to have seen the faces of those cops when you ran right through that brick wall; that's one police report that'll never get filed."

"Then why don't you let me take the money and go out and *buy* you some real coke?"

He shook his head again, that ominous glint in his eyes. "It's not the money—that's just paper. It's not even getting the coke anymore. It's the *principle* of the thing."

If I'd been a bit nearer, I'd have spit in his eye. "Why you dumb ersatz nigger!" I snarled, losing the ragged edge of my temper. "You're a terrific one to be talking about *principles. You paid for the whole transaction in funny money.* You stiffed *me.*"

He shrugged. "Your people never would've noticed anything odd about that money. But that doesn't matter anyway. What *matters* is—*you don't fuck around with the Time Corps.* Never, ever, not even when the only mission we're on is a clandestine dope run. You've screwed over the Time Corps, and we're going to take it out of your hide, I promise you." He smiled that thin and icy smile again, and it cut like a razor. "We'll get that one-hundred thousand dollars worth of use out of you, Jerry—*one way or another.*"

I tried to keep my face still, but a hundred dreadful images were skittering behind my eyes, and he probably knew it: me as a galley slave, tied to a giant oar while the salt sea spray stings the festering whip-scars on my back; me as a mine slave, working deep underground, never seeing the sun, lungs straining at the foul air, my back gnarled, my hands torn and bleeding; me as a medieval serf, struggling to pull a primitive plow through the unturned soil, sweating and groaning like a mule; me being disemboweled, crucified, having my eyes put out, having molten gold poured down my throat. . . . No doubt a race of time-travellers could arrange for any of those fates—history is large enough to swallow thousands of wretches like me down into nameless oblivion, and no doubt it had. Was Judge Crater now a kitchen slave in ancient Carthage? Did Ambrose Bierce now spend his time shoveling out manure piles in some barnyard in Celtic Britain?

We'll get one-hundred thousand dollars worth of use out of you— *one way or another.*

Think, damnit, *think.* Let's see the Giant Brain get you out of *this* one, kid.

My mind raced like a car engine does when someone has the accelerator and the brake simultaneously floored.

I stared unflinchingly into Stringy's ice-pale eyes for one heartbeat, two heartbeats, three, and then slowly, oh so slowly, I allowed a smile to form on my face, a beatific smile, a knowing smile, a smile that I managed to make both mocking and conspiratorial all at the same time.

"Tell me, Stringy," I said lazily, "do you ever *meddle* with the One and Proper Chain of Events instead of just preserving the *status quo*? Do you ever *tinker* with it, just a little bit, here and there, now and then? Do you ever beat the bad guys to the punch by changing something *first*?"

"Well . . ." Stringy said. He looked uneasy.

"You know something, Stringy?" I said, still in that same dreamy, drifting, conversational tone. "I'm one of the few guys in the world who can pull off the Big Con—can't be more than five or six others who can handle it, and I'm the best of them. There can't *ever* have been many, not in any age. And I took you with it, Stringy—you know that I did. I took you with it clean. And you know just as well as

I do that if it hadn't been for an Act of God, a million-to-one accident, you never even would have tumbled to the fact that I took you."

"Well . . ." Stringy said. "Maybe so. . . ."

I felt a rush of fierce singing joy and carefully hid it. I was going to do it! I was going to *con* the sonofabitch. I was going to take him! With the odds stacked overwhelmingly in his favor, still I was going to take him!

I metaphorically rolled up my sleeves and settled down to *talk* better and faster than I had ever talked before.

Now, years later by my own subjective life clock, I sometimes wonder just who was conning whom. I think that Stringy—not actually his name, of course; but then, neither is my name Jerry—was playing me like a virtuoso angler with a record trout on the line from the moment I came stumbling through the timescreen, playing on my fear and anger and disorientation, letting me run up against black despair and then see just the faintest glimmer of hope beyond, conning me into thinking I was conning him into letting me do what he'd wanted me to do all along: or, at any rate, as soon as he had realized what sort of man I was.

Good recruits for the more exotic branches of the Time Corps are hard to come by in any age, just as I'd said, and Stringy was—and is—a very subtle fellow indeed. I always enjoy working with him, and one of the fringe benefits—for Stringy's taste for snow was real enough—is the plenitude of high-quality dope he always manages to gather unto himself.

Ironically, my specialty within the Corps has become the directing of operations where the button is *supposed* to come hot, where the marks are *supposed* to realize that they are being conned; their resultant fury, if adroitly directed toward the proper target, can have some very interesting effects indeed.

As with the South Sea Bubble scandal, for instance, which brought Walpole—no friend of Bolingbroke's—into power, as a minor result of which—one of many, many results which echoed down the time-lines for centuries—a certain motion picture starring Errol Flynn was never made, or even contemplated. Or with the Teapot Dome scandal, as a result of which—a small result among many more significant and long-term results—Harding's name is not attached to a certain dam in Colorado, and never has been.

My latest operation is something that will come to be called Watergate. You haven't heard of it yet—you *couldn't* have heard of it yet. But just give it time—you will.

SNOW JOB

This story is an artifact of a high-energy, high-production period of mine. Although I'd already started to come out of a long dry spell by the beginning of 1979, it wasn't, paradoxically enough, until I nearly died at the end of 1980, was hospitalized for a while, and then released, that I really shifted into high gear. When I was released from the hospital into the crisp, clear winter days of early January 1981, I found myself crackling with creative energy, and during the next two or three years I turned out more than twenty stories, both solo and collaborative, as well as a fair amount of critical writing, several anthologies, and a largish body of stuff that has yet to be completed, including chunks of a couple of novels. This was the most fertile production period I'd ever enjoyed, rivaled only by a similar high-production period from 1971 to 1973.

Michael's anecdote about the origin of this story is true. I'm embarrassed to say that the writing of it was something of a stunt; I was showing off, flexing my creative muscles — if I'd been in a low-energy period instead, I probably never would have attempted to do what I did. I was browsing through old files, and I happened to pick up the first chapter of an abortive novel Michael had begun and then abandoned the year before. Called "The Button Comes Hot," the bulk of the chapter was taken up by a long description of an intricately-detailed coke-scam which was being run by a young con artist. The coke-scam scene was really well-done, and it occurred to me that it was a shame to *waste* it just because it was embedded in the now-extraneous plotline of a novel that had faltered and died. All at once, with a rush of mischievous excitement, I saw how I could save the coke-scam scene and build a viable science fiction story   139 around it, and, better still, that I could do it all *without having to tell Michael about it.*

I snipped the coke-scam scene out of the novel fragment, added a time-travel plot at the beginning and end of it, and did a unifying draft, taking particular care to feather over the joins where I had put the two drafts together, so that they melded as seamlessly as possible. I had fun coming up with the details of the alternate-world scams — especially the Errol Flynn movie that was never made on *this* timeline because of them — and inventing the sardonic, drawling dialogue of the coke-sniffing time-traveller. I worked on the story all day on February 10, 1981, and then stayed up most of the night typing up a clean draft. I was just finishing up when Michael arrived the next day — I had been expecting him, which was why I was hurrying to finish — and I chuckled fiendishly to myself as he rang the doorbell. *Won't he be surprised!* I thought.

He was.

Although this is really an innocuous little thing, nobody in the genre would touch this story with a ten-foot pole. It finally sold to *High Times,* appearing in an issue with a girlie-magazine-like gatefold of a marijuana plant. Later on, it was reprinted in *Isaac Asimov's Science Fiction Magazine,* after Shawna McCarthy had taken over as editor there.

SEND NO MONEY

SUSAN CASPER & GARDNER DOZOIS

SEND NO MONEY! the postcard said, in dark blue letters against a bright orange background. Judy smiled, and pushed it into the stack. She liked her junk mail. Certainly it was less depressing than the load of bills that made up the bulk of her mail. She especially liked the computer-generated "personalized" ones, eternally optimistic, that excitedly announced "You may have won a million dollars!" (Only Maybe Not), or the ones that promised to send you something "Absolutely Free!" for only $2 plus shipping and handling, or the ones that enclosed sample swatches of material, or paperthin slices of stale-looking fruitcake, or slightly squashed bits of cheese wrapped up in cellophane. Today's stack of junk mail was particularly large. Who *knew* what might be in it?

She carried the mail inside, hung her coat neatly in the closet, and then went in search of something to eat. The freezer was packed with frozen foods of the "gourmet dinner" variety. She stared at them listlessly, unable to work up any enthusiasm. Too much trouble after the kind of day she'd had at work. She settled for cold leftover spaghetti and a glass of milk. Sighing, she carried the food over to the table. Lately, it seemed like deciding what to have for dinner was the most important decision of her day; certainly it was the day's most *exciting* moment, with the possible exception of the "Dark

Shadows" reruns on TV. . . . Well, whose fault was *that*? she asked herself. Ginny and Lois weren't eating leftovers tonight, were they? They had gone to dinner at Le Boeuf, and then on to Spangles for dancing, and they had wanted her to come too. In fact, Ginny had spent the whole last week trying to talk her into it. Why had she refused?

The fact was, she was tired of the whole dating scene — the bars, the banal small talk, the clichéd pick-up lines, the loud insipid music, the leering faces. Anyway, all you ever seemed to meet were nerds, or narcissistic romeos in mirror sunglasses, or prowling husbands in clever plastic disguises. . . .

So *this* is better? she thought. *Oh* yeah. Right. Sighing again, she sat down to go through the mail while she ate. Simple Pleasures . . . but at least there was no cover charge.

It seemed like a fairly typical assortment. The first three envelopes were bills, from, respectively, the electric company, the phone company, and the credit-card company. One was *awful*, the others not as bad as she had feared. There was an unordered catalogue from one of those "naughty underwear" places; a solicitation from a local animal-rescue shelter; a "Vote for So-and-So" political flyer; an offer of 20% off on a diamond engagement ring with a genuine imitation diamond — guaranteed absolutely undetectable from the real thing at fifty feet or more — addressed to Mr. J. B. Pender; an offer of "personalized" ballpoint pens that promised an enormous money-saving discount on orders of 100 or more; and, finally, a little green postcard.

Green? She could have *sworn* that it had been orange. Or had there been *two* postcards, and she'd somehow dropped the orange one somewhere on the way in? She ate a forkful of spaghetti, and prodded the postcard idly with her finger. Strange. . . . No company name, no return address. It was one of those "personalized" come-ons, and the front of the card shouted MS. JUDY PENDER!! in enormous glittery letters. She turned it over.

The card said: MS. JUDY PENDER, WHY ARE YOU SITTING THERE EATING COLD SPAGHETTI WHEN YOU *COULD* BE OUT HAVING THE TIME OF YOUR LIFE?

Whoo. She was startled enough to drop the card and sit back suddenly in her chair. Pretty strange. What were the odds against her reading that *particular* come-on pitch just at the exact moment that she actually *did* happen to be eating some cold spaghetti? Pretty astronomical. She tittered nervously, then began to laugh, perhaps a shade too loudly. Mindboggling coincidences *did* happen, she knew that. But this one was weird. *Ripley's Believe It or Not* would love it. They'd publish it right next to "Man Who Grew A Potato in the Shape of Anita Ekberg" and "Replica of the *Titanic* Made Entirely Out of Old Fingernail Parings."

Still chuckling, she quickly finished her spaghetti. Almost time for her nightly fix of "Dark Shadows" reruns. She reached out and picked up the postcard again.

This time it said: IS A NIGHT SPENT WATCHING "DARK SHADOWS" RERUNS REALLY *ALL* YOU WANT OUT OF LIFE?

She dropped the card again.

She found that, without realizing it, she had pushed herself away from the table and was standing bolt upright, quivering, like a garden rake that's been stepped on.

Her mind was blank for several heartbeats, and then she began casting frantically about for explanations. She'd just *missed* that part of the text the first time she'd read the card, skipped right over it. Sure, that was it. And as for the card mentioning "Dark Shadows." ... Well, coincidences *did* happen. Remember that. A man drops his watch in the ocean and twenty years later finds it inside the belly of a fish he's just caught; another one jumps off the Empire State Building, and survives because he happens to land on top of the long-lost twin brother he hasn't seen since they both were five. . . . It Happens All The Time. Or—and she grabbed for this one eagerly, although the ultimate implications of it were somewhat unflattering —she was just statistically *predictable*, normal, average, humdrum, easy meat for the trend-spotters and social analysts. Doubtless her habits were far from unique. Probably there were *millions* of bored young women just like her who spent their evenings eating cold spaghetti and watching "Dark Shadows." Hence the card, addressed to her statistical *type*, a profile she just happened to fit embarrassingly well. . . .

Nevertheless, she didn't touch the card again.

Leaving it where it lay, she bustled nervously around, putting the spaghetti bowl into the sink to soak, picking up last Sunday's paper (which was still strewn over the end of the couch), emptying the ashtrays, annoyedly pushing the term "displacement activity" out of her head every time it forced its way into it.

After a while, she began to get tired. She glanced at the television, but whoever the Machiavellian social researcher responsible for the postcard was, she'd be damned if she'd prove him *right*. Besides, "Dark Shadows" was almost over anyway. The only thing on now were "M*A*S*H" reruns, and she'd always thought that Hawkeye was a wimp, like one of those oh-so-sincere-and-sensitive types from the singles bars who suddenly turned into married men when the full moon came out. She could survive a night without television just fine, thank you. Decisively, Judy went into the bedroom to get the book she'd been reading and to pick up her double-acrostic magazine, and then headed back toward her favorite armchair.

On her way past the table, she glanced suspiciously at the card again—and it was *red*. Bright fire-engine red! It had been *green* before, hadn't it? She stood swaying in shock, trying to remember. Had it? Yes, dammit, it *had* been green, bright apple green. There was no doubt about that.

Unfortunately, there was also no doubt that the card was now *red*.

Shakily, Judy sat down. One part of her mind was keeping up a stream of desperate speculation about dyes that faded from one color to another, perhaps depending on the length of time they'd been exposed to light, but that was so obviously a last-ditch—and rather ineffectual—defensive effort on behalf of Rationality that she didn't pay much attention to it. Slowly, with immense trepidation, as if it were a venomous insect, she picked up the card again, this time with only two fingers, holding it as far away from herself as she could and still make out the words.

This time, in spangly gold letters, it said: SURE *THE GULAG ARCHIPELAGO* IS A GOOD BOOK, BUT WOULDN'T YOU RATHER PUT ON YOUR BLUE CHANEL DRESS—THE SLINKY ONE WITH THE GOLD GLITTER SASH—AND THE GOLD HOOP EARRINGS YOU BOUGHT AT THE CRAFTS FAIR, AND GO *OUT* ON THE TOWN FOR A ROMANTIC EVENING AT DELANEY'S OR KARISMA? INSTEAD OF STARTING ANOTHER ONE OF THOSE STUPID CROSS-WORD PUZZLE MAGAZINES, WOULDN'T YOU RATHER BE OUT STARTING UP A "MEANINGFUL RELATIONSHIP"?

Her hand began to tremble, vibrating the card into unreadability. By the time she steadied it down again, it read: WE CAN FIND THE PERFECT MATE FOR *YOU!*

Moving with exaggerated caution, as if it might explode, she lowered the card to the tabletop. She wiped her hands on her thighs. Her mouth was dry.

The card changed to a soft chocolate brown, this time before her eyes. In urgent red letters, it now said: WE CAN HELP YOU

FIND THE MAN OF YOUR DREAMS! SATISFACTION GUAR-ANTEED! MANY, MANY YEARS OF EXPERIENCE! STAFF OF EXPERTS!

That faded and was replaced by: SEND NO MONEY!

Followed, after a pause, in a somewhat more subdued script, by: *Magic Mates . . . a division of Elf Hill Corp.*

To her own surprise, much of Judy's fear was draining rapidly away, to be replaced by a drifting, dreamlike bemusement. Could this *really* be happening? Had someone sifted LSD into the grated parmesan cheese she'd used on the spaghetti? Her rational mind kept throwing up feverish high-tech speculations about wireless telegraphy and time-release invisible inks, but she no more believed them than she really believed that she was dreaming, or hallucinating, or crazy. Instead, she was beginning to feel a curious tranced calm, a bemused nonchalance. Oh, magic. Of course.

Can you guys read my mind? she thought, trying to project her thoughts *at* the card, the way they do in sci-fi movies, keeping her lips firmly shut.

Do you know what I'm thinking? Hello? Hello in there . . . ?

The card didn't answer.

No mind-reading, then. Still, there was no *way* that the postcard could know all that stuff about her unless they had her under some sort of magical observation. Maybe they really *could* do what they said they could do. . . .

"Well," she said aloud. "I don't know. I don't really *need*—"

COME NOW, MS. PENDER, the card said, brown letters on gold this time. WE *KNOW* YOU DREAM ABOUT YOUR PERFECT MAN ALL THE TIME. YOU CERTAINLY TALK TO YOUR GIRLFRIENDS ABOUT HIM OFTEN ENOUGH. DON'T WOR-RY, WE *KNOW* WHAT YOU WANT. TALL AND SLENDER, WITH GRAY EYES. WAVY BROWN HAIR, RIGHT? GLASSES. NO MUSTACHE. WITTY. ARTICULATE. SENSITIVE YET MASCULINE. DECISIVE YET UNDERSTANDING. NOT MARRIED. RIGHT? WELL, WE CAN *FIND* HIM FOR YOU! SATISFACTION GUARANTEED! THIRTY-DAY TRIAL PERI-OD! SEND NO MONEY! DEAL'S OFF IF YOU DON'T LIKE HIM! GIVE IT A TRY!

"Well . . ."Judy said, feeling only a distant twinge of wonder that she was sitting here talking to a postcard.

OH, GO AHEAD, the postcard said. YOU KNOW YOU'RE AS HORNY AS A GOAT. . . .

"Well," Judy said weakly. "I really *shouldn't*. . . ."

145

The postcard went blank. Then, in large block letters, formal and somewhat severe, as though it were growing impatient with her, there appeared:

DO YOU WANT THIS SERVICE?

yes   no

☐   ☐

CHECK ONE.

Hesitantly, feeling an odd little chill run up her spine, she checked the square for "yes."

The doorbell rang.

Early one Saturday morning, a month later, Judy awoke to the soft, liquid trilling of birdsong. The sun had not reached the bedroom window yet, and the room was still in shadow, but hot bright sunlight was already touching the roof of the house across the street, turning tile and mortar and brick to gold. The wedge of sky she could see was a clear bright blue. It was going to be another beautiful day, more like May than March.

Mark snored softly beside her, and she raised herself up on one elbow to look down at him for a moment, smiling fondly. Even his *snores* were melodic!

Moving carefully, so as not to wake him, she got up and threw on a bathrobe, and quietly let herself out of the bedroom. She would make breakfast, a big weekend breakfast, and serve it to him in bed, along with maybe one or two other items. . . .

The thought made her smile as she padded into the kitchen to start the coffee perking, but when she popped into the front room to pick up a sheet of newspaper to drain the bacon on, her smile died at once.

There was a little green postcard lying on the throw rug next to the front door, as though someone had ignored the box outside and pushed it through the mail slot instead.

She knew at once what it was, of course.

Judy and Mark had been dating for a month now, ever since his car had broken down outside, and he'd rung her doorbell to ask if he could use the phone. They'd been fascinated with each other at once. Mark was *perfect*. It was almost *scary* how perfect he was. Never had she jibed better with a man. They like the same books, the same movies, the same music, the same foods, enjoyed the same kind of quirky humor, shared the same kinds of dreams and aspirations, disagreeing just enough to add a touch of spice to the relationship, but never enough to make them seriously squabble or fight. Physically, they couldn't possibly have been more compatible.

The month had gone by for Judy in a blur of excitement and happiness. She had done her best to forget about the magic postcard, thrust it out of her mind, and deny its reality. That had been made easier by the fact that the postcard itself had disappeared right after that first evening, although at one point she tore the house apart looking for it. She sighed. Out of sight, out of mind. People were *always* willing to be lulled into forgetting about unpleasant or inconvenient facts, and she was no exception. For long stretches of time, she had almost managed to convince herself that it had never happened at all—or that, at most, it had been some strange sort of waking dream. . . . But always, sooner or later, she would seem to hear a dry little voice in her head whispering THIRTY-DAY TRIAL PERIOD!, and then she would *know* better, and she would feel a chill of apprehension.

And now here was the postcard—or another just like it—turning up again, right on schedule. She had had her month's free trial, and now, having hooked her on the product, they were about to reel her in and scoop her up in a net and clean and gut her. Here came the price tag. Here came *the catch*. She *knew* it. In every sales pitch, behind every "free offer," there was always a catch. There was *always* a price tag. Why hadn't she remembered that? The sweeter and more generous the deal seemed, the higher the price tag was likely to be. They—whoever They were—weren't in business for their *health*, after all. . . .

Unsteadily, she sat down in one of her beat-up old armchairs, keeping her eyes riveted on that innocent-looking little postcard, as if it might slither sinisterly away under the highboy if she looked away for a second. She even knew who They were, had always known, really, although she'd tried to suppress that knowledge, too. Elves. Leprechauns. The Little People. The Good Folk. . . .

Faëries, of course, Of *course* faëries. Who else?

The knowledge did not reassure her. Now that it was too late, she found herself remembering all the folktales and fairy stories she'd read as a child: the Brothers Grimm, Hans Christian Andersen, Charles Perrault, Yeats's collection of Irish folklore, *The Blue Fairy Book*. . . . All of them agreed on one thing: faëries were worse than used-car-salesmen. No matter how wonderful the service they performed, there was *always* a price, and it was usually far more than you were willing to pay.

With a sudden flurry of the heart, she even thought that she knew *what* the price would be. . . .

Compressing her lips into a thin hard line, Judy got up and walked determinedly over to the front door. Hesitating only for the smallest fraction of a second, she picked up the postcard and held it up to the light.

In fine copperplate letters, it said: MS. JUDY PENDER, YOUR THIRTY-DAY TRIAL PERIOD IS OVER! DID THE SERVICE MEET YOUR EXPECTATIONS? ARE YOU SATISFIED WITH THE PRODUCT?

"No," Judy said weakly, her voice lacking conviction even to her own ears. "No, I'm not at all satisfied. . . ."

OH, COME NOW, MS. PENDER, the postcard chided in somehow tired-looking letters. She could almost hear it sigh. DON'T DISSEMBLE. WE *KNOW* BETTER THAN *THAT!*

Judy—who with Mark had found herself easily and naturally acting out several sexual fantasies she had never even thought of *mentioning* to any other man—began to blush.

THAT'S BETTER, the card said, in florid purple ink this time. IN FACT, WE KNOW PERFECTLY WELL THAT THE PRODUCT MORE THAN FULFILLS YOUR EVERY EXPECTATION. YOUR EVERY DREAM, FOR THAT MATTER. WE'RE EXPERTS. WE *KNOW* WHAT WE'RE DOING—IT'S OUR *BUSINESS,* AFTER ALL. SO LET'S HAVE NO MORE EVASIVENESS, MS. PENDER. MARK PROPOSED LAST NIGHT, CORRECT? AND YOU ACCEPTED. SO IT'S TIME, AND PAST TIME, TO ENTER INTO A BINDING AGREEMENT CONCERNING *PAYMENT* FOR THIS SERVICE. . . .

"All right," she said through tight lips. "Tell me. Just what is it you want?"

FOR SERVICES RENDERED . . . said the card, and seemed to pause portentously . . . YOUR FIRSTBORN CHILD.

"I *knew* it!" Judy cried. "I *knew* that's what it was going to be! You're *crazy!*"

IT'S THE TRADITIONAL PRICE, the card said. NOT AT ALL EXCESSIVE, REALLY, CONSIDERING ALL WE'VE DONE TO CHANGE YOUR LIFE FOR THE BETTER.

"I won't do it!" Judy said.

YOU DON'T HAVE MUCH CHOICE, the card said. YOU HAVE TO PAY YOUR DEBT TO US AT ONCE IF YOU DON'T WANT

THE PRODUCT . . . SHIPPED BACK, AS IT WERE.

"Mark *loves* me," Judy said fiercely. "It's too late for you to change that *now*".

DON'T KID YOURSELF, MS. PENDER, the card said. IF WE CAN'T FINALIZE A BINDING AGREEMENT RIGHT NOW, YOU'LL HAVE AN EXTREMELY BITTER FIGHT WITH HIM THIS VERY MORNING. NO MATTER HOW HARD YOU TRY TO AVOID IT, IT *WILL* HAPPEN. HE'LL WALK OUT OF HERE, AND YOU'LL NEVER SEE HIM AGAIN. WE GUARANTEE *THAT*.

"But, my firstborn *child*. . . ." Judy whispered.

A HIGH PRICE INDEED, the card gloated. AH, YES. A VERY HIGH PRICE. BUT THINK. . . . REMEMBER. . . . BE *HONEST* WITH YOURSELF. DO YOU REALLY WANT TO GO BACK TO "DARK SHADOWS" AND COLD SPAGHETTI? NOW THAT YOU'VE MET MARK, COULD YOU REALLY LIVE WITHOUT HIM?

"No," Judy said, in the smallest of voices.

WE THOUGHT NOT, the card said smugly.

Judy groped behind her for a chair, and sank into it. She dropped the card on the coffee table, and buried her face in her hands. After a moment or two, she raised her head wearily and looked over at the card again. It said: COME, COME, MS. PENDER. IT'S NOT REALLY SUCH A TRAGEDY. BABIES ARE NUISANCES, ANYWAY. THEY SQUALL AND STINK, THEY CRAYON ON YOUR WALLS AND VOMIT ON YOUR CARPET. . . . THEY WEIGH YOU *DOWN*, MS. PENDER. YOU'LL BE BETTER OFF WITHOUT IT, REALLY. YOU OUGHT TO BE GLAD WE'LL BE TAKING IT OFF YOUR HANDS. ALL THE MORE TIME YOU'LL BE ABLE TO SPEND WITH MARK. . . .

There was a long pause, and then, in tacit surrender, Judy said, "Why in the world did you guys ever get into this *mail-order* scam?" Her voice was flat and weary, bitter and dull. "It doesn't seem your style, somehow. . . ."

MODERNIZATION IS A MUST, MS. PENDER, the card said. THE OLD WAYS JUST AREN'T VERY EFFECTIVE ANYMORE. WE HAVE TO KEEP UP WITH THE TIMES TOO, YOU KNOW. It paused. NOW . . . ENOUGH SHILLY-SHALLYING, MS. PENDER. YOU MUST DECIDE NOW. IF YOU AGREE TO PAY THE PRICE FOR OUR SERVICE—TO SPECIFY: YOUR FIRSTBORN CHILD—THEN SIGN HERE. . . .

A dotted signature line appeared on the postcard.   149

Judy stared at it, her face haggard, and then slowly, hesitantly, reluctantly, with many a stop and start, she picked up a pen and leaned forward.

She signed her name.

After a moment, the card vanished, disappearing with a smug little pop.

Everything was quiet. Everything was still.

Judy held her breath for a few moments, then slowly let it out. She wiped her brow. Slowly, she began to smile.

She had had her tubes tied two years ago because it was the cheapest and surest form of birth control. It was a good thing that the Wee Folk didn't *really* keep up with the times. . . .

Whistling cheerfully, she strolled into the kitchen and finished making breakfast.

■
■
■
■
■

SEND NO MONEY

Susan thought up the idea for this story, worked on it as a solo piece for a while, got stuck on it, and asked me if I wanted to collaborate on it with her. I was the most intrigued here by the idea of a junk-mail come-on that actually *talked* to you, interactively, changing its printed message to fit the situation and your response, and I had fun helping her come up with the chiding, somewhat scornful "dialogue" of the card. I started work on the story on February 29, 1984, a few days after Susan had started it, and we finished work on it on March 2, 1984.

This is one of several stories that I've worked—"Golden Apples of the Sun" and "Afternoon At Schrafft's" are two others—that strike me as legitimate modern updates of *Unknown*-style fantasies—that is, as stories that *might* have fit in to the famous fantasy magazine *Unknown* if it had survived the wartime paper shortage that killed it and was instead still publishing today, in the '90s. I like this kind of story; Jack and I frequently reprint *Unknown* stories in our fantasy anthologies for Ace, and I buy good new stories of this type for *IAsfm* when I can find them. It says something, I think, that people are still producing recognizable *Unknown*-style fantasies nearly forty years after the magazine died—many of them by writers who weren't even born yet when the magazine was on the newsstands!

We sold this story to Shawna McCarthy, very nearly the last thing she bought before relinquishing her editorship of *Isaac Asimov's Science Fiction Magazine*, and it appeared there in the Mid-December 1985 issue.

Playing the Game

GARDNER DOZOIS & JACK DANN

The woods that edged the north side of Leister-shire belonged to the cemetery, and if you looked westward toward Owego, you could see marble mausoleums and expensive monuments atop the hills. The cemetery took up several acres of carefully mown hillside, and bordered Jefferson Avenue, where well-kept wood-frame houses faced the rococo, painted headstones of the Italian section.

West of the cemetery there had once been a district of brownstone buildings and small shops, but for some time now there had been a shopping mall there instead; east of the cemetery, the row of dormer-windowed old mansions that Jimmy remembered had been replaced by an ugly brick school building and a fenced-in schoolyard where kids never played. The cemetery itself, though — that never changed, that had always been there, exactly the same for as far back as he could remember, and that made the cemetery a pleasant place to Jimmy Rodgers, a refuge, a welcome island of stability in a rapidly changing world where change itself was often unpleasant and sometimes menacing.

Jimmy Rodgers lived in Old Town most of the time, just down the hill from the cemetery, although sometimes they lived in Passdale or Southside or even Durham. Old Town was a quiet residential neighborhood of whitewashed narrow-fronted houses and steep cobbled streets that were lined with oak and maple trees; things changed slowly there also, unlike the newer districts downtown, where it seemed that new parking garages or civic buildings popped out of the ground like mushrooms after a rain—only rarely did a new building appear in Old Town, or an old building vanish. For this reason alone, Jimmy much preferred Old Town to Passdale or Southside, and was always relieved to be living there once again. True, he usually had no friends or school chums in the neighborhood, which consisted mostly of first-and-second generation Poles who worked for the Leistershire shoe factories, which had recently begun to fail; sometimes when they lived in Old Town Jimmy got to play with a lame Italian boy who was almost as much of an outcast in the neighborhood as Jimmy was, but the Italian boy had been gone for the last few days, and Jimmy was left alone again. He didn't really mind being alone all that much, most of the time, anyway—he was a solitary boy by nature.

The whole Rodgers family tended to be solitary, and usually had little to do with the close-knit, church-centered life of Old Town, although sometimes his mother belonged to the PTA or the Ladies' Auxiliary, and once Jimmy had been amazed to discover that his father had joined the Rotary Club. Jimmy's father usually worked for Weston Computers in Owego, although Jimmy could remember times, unhappier times, when his father had worked as a CPA in Endicott or even as a shoe salesman in Manningtown. Jimmy's father had always been interested in history, that was another constant in Jimmy's life, and sometimes he did volunteer work for the Catholic Integration League. He never had much time to spend with Jimmy, wherever they lived, wherever he worked—that was another thing that didn't change. Jimmy's mother usually taught at the elementary school, although sometimes she worked as a typist at home, and other times, the bad times again, she stayed at home and took "medicine" and didn't work at all.

That morning when Jimmy woke up, the first thing he realized was that it was summer, a fact testified to by the brightness of the sunshine and the balminess of the air that came in through the open window, making up for his memory of yesterday, which had been gray and cold and dour. He rolled out of bed, surprised for a moment to find himself on the top tier of a bunk bed, and plumped down to the floor hard enough to make the soles of his feet tingle; at the last few places they had lived, he hadn't had a bunk bed, and he wasn't used to waking up that high off the ground. Sometimes he had trouble finding his clothes in the morning, but this time it seemed that he had been conscientious enough to hang them all up the night before, and he came across a blue shirt with a zigzag green stripe that he had not seen in a long time. That seemed like a good omen to him, and cheered him. He put on the blue shirt, puzzled out the knots he could not remember leaving in his shoelaces. Still blinking sleep out of his eyes, he hunted futilely for his toothbrush—it always took a while for his mind to clear in the morning, and he could be confused and disoriented until it did, but eventually memories began to seep back in, as they always did, and he sorted through them, trying to keep straight which house this was out of all the ones he had lived in, and where he kept things here.

Of course. But who would ever have thought that he'd keep it in an old coffee can under his desk!

Downstairs, his mother was making French toast, and he stopped in the archway to watch her as she cooked. She was a short, plump, dark-eyed, olive-complexioned woman who wore her oily black hair pulled back in a tight bun. He watched her intently as she fussed over the hot griddle, noticing her quick nervous motions, the irritable way she patted at loose strands of her hair; her features were tightly-drawn, her nose was long and straight and sharp, as though you could cut yourself on it, and she seemed all angles and edges today. Jimmy's father had been sitting sullenly over his third cup of coffee, but as Jimmy hesitated in the archway, he got to his feet and began to get ready for work. He was a thin man with a pale complexion and a shock of wiry red hair, and Jimmy bit his lip in disappointment as he watched him, keeping well back and hoping not to be noticed—he could tell from the insignia on his father's briefcase that his father was working in Endicott today, and those times when his father's job was in Endicott were among the times when both of his parents would be at their most snappish in the morning.

He slipped silently into his chair at the table as his father stalked wordlessly from the room, and his mother served him his French toast, also wordlessly, except for a slight sullen grunt of acknowledgment. This was going to be a bad day—not as bad as those times when his father worked in Manningtown and his mother took her "medicine," not as bad as some other times that he had no intention of thinking about at all, but unpleasant enough, right on the edge of acceptability. He shouldn't have given in to tiredness and come inside yesterday, he should have kept playing the Game. . . . Fortunately, he had no intention of spending much time here today.

Jimmy got through his breakfast with little real difficulty, except that his mother started in on her routine about why didn't he call Tommy Melkonian, why didn't he go swimming or bike riding, he was daydreaming his summer away, it wasn't natural for him to be by himself all the time, he needed friends, it hurt her and made her feel guilty to see him moping around by himself all the time . . . and so on. He made the appropriate noises in response, but he had no intention of calling Tommy Melkonian today, or of letting her call him for him. He had only played with Tommy once or twice before, the last time being when they lived over on Clinton Street, Tommy hadn't been around before that, but he didn't even *like* Tommy all that much, and he certainly wasn't going to waste the day on him. Sometimes Jimmy had given in to temptation and wasted whole days playing jacks or kick-the-can with other kids or going swimming or flipping baseball cards, sometimes he'd frittered away a week like that without once playing the Game, but in the end he always returned dutifully to playing the Game again, however tired of it all he sometimes became, and the Game had to be played alone.

Yes, he was definitely going to play the Game today—there was certainly no incentive to hang around here, and the Game seemed to be easier to play on fine warm days anyway, for some reason.

So as soon as he could, Jimmy slipped away. For a moment, he confused this place with the house they sometimes lived in on Ash Street, which was very similar in layout and where he had a different secret escape route to the outside, but at last he got his memories straightened out. He snuck into the cellar while his mother was busy elsewhere, and through the back cellar window, under which he had placed a chair so that he could reach the cement overhang and climb out onto the lawn. He cut across the neighbors' yards to Charles Street, and then over to Floral Avenue, a steep macadam dead-end road. Beyond was the start of the woods that belonged to the cemetery. Sometimes the mudhills below the woods would be guarded by a mangy black-and-brown dog that would bark and snarl at him and chase him, and he walked faster, dreading the possibility.

But once in the woods, in the cool brown and green shade of bole and leaf, he knew he was safe, safe from everything, and his pace slowed. The first tombstone appeared, half-buried in mulch and stained with green moss, and he patted it fondly, as if it were a dog. He was in the cemetery now, where it had all begun so long ago. Where he had first played the Game.

Moving easily, he climbed up toward the crown of woods, a grassy knoll that poked up above the surrounding trees, the highest point in the cemetery. Even after all he had been through, this was still a magic place for him — never had he feared spooks or ghouls while he was here, even at night, although often as he walked along, as now, he would peer up at the gum-gray sky through branches that interlocked like the fingers of witches and pretend that monsters and secret agents and dinosaurs were moving through the woods around him, that the stunted azalea bushes concealed pirates or orcs . . . but these were only small games, mood-setting exercises to prepare him for the playing of the Game itself, and they fell away from him like a shed skin as he came out onto the grassy knoll and the landscape opened up below.

Jimmy stood entranced, feeling the warm hand of the sun on the back of his head, hardly breathing, listening to the chirruping of birds, the scratching of katydids, the long sighing rush of wind through oak and evergreen. The sky was blue and high and cloudless, and the Susquehanna River gleamed below like a mirror snake, burning silver as it wound through the rolling, hilly country. Slowly, he began to play the Game. How had it been, that first time that he had played the Game, inadvertently, not realizing what he was doing, not understanding that he was playing the Game or what Game he was playing until after he had already started playing . . . ? How had it been? Had everything looked like this? He decided that the sun had been lower in the sky that day, that the air had been hazier, that there had been a mass of clouds on the eastern horizon, and he flicked through mental pictures of the landscape as if he were riffling through a deck of cards with his thumb, until he found one that seemed to be right. Obediently, the sky grew darker, but the shape and texture of the clouds were not right, and he searched until he found a better match. It had been somewhat colder, and there had been a slight breeze. . . . So far it had been easy, but there were more subtle adjustments to be made. Had there been four smokestacks or five down in Southside? Four, he decided, and took one away. Had that radio tower been on the crest of that particular distant hill? Or on *that* one? Had the bridge over the Susquehanna been nearer or further away? Had that EXXON sign been there, at the corner of Cedar Road? Or had it been an ESSO sign? His green shirt had changed to a brown shirt by now, and he changed it further, to a red pinstriped shirt, trying to remember. Had that ice cream stand been there? He decided that it had not been. His skin was dark again now, although his hair was still too straight. . . . Had the cemetery fence been a wrought-iron fence or a hurricane 157 fence? Had there been the sound of a factory whistle blowing? Or the smell of sulphur in the air? Or the smell of pine . . . ?

He worked at it until dusk, and then, drained, he came back down the hill again.

The shopping-mall was till there, but the school and schoolyard had vanished this time, to be replaced by the familiar row of stately, dormer-windowed old mansions. That usually meant that he was at least close. The house was on Schubert Street this evening, several blocks over from where it had been this morning, and it was a two-story, not a three-story house, closer to his memories of how things had been before he'd started playing the Game. The car outside the house was a '78 Volvo — not what he remembered, but closer than the '73 Buick from this morning. The windshield bore an Owego parking sticker, and there was some Weston Computer literature tucked under the eyeshade, all of which meant that it was probably safe to go in; his father wouldn't be a murderous drunk this particular evening.

Inside the parlor, Jimmy's father looked up from his armchair, where he was reading Fuller's *Decisive Battles of the Western World,* and winked. "Hi, sport," he said, and Jimmy replied "Hi, Dad." At least his father was a black man this time, as he should be, although he was much fatter than Jimmy ever remembered him being, and still had this morning's kinky red hair, instead of the kinky black hair he should have. Jimmy's mother came out of the kitchen, and she was thin enough now, but much too tall, with a tiny upturned nose, blue eyes instead of hazel, hair more blond than auburn. . . .

"Wash up for dinner, Jimmy," his mother said, and Jimmy turned slowly for the stairs, feeling exhaustion wash through him like a bitter tide. She wasn't *really* his mother, they weren't *really* his parents. . . . He had come a lot closer than this before, lots of other times. . . . But always there was some small detail that was *wrong,* that proved that that particular probability-world out of the billions of probability-worlds was *not* the one he had started from, was not *home.* Still, he had done much worse than this before, too. . . . At least this wasn't a world where his father was dead, or an atomic war had happened, or his mother had cancer or was a drug-addict, or his father was a brutal drunk, or a Nazi, or a child molester. . . . This would do, for the night. . . . He would settle for this, for tonight. . . . He was so tired. . . .

In the morning, he would start searching again.

Someday, he would find them.

PLAYING THE GAME

This started off as a story by Jack called "The Alpha Tree," about a boy who could see into alternate universes. Jack had gotten stalled on it after a few pages, and passed it along to me to see what I could do with it. I started work on it on May 12, 1981, only a few days after having finished working on "Down Among The Dead Men." I skewed Jack's idea somewhat, building the story instead around a concept that had long fascinated me — an intuition of how easy it would be to become lost among the billions of probability-worlds that are born and die around us every second of every day. Once you had started travelling among them, could you ever *really* be sure that you had returned home again? Quantum uncertainty would seem to indicate that you could never really be *certain* that you were really back where you'd started from, no matter how close a match it seemed. What would be the emotional consequences of that for the traveller?

The work went quickly. I took Jack's incomplete draft to pieces and built it into the new framework of the story (it survives most nearly intact in the opening two pages, and in the description of Jimmy's journey to the grassy knoll in the cemetery), added about twice again as much material of my own interstitially, and then did a smoothing and homogenizing draft to blend his pages and mine together as seamlessly as possible.

I had the most fun here playing with seemingly-innocuous statements that the reader would take at face value while reading the story initially — "only rarely did a new building appear in Old Town, or an old building vanish"; "Jimmy's father usually worked for Weston Computers in Owego, although Jimmy could remember times when

159

his father had worked as a CPA in Endicott or even as a shoe-salesman in Manningtown"; "but the Italian boy had been gone for the last few days"—but that would have a very different and literal meaning when he went back and looked at them again, this time knowing what the story was about. This technique—giving the reader the information he needs to figure out the real situation, but distracting him from examining it closely enough to tumble before he's supposed to tumble; hiding things in plain sight—is a favorite of mine, and I've used it to one degree or another in many different stories.

I finished this in one long session. It bounced around for a few months, and finally sold to *The Twilight Zone Magazine*. It later was reprinted in *Great Stories From The Twilight Zone Magazine* and in Donald A. Wollheim's *The 1983 Annual World's Best SF*.

NEW KID
ON THE BLOCK

SUSAN CASPER

We came up with "The Clowns" after a stomach-stretching dinner at a local steak house. Whenever Gardner and I discuss the events of that evening we sound a lot like Maurice Chevalier and Hermione Gingold doing a skewed rendition of "Ah Yes, I Remember It Well." And if Jack were present he'd smilingly agree with both of us, not from a sense of diplomacy, but simply because his memory isn't any better than ours.

Actually, I had known Gardner, Jack, Michael, and Jay (Jack Haldeman) for years without ever becoming part of the writing circle. I swore up and down, to anyone who would listen, that I never wanted to write, never would write, that all writers were crazy. I believed it, too. (I was probably right.) I had tried my hand at a novel when I was a teenager, heavily inspired by the works of Harold Robbins and then given up, for good, I thought. But, I did hate the fact that I was semi-excluded from the patter that went on around me constantly. Perhaps it was that fact that set me to put my first little story on paper in 1983, though I truly believe that writing is a contagious disease with a very long incubation period and that I had caught it years before without knowing. What I truly don't know is whatever possessed me to show that awful little story to Jack Dann and Gardner, but it was their encouragement that led me to keep on trying.

I was as yet an unsold writer when I started the piece that would become my first collaboration. I had started a story about a suburban housewife who notices a unicorn running down the street. So far so good, but where do I go with it. I showed the fragment to Gardner and we discussed some ideas, none of which struck sparks. The piece sat in my drawer for months, untouched. I awoke one morning

161

to find Gardner smiling at me nervously. He had obviously been up all night and there was a curious look in his eyes. I honestly don't remember what I thought he was up to, but it was neither my birthday nor our anniversary. I waited him out. "You weren't planning to *finish* that unicorn piece you had lying around, were you?" he asked. Thus "The Stray" was born.

"The Clowns" was another story. I do know that I wasn't exactly *invited* into this collaboration. Dragooned would be a better term.

Jack Dann had come down to visit for a weekend or so, and Michael had been over for most of the day. The three of them were wrapped up in discussing their various projects. It had never occurred to me to become involved in the "Fiction Factory" as they jokingly called their collaborative team. For one thing, I was the new kid on the block, careerwise, and for another, they wrote mostly science fiction, while my work tended to be either fantasy or horror. But there was another reason why I was reluctant to become involved. After all, if things weren't going well, Jack and Michael could always go home and cool off. But if Gardner and I had differences, well, we still had to sit across from each other at the dinner table. Too risky. So, mostly I tried to keep busy while they worked, and tried even harder (usually vainly) to enforce a no-business-at-dinner rule that we had worked out. And we didn't work that night, as I recall — at least not at first. We had a large dinner that left us all hazy and groaning, then spent the evening discussing weird things that had happened to us. That was when Gardner brought up the story of "this guy in the Village who kept seeing clowns." Jack's eyes began to glow. He turned to me. "And you write horror, don't you? This is perfect," he said. He roughed out the general idea, using two kids as protagonists and wrote an opening paragraph. I know that Gardner remembers being left out of the discussion, but it's my memory that he was always included. I seem to recall that he had planned to write this one by himself and we had stolen his idea. So, I'm a thief. I admit it. Half a thief, anyway.

In some ways it was one of the easiest pieces I've ever worked on, because when the going got tough I could turn it over to someone else. Also, it is easier, at least for me, to see where someone else has taken a wrong turn than it is to define the mistakes I've made myself. Or maybe the story just got to me. I expected that being *the new kid on the block* my ideas would get overruled a lot, but in some ways it was Gardner and I who rode roughshod over Jack because we could discuss our ideas more easily and present him with a united front — not that we did this intentionally, it just worked out that way. We really had few disagreements on where to go with the piece. I think we turned out a good piece of fiction, and I learned a lot from the experience.

Of course, while all this was going on, we were each working on our solo fiction. It was not long after we got started on "The Clowns" that I came up with another idea for a modern fairytale. It started with the postcard, but again, I wasn't quite sure where it should go. I roped Gardner in on this one from the beginning. I discussed it with him and he had some very good ideas. We talked about what to do with it and where it should go and we worked on it in turns, with Gardner doing the final, smoothing draft.

Collaborating with these guys has been fun and I sincerely hope that we get to do it again. Unfortunately, writing novels, editing and individual work has kept us all busy. Jack is unable to come to Philadelphia as often as he once did, and Binghamton is just as far for us. But we all look forward to the day when we can get rolling again.

"Jack, Gardner, I have this idea . . ."

The tray

SUSAN CASPER & GARDNER DOZOIS

You always think of a unicorn as a horse with a horn, I reflected as it galloped past my window, and this *did* look quite a bit like a horse, but in some odd indefinable way it also looked just as much like a giant cat, or an otter, or a fox, or like any other sleek, smooth-furred, swift-moving, graceful creature. I opened the window, and leaned out for a better look. Yes, it was a unicorn, all right. It was silver (silver, not gray—there was a definite metallic sheen to its coat), with a cream-colored mane and tail. The single horn was gleaming white, and spiraled, and very long. In spite of the Unicorn Tapestry pictures, it had no fringy little billygoat beard—in fact, a goat was one of the few sorts of creatures it *didn't* look like.

I didn't waste a minute thinking that I was crazy. The natural assumption was that someone was making a movie outside, and that this was something whomped-up by the Special Effects Department, like those poor elephants that had to stand around wearing fur overcoats in *Star Wars*. Or perhaps it was a publicity stunt. It probably said EAT AT JOE'S in huge neon letters on the other side.

I had some shopping to do anyway, and so this seemed like the perfect time to go out. I grabbed my purse and let myself out the front door. The unicorn was just cantering back down the block, returning in the direction from which it had come. *Too bad Jenny goes over to Stacey's house on Sundays,* I thought, watching it run gracefully along. She was six, and she would have loved this. Then the unicorn saw me, and stopped. It daintily raised one foot, like a setter pointing, and then it tilted its head back and flared its nostrils. It was smelling me, catching my scent on the breeze.

Then it looked at me, right at me, and, still staring at me, pawed impatiently at the ground with one silver hoof, as if it were waiting for something.

As if it were waiting for *me.*

Its movements were flowing, graceful, completely natural. A pretty damn good mockup, I thought, feeling the first pangs of doubt. There didn't seem to be any cameraman in evidence — in fact, there was no one around at all this time of the morning. So, at the risk of ruining somebody's long shot, I started walking toward him. He snorted, tossed his head, and shuffled his front legs nervously. I stopped, startled, less sure by the second that this was a publicity stunt or a movie gimmick, but he wasn't running away, and didn't really *look* very dangerous — he was still staring at me gravely, with bright, intelligent eyes — and so, hesitantly, I started walking toward him again.

He snorted again when I was a few steps away, softly, a gentle whickering sound, and then I was beside him, gingerly stretching out my hand, and then I was *touching* him.

He was covered with some sort of thick silky hair or fine-grained fur, and he was softer than anything I had ever touched, softer than the finest Angora. He was warm to the touch, and I could feel muscles twitch under his coat from time to time as he shifted position slightly. This close to him, I could hear him breathing, a deep, rhythmical sound, and I could smell him — a warm, spicy odor, not at all horselike, not at all unpleasant. I could feel his warm breath on my face. There could be no doubt anymore. This was no mechanical mockup — this was real.

Bemused, I stroked him, rubbing my hand through his thick mane, patting the graceful arch of his neck. He made a sighing sound of contentment and leaned into my fingers. We were almost eye to eye now, and his eyes watched me steadily and thoughtfully as I patted him — his eyes were large and liquid and extraordinarily beautiful, silver on ebony, flecked with specks of molten gold, like no eyes I had ever seen. I scratched his head, and then, gingerly, I brushed at the base of his horn with my fingers, but I could find no seam or junction; as far as I could tell, it grew naturally out of his forehead. Surely it would be more obvious than that if the horn had been grafted on surgically, and besides, grafted onto *what?* I knew of no breed of horse in the world that was even remotely like this—if it even *was* a horse in the first place. Right now it seemed to be purring, a decidedly unhorselike thing to do.

I had been right the first time: it was a unicorn. Plain and simple as that—nothing else but exactly what it was. I kept stroking him, and he nuzzled against my hand in a way that made me wish I had a carrot to give him. "I thought you guys were only supposed to let virgins touch you." I said ruefully, ruffling his mane. "Well," I continued, "I hate to tell you this, but this time you blew it. A virgin I am not. You're too late. By about fifteen years, too late. You should have come around while I was still at Swarthmore." But the dumb beast didn't seem to care. He whickered and butted his nose against my shoulder, and I took this for my cue to scratch him behind the ears—which indeed it seemed to be, for he bent his neck and sighed with pleasure. I kept scratching. He rested his head lightly on my shoulder, rolling his huge eyes and looking soulfully up at me, and then he licked me on the cheek.

I kept on patting the unicorn for what seemed like hours—and perhaps it was. But at last I began to become aware of the passage of time again. It was getting on toward afternoon, and I had things to do before Jenny got home.

I had found a unicorn, but unicorn or no unicorn, I still had to go to the Pathmark.

I stepped back away from him, and he stepped right after me, nuzzling at my hands. "Well . . ." I said. "Well, it's been lovely . . . but I have to go now. I've got shopping. . . ." He was staring at me, his eyes still bright and soulful, and suddenly I felt like a fool, standing there making polite social excuses to a mythological creature. "Okay, then," I said briskly, and I gave him one last solid pat on the neck in farewell. "Gotta go now. Goodbye!" And I turned, briskly, and briskly walked away.

I hadn't gotten very far when I heard clopping footsteps behind me, and looked around. He was following me. I stopped, feeling a trace of uneasiness. "Sorry, boy." I said firmly. "I've got to go now." He came up and nuzzled me again, and I made shooing motions at him. "Go away, now! Go on—git! Shoo!" But he didn't shoo—he just stood there and stared at me, his eyes sad and wet.

Exasperated, I turned and walked away again, walking much faster this time, but, sure enough, he kept following me. I began to run, and behind me I could hear him break into a trot. No way I was going to outrun that great beast, but fortunately I knew an easy way to lose him. A bit breathless — I'm not the jogging type, generally — I reached the place where my car was parked, and climbed into it, slamming the door behind me. Quickly, I started the car and drove away. I could see the unicorn in the rear-view mirror — he was standing by the curb and staring after me, craning his neck, looking faintly puzzled. I felt a pang of sadness, and hoped that he would find his way home again, wherever home was. . . .

The supermarket was a madhouse, as usual, and by the time I got out of there I was tired and irritable, and the encounter with the unicorn was already beginning to seem like some strange waking dream, the vivid colors of it leached away by the world's petty gray routine.

I thought about it all the way home, wondering now if it had happened at all. I had just about decided it could not have happened, when I got out of the car and saw the unicorn again.

Not only was he still waiting there patiently for me, but my daughter Jenny was actually sitting on his back, drumming her little heels gleefully against his shaggy ribs.

My heart lurched; surprise, a momentary touch of fear that quickly faded, dismay, irritation — and a strange kind of relief, a guilty joy at seeing him again.

My daughter waved. She jumped down from the unicorn's back and rushed toward me like a small excited whirlwind, hugging me, spinning around me wildly, nearly knocking me over. "Mommy!" she yelled. "Mommy, *can we keep it?*"

"We most certainly can *not*," I said indignantly, but Jenny had already scooted back to the unicorn, and was doing a sort of mad little dance of joy around it, whining in excitement, like a puppy. "Jenny!" I called sternly. "We *can not* keep it!" The unicorn whickered softly in greeting me as I came slowly up to it, and reached out to nuzzle my hands. "None of *that*," I said grumpily. I glanced at my wildly capering daughter, and then leaned forward to whisper exasperatedly into the unicorn's ear. "Listen! Let me tell you *again*. I am *not* a virgin, understand? *Not.* There was Steve, and Robbie, and Sam, and Trevor, and Herbie, that slimy little toad. . . ." The unicorn licked my face, a touch as soft as a falling leaf. "You've made some kind of mistake," I continued doggedly. "You shouldn't be here, not with *me*. Find somebody else. Or go back to whatever fairy tale you galloped out of. . . ." The unicorn looked at me reproachfully, and my voice faltered to a stop.

My daughter had gotten tired of dancing. She had buried her face in the unicorn's mane, and was hugging him tightly; he nuzzled her hair, and licked her on the ear. "Oh, Mommy," she whispered. "He's *wonderful*. He's the most wonderful thing I've ever seen. . . ."

"Well, we can't keep him," I said weakly. "So don't get too attached to him."

But already it was starting to rain, a sooty city rain that left streaks along the unicorn's shining silver flanks. The unicorn was staring at me with his great sad eyes, and I felt myself beginning to melt.

"Oh, Mommy, it's *raining*. We can't leave him out in the *rain*—"

The garage door was big enough to get him inside with no problem. At first I'd meant to make him stay in the garage, but Jenny pointed out that the door into the basement floor was almost as large as the garage door itself, and after a while I relented, and let the unicorn squeeze himself through that door too. There were only a couple of interconnected rumpus rooms down there, and the only thing of any value was Herbie's pool table, unused since the divorce, and *that* the unicorn could smash to flinders for all I cared.

"All right Jenny, but remember, it's only for tonight. . . ."

Of course, we kept him.

Actually, he turned out to be remarkably little trouble. He seemed content to stay downstairs most of the time, as long as we visited him frequently and patted him a lot, and after a while we noticed that he didn't seem to either eat or eliminate, so two of the major problems that would have arisen if we'd been keeping an ordinary horse in our rumpus room never came up at all. To my relief, he didn't insist on trying to follow me to work on Monday, and although I half-hoped that when I came back from the office that evening, he'd be gone, I was also a bit more than half-glad when I came down the basement steps and heard him whinny to me in greeting.

Some of my friends adjusted with amazing ease to the fact that I now had a unicorn living in the basement, and those who *couldn't* adjust soon stopped coming around at all. One of those who couldn't adjust was Ralph, the guy I was seeing at the time, and I was broken up about that for a day or two, but the unicorn snorted and gave me a look that seemed to say, *him* you're better off without, you can do better than *that*, and after a while I came to agree with him.

Jenny and I spent many evenings brushing the unicorn's beautiful coat and trying to think of a name for him, but although we made up list after list, none of the names seemed to fit. Mythological creatures are so intensely *themselves* that names are superfluous, I guess. "The unicorn" was all the name he needed.

So we settled down together, the months went by, and we had our first dusting of snow.

I was making tuna salad one frosty winter morning when Jenny came running excitedly into the kitchen. "Mommy!" she said breathlessly. "Mommy, the unicorn went into the closet!"

"That's nice," I said, continuing to dice an onion.

"And he's making a *nest* in there, and everything!"

"Uh-oh," I said. I put down the knife and rushed out of the room, Jenny scampering at my heels.

It was the large walk-in storage closet in the basement, but it was still a closet, and the unicorn had made a nest in there all right, pulling down old coats and dresses and treading and pawing them all into a nice fluffy mound. I leaned wearily against the doorjamb—I had been through this before with innumerable tabby cats, and knew what to expect, but Jenny was peeking timidly around my hip and saying in a hushed little voice, "Mommy, what *is* it?" and so I sighed, and knelt, and peered more closely myself.

Inside the warm semi-darkness of the storage closet, the unicorn softly whickered. She looked tired and rumpled and very proud of herself.

Of course, she had kittens in there. Kittens, colts, foals, whatever you want to call them. Babies. Baby unicorns.

There were five of them white as snow and about the size of cocker spaniels, nuzzling up against their mother's side. Their stubby little horns were still covered with furry velvet, and except for the fact that they were squirming and moving about, they looked just like the unicorn plush toys you sometimes see in the more imaginative gift shops.

"Funny," I said, "you didn't *look* pregnant." I met the unicorn's liquid eyes, and she stared back at me serenely and guilelessly. "So, old girl," I said ruefully. "You weren't a virgin either, were you? No wonder you didn't care."

The unicorn whickered again and blew out its lips with a soft snorting sound, and I sighed. I thought of the snow that was gusting around outside. No wonder you wanted a place to live—you might not be so hot at recognizing virgins, but you sure knew a sucker when you saw one. The unicorn rested her head in my lap, staring lovingly up at me out of her enormous eyes, and gently licked my hand with her velvet tongue.

Jenny was leaning by me now, her eyes as wide as saucers, her face soft with wonder. "Oh, *Mommy* . . ." she breathed. "Oh, Mommy, they're so *pretty—*"

170

The babies were squeaking and squirming about, making little mewing noises, and one of them nuzzled its mole-soft nose trustingly into my hand, searching blindly for milk, gently nibbling me with its soft little lips. . . .

I sighed again.

So this week I put an ad in the paper:

UNICORNS — FREE TO GOOD HOMES.

But somehow I don't think we're going to get many replies.

A F T E R W O R D   T O
THE STRAY

Susan started this and got stalled on it, and a few days later, while she was sleeping, I picked it up off her desk and finished it for her. This was a pretty nervy and presumptuous thing for me to do, since I hadn't even asked her if I could work on it, and I got a bit uneasy about what her reaction to this would be, after it was too late, but she was in a generous mood that morning (or else stunned by the sheer *chutzpah* of what I'd done), and let me live. The story was finished on April 24, 1982.

"The Stray" turned out to be a bit more nakedly sentimental than either of us was entirely comfortable with, certainly more sentimental than either of our solo work, but this was what seemed to be called-for by the tone and mood of the story, so we went with it. If the story is too sentimental for *your* taste, you can, if you wish, imagine the unicorn running amuck at the end and skewering the mother and daughter with its horn, or, perhaps, picture the mother going berserk with a chainsaw and slicing and dicing the unicorn to a blood-soaked mass of bones and flesh. The way the horror market is these days, we probably could sell either of *those* variants, too.

The story sold to the ill-fated second issue of *Imago,* a fantasy magazine which died stillborn and never even produced the first issue. A few years later, Tappan King bought it, and it appeared in the December 1987 issue of *The Twilight Zone Magazine.*

The 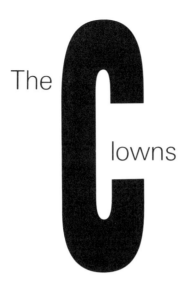lowns

GARDNER DOZOIS, JACK DANN, & SUSAN CASPER

The C. Fred Johnson Municipal Pool was packed with swimmers, more in spite of the blazing sun and wet, muggy heat than because of them.

It was the dead middle of August, stiflingly hot, and it would have made more sense to stay inside — or, at the very least, in the shade — than to splash around in the murky, tepid water. Nevertheless, the pool was crowded almost shoulder to shoulder, especially with kids — there were children everywhere, the younger ones splashing and shouting in the shallow end, the older kids and the teenagers jumping off the high dive or playing water polo in the deep end. Mothers sat in groups and chatted, their skins glistening with suntan oil and sweat. The temperature was well above 90, and the air seemed to shimmer with the heat, like automobile exhaust in a traffic jam.

David Shore twisted his wet bath towel and snapped it at his friend Sammy, hitting him on the sun-reddened backs of his thighs.

"Ow!" Sammy screamed. "You dork! Cut it out!" David grinned and snapped the towel at Sammy again, hitting only air this time but producing a satisfyingly loud *crack*. Sammy jumped back, shouting, "Cut it out! I'll tell! I'll *tell!* I mean it."

Sammy's voice was whining and petulant, and David felt a spasm of annoyance. Sammy was his friend, and he didn't have so many friends that he wasn't grateful for that, but Sammy was *always* whining. What a baby! That's what he got for hanging out with little kids—Sammy was eight, two years younger than David—but since the trouble he'd had last fall, with his parents almost breaking up and he himself having to go for counseling, he'd been ostracized by many of the kids his own age. David's face darkened for a moment, but then he sighed and shook his head. Sammy was all right, really. A good kid. He really shouldn't tease him so much, play so many jokes on him. David smiled wryly. Maybe he did it just to hear him *whine*—

"Don't be such a baby," David said tiredly, wrapping the towel around his hand. "It's only a *towel*, dickface. It's not gonna kill you if—" Then David stopped abruptly, staring blankly off beyond Sammy, toward the bathhouse.

"It *hurt*," Sammy whined. "You're a real dork, you know that, Davie? How come you have to—" And then Sammy paused, too, aware that David wasn't paying any attention to him anymore. "Davie?" he said. "What's the matter?"

"Look at *that*," David said in an awed whisper.

Sammy turned around. After a moment, confused, he asked, "Look at what?"

"There!" David said, pointing toward a sun-bleached wooden rocking chair.

"*Oh*, no, you're not going to get *me* again with *that* old line," Sammy said disgustedly. His face twisted, and this time he looked as if he were really getting mad. "The wind's making that chair rock. It can rock for hours if the wind's right. You can't scare me that easy! I'm not a *baby*, you know!"

David was puzzled, Couldn't Sammy *see*? What was he—blind? It was as plain as anything. . . .

There was a clown sitting in the chair, sitting and rocking, watching the kids in the swimming pool.

The clown's face was caked with thick white paint. He had a bulb nose that was painted blood red, the same color as his broad, painted-on smile. His eyes were like chips of blue ice. He sat very still, except for the slight movement of his legs needed to rock the beat-up old chair, and his eyes never left the darting figures in the water.

David had seen clowns before, of course; he'd seen plenty of them at the Veterans' Arena in Binghamton when the Barnum & Bailey Circus came to town. Sammy's father was a barber and always got good tickets to everything, and Sammy always took David with him. But this clown was *different*, somehow. For one thing, instead of

174

performing, instead of dancing around or cakewalking or somersault-ing or squirting people with a Seltzer bottle, this clown was just sitting quietly by the pool, as if it were the most normal thing in the world for him to be there. And there was something else, too, he realized. *This* clown was all in black. Even his big polka-dotted bow tie was black, shiny black dots against a lighter gray-black. Only his gloves were white, and they were a pure, eye-dazzling white. The contrast was startling.

"Sammy?" David said quietly. "Listen, this is important. You *really* think that chair is empty?"

"Jeez, grow *up*, will ya?" Sammy snarled. "What a dork!" He turned his back disgustedly on David and dived into the pool.

David stared thoughtfully at the clown. Was Sammy trying to kid him? Turn the tables on him, get back at him for some of *his* old jokes? But David was sure that Sammy wasn't smart enough to pull it off. Sammy *always* gave himself away, usually by giggling.

Odd as it seemed, Sammy really *didn't* see the clown.

David looked around to see who else he could ask. Certainly not Mr. Kreiger, who had a big potbelly and wore his round wire-rimmed glasses even in the water and who would stand for hours in the shallow end of the pool and splash himself with one arm, like an old bull elephant splashing water over itself with its trunk. No. Who else? Bobby Little, Jimmy Seikes and Andy Freeman were taking turns diving and cannonballing from the low board, but David didn't want to ask *them* anything. That left only Jas Ritter, the pool life-guard, or the stuck-up Weaver sisters.

But David was beginning to realize that he didn't really *have* to ask anybody. Freddy Schumaker and Jane Gelbert had just walked right by the old rocking chair, without looking at the clown, without even glancing at him. Bill Dwyer was muscling himself over the edge of the pool within inches of the clown's floppy oblong shoes, and he wasn't paying any attention to him, either. That just wasn't possible. No matter how supercool they liked to pretend they were, there was no *way* that kids were going to walk past a clown without even *glancing* at him.

With a sudden thrill, David took the next logical step. Nobody could see the clown except *him*. Maybe he was the only one in the world who could see him!

It was an exhilarating thought. David stared at the clown in awe. Nobody else could see him! Maybe he was a *ghost*, the ghost of an old circus clown, doomed to roam the earth forever, seeking out kids like the ones he'd performed for when he was alive, sitting in the sun and watching them play, thinking about the happy days when the circus had played this town.

That was a *wonderful* idea, a lush and romantic idea, and David shivered and hugged himself, feeling goose flesh sweep across his skin. He could see a *ghost!* It was wonderful! It was magic! Private, secret magic, his alone. It meant that he was *special.* It gave him a strange, secret kind of power. Maybe nobody else in the *universe* could see him —

It was at this point that Sammy slammed into him, laughing and shouting, "I'll learn *you*, sucker!" and knocked him into the pool.

By the time David broke the surface, sputtering and shaking water out of his eyes, the clown was gone and the old rocker was rocking by itself, in the wind and the thin, empty sunshine.

After leaving the pool, David and Sammy walked over the viaduct — there was no sign of any freight trains on the weed-overgrown tracks below — and took back-alley short cuts to Curtmeister's barber-shop.

"Hang on a minute," Sammy said and ducked into the shop. Ordinarily, David would have followed, as Sammy's father kept gum and salt-water taffy in a basket on top of the magazine rack, but today he leaned back against the plate-glass window, thinking about the ghost he'd seen that morning, *his* ghost, watching as the red and blue stripes ran eternally up around the barber pole. How fascinated he'd been by that pole a few years ago, and how simple it seemed to him now.

A clown turned the corner from Avenue B, jaywalking casually across Main Street.

David started and pushed himself upright. The ghost again! or was it? Surely, *this* clown was shorter and squatter than the one he'd seen at the pool, though it was wearing the same kind of black costume, the same kind of white gloves. Could this be *another* ghost? Maybe there was a whole *circus*ful of clown ghosts wandering around the city.

"David!" a voice called, and he jumped. It was old Mrs. Zabriski, carrying two bulging brown-paper grocery bags, working her way ponderously down the sidewalk toward him, puffing and wheezing, like some old, slow tugboat doggedly chugging toward its berth. "Want to earn a buck, David?" she called.

The clown had stopped right in the middle of Main Street, standing nonchalantly astride the double white divider line. David watched him in fascination.

"David?" Mrs. Zabriski said impatiently.

Reluctantly, David turned his attention back to Mrs. Zabriski. "Gosh, I'm sorry, Mrs. Zabriski. Gosh, I'm sorry, Mrs. Z.," he said. A buck would be nice, but it was more important to keep an eye on the clown. "I— ah, I promised Sammy that I'd wait out here for him."

Mrs. Zabriski sighed. "OK, David," she said. "Another time, then." She looked across the street to see what he was staring at, looked back puzzledly. "Are you all right, David?"

"Yeah. Honest, Mrs. Z.," he said, without looking around. "Really. I'm fine."

She sighed again with doughy fatalism. And then she started across the street, headed directly for the clown.

It was obvious to David that *she* didn't see him. He was standing right in front of her, grimacing and waving his arms and making faces at her, but she didn't even slow down—she would have walked right into him if he hadn't ducked out of the way at the last moment. After she passed, the clown minced along behind her for a few steps, doing a cruel but funny imitation of her ponderous, waddling walk, pretending to spank her on her big, fat rump.

David stifled a laugh. This was better than the circus! But now the clown seemed to have grown bored with mocking Mrs. Zabriski and began drifting slowly away toward the far side of Main Street.

David wanted to follow, but he suddenly realized, with a funny little chill, that he didn't want to do it alone. Even if it was the ghost of a clown, a funny and entertaining ghost, it was still a *ghost*, after all. Somehow, he'd have to get Sammy to come with him. But how could he explain to Sammy what they were doing? Not that it would matter if Sammy didn't come out of the shop soon—the clown was already a block away.

Anxiously, he peered in through the window until he managed to catch Sammy's attention, then waved to him urgently. Sammy held up his index finger and continued his conversation with his father. "Hurry up, dummy," David muttered under his breath. The clown was getting farther and farther away, almost out of sight now. Hurry up. David danced impatiently from one foot to the other. Hurry *up*.

But when Sammy finally came running out of the barbershop with the news that he'd talked his father into treating them both to a movie, the clown was gone.

By the time they got to the movie theater, David had pretty much gotten over the disappointment of losing the clown. At least it was a pretty good show—cartoons and a space-monster movie. There was a long line in front of the ticket window, a big crowd of kids—and even a few adults—waiting to get into the movie.

They were waiting in the tail of the line when the clown—or *a* clown—appeared again across the street.

"Hey, Davie!" Sammy said abruptly. "Do you see what *I* see?" And Sammy waved to the clown.

David was startled—and somewhat dismayed—by the strength of the surge of disappointment and jealousy that shot through him. If *Sammy* could see them, too, then David wasn't *special* anymore. The whole thing was ruined.

Then David realized that it wasn't the clown that Sammy was waving to.

He was waving to the old man who was waiting to cross the street, standing just in *front* of the clown. Old Mr. Thorne. He was at least a million years old, David knew. He'd played for the Boston Braves back before they'd even had *television,* for cripes' sake. But he loved children and treated them with uncondescending courtesy and in turn was one of the few adults who were really respected by the kids. He was in charge of the yo-yo contests held in the park every summer, and he could make a yo-yo sleep or do around the world or over the falls or walking the dog better than anyone David had ever seen, including the guy who sold the golden yo-yos for the Duncan Company.

Relieved, David joined Sammy in waving to his old friend, almost —but not quite—forgetting the clown for a moment. Mr. Thorne waved back but motioned for them to wait where they were. It was exciting to see the old man again. It would be worth missing the movie if Mr. Thorne was in the mood to buy them chocolate malteds and reminisce about the days when he'd hit a home run off the immortal Grover Cleveland Alexander.

Just as the traffic light turned yellow, an old flat-bed truck with a dented fender came careening through the intersection.

David felt his heart lurch with sudden fear—But it was all right. Mr. Thorne saw the truck coming, he was still on the curb, he was safe. But then the clown stepped up close behind him. He grabbed Mr. Thorne by the shoulders. David could see Mr. Thorne jerk in surprise as he felt the white-gloved hands close over him. Mr. Thorne's mouth opened in surprise, his hands came fluttering weakly up, like startled birds. David could see the clown's painted face grinning over the top of Mr. Thorne's head. That wide, unchanging, painted-on smile.

Then the clown threw Mr. Thorne in front of the truck.

There was a sickening wet *thud*, a sound like that of a sledge-hammer hitting a side of beef. The shriek of brakes, the squeal of flaying tires. A brief, unnatural silence. Then a man said, "Jesus Christ!" in a soft, reverent whisper. A heartbeat later, a woman started to scream.

Then everyone was shouting, screaming, babbling in a dozen confused voices, running forward. The truck driver was climbing down from the cab, his face stricken; his mouth worked in a way that might have been funny in other circumstances, opening and closing, opening and closing—then he began to cry.

All you could see of Mr. Thorne was one arm sticking out from under the truck's rear wheels at an odd angle, like the arm of a broken doll.

A crowd was gathering now, and between loud exclamations of horror, everyone was already theorizing about what had happened: Maybe the old man had had a heart attack; maybe he'd just slipped and fallen; maybe he'd tripped over something. A man had thrown his arm around the shoulders of the bitterly sobbing truck driver; people were kneeling and peering gingerly under the truck; women were crying; little kids were shrieking and running frenziedly in all directions. Next to David, Sammy was crying and cursing at the same time, in a high and hysterical voice.

Only David was not moving.

He stood as if frozen in ice, staring at the clown.

All unnoticed, standing alone behind the ever-growing crowd, the clown was laughing.

Laughing silently, in unheard spasms that shook his shoulders and made his bulb nose jiggle. Laughing without sound, with his mouth wide-open, bending forward to slap his knees in glee, tears of pleasure running down his painted cheeks.

Laughing.

David felt his face flame. Contradictory emotions whipped through him: fear, dismay, rage, horror, disbelief, guilt. Guilt. . . .

The fucking clown was *laughing*—

All at once, David began to run, motionless one moment and running flat-out the next, as if suddenly propelled from a sling. He could taste the salty wetness of his own tears. He tried to fight his way through the thickening crowd, to get by them and *at* the clown. He kept bumping into people, spinning away, sobbing and cursing, then slamming into someone *else*. Someone cursed him. Someone else grabbed him and held him, making sympathetic, soothing noises — it was Mr. Gratini, the music teacher, thinking that David was trying to reach Mr. Thorne's body.

Meanwhile, the clown had stopped laughing. As if suddenly re-membering another appointment, he turned brusquely and strode away.

"David, wait, there's nothing you can do. . . ." Mr. Gratini was saying, but David squirmed wildly, tore himself free, ran on.

By the time David had fought his way through the rest of the crowd, the clown was already a good distance down Willow Street, past the bakery and the engraving company with the silver sign in its second-story window.

The clown was walking faster now, was almost out of sight. Pant-ing and sobbing, David ran after him.

He followed the clown through the alleys behind the shoe factories, over the hump of railroad tracks, under the arch of the cement viaduct that was covered with spray-painted graffiti. The viaduct was dark, its pavement strewn with candy wrappers and used con-doms and cigarette butts. It was cool inside and smelled of dampness and cinders.

But on the other side of the viaduct, he realized that he'd lost the clown again. Perhaps he had crossed the field . . . though, surely, David would have seen him do that. He could be anywhere; this was an old section of town and streets and avenues branched off in all directions.

David kept searching, but he was getting tired. He was breathing funny, sort of like having the hiccups. He felt sweaty and dirty and exhausted. He wanted to go home.

What would he have done if he'd *caught* the clown?

All at once, he felt cold.

There was nobody around, seemingly for miles — the streets were as deserted as those of a ghost town. Nobody around, no one to help him if he were attacked, no one to hear him if he cried for help.

The silence was thick and dusty and smothering. Scraps of paper blew by with the wind. The sun shimmered from the empty side-walks.

David's mouth went dry. The hair rose bristlingly on his arms and legs.

The clown suddenly rounded the corner just ahead, coming swiftly toward him with a strange, duckwalking gait.

David screamed and took a quick step backward. He stumbled and lost his balance. For what seemed like an eternity, he teetered precariously, windmilling his arms. Then he crashed to the ground.

The fall hurt and knocked the breath out of him, but David almost didn't notice the pain. From the instant he'd hit the pavement, the one thought in his head had been, *Had he given himself away?* Did the clown now *realize* that David could *see* him?

Quickly, he sat up, clutching his hands around his knee and rocking back and forth as if absorbed in pain. He found that he had no difficulty making himself cry, and cry loudly, though he didn't feel the tears the way he had before. He carefully did not turn his head to look at the clown, though he did sneak a sidelong peek out of the corner of his eye.

The clown had stopped a few yards away and was watching him—standing motionlessly and *staring* at him, fixedly, unblinkingly, with total concentration, like some great, black, sullen bird of prey.

David hugged his skinned knee and made himself cry louder. There was a possibility that he hadn't given himself away—that the clown would think he'd yelled like that *because* he'd tripped and fallen down and not because he'd seen him come dancing around the corner. The two things had happened closely enough together that the clown *might* think that. Please, God, let him think that. Let him believe it.

The clown was still watching him.

Stiffly, David got up. Still not looking at the clown, he made himself lean over and brush off his pants. Although his mouth was still as dry as dust, he moistened his lips and forced himself to swear, swear out loud, blistering the air with every curse word he could think of, as though he were upset about the ragged hole torn in his new blue jeans and the blood on his knee.

He kept slapping at his pants a moment longer, still bent over, wondering if he should suddenly break and run now that he was on his feet again, make a flat-out dash for freedom. But the clowns were so *fast*. And even if he *did* escape, then they would *know* that he could see them.

Compressing his lips into a hard, thin line, David straightened up and began to walk directly toward the clown.

Closer and closer. He could sense the clown looming enormously in front of him, the cold blue eyes still staring suspiciously at him. Don't look at the clown! Keep walking casually and *don't look at him*. David's spine was as stiff as if it were made of metal, and his head ached with the effort not looking. He picked a spot on the sidewalk and stared at it, thrust his hands into his pockets with elaborate casualness and somehow forced his legs to keep walking. Closer. Now he was close enough to be grabbed, if the clown wanted to grab him. He was right next to him, barely an arm's length away. He could *smell* the clown now — a strong smell of greasepaint, underlaid with a strange, musty, earthen smell, like old wet leaves, like damp old wallpaper. He was suddenly *cold*, as cold as ice; it was all he could do to keep from shaking with the cold. Keep going. Take one more step. Then one more. . . .

As he passed the clown, he caught sight of an abrupt motion out of the corner of his eye. With all the will he could summon, he forced himself not to flinch or look back. He kept walking, feeling a cold spot in the middle of his back, *knowing* somehow that the clown was still staring at him, staring after him. *Don't* speed up. Just keep walking. Papers rustled in the gutter behind him. Was there a clown walking through them? Coming up behind him? About to *grab* him? He kept walking, all the while waiting for the clown to *get* him, for those strong cold hands to close over his shoulders, the way they had closed over the shoulders of old Mr. Thorne.

He walked all the way home without once looking up or looking around him, and it wasn't until he had gotten inside, with the door locked firmly behind him, that he began to tremble.

David had gone upstairs without eating dinner. His father had started to yell about that — he was strict about meals — but his mother had intervened, taking his father aside to whisper something about "trauma" to him — both of them inadvertently shooting him that uneasy walleyed look they sometimes gave him now, as if they weren't sure he mightn't suddenly start drooling and gibbering if they said the wrong thing to him, as if he had something they might *catch* — and his father had subsided, grumbling.

Upstairs, he sat quietly for a long time, thinking hard.

The clowns. Had they just come to town, or had they always been there and he just hadn't been able to *see* them before? He remembered when Mikey had broken his collarbone two summers ago, and when Sarah's brother had been killed in the motorcycle accident, and when that railroad yardman had been hit by the freight train. Were the clowns responsible for those accidents, too?

He didn't know. There was one thing he *did* know, though: Something had to be done about the clowns.

He was the only one who could see them.

Therefore, *he* had to do something about them.

He was the only one who could see them, the only one who could *warn* people. If he didn't do anything and the clowns hurt somebody else, then *he*'d be to blame. Somehow, he *had* to stop them.

How?

David sagged in his chair, overwhelmed by the immensity of the problem. *How?*

The doorbell rang.

David could hear an indistinct voice downstairs, mumbling something, and then hear his mother's voice, clearer, saying, "I don't know if David really feels very much like having company right now, Sammy."

Sammy—

David scooted halfway down the stairs and yelled, "Ma! No, Ma, it's OK! Send him up!" He went on down to the second-floor landing, saw Sammy's face peeking tentatively up the stairs and motioned for Sammy to follow him up to his room.

David's room was at the top of the tall, narrow old house, right next to the small room that his father sometimes used as an office. There were old magic posters on the walls—Thurston, Houdini, Blackstone: King of Magicians—a Duran Duran poster behind the bed and a skeleton mobile of a Tyrannosaurus hanging from the overhead lamp. He ushered Sammy in wordlessly, then flopped down on top of the *Star Wars* spread that he'd finally persuaded his mother to buy for him. Sammy pulled out the chair to David's desk and began to fiddle abstractedly with the pieces of David's half-assembled Bell X-15 model kit. There were new dark hollows under Sammy's eyes and his face looked strained. Neither boy spoke.

"Mommy didn't want to let me out," Sammy said after a while, sweeping the model pieces aside with his hand. "I told her I'd feel better if I could come over and talk to you. It's really weird about Mr. Thorne, isn't it? I can't believe it, the way that truck *smushed* him, like a tube of toothpaste or something." Sammy grimaced and put his arms around his legs, clasping his hands together tightly, rocking back and forth nervously. "I just can't believe he's gone."

David felt the tears start and blinked them back. Crying wouldn't help. He looked speculatively at Sammy. He certainly couldn't tell his *parents* about the clowns. Since his "nervous collapse" last fall, they were already afraid that he was a nut.

"Sammy," he said. "I have to tell you something. Something important. But first you have to *promise* not to tell anybody. No matter what, no matter how crazy it sounds, you've got to promise!"

"Yeah?" Sammy said tentatively.

"No—first you've got to promise."

"OK, I *promise*," Sammy said, a trace of anger creeping into his voice.

"Remember this afternoon at the swimming pool, when I pointed at that rocking chair, and you thought I was pulling a joke on you? Well, I *wasn't*. I did see somebody sitting there. I saw a clown."

Sammy looked disgusted. "I see a clown right now," he grated.

"Honest, Sammy I *did* see a clown. A clown, all made up and in costume, just like at the circus. And it was a clown—the same one, I think—who pushed Mr. Thorne in front of that truck."

Sammy just looked down at his knees. His face reddened.

"I'm not lying about this, I swear. I'm telling the truth this time; honest, Sammy, I really am—"

Sammy made a strange noise, and David suddenly realized that he was *crying*.

David started to ask him what the matter was, but before he could speak, Sammy had rounded fiercely on him, blazing. "You're nuts! You *are* a loony, just like everybody says! No wonder nobody will play with you. Loony! Fucking *loony!*"

Sammy was screaming now, the muscles in his neck cording. David shrank away from him, his face going ashen.

They stared at each other. Sammy was panting like a dog, and tears were running down his cheeks.

"Everything's . . . some kind of . . . *joke* to you, isn't it?" Sammy panted. "Mr. Thorne was my *friend*. But you . . . you don't care about *anybody!*" He was screaming again on the last word. Then he whirled and ran out of the room.

David followed him, but by the time he was halfway down the stairs, Sammy was already out the front door, slamming it shut behind him.

"What was *that* all about?" David's mother asked.

"Nothing," David said dully. He was staring through the screened-in door, watching Sammy run down the sidewalk. Should he chase him? But all at once it seemed as if he were too tired to move; he leaned listlessly against the doorjamb and watched Sammy disappear from sight. Sammy had left the gate of their white picket fence unlatched, and it swung back and forth in the wind, making a hollow slamming sound.

How could he make anyone else believe him if he couldn't even convince *Sammy?* There was nobody left to tell.

David had a sudden, bitter vision of just how lonely the rest of the summer was going to be without even Sammy to play with. Just him, all by himself, all summer long.

Just him . . . and the clowns.

∎ ∎ ∎

David heard his parents talking as he made his way down to breakfast the next morning and paused just outside the kitchen archway to listen.

"Was the strangest thing," his mother was saying.

"What was?" David's father grumbled. He was hunched over his morning coffee, glowering at it, as if daring it to cool off before he got around to drinking it. Mr. Shore was often grouchy in the morning, though things weren't as bad anymore as they'd been last fall, when his parents had often screamed obscenities at each other across the breakfast table—not as bad as that one terrible morning, the morning David didn't even want to think about, when his father had punched his mother in the face and knocked two of her teeth out, because the eggs were runny. David's mother kept telling him that his father was under a lot of "stress" because of his new job—he used to sell computers, but now he was a stockbroker trainee.

"What was?" David's father repeated irritably, having gotten no reply.

"Oh, I don't know," David's mother said. "It's just that I was thinking about that poor old woman all night. I just can't get her out of my mind. You know, she kept swearing somebody pushed her."

"For Christ's sake!" David's father snapped. "Nobody *pushed* her. She's just getting senile. She had heavy bags to carry and all those stairs to climb, that's all." He broke off, having spotted David in the archway. "David, don't *skulk* like that. You know I hate a sneak. In or out!"

David came slowly forward. His mouth had gone dry again and he had to moisten his lips to be able to speak. "What—what were you talking about? Did something happen? Who got hurt?"

"Marty!" David's mother said sharply, glancing quickly and significantly at David, frowning, shaking her head.

"Damn it, Anna," David's father grumbled. "Do you really think that the kid's gonna curl up and die if he finds out that Mrs. Zabriski fell down a flight of stairs? What the hell does he care?"

"*Marty!*"

"He doesn't even know her, except to say hello to, for Christ's sake! Accidents happen all the time; he might just as well get used to that—"

David was staring at them. His face had gone white. "Mrs. Zabriski?" he whispered. "Is—is she *dead?*"

His mother gave her husband a now-look-what-you've-done glare and moved quickly to put an arm around David's shoulder. "No, honey," she said soothingly, in that nervous, almost *too* sympathetic voice she used on him now whenever she thought he was under stress. "She's going to be OK. Just a broken leg and a few bruises. She fell down the stairs yesterday on her way back from the grocery store. Those stairs are awfully steep for a woman her age. She tripped, that's all."

David bit his lip. Somehow, he managed to blink back sudden bitter tears. *His* fault! If he'd carried her bags for her, like she'd wanted him to, like she'd *asked* him to, then she'd have been all right; the clown wouldn't have gotten her.

For Mrs. Zabriski hadn't tripped. He knew that.

She'd been *pushed*.

By the time David got to Sammy's house, there was no one home. Too late! His father had reluctantly let David off the hook about eating breakfast — the very thought of eating made him ill — but had insisted in his I'm-going-to-brook-no-more-nonsense voice, the one he used just before he started hitting, that David wash the breakfast dishes, and that had slowed him up just enough. He'd hoped to catch Sammy before he left for the pool, try to talk to him again, try to get him to at least agree to keep quiet about the clowns.

He made one stop, in the Religious Book Store and Reading Room on Main Street, and bought something with some of the money from his allowance. Then, slowly and reluctantly, trying to ignore the fear that was building inside him, he walked to the swimming pool.

Sammy was already in the water when David arrived.

The pool was crowded, as usual. David waved halfheartedly to Jas, who was sitting in the high-legged lifeguard's chair. Jas waved back uninterestedly; he was surveying his domain through aluminum sunglasses, his nose smeared with zinc oxide to keep it from burning.

And — yes — the clown was there! Way in the back, near the refreshment stand. Lounging quietly against a wall and watching the people in the pool.

David felt his heart start hammering. Moving slowly and — he hoped — inconspicuously, he began to edge through the crowd toward Sammy. The clown was still looking the other way. If only —

But then Sammy saw David. "Well, well, *well*," Sammy yelled, "if it isn't David Shore!" His voice was harsh and ugly, his face flushed and twisted. David had never seen him so bitter and upset. "Seen any more *clowns* lately, Davie?" There was real hatred in his voice. "Seen any more killer invisible clowns, Davie? You loony! You fucking loony!"

David flinched, then tried to shush him. People were looking around, attracted by the shrillness of Sammy's voice.

The clown was looking, too. David saw him look at Sammy, who was still waving his arms and shouting, and then slowly raise his head, trying to spot who Sammy was yelling at.

David ducked aside into the crowd, half squatting down, dodging behind a couple of bigger kids. He could *feel* the clown's gaze pass overhead, like a scythe made of ice and darkness. Shut up, Sammy, he thought desperately. Shut up. He squirmed behind another group of kids, bumping into somebody, heard someone swear at him.

"Daa — vie!" Sammy was shouting in bitter mockery. "Where are all the clowns, Davie? You seen any clowning around here *today*, Davie? Huh, Davie?"

The clown was walking toward Sammy now, still scanning the crowd, his gaze relentless and bright.

Slowly, David pushed his way through the crowd, moving away from Sammy. Bobby and Andy were standing in line at the other end of the pool, waiting to jump off the board. David stepped up behind Andy, pretending to be waiting in line, even though he hated diving. Should he leave the pool? Run? That would only make it easier for the clown to spot him. But if he left, maybe Sammy would shut *up*.

"You're crazy, David Shore!" Sammy was yelling. He seemed on the verge of tears — he had been very close to Mr. Thorne. "You know that? You're fucking *crazy. Bats in the belfry*, Davie —"

The clown was standing on the edge of the pool, right above Sammy, staring down at him thoughtfully.

Then Sammy spotted David. His face went blank, as though with amazement, and he pointed his finger at him. "David! *There's a clown behind you!*"

Instinctively, knowing that it was a mistake even as his muscles moved but unable to stop himself, David whipped his head around and looked behind him. Nothing was there.

When he turned back, the clown was staring at him.

Their eyes met, and David felt a chill go through him, as if he had been pierced with ice.

Sammy was breaking up, hugging himself in glee and laughing, shrill, cawing laughter with a trace of hysteria in it. "Jeez-*us*, Davie!" he yelled. "You're just not playing with a full deck, are you, Davie? You're —"

The clown knelt by the side of the pool. Moving with studied deliberation, never taking his eyes off David, the clown reached out, 187 seized Sammy by the shoulders—Sammy jerked in surprise, his mouth opening wide—and slowly and relentlessly forced him under the water.

"Sammy!" David screamed.

The clown was leaning out over the pool, eyes still on David, one arm thrust almost shoulder-deep into the water, holding Sammy under. The water thrashed and boiled around the clown's outthrust arm, but *Sammy wasn't coming back up—*

"Jason!" David shrieked, waving his arms to attract the lifeguard's attention and then pointing toward the churning patch of water. "Ja-*son!* Help! Help! Somebody's *drowning!*" Jason looked in the direction David was pointing, sat up with a start, began to scramble to his feet—

David didn't wait to see any more. He hit the water in a clumsy dive, almost a belly-whopper, and began thrashing across the pool toward Sammy, swimming as strongly as he could. Half blinded by spray and by the wet hair in his eyes, half dazed by the sudden shock of cold water on his sun-baked body, he almost rammed his head into the far side of the pool, banging it with a wildly flailing hand instead. He recoiled, gasping. The clown was right above him now, only a few feet away. The clown turned his head to look at him, still holding Sammy under, and once again David found himself shaking with that deathly arctic cold. He kicked at the side wall of the pool, thrusting himself backward. Then he took a deep breath and went under.

The water was murky, but he was close enough to see Sammy. The clown's white-gloved hand was planted firmly on top of Sammy's head, holding him under. Sammy's eyes were open, strained wide, bulging almost out of his head. Dreadfully, they seemed to see David, recognize him, appeal mutely to him. Sammy's hands were pawing futilely at the clown's arm, more and more weakly, slowing, running down like an unwound clock. Even as David reached him, Sammy's mouth opened and there was a silvery explosion of bubbles.

David grabbed the clown's arm. A shock went through him at the contact, and his hands went cold, the bitter cold spreading rapidly up his arms, as if he were grasping something that avidly sucked the heat from anything that touched it. David yanked at the clown's arm with his numbing, clumsy hands, trying to break his grip, but it was like yanking on a steel girder.

A big white shape barreled by him like a porpoise, knocking him aside. Jas.

David floundered, kicked, broke the surface of the water. He shot up into the air like a Polaris missile, fell back, took a great racking breath, another. Sunlight on water dazzled his eyes, and everything was noise and confusion in the open air, baffling after the muffled underwater silence. He kicked his feet weakly, just enough to keep him afloat, and looked around.

Jas was hauling Sammy out of the pool. Sammy's eyes were still open, but now they looked like glass, like the blank, staring eyes of a stuffed animal; a stream of dirty water ran out of his slack mouth, down over his chin. Jas laid Sammy out by the pool edge, bent hurriedly over him, began to blow into his mouth and press on his chest. A crowd was gathering, calling out questions and advice, making little wordless noises of dismay.

The clown had retreated from the edge of the pool. He was standing some yards away now, watching Jas labor over Sammy.

Slowly, he turned his head and looked at David.

Their eyes met again, once again with that shock of terrible cold, and this time the full emotional impact of what that look implied struck home as well.

The clowns *knew* that he could see them.

The clowns knew who he *was*.

The clowns would be after *him* now.

Slowly, the clown began to walk toward David, his icy blue eyes fixed on him.

Terror squeezed David like a giant's fist. For a second, everything went dark. He couldn't remember swimming back across to the other side of the pool, but the next thing he knew, there he was, hauling himself up the ladder, panting and dripping. A couple of kids were looking at him funny; no doubt he'd shot across the pool like a torpedo.

The clown was coming around the far end of the pool, not running but walking fast, still staring at David.

There were still crowds of people on this side of the pool, too, some of them paying no attention to the grisly tableau on the far side, most of them pressed together near the pool's edge, standing on tiptoe and craning their necks to get a better look.

David pushed his way through the crowd, worming and dodging and shoving, and the clown followed him, moving faster now. The clown seemed to flow like smoke around people without touching them, never stumbling or bumping into anyone even in the most densely packed part of the crowd, and he was catching up. David kept looking back, and each time he did, the widely smiling painted face was closer behind him, momentarily bobbing up over the sunburned shoulders of the crowd, weaving in and out. Coming relentlessly on, pressing *closer*, all the while never taking his eyes off him.

The crowd was thinning out. He'd never make it back around the end of the pool before the clown caught up with him. Could he possibly outrun the clown in the open? Panting, he tried to work his hand into the pocket of his sopping-wet jeans as he stumbled along. The wet cloth resisted, resisted, and then his hand was inside the pocket, his fingers touching metal, closing over the thing he'd bought at the store on his way over.

Much too afraid to feel silly or self-conscious, he whirled around and held up the crucifix, extended it at arm's length toward the clown.

The clown stopped.

They stared at each other for a long, long moment, long enough for the muscles in David's arm to start to tremble.

Then, silently, mouth open, the clown started to laugh.

It wasn't going to work—

The clown sprang at David, spreading his arms wide as he came.

It was like a wave of fire-shot darkness hurtling toward him, getting bigger and bigger, blotting out the world—

David screamed and threw himself aside.

The clown's hand swiped at him, hooked fingers grazing his chest like stone talons, tearing free. For a moment, David was enveloped in arctic cold and that strong musty smell of dead leaves, and then he was rolling free, scrambling to his feet, *running—*

He tripped across a bicycle lying on the grass, scooped it up and jumped aboard it all in one motion, began to pedal furiously. Those icy hands clutched at him again from just a step behind. He felt his shirt rip; the bicycle skidded and fishtailed in the dirt for a second; and then the wheels bit the ground and he was away and picking up speed.

When he dared to risk a look back, the clown was staring after him, a look thoughtful, slow and icily intent.

David left the bicycle in a doorway a block from home and ran the rest of the way, trying to look in all directions at once. He trudged wearily up the front steps of his house and let himself in.

His parents were in the front room. They had been quarreling, but when David came into the house they broke off and stared at him. David's mother rose rapidly to her feet, saying, "David! Where *were* you? We were so worried! Jason told us what happened at the pool."

David stared back at them. "Sammy?" he heard himself saying, knowing it was stupid to ask even as he spoke the words but unable to keep himself from feeling a faint stab of hope. "Is Sammy gonna be all right?"

His parents exchanged looks.

David's mother opened her mouth and closed it again, hesitantly, but his father waved a hand at her, sat up straighter in his chair and said flatly, "Sammy's dead, David. They think he had some sort of seizure and drowned before they could pull him out. I'm sorry. But that's the way it is."

"Marty!" David's mother protested.

"It's part of life, Anna," his father said. "He's got to learn to face it. You can't keep him wrapped up in cotton wool, for Christ's sake!"

"It's all right," David said quietly. "I knew he *had* to be. I just thought maybe . . . somehow. . . ."

There was a silence, and they looked at each other through it. "At any rate," his father finally said, "we're proud of you, David. The lifeguard told us you tried to save Sammy. You did the best you could, did it like a man, and you should be proud of that." His voice was heavy and solemn. "You're going to be upset for a while, sure— that's only normal—but someday that fact's going to make you feel a lot better about all this, believe me."

David could feel his lips trembling, but he was determined not to cry. Summoning all his will to keep his voice steady, he said, "Mom . . . Dad . . . if I . . . *told* you something—something that was really *weird*—would you believe me and not think I was going nuts again?"

His parents gave him that uneasy, wall-eyed look again. His mother wet her lips, hesitantly began to speak, but his father cut her off. "Tell your tall tales later," he said harshly. "It's time for supper."

David sagged back against the door panels. They *did* think he was going nuts again, had probably been afraid of that ever since they heard he had run wildly away from the pool after Sammy drowned. He could *smell* the fear on them, a sudden bitter burnt reek, like scorched onions. His mother was still staring at him uneasily, her face pale, but his father was grating, "Come on, now, wash up for supper. Make it snappy!" He wasn't going to *let* David be nuts, David realized; he was going to *force* everything to be "normal," by the sheer power of his anger.

"I'm not hungry," David said hollowly. "I'd rather just lie down." He walked quickly by his parents, hearing his father start to yell, hearing his mother intervene, hearing them start to quarrel again behind him. He didn't seem to care anymore. He kept going, pulling himself upstairs, leaning his weight on the wrought-iron banister. He was bone-tired and his head throbbed.

In his room, he listlessly peeled off his sweat-stiff clothes. His head was swimming with the need to sleep, but he paused before turning down the bedspread, grimaced and shot an uneasy glance at the window. Slowly, he crossed the room. Moving in jerks and starts, as though against his will, he lifted the edge of the curtain and looked out.

There was a clown in the street below, standing with that terrible motionless patience in front of the house, staring up at David's window.

David was not even surprised. Of *course* the clowns would be there. They'd heard Sammy call his name. They'd found him. They knew where he lived now.

What was he going to *do?* He couldn't stay inside all summer. Sooner or later, his parents would *make* him go out.

And then the clowns would *get* him.

David woke up with a start, his heart thudding.

He pushed himself up on one elbow, blinking in the darkness, still foggy and confused with sleep. What had happened? What had wakened him?

He glanced at the fold-up travel clock that used to be his dad's; it sat on the desk, its numbers glowing. Almost midnight.

Had there been a noise? There *had* been a noise, hadn't there? He could almost remember it.

He sat alone in the darkened room, still only half-awake, listening to the silence.

Everything was silent. Unnaturally silent. He listened for familiar sounds; the air conditioner swooshing on, the hot-water tank rumbling, the refrigerator humming, the cuckoo clock chiming in the living room. Sometimes he could hear those sounds when he awakened in the middle of the night. But he couldn't hear them now. The crickets weren't even chirruping outside, nor was there any sound of passing traffic. There was only the sound of David's own breathing, harsh and loud in his ears, as though he were underwater and breathing through scuba gear. Without knowing why, he felt the hair begin to rise on the back of his neck.

The clowns were in the house.

That hit him suddenly, with a rush of adrenalin, waking him all the way up in an eyeblink.

He didn't know how he knew, but he *knew*. Somehow, he had thought that houses were *safe*, that the clowns could only be outside. But they were here. They were in the house. Perhaps they were here in the *room*, right now. Two of them, eight, a dozen. Forming a circle around the bed, staring at him in the darkness with their opaque and malevolent eyes.

He burst from the bed and ran for the light switch, careening blindly through blackness, waiting for clutching hands to grab him in the dark. His foot struck something — a toy, a shoe — and sent it clattering away, the noise making him gasp and flinch. A misty ghost shape seemed to move before him, making vague, windy gestures, more sensed than seen. He ducked away, dodging blindly. Then his hand was on the light switch.

The light came on like a bomb exploding, sudden and harsh and overwhelmingly bright. Black spots flashed before his eyes. As his vision re-adjusted, he jumped to see a face only inches from his own — stifling a scream when he realized that it was only his reflection in the dresser mirror. That had also been the moving, half-seen shape.

There was no one in the room.

Panting with fear, he slumped against the dresser. He'd instinctively thought that the light would help, but somehow it only made things worse. It picked out the eyes and the teeth of the demons in the magic posters on the walls, making them gleam sinisterly, and threw slowly moving monster shadows across the room from the dangling Tyrannosaurus mobile. The light was harsh and spiky, seeming to bounce and ricochet from every flat surface, hurting his eyes. The light wouldn't save him from the clowns, wouldn't keep them away, wouldn't banish them to unreality, like bad-dream bogeymen — it would only help them *find* him.

He was making a dry little gasping noise, like a cornered animal. He found himself across the room, crouching with his back to the wall. Almost without thinking, he had snatched up the silver letter-opener knife from his desk. Knife in hand, lips skinned back over his teeth in an animal snarl, he crouched against the wall and listened to the terrible silence that seemed to press in against his eardrums.

They were coming for him.

He imagined them moving with slow deliberation through the darkened living room downstairs, their eyes and their dead-white faces gleaming in the shadows, pausing at the foot of the stairs to look up toward his room and then, slowly, slowly — each movement as intense and stylized as the movements of a dance — beginning to climb ... the stairs creaking under their weight ... coming *closer*. ...

David was crying now, almost without realizing that he was. His heart was thudding as if it would tear itself out of his chest, beating faster and faster as the pressure of fear built up inside him, shaking him, chuffing out, "*Run, run, run!* Don't let them trap you in here! *Run!*"

Before he had realized what he was doing, he had pulled open the door to his room and was in the long corridor outside.

Away from the patch of light from his doorway, the corridor was deadly black and seemed to stretch endlessly away into distance. Slowly, step by step, he forced himself into the darkness, one hand on the corridor wall, one hand clutching the silver knife. Although he was certain that every shadow that loomed up before him would turn out to be a silently waiting clown, he didn't even consider switching on the hallway light. Instinctively, he knew that the darkness would hide him. Make no noise, stay close to the wall. They might miss you in the dark. Knife in hand, he walked on down the hall, feeling his fingertips rasp along over wood and tile and wallpaper, his eyes strained wide. Into the darkness.

His body knew where he was going before he did. His parents' room. He wasn't sure if he wanted his parents to protect him or if he wanted to protect *them* from a menace they didn't even know existed and couldn't see, but through his haze of terror, all he could think of was getting to his parents' room. If he could beat the clowns to the second floor, hide in his parents' room, maybe they'd miss him; maybe they wouldn't look for him there. Maybe he'd be safe there ... safe ... the way he used to feel when a thunderstorm would wake him and he'd run sobbing down the hall in the darkness to his parents' room and his mother would take him in her arms.

The staircase, opening up in a well of space and darkness, was more felt than seen. Shoulder against the wall, he felt his way down the stairs, lowering one foot at a time, like a man backing down a ladder. The well of darkness rose up around him and slowly swallowed him. Between floors, away from the weak, pearly light let in by the upstairs-landing window, the darkness was deep and smothering, the air full of suspended dust and the musty smell of old carpeting. Every time the stairs creaked under his feet, he froze, heart thumping, certain that a clown was about to loom up out of the inky blackness, as pale and terrible as a shark rising up through black midnight water.

He imagined the clowns moving all around him in the darkness, swirling silently around him in some ghostly and enigmatic dance, unseen, their fingers not quite touching him as they brushed by like moth wings in the dark . . . the bushy fright wigs puffed out around their heads like sinister nimbi . . . the ghostly white faces, the dead-black costumes, the gleaming-white gloves reaching out through the darkness.

He forced himself to keep going, fumbling his way down one more step, then another. He was clutching the silver knife so hard that his hand hurt, holding it up high near his chest, ready to strike out with it.

The darkness seemed to open up before him. The second-floor landing. He felt his way out onto it, sliding his feet flat along the floor, like an ice skater. His parents' room was only a few steps away now. Was that a noise from the floor below, the faintest of sounds, as if someone or something were slowly climbing up the stairs?

His fingers touched wood. The door to his parents' room. Trying not to make even the slightest sound, he opened the door, eased inside, closed the door behind him and slowly threw the bolt.

He turned around. The room was dark, except for the hazy moonlight coming in the window through the half-opened curtains; but after the deeper darkness of the hall outside, that was light enough for him to be able to see. He could make out bulky shapes under the night-gray sheets, and, and as he watched, one of the shapes moved slightly, changing positions.

They were there! He felt hope open hot and molten inside him, and he choked back a sob. He would crawl into bed between them as he had when he was a very little boy, awakened by nightmares . . . he would nestle warmly between them . . . he would be *safe*.

"Mom?" he said softly. "Dad?" He crossed the room to stand beside the bed. "Mom?" he whispered. Silence. He reached out hesitantly, feeling a flicker of dread even as he moved, and slowly pulled the sheet down on one side —

And there was the clown, staring up at him with those terrible, opaque, expressionless blue eyes, smiling his unchanging painted smile.

David plunged the knife down, feeling it bite into the spongy resistance of muscle and flesh. Yet even as the blow struck home, he felt cold, strong hands, white-gloved hands, close over his shoulders from behind.

THE CLOWNS

I became involved in this particular collaboration in self-defense. For years, I'd been carrying around in my head the memory of talking to an acquaintance in the West Village in New York City sometime in 1970 or early 1971, and the weird story that he had told me — with total conviction — about how he was being followed everywhere by sinisterly smiling-clowns that were invisible to everybody else; about how he had been alone in his apartment, and had gone into the bathroom, and found a clown in there, sitting on the toilet and silently grinning at him; about how he had been riding on his motorcycle, and felt cold arms close around his middle, and looked behind him, and a clown was there, riding behind him on the motorcycle, clutching him around the waist, grinning at him.... As I said, the guy told me all this earnestly, matter-of-factly, with a kind of weird tranced calm, and I felt the hairs rise up on the back of my neck as I listened to him; he was heavily into drugs, his eyes had become opaque and shiny, the smell of Bad Karma was on him, and he was clearly doomed — in fact, I never saw him again after that.

At any rate, Jack was down for a visit one weekend, I think it was the weekend of November 11-13, 1983, and one evening Jack and Susan and I were sitting around talking about Weird Stuff, the sort of conversation where someone is likely to start humming the old *Twilight Zone* theme ("doduedoduedoduedodue . . ."), and at one point I related the clown anecdote.

Jack's eyes bugged out, "Wow!" he said. "What a great idea for a *story!*" And before I knew what was happening, Jack and Susan were eagerly discussing a plot, and then they were off in the living room, pounding out a rough draft of the first couple of pages on my typewriter.

I was somewhat miffed. They were writing *my* story, on *my* typewriter, and they hadn't even invited me to join them in the collaboration! I sulked about this for a day or so, while Jack and Susan became more enthusiastic and it became more and more obvious that they actually *were* going to write this thing, and it became more and more clear to me that if I was going to get any mileage at all out of this material that I'd carried around in my head for so long, I'd better put my oar in fast. So I dealt myself into the collaboration, and, after I picked up the tab for Hot Fudge Sundaes at *More Than Just Ice Cream*, Susan and Jack acquiesced.

Jack took the first crack at the story, and we received a partial draft from him, consisting mostly of the opening and the middle sequences, on December 12, 1983. Susan then did a draft, adding most of the scenes with David's parents, and adding early versions of the pushing-in-front-of-the-truck scene and the second swimming-pool scene. They may have passed the story back and forth between them a few more times, too; I'm not sure. At any rate, my calendar shows that I started work on the story myself on March 11, 1984. I fleshed out the opening section, the initial pool section, and the truck section, and then Susan and I worked at hammering out an ending, going back and forth between ourselves with several drafts; that took most of March. Then, during the end of August and the first half of September (I was working on other projects in the meantime), I did my usual unifying draft, adding a few new scenes and adding things interstitially throughout. The second swimming-pool scene and the ending were redrafted again several times, with some more input from Susan and Jack. The story was finished on September 24, 1984, and later that year, on December 27th, I did a fairly extensive cutting job on the story, at the prompting of Alice K. Turner of *Playboy.*

My major contribution to the story, I think, was in altering its pacing. I reworked the pacing of several scenes — notably the skinned-knee scene, the truck scene, the second swimming pool scene, and the ending sequence — in an effort to inject more suspense into the story, crank the tension and suspense up to the maximum by using the same kind of techniques that you'd use in a suspense film, a Hitchcock movie, say . . . and, in this, I think that I was moderately successful.

"The Clowns" appeared in *Playboy* in 1985.

olden Apples
of the Sun

GARDNER DOZOIS, JACK DANN, & MICHAEL SWANWICK

Few of the folk in Faërie would have anything to do with the computer salesman. He worked himself up and down one narrow, twisting street after another, until his feet throbbed and his arms ached from lugging the sample cases, and it seemed like days had passed rather than hours, and *still* he had not made a single sale. Barry Levingston considered himself a first-class sales-man, one of the *best*, and he wasn't used to this kind of failure. It discouraged and frustrated him, and as the afternoon wore endlessly on — there was something funny about the way time passed here in Faërie; the hazy, bronze-colored Fairyland sun had hardly moved at all across the smoky amber sky since he'd arrived, although it should certainly be evening by *now* — he could feel himself beginning to lose that easy confidence and unshakable self-esteem that are the successful salesman's most essential stock-in-trade. He tried to tell himself that it wasn't really *his* fault. He was working under severe restrictions, after all. The product was new and unfamiliar to this particular market, and he was going "cold sell." There had been no telephone solicitation programs to develop leads, no ad campaigns, not so much as a demographic study of the market potential. Still, his total lack of success was depressing.

The village that he'd been trudging through all day was built on and around three steep, hive-like hills, with one street rising from the roofs of the street below. The houses were piled chockablock atop each other, like clusters of grapes, making it almost impossible to even find — much less *get* to — many of the upper-story doorways. Sometimes the eaves grew out over the street, turning them into long, dark tunnels. And sometimes the streets ran up sloping house-sides and across rooftops, only to come to a sudden and frightening *stop* at a sheer drop of five or six stories, the street beginning again as abruptly on the far side of the gap. From the highest streets and stairs you could see a vista of the surrounding countryside: a hazy golden-brown expanse of orchards and forests and fields, and, on the far horizon, blue with distance, the jagged, snow-capped peaks of a mighty mountain range — except that the mountains didn't always seem to be in the same *direction* from one moment to the next; sometimes they were to the west, then to the north, or east, or south; sometimes they seemed much closer or further away; sometimes they weren't there at *all*.

Barry found all this unsettling. In fact, he found the whole *place* unsettling. Why go *on* with this, then? he asked himself. He certainly wasn't making any headway. Maybe it was because he overtowered most of the fairyfolk — maybe they were sensitive about being so *short*, and so tall people annoyed them. Maybe they just didn't like humans; humans *smelled* bad to them, or something. Whatever it was, he hadn't gotten more than three words of his spiel out of his mouth all day. Some of them had even slammed doors in his face — something he had almost forgotten *could* happen to a salesman.

Throw in the towel, then, he thought. But . . . no, he *couldn't* give up. Not yet. Barry sighed, and massaged his stomach, feeling the acid twinges in his gut that he knew presaged a savage attack of indigestion later on. This was virgin territory, a literally untouched route. Gold waiting to be mined. And the Fairy Queen had given this territory to *him*. . . .

Doggedly, he plodded up to the next house, which looked something like a gigantic acorn, complete with a thatched cap and a crazily twisted chimney for the stem. He knocked on a round wooden door.

A plump, freckled fairy woman answered. She was about the size of an earthly two-year-old, but a transparent gown seemingly woven of spidersilk made it plain that she was no child. She hovered a few inches above the doorsill on rapidly beating hummingbird wings.

"Aye?" she said sweetly, smiling at him, and Barry immediately felt his old confidence return. But he didn't permit himself to become excited. That was the quickest way to lose a sale.

"Hello," he said smoothly. "I'm from Newtech Computer Systems, and we've been authorized by Queen Titania, the Fairy Queen *herself*, to offer a *free* installation of our new home computer system—"

"That wot I not of," the fairy said.

"Don't you even know what a computer *is*?" Barry asked, dismayed, breaking off his spiel.

"Aye, I fear me, 'tis even so," she replied, frowning prettily. "In sooth, I know not. Belike you'll tell me of't, fair sir."

Barry began talking feverishly, meanwhile unsnapping his sample case and letting it fall open to display the computer within. "—balance your household accounts," he babbled. "Lets you organize your recipes, keep in touch with the stock market. You can generate full-color graphics, charts, graphs. . . ."

The fairy frowned again, less sympathetically. She reached her hand toward the computer, but didn't quite touch it. "Has the smell of metal on't," she murmured. "Most chill and adamant." She shook her head. "Nay, sirrah, 'twill not serve. 'Tis a thing mechanical, a clockwork, meet for carillons and orreries. Those of us born within the Ring need not your engines philosophic, nor need we toil and swink as mortals do at such petty tasks an you have named. Then wherefore should I buy, who neither strive nor moil?"

"But you can play *games* on it!" Barry said desperately, knowing that he was losing her. "You can play Donkey Kong! You can play *Pac-Man! Everybody* likes to play Pac-Man—"

She smiled slowly at him sidelong. "I'd liefer more delightsome games," she said.

Before he could think of anything to say, a long, long, *long* green-gray arm came slithering out across the floor from the hidden interior of the house. The arm ended in a knobby hand equipped with six grotesquely long, tapering fingers, now spreading wide as the hand reached out toward the fairy. . . .

Barry opened his mouth to shout a warning, but before he could, the long arm had wrapped bonelessly around her ankle, not once but *four* times around, and the hand with its scrabbling spider fingers had closed over her thigh. The arm yanked back, and she tumbled forward in the air, laughing. "Ah, loveling, can you not wait?" she said with mock severity. The arm tugged at her. She giggled. "Certes, meseems you cannot!"

As the arm pulled her, still floating, back into the house, the fairy woman seized the door to slam it shut. Her face was flushed and preoccupied now, but she still found a moment to smile at Barry. "Farewell, sweet mortal!" she cried, and winked. "Next time, mayhap?"

The door shut. There was a muffled burst of giggling within. Then silence.

The salesman glumly shook his head. This was a goddam tank town, was what it was, he thought. Here there were no nicknacks and bric-a-brac lining the windows, no cast-iron flamingos and eave-climbing plaster kitty cats, no mailboxes with fake Olde English calligraphy on them—but in spite of that it was still a tank town. Just another goddamn middle-class neighborhood with money a little tight and the people running scared. Place like this, you couldn't even *give* the stuff away, much less make a sale. He stepped back out into the street. A fairy knight was coming down the road toward him, dressed in green jade armor cunningly shaped like leaves, and riding an enormous frog. Well, why not? Barry thought. He wasn't having a lot of luck door-to-door.

"Excuse me, sir!" Barry cried, stepping into the knight's way. "May I have a moment of your—"

The knight glared at him, and pulled back suddenly on his reins. The enormous frog reared up, and leaped straight into the air. Gigantic, leathery, bat-like wings spread, caught the thermals, carried mount and rider away.

Barry sighed and trudged doggedly up the cobblestone road toward the next house. No matter what happened, he wasn't going to quit until he'd finished the street. That was a compulsion of his . . . and the reason he was one of the top cold-sell agents in the company. He remembered a night when he'd spent five hours knocking on doors without a single sale, or even so much as a kind *word*, and then suddenly he'd sold $30,000 worth of merchandise in an hour . . . suddenly he'd been golden, and they couldn't say no to him. Maybe that would happen today, too. Maybe the next house would be the beginning of a run of good luck. . . .

The next house was shaped like a gigantic ogre's face, its dark wood forming a yawning mouth and heavy-lidded eyes. The face was made up of a host of smaller faces, and each of *those* contained other, even smaller faces. He looked away dizzily, then resolutely climbed to a glowering, thick-nosed door and knocked right between the eyes—eyes which, he noted uneasily, seemed to be studying him with interest.

A fairy woman opened the door—below where he was standing. Belatedly, he realized that he had been knocking on a dormer; the top of the door was a foot below him.

This fairy woman had stubby, ugly wings. She was lumpy and gnarled, and her skin was the texture of old bark. Her hair stood straight out on end all around her head, in a puffy nimbus, like the Bride of Frankenstein. She stared imperiously up at him, somehow managing to seem to be staring *down* her nose at him at the same time. It was quite a nose, too. It was longer than his hand, and sharply pointed.

"A great ugly lump of a mortal, an I mistake not!" she snapped. Her eyes were flinty and hard. "What's toward?"

"I'm from Newtech Computer Systems," Barry said, biting back his resentment at her initial slur, "and I'm selling home computers, by special commission of the Queen—"

"Go to!" she snarled. "Seek you to cozen me? I wot *not* what abnormal beast that be, but I have no need of mortal kine, nor aught else from your loathly world! Get you gone!" She slammed the door under his feet. Which somehow was every bit as bad as slamming it in his face.

"Sonofa*bitch!*" Barry raged, making an obscene gesture at the door, losing his temper at last. "You goddamn flying fat pig!"

He didn't realize that the fairy woman could hear him until a round crystal window above his head flew open, and she poked her head out of it, nose first, buzzing like a jarful of hornets. "Wittold!" she shrieked. "Caitiff rogue!"

"Screw off, lady," Barry snarled. It had been a long, hard day, and he could feel the last shreds of self-control slipping away. "Get back in your goddamn hive, you goddamn Pinocchio-nosed mosquito!"

The fairy woman spluttered incoherently with rage, then became dangerously silent. "So!" she said in cold passion. "*Noses*, is't? Would vilify *my* nose, knave, whilst your *own* be uncommon squat and vile? A tweak or two will remedy *that*, I trow, and exchange the worse for the better!"

So saying, she came buzzing out of her house like an outraged wasp, streaking straight at the salesman.

Barry flinched back, but she seized hold of his nose with both hands and tweaked it savagely. Barry yelped in pain. She shrieked out a high-pitched syllable in some unknown language and began flying backward, her wings beating furiously, *tugging* at his nose.

He felt the pressure in his ears change with a sudden *pop*, and then, horrifyingly, he felt his face beginning to *move* in a strangely fluid way, flowing like water, swelling out and out and *out* in front of him.

The fairy woman released his nose and darted away, cackling gleefully.

Dismayed, Barry clapped his hands to his face. He hadn't realized that these little buggers could *all* cast spells — he'd thought that kind of magic stuff was reserved for the Queen and her court. Like cavorting in hot tubs with naked starlets and handfuls of cocaine, out in Hollywood — a prerogative reserved only for the Elite. But when his hands reached his nose, they almost couldn't close around it. It was too large. His nose was now nearly two feet long, as big around as a Polish sausage, and covered with bumpy warts.

He screamed in rage. "Goddammit, lady, come back here and *fix* this!"

The fairy woman was perching half-in and half-out of the round window, lazily swinging one leg. She smiled mockingly at him. "There!" she said, with malicious satisfaction. "Art *much* improved, methinks! Nay, thank me not!" And, laughing joyously, she tumbled back into the house and slammed the crystal window closed behind her.

"Lady!" Barry shouted. Scrambling down the heavy wooden lips, he pounded wildly on the door. "Hey, look, a joke's a joke, but I've got *work* to do! *Lady!* Look, lady, I'm *sorry*," he whined. "I'm sorry I swore at you, honest! Just come out here and *fix* this and I won't bother you anymore. Lady, *please!*" He heaved his shoulder experimentally against the door, but it was as solid as rock.

An eyelid-shaped shutter snapped open above him. He looked up eagerly, but it wasn't the lady; it was a fat fairy man with snail's horns growing out of his forehead. The horns were quivering with rage, and the fairy man's face was mottled red. "Pox take you, boy, and your cursed brabble!" the fairy man shouted. "When I am fore-done with weariness, must I be roused from honest slumber by your hurble-burble?" Barry winced; evidently he had struck the Faërie equivalent of a night-shift worker. The fairy man shook a fist at him. "Out upon you, miscreant! By the Oak of Mughna, I demand SILENCE!" The window snapped shut again.

Barry looked nervously up at the eyelid-window, but somehow he *had* to get the lady to come out and fix this goddamn *nose*. "Lady?" he whispered. "*Please*, lady?" No answer. This wasn't working at all. He'd have to change tactics, and take his chances with Snailface in the next apartment. "LADY!" he yelled. "OPEN UP! I'M GOING TO STAND HERE AND SHOUT AT THE TOP OF MY LUNGS

UNTIL YOU COME OUT! YOU WANT THAT? DO YOU?"

The eyelid flew open. "This passes bearing!" Snailface raged. "Now Cernunnos shrivel me, an I chasten not this boistous doltard!"

"Listen, mister, I'm *sorry*", Barry said uneasily, "I don't mean to wake you up, honest, but I've *got* to get that lady to come out, or my ass'll really be grass!"

"Your *arse*, say you?" the snail-horned man snarled. "Marry, since you would have it so, why, by Lugh, I'll do it, straight!" He made a curious gesture, roared out a word that seemed to be all consonants, and then slammed the shutter closed.

Again, there was a *popping* noise in Barry's ears, and a change of pressure that he could feel throughout his sinuses. *Another* spell had been cast on him.

Sure enough, there was a strange, prickly sensation at the base of his spine. "Oh, no!" he whispered. He didn't really want to look—but at last he forced himself to. He groaned. He had sprouted a long green tail. It looked and smelled suspiciously like grass.

"Ha! Ha!" Barry muttered savagely to himself. "Very funny! *Great* sense of humor these little winged people've got!"

In a sudden spasm of range, he began to rip out handfuls of grass, trying to *tear* the loathsome thing from his body. The grass ripped out easily, and he felt no pain, but it grew back many times faster than he could tear it free—so that by the time he decided that he was getting nowhere, the tail trailed out six or seven feet behind him.

What was he going to do *now*?

He stared up at the glowering house for a long, silent moment, but he couldn't think of any plan of action that wouldn't just get him in *more* trouble with *someone*.

Gloomily, he gathered up his sample cases, and trudged off down the street, his nose banging into his upper lip at every step, his tail dragging forlornly behind him in the dust. Be damned if this wasn't even worse than cold-selling in *Newark*. He wouldn't have believed it. But *there* he had only been mugged and had his car's tires slashed. *Here* he had been hideously disfigured, maybe for life, and he wasn't even making any *sales*.

He came to an intricately carved stone fountain, and sat wearily down on its lip. Nixies and water nymphs laughed and cavorted within the leaping waters of the fountain, swimming just as easily up the spout as down. They cupped their pretty little green breasts and called invitingly to him, and then mischieviously spouted water at his tail when he didn't answer, but Barry was in no mood for them, and resolutely ignored their blandishments. After a while they went back to their games and left him alone.

Barry sighed, and tried to put his head in his hands, but his enormous new nose kept getting in the way. His stomach was churning. He reached into his pocket and worried out a metal-foil packet of antacid tablets. He tore the packet open, and then found—to his disgust—that he had to lift his sagging nose out of the way with one hand in order to reach his mouth. While he chewed on the chalky-tasting pills, he stared glumly at the twin leatherette bags that held his demonstrator models. He was beaten. Finished. Destroyed. *Ruined.* Down and out in Faërie, at the ultimate rock bottom of his career. What a bummer! What a *fiasco!*

And he had had such high hopes for this expedition, too. . . .

Barry never really understood why Titania, the Fairy Queen, spent so much of her time hanging out in a sleazy little roadside bar on the outskirts of a jerkwater South Jersey town—perhaps *that* was the kind of place that seemed exotic to *her*. Perhaps she like the rotgut hooch, or the greasy hamburgers—just as likely to be "venison-burgers," really, depending on whether somebody's uncle or backwoods cousin had been out jacking deer with a flashlight and a 30.30 lately—or the footstomping honky-tonk music on the jukebox. Perhaps she just had an odd sense of humor. Who knew? *Not* Barry.

Nor did Barry ever really understand what *he* was doing there— it wasn't really his sort of place, but he'd been on the road with a long way to go to the next town, and a sudden whim had made him stop in for a drink. *Nor* did he understand why, having stopped in in the first place, he had then gone *along* with the gag when the beat-up old barfly on his left had leaned over to him, breathing out poisonous fumes, and confided "*I'm* really the Queen of the Fairies, you know." Ordinarily, he would have laughed, or ignored her, or said something like "And *I'm* the Queen of the May, sleazeball." But he had done none of these things. Instead, he had nodded gravely and courteously, and asked her if he could have the honor of lighting the cigarette that was wobbling about in loopy circles in her shaking hand.

Why did he do this? Certainly it hadn't been from even the *remotest* desire to get into the Queen's grease-stained pants—in her earthly incarnation, the Queen was a grimy, gray-haired, broken-down rummy, with a horse's face, a dragon's breath, cloudy agate eyes, and a bright-red rumblossom nose. No, there had been no ulterior motives. But he had been in an odd mood, restless, bored, and stale. So he had played up to her, on a spur-of-the-moment whim, going along with the gag, buying her drinks and lighting cigarettes for her, and listening to her endless stream of half-coherent talk, all the while solemnly calling her "Your Majesty" and "Highness," getting a kind of role-playing let's-pretend kick out of it that he hadn't known since he was a kid and he and his sister used to play "grown-up dress-up" with the trunk of castoff clothes in the attic.

So that when midnight came, and all the other patrons of the bar froze into freeze-frame rigidity, paralyzed in the middle of drinking or shouting or scratching or shoving, and Titania manifested herself in the radiant glory of her *true* form, nobody could have been more surprised than *Barry*.

"My God!" he'd cried. "You really *are*—"

"The Queen of the Fairies," Titania said smugly. "You bet your buns, sweetie. I *told* you so, didn't I?" She smiled radiantly, and then gave a ladylike hiccup. The Queen in her new form was so dazzlingly beautiful as to almost hurt the eye, but there was still a trace of rotgut whiskey on her breath. "And because *you've* been a most true and courteous knight to one from whom you thought to see no earthly gain, I'm going to grant you a *wish*. How about *that*, kiddo?" She beamed at him, then hiccuped again; whatever catabolic effect her transformation had had on her blood-alcohol level, she was obviously still slightly tipsy.

Barry was flabbergasted. "I can't believe it," he muttered. "I come into a bar, on *im*pulse, just by *chance*, and the very very first person I sit down next to turns out to be—"

Titania shrugged. "That's the way it goes, sweetheart. It's the Hidden Hand of Oberon, what you mortals call 'synchronicity.' Who knows what'll eventually come of this meeting—tragedy or comedy, events of little moment or of world-shaking weight and worth? Maybe even *Oberon* doesn't know, the silly old fart. Now, about that *wish*—"

Barry thought about it. What *did* he want? Well, he was a *salesman*, wasn't he? New worlds to conquer. . . .

Even Titania had been startled. She looked at him in surprise and then said, "Honey, I've been dealing with mortals for a lot of years now, but nobody ever asked for *that* before. . . ."

Now he sat on cold stone in the heart of the Faërie town, and groaned, and cursed himself bitterly. If only he hadn't been so ambitious! If only he'd asked for something *safe*, like a swimming pool or a Ferrari. . . .

Afterward, Barry was never sure how long he sat there on the lip of the fountain in a daze of despair—perhaps literally for weeks; it *felt* that long. Slowly, the smoky bronze disk of the Fairyland sun sank beneath the horizon, and it became night, a warm and velvety night whose very darkness seemed somehow luminous. The nixies had long since departed, leaving him alone in the little square with the night and the plashing waters of the fountain. The strange stars of Faërie swam into the sky, witchfire crystals so thick against the velvet blackness of the night that they looked like phosphorescent plankton sparkling in some midnight tropic sea. Barry watched the night sky for a long time, but he could find none of the familiar constellations he knew, and he shivered to think how far away from home he must be. The stars *moved* much more rapidly here than they did in the sky of Earth, crawling perceptibly across the black bowl of the night even as you watched, swinging in stately procession across the sky, wheeling and reforming with a kind of solemn awful grandeur, eddying and whirling, swirling into strange patterns and shapes and forms, spiral pinwheels of light. Pastel lanterns appeared among the houses on the hillsides as the night deepened, seeming to reflect the wheeling, blazing stars above.

At last, urged by some restless tropism, he got slowly to his feet, instinctively picked up his sample cases, and set off aimlessly through the mysterious night streets of the Faërie town. Where was he going? Who knew? Did it matter any more? He kept walking. Once or twice he heard faint, far snatches of fairy music—wild, sad, yearning melodies that pierced him like a knife, leaving him shaken and melancholy and strangely elated all at once—and saw lines of pastel lights bobbing away down the hillsides, but he stayed away from those streets, and did his best not to listen; he had been warned about the bewitching nature of fairy music, and had no desire to spend the next hundred or so years dancing in helpless enchantment within a fairy ring. Away from the street and squares filled with dancing pastel lights and ghostly will-o'-the-wisps—which he avoided —the town seemed dark and silent. Occasionally, winged shapes swooped and flittered overhead, silhouetted against the huge mellow silver moon of Faërie, sometimes seeming to fly behind it for several wingbeats before flashing into sight again. Once he met a fellow pedestrian, a monstrous one-legged creature with an underslung jaw full of snaggle teeth and one baleful eye in the middle of its forehead that blazed like a warning beacon, and stood unnoticed in the shadows, shivering, until the fearsome apparition had hopped by. Not paying any attention to where he was going, Barry wandered blindly downhill. He couldn't think at all—it was as if his brain had turned to ash. His feet stumbled over the cobblestones, and only by bone-deep instinct did he keep hold of the sample cases. The street ended in a long curving set of wooden stairs. Mechanically, dazedly, he followed them down. At the bottom of the stairs, a narrow path led under the footing of one of the gossamer bridges that looped like slender gray cobwebs between the fairy hills. It was cool and dark here, and almost peaceful. . . .

"AAAARRRRGGHHHHH!"

Something *enormous* leaped out from the gloom, and enveloped him in a single, scaly green hand. The fingers were a good three feet long each, and their grip was as cold and hard as iron. The hand lifted him easily into the air, while he squirmed and kicked futilely.

Barry stared up into the creature's face. "Yop!" he said. A double row of yellowing fangs lined a frog-mouth large enough to swallow him up in one gulp. The blazing eyes bulged ferociously, and the nose was a flat smear. The head was topped off by a fringe of hair like red worms, and a curving pair of ram's horns.

"Pay *up* for the use a my bridge," the creature roared, "or by Oberon's dirty socks, I'll crunch you whole!"

It never ends, Barry thought. Aloud, he demanded in frustration, "What bridge?"

"A wise guy!" the monster sneered. "*That* bridge, whadda ya *think?*" He gestured upward scornfully. "The bridge *over* us, dummy! The Bridge a Morrig the Fearsome! *My* bridge. I got a royal commission says I gotta right ta collect toll from *every* creature that sets foot on it, and you better believe that means *you*, buddy. I got you dead to rights. So cough up!" He shook Barry until the salesman's teeth rattled. "Or *else!*"

"But I *haven't* set foot on it!" Barry wailed. "I just walked *under* it!"

"Oh," the monster said. He looked blank for a moment, scratching his knobby head with his free hand, and then his face sagged. "Oh," he said again, disappointedly. "Yeah. I guess you're right. Crap." Morrig the Fearsome sighed, a vast noisome displacement of air. Then he released the salesman. "Jeez, buddy, I'm sorry," Morrig said, crestfallen. "I shouldn't'a'oughta have jerked ya around like that. I guess I got overanxious or sumpthin. Jeez, mac, you know how it is. Tryin' to make a buck. The old grind. It gets me down."

Morrig sat down discouragedly and wrapped his immensely long and muscular arms around his knobby green knees. He brooded for a moment, then jerked his thumb up at the bridge. "That bridge's my only source a income, see?" He sighed gloomily. "When I come down from Utgard and set up this scam, I think I'm gonna get *rich.* 209

Got the royal commission, all nice an' legal, everybody gotta *pay* me, right? Gonna clean *up*, right?" He shook his head glumly. "*Wrong*. I ain't making a lousy *dime*. All the locals got *wings*. Don't use the bridge at *all*." He spat noisily. "They're cheap little snots, these fairy-folk are."

"*Amen*, brother," Barry said, with feeling. "I know *just* what you mean."

"Hey!" Morrig said, brightening. "You care for a snort? I got a jug a hooch right here."

"Well, actually . . ." Barry said reluctantly. But the troll had already reached into the gloom with one long, triple-jointed arm, and pulled out a stone crock. He pried off the top and took a long swig. Several gallons of liquid gurgled down his throat. "Ahhhh!" He wiped his thin lips. "That hits the spot, alright." He thrust the crock into Barry's lap. "Have a belt."

When Barry hesitated, the troll rumbled, "Ah, go ahead, pal. Good for what ails ya. You got troubles too, aintcha, just like me — I can tell. It's the lot a the workin' man, brother. Drink up. Put hair on your *chest* even if you ain't got no dough in your *pocket*." While Barry drank, Morrig studied him cannily. "You're a mortal, aintcha, bud?"

Barry half-lowered the jug and nodded uneasily.

Morrig made an expansive gesture. "Don't worry, pal. *I* don't care. I figure all a us workin' folks gotta stick *together*, regardless a race er creed, or the bastards'll grind us *all* down. Right?" He leered, showing his huge, snaggly, yellowing fangs in what Barry assumed was supposed to be a reassuring grin. "But, say, buddy, if you're a mortal, how come you got a funny nose like that, an a tail?"

Voice shrill with outrage, Barry told his story, pausing only to hit the stone jug.

"Yeah, buddy," Morrig said sympathetically. "They really worked you over, didn't they?" He sneered angrily. "Them bums! Just *like* them little snots to gang up ona guy who's just tryin' ta make an honest buck. Whadda *they* care about the problems a the workin' man? Buncha booshwa snobs! Screw 'em all!"

They passed the seemingly bottomless stone jug back and forth again. "Too bad *I* can't do none a that magic stuff," Morrig said sadly, "or I'd fix ya right up. What a shame." Wordlessly, they passed the jug again. Barry sighed. Morrig sighed too. They sat in gloomy silence for a couple of minutes, and then Morrig roused himself and said, "*What* kinda scam is it you're tryin' ta run? I ain't never heard a it before. Lemme see the merchandise."

"What's the point — ?"

"C'mon," Morrig said impatiently. "I wantcha ta show me the goods. Maybe *I* can figure out a way ta move the stuff."

Listlessly, Barry snapped open a case. Morrig leaned forward to study the console with interest. "Kinda pretty," the troll said; he sniffed at it. "Don't smell too bad, either. Maybe make a nice planter, or sumpthin."

"*Planter?*" Barry cried; he could hear his voice cracking in outrage. "I'll have you know this is a piece of high technology! Precision machinery!"

Morrig shrugged. "Okay, bub, make it march."

"Ah," Barry said. "I need someplace to plug it in. . . ."

Morrig picked up the plug and inserted it in his ear. The computer's CRT screen lit up. "Okay," Morrig said. "Gimme the pitch. What's it do?"

"Well," Barry said slowly, "let's suppose that you had a bond portfolio worth $2,147 invested at 8¾ % compounded daily, over eighteen months, and you wanted to calculate—"

"Two thousand four hundred forty-three dollars and sixty-eight and seven-tenths cents," said the troll.

"Hah?"

"That's what it works out to, pal. Two hundred ninety-six dollars and change in compound interest."

With a sinking sensation, Barry punched through the figures and let the system work. Alphanumerics flickered on the CRT: $296.687.

"Can *everybody* in Faërie do that kind of mental calculation?" Barry asked.

"Yeah," the troll said. "But so what? No big deal. Who *cares* about crap like that anyway?" He stared incredulously at Barry. "Is *that* all that thing does?"

There was a heavy silence.

"Maybe you oughta reconsider that idea about the planters. . . ." Morrig said.

Barry stood up again, a trifle unsteady from all the hooch he'd taken aboard. "Well, that's *really* it, then," he said. "I might just as well chuck my samples in the river—I'll never sell in *this* territory. Nobody needs my product."

Morrig shrugged. "What do *you* care how they use 'em? You oughta sell 'em first, and then let the *customers* find a use for 'em afterward. That's logic."

Fairy logic, perhaps, Barry thought. "But how can you *sell* something without first convincing the customer that it's useful?"

"Here." Morrig tossed off a final drink, gave a bone-rattling belch, and then lurched ponderously to his feet, scooping up both sample cases in one hand. "Lemme show you. Ya just gotta be *forceful.*"

The troll started off at a brisk pace, Barry practically having to run to keep up with his enormous strides. They climbed back up the curving wooden steps, and then Morrig somehow retraced Barry's wandering route through the streets of Faërie town, leading them unerringly back to the home of the short-tempered, Pinocchio-nosed fairy who had cast the first spell on Barry—the Hag of Blackwater, according to Morrig.

Morrig pounded thunderously on the Hag's door, making the whole house shake. The Hag snatched the door open angrily, snarling, "What's to—GACK!" as Morrig suddenly grabbed her up in one enormous hand, yanked her out of the house, and lifted her up to face level.

"Good evenin', m'am," Morrig said pleasantly.

"A murrain on you, lummox!" she shrieked. "Curst vile rogue! Release me at once! At *once,* you foul scoundrel! I'll—BLURK." Her voice was cut off abruptly as Morrig tightened his grip, squeezing the breath out of her. Her face turned blood-red, and her eyes bulged from her head until Barry was afraid that she was going to pop like an overripe grape.

"Now, *now,* lady," Morrig said in a gently childing tone. "Let's keep the party polite, okay? You know your magic's too weak to use on *me.* And you shouldn't'a'oughta use no hard language. We're just two workin' stiffs tryin' ta make a honest buck, see? You give us the bad mouth, and, say, it just might make me *sore.*" Morrig began shaking her, up and down, back and forth, his fist moving with blinding speed, shaking her in his enormous hand as if she were a pair of dice he was about to shoot in a crap game. "AND YOU WOULDN'T WANT TA MAKE ME SORE, NOW, WOULD YOU, LADY?" Morrig bellowed. "WOULD YOU?"

The Hag was being shaken so hard that all you could see of her was a blur of motion. "Givors!" she said in a faint little voice. "Givors, I pray you!"

Morrig stopped shaking her. She lay gasping and disheveled in his grasp, her eyes unfocused. "There!" Morrig said jovially, beaming down at her. "That's better, ain't it? Now I'm just gonna start all over again." He paused for a second, and then said brightly, "'Evenin', m'am! I'm sellin' . . . uh . . ." He scratched his head, looking baffled, then brightened. ". . . compukers!" He held up a sample case to show her; she stared dazedly at it. "Now I could go on and on about how swell these compukers are, but I can see you're *already* anxious ta buy, so there ain't no need ta waste yer valuable time like that. Ain't that right?" When she didn't answer, he frowned and gave her a little shake. "Ain't that *right?*"

"A-aye," she gibbered. "Aye!"

Morrig set her down, keeping only a light grip on her shoulder, and Barry broke out the sales forms. While she was scribbling frantically in the indicated blanks, Morrig rumbled, "And, say, now that we're all gettin' along so good, how's about takin' your spell offa my friend's nose, just as a gesture a good will? You'll do that little thing for me, *won'tcha?*"

With ill grace, the Hag obliged. There was a *pop*, and Barry exulted as he felt his nose shrink down to its original size. *Part* of the way home, anyway! He collected the sales forms and returned the receipts. "You can let go of her now," he told Morrig.

Sullenly, the Hag stalked back into her house, slamming the door behind her. The door vanished, leaving only an expanse of blank wood. With a freight-train rumble, the whole house sank into the ground and disappeared from sight. Grass sprang up on the spot where the house had been, and started growing furiously.

Morrig chuckled. Before they could move on, another fairy woman darted out from an adjacent door. "What bought the Hag of Blackwater, so precious that straight she hastens to hide herself away with it from prying eyes?" the other fairy asked. "Must indeed be something wondrous rare, to make her cloister herself with such dispatch, like a mouse to its hole, and then pull the very hole in after her! Aye, she knew I'd be watching, I doubt not, the selfish old bitch! Ever has she been jealous of my Art. Fain am I to know what the Hag would keep from my sight. Let *me* see your wares."

It was *then* that Barry had his master-stroke. "I'm sorry," he said in his snidest voice, "but I'm afraid that I can't show it to *you*. We're selling these computers by *exclusive* license of the *Queen*, and of course we can't sell them to just *anyone*. I'm afraid that we certainly couldn't sell *you* one, so—"

"What!" the fairy spluttered. "*No one* is better connected at Court than I! You *must* let me buy! An you do *not*, the Queen's majesty shall hear of this!"

"Well," said Barry doubtfully, "I don't know. . . ."

Barry and Morrig made a great team. They were soon surrounded by a swarm of customers. The demand became so great that they had no trouble talking Snailface into taking his spell off Barry as part of the price of purchase. In fact, Snailface became so enthusiastic about computers that he bought *six* of them. Morrig had been right. Who cared what they used them for, so long as they *bought* them? That was *their* problem, wasn't it?

In the end, they only quit because they had run out of sales forms.

Morrig had a new profession, and Barry returned to Earth a happy man.

Soon Barry had (with a little help from Morrig, who was still hard at work, back in Faërie) broken all previous company sales records, many times over. Barry had convinced the company that the flood-tide of new orders was really coming from heretofore untouched backwoods regions of West Virginia, North Carolina, and Tennessee, and everyone agreed that it was simply *amazing* how many hillbillies out there in the Ozarks had suddenly decided that they wanted home computer systems. Business was booming. So, when, months later, the company opened a new branch office with great pomp and ceremony, Barry was there, in a place of honor.

The sales staff stood respectfully watching as the company president himself sat down to try out one of the gleaming new terminals. The president had started the company out of his basement when home computers were new and he was only a college dropout from Silicon Valley, and he was still proud of his programming skills.

But as the president punched figures into the keyboard, long, curling, purple moose antlers began to sprout from the top of his head.

The sales staff stood frozen in silent horror. Barry gasped; then, recovering swiftly, he reached over the president's shoulder to hit the cancel key. The purple moose horns disappeared.

The Old Man looked up, puzzled. "Is anything wrong?"

"Only a glitch, sir," Barry said smoothly. But his hand was trembling.

He was afraid that there were going to be more such glitches. The way sales were booming—a *lot* more.

Evidently, the fairyfolk had finally figured out what computers were *really* for. And Barry suddenly seemed to hear, far back in his head, the silvery peals of malicious elven laughter.

It was a *two*-way system, after all. . . .

GOLDEN APPLES OF THE SUN

Michael's account of the origin of this story is fundamentally accurate, although I recall that it was preceded by some discussion about Jack's announced desire to write a story that made use of his recent experiences as a door-to-door salesman. (Jack was then working for a cable TV company, doing door-to-door soliciting people to have cable installed, and very successful he was at it, too; Jack, in fact, is a terrific salesman, able to sell almost anything to almost anybody — which is interesting, since it would be difficult to imagine two *worse* salesmen than Michael and me.) At any rate, when I made my joke about the Queen of the Fairies, it was immediately apparent to everyone that this dovetailed neatly with Jack's desire to write a door-to-door salesman story, and the core idea and plot of the story developed rapidly.

Jack did the first partial draft of the story, and the bulk of the material throughout the door-to-door selling sequence is fundamentally his. Michael then did a draft of the story, extending the storyline, adding new plot elements — Morrig the Fearsome was wholly of Michael's devising, for instance, although having him talk like a '30s Socialist or Labor Union Organizer was my idea — and finishing the story in rough draft.

I then did my usual unifying draft, working on the story pretty steadily for about a week even though I was laid up flat on my back in bed as a result of having suffered a major back-spasm. Although I did contribute some new sections of my own — most notably the scene in which Barry runs into Titania in a rundown roadside bar in South Jersey — it seems to me that my major contribution to the story was probably in fluffing up the texture here and there, and shining up the detailwork. I spent a good deal of time working out

215

the pseudo-Spenserian dialect most of the Faërie folk speak, for instance, and digging obscure references out of books of mythology and fairy lore — "By the Oak of Mughna," "Cernunnos shrivel me" — for the characters to sprinkle through their dialogue. I also thought that a story set in Faërie should feature moments of wonder and lyricism as well as the funny stuff, and so I did my best to work some evocative touches in here and there, notably in the scene after Barry wakes up at the fountain and wanders off through the Faërie town. The fairy knight riding the batwinged frog was solely Michael's invention, and, of course, the hopping one-eyed creature is an old friend of Jack's, to whom he has given employment in at least one other story.

Michael has told the story of our cutting the manuscript for *Penthouse*. The cut version was published in the March 1984 issue as "Virgin Territory," a name none of us particularly liked (if it was intended to convey the wink wink nudge nudge impression that the story was salacious, there must have been a *lot* of disappointed *Penthouse* readers out there that month). The story was later picked up by Art Saha for *The Year's Best Fantasy Stories: 11*, where it appeared under the original title, "Golden Apples of the Sun" (which someone at the magazine told me we couldn't use because it "was a quote from a Ray Bradbury story"), with some of the cut material restored.

Michael has already claimed unblushing responsibility for the appalling pun concealed in the title — so be sure to blame *him* for it.

RUNNING WILD

JACK DANN

Between 1981 and 1985 I wrote ten stories with the talented people who appear between these covers.

How the hell did we do it?

We are all very private people, and our work habits are somewhat similar: we sit down at our respective desks, stare at our computer screens or blank typewriter pages, look for anything we can find to distract us from the agonizing task at hand; and then slowly — and with nightmarish visions of writer's block a'dancing in our heads — we eke out the words. We work . . . and slowly, patiently rework.

Gardner is a night-person; his metabolism can still function at 4 A.M. Many a night I've dozed on the couch to the tapping of his typewriter. The cats would be padding about, Gardner would be hunkered over his ancient Remington typewriter on the manuscript-strewn kitchen table, while cats navigated between the precarious piles and padded around the room, as if impatient for him to complete the story.

My habit is to be up at 6 A.M. I prefer the dusty morning light, the first taste of fresh coffee, my portable television playing silently on my desk, the words of a current story or novel an amber glow on the implacable, black CRT screen sitting atop my old executive desk.

The whole day stretches before me, full of promise. The phone does not ring in the early hours, and if it does, my answering machine is set to one ring. And that's how I work, eking out two to four pages a day, sitting alone and slowly, slowly pounding out the words.

But collaborations . . . indeed, *they* are a different animal altogether.

■ ■ ■

I remember a visit to Gardner and Sue's apartment in Philadelphia in March of 1981. We had spent the weekend informally workshopping stories and novels, schmoozing, going downtown, eating at my favorite restaurants, seeing friends, and constantly talking shop. I suppose that this is about as close to writers' heaven as we get. Memory serves me that the weekend was topped off by a party with Michael Swanwick, Marianne Porter, Tess Kissinger, and Bob Walters—however, Gardner doesn't remember it that way. He thinks that, at best, Michael was the only other guest at the house that night. Well, taking the chance that I might be fictionalizing the past—something we all tend to do—this is the way *I* remember it:

While the party was in full swing, (but then who knows, maybe it *was* just Michael sitting there, big-as-life, throwing spitballs at me), I was sitting at the kitchen table, typing furiously at a story that was to become "Down Among the Dead Men."

Yet, when I'm writing at home, I can't concentrate if the television downstairs is on too loud, much less work in the midst of a party. I tend to yell and "behave in a self-involved manner," as my wife Jeanne puts it.

Could this be the same person who was sitting in Gardner and Sue's living room and typing furiously on Gardner's paleolithic typewriter while exchanging jokes, bad puns, and blunted witticisms with his friends?

The story I was writing, "Down Among the Dead Men," is a grittily realistic horror story about life in a concentration camp. How could it have been written—or how could the first eight or nine pages have been written—under those circumstances?

Background: I had written a story entitled "Camps," in 1979, which was quite popular. Gardner told me that he had an idea for a story set in a camp; and since I had already done the background work, it seemed to him that it would be a natural collaboration. His idea was of a vampire preying on other inmates. The difficulty was that he felt that the vampire should be an inmate rather than a guard.

My first reaction was very negative, but subtle, smooth, silver-tongued Gardner can be very persuasive. (Again, regarding the shifts memory can wreak with reality, Gardner recalls that I was initially enthusiastic about the idea; so here we are again!) He gently suggested I "just take a shot at it. Don't worry about it, just write whatever comes into your head. We can fix everything up later."

We were discussing it when the guests arrived; and in a fit of perverse humor, I sat down and began typing.

For, you see, I had nothing to lose.

And *because* there was a party going on, and because I wasn't really taking this story seriously, the words flowed strong and fresh. I felt as if I were simply an observer watching the story unfold.

"Down Among the Dead Men" turned out to be one of our most serious stories, and perhaps one of the best. It dealt without compromise with difficult, explosive material; but perhaps the key here is that the idea of collaborating—no matter how difficult or wild or outré the material—fooled this writer into believing it would be easy to write.

As opposed to sweating blood eking out a novel or a solo story, I perceived this to be *fun!*

Why?

Because I was relieved of responsibility.

Everything I wrote could be fixed if need be.

This was complete, unadulterated freedom.

This was the way writing was supposed to be: a joyous exhalation of words, the pounding of fingers on keys, the rush of unfettered imagination without any worry about that leaden, ugly, fear-inspiring, ego-containing monster: craft.

But I had only fooled myself—or Gardner, that prestidigitator par excellence, had fooled me—into thinking that I could break all the ties that bind.

Whatever I fucked-up could be fixed. So why worry?

And in fact it is true.

Once we had material to work with, everything *could* be fixed. But in those eight or nine pages that I typed so quickly that night, there was little that needed changing. For the craft that narrows and focuses you also sticks to you; you can no more shake it off than you can the flesh on your bones.

But for a while, when I was in the "trance of collaboration," I thought I could shake all limits. I could write *anything*. As a result the words just bubbled up out of my unconscious. I had put the little man inside my head, my lifelong editor, to sleep for a short, precious while.

And that is a wonderful, one-of-a-kind, running wild, no-one-can-touch-me-now freedom.

I could do it because Gardner was there. . . .

Just as in other collaborative stories Gardner and Michael and Jay and Sue and Jeanne and Barry were there.

Just as I've been there for them.

You simply can't fall down. . . .

Well, maybe you can; but if you do, if the story turns out to be bombsville, well you're not alone, honey.

Sumbitch if that bomb of a story wasn't Michael's fault. Or Gardner's fault. Or Sue's fault.

Because *my* part was just fine (even if I can't tell which part mine was)!

I've been on both sides of collaborations . . . and in the middle, too! I am more comfortable with the first stage, doing the original draft, for then I don't have to muck around with anyone else's words. But before any words are put to paper, the idea is expanded into a plot. Difficult as plotting might be when one is working alone, there is a certain synergy that develops when you start brainstorming with others. Ideas seem to take fire. Someone offers a suggestion; another runs with it. And somehow plot, theme, character, and background begin to take form.

It *feels* like magic.

It certainly isn't work, even though it can be exhausting and unnerving.

Usually, when I collaborate with my friend Barry N. Malzberg, he does first cut and I do the final polish. To have the words already there before you, to be able to rework them—no matter how much you expand the material—feels more like editing than writing. You don't have that cold-sweat panic of staring at a blank page and wondering how in God's name you are going to fill it up with words, much less produce prose that is elegant, comprehensible, and brilliant. And since you're wearing an editor's hat, it's natural to write pages and pages of ''interstitial'' prose. After all, you are merely doing the editorial job of connecting one scene to another, never mind that you have created thirty pages of your own scenes in-between.

You've been duped into believing that the hard work has already been done.

I always feel that Barry did all the hard work of putting pen to paper, even when *my* draft weighs in at twice the length.

Although I can't speak for Gardner, I imagine he might feel something like that, for he usually takes last cut when we work together. That has been comfortable for us. It worked out naturally. And I like getting to do the easy part: the first draft. I should mention that once a story is in motion, everyone involved will do first draft material, for we take turns writing various sections and polishing others. (Remember, I wrote the first nine pages of ''Down Among the Dead Men,'' and then Gardner carried the ball, with me only drafting material here and there and reworking for background continuity.)

Usually a story gets passed back and forth so many times, I sometimes find it difficult to discern who wrote what. When we work with Michael and Susan, *they* usually do first cut—after all, they've got so much more energy than we old farts. And then I really beat the game by mucking about in the middle, writing scenes here and there, knowing that the initial hard work has already been done, and the final polish *will* be done, and I'll still get my share of the profits!

Gardner called today to see how I was coming along with this memoir. (You know what pests editors can be. They actually expect projects to be completed by deadlines.) But there are so many deadlines now. Perhaps we shouldn't complain; but it is a sad marker, (only because we still think of ourselves as the Young Turks!) for we are definitely in middle life, right in the hurly-burly of it all; and time, which we've so successfully filled with work and family, becomes compressed. We reminisce on the phone, discuss a story we worked on, only to discover that it's been five years since we wrote it.

But this book seems to have juiced us up once again.

This time Gardner and I discussed plots and counterplots for a new story called ''The Wall.'' Then Susan picked up the phone and we discussed expanding our *Playboy* story ''The Clowns'' into a novel. We discussed other projects that had been lying dormant these last few, busy years. We started planning other novels. We made a pact to get together and once again talk the talk. To make the stuff we so fondly remember, the kind of memories that Michael recounted in his memoir, which had me chuckling for hours.

Hey, Michael, be warned, the good times are coming back.

Although I won't have a Special Corona cigar clamped in my teeth (Sigh, how I miss cigars!), you may consider this fair warning: soon I'll be leaning close to you while we're in the creative throes of working up another story, and you'll wince from the odor of garlic on my breath and recoil in horror from my unshaven, gleeful, wild-eyed visage as I tell you once again that ''This, my friend, is as good as it gets!''

Hallelujah.

Down
Among the Dead Men

GARDNER DOZOIS & JACK DANN

Bruckman first discovered that Wernecke was a vampire when they went to the quarry that morning.

He was bending down to pick up a large rock when he thought he heard something in the gully nearby. He looked around and saw Wernecke huddled over a *Musselmänn,* one of the walking dead, a new man who had not been able to wake up to the terrible reality of the camp.

"Do you need any help?" Bruckman asked Wernecke in a low voice.

Wernecke looked up, startled, and covered his mouth with his hand, as if he were signing to Bruckman to be quiet.

But Bruckman was certain that he had glimpsed blood smeared on Wernecke's mouth. "The *Musselmänn,* is he alive?" Wernecke had often risked his own life to save one or another of the men in his barrack. But to risk one's life for a *Musselmänn?* "What's wrong?"

"Get away."

All right, Bruckman thought. Best to leave him alone. He looked pale, perhaps it was typhus. The guards were working him hard enough, and Wernecke was older than the rest of the men in the work-gang. Let him sit for a moment and rest. But what about that blood . . . ?

223

"Hey, you, what are you doing?" one of the young SS guards shouted to Bruckman.

Bruckman picked up the rock and, as if he had not heard the guard, began to walk away from the gully, toward the rusty brown cart on the tracks that led back to the barbed-wire fence of the camp. He would try to draw the guard's attention away from Wernecke.

But the guard shouted at him to halt. "Were you taking a little rest, is that it?" he asked, and Bruckman tensed, ready for a beating. This guard was new, neatly and cleanly dressed—and an unknown quantity. He walked over to the gully and, seeing Wernecke and the *Musselmänn*, said, "Aha, so your friend is taking care of the sick." He motioned Bruckman to follow him into the gully.

Bruckman had done the unpardonable—he had brought it on Wernecke. He swore at himself. He had been in this camp long enough to know to keep his mouth shut.

The guard kicked Wernecke sharply in the ribs. "I want you to put the *Musselmänn* in the cart. Now!" He kicked Wernecke again, as if as an afterthought. Wernecke groaned, but got to his feet. "Help him put the *Musselmänn* in the cart," the guard said to Bruckman; then he smiled and drew a circle in the air—the sign of smoke, the smoke which rose from the tall gray chimneys behind them. This *Musselmänn* would be in the oven within an hour, his ashes soon to be floating in the hot, stale air, as if they were the very particles of his soul.

Wernecke kicked the *Musselmänn*, and the guard chuckled, waved to another guard who had been watching, and stepped back a few feet. He stood with his hands on his hips. "Come on, dead man, get up or you're going to die in the oven," Wernecke whispered as he tried to pull the man to his feet. Bruckman supported the unsteady *Musselmänn*, who began to wail softly. Wernecke slapped him hard. "Do you want to live, *Musselmänn*? Do you want to see your family again, feel the touch of a woman, smell grass after it's been mowed? Then *move*." The *Musselmänn* shambled forward between Wernecke and Bruckman. "You're dead, aren't you *Musselmänn*," goaded Wernecke. "As dead as your father and mother, as dead as your sweet wife, if you ever had one, aren't you? Dead!"

The *Musselmänn* groaned, shook his head, and whispered, "Not dead, my wife. . . ."

"Ah, it talks," Wernecke said, loud enough so the guard walking a step behind them could hear. "Do you have a name, corpse?"

"Josef, and I'm not a *Musselmänn*."

224 "The corpse says he's alive," Wernecke said, again loud enough for

the SS guard to hear. Then in a whisper, he said, "Josef, if you're not a *Musselmänn*, then you must work now, do you understand?" Josef tripped, and Bruckman caught him. "Let him be," said Wernecke. "Let him walk to the cart himself."

"Not the cart," Josef mumbled. "Not to die, not—"

"Then get down and pick up stones, show the fart-eating guard you can work."

"Can't. I'm sick, I'm . . ."

"*Musselmänn!*"

Josef bent down, fell to his knees, but took hold of a stone and stood up with it.

"You see," Wernecke said to the guard, "it's not dead yet. It can still work."

"I told you to carry him to the cart, didn't I," the guard said petulantly.

"Show him you can work," Wernecke said to Josef, "or you'll surely be smoke."

And Josef stumbled away from Wernecke and Bruckman, leaning forward, as if following the rock he was carrying.

"Bring him *back!*" shouted the guard, but his attention was distracted from Josef by some other prisoners, who, sensing the trouble, began to mill about. One of the other guards began to shout and kick at the men on the periphery, and the new guard joined him. For the moment, he had forgotten about Josef.

"Let's get to work, lest they notice us again," Wernecke said.

"I'm sorry that I—"

Wernecke laughed and made a fluttering gesture with his hand— smoke rising. "It's all hazard, my friend. All luck." Again the laugh. "It was a venial sin," and his face seemed to darken. "Never do it again, though, lest I think of you as bad luck."

"Eduard, are you all right?" Bruckman asked. "I noticed some blood when—"

"Do the sores on your feet bleed in the morning?" Wernecke countered angrily. Bruckman nodded, feeling foolish and embarrassed. "And so it is with my gums, now go away, unlucky one, and let me live."

They separated, and Bruckman tried to make himself invisible, tried to think himself into the rocks and sand and grit, into the choking air. He used to play this game as a child; he would close his eyes, and since *he* couldn't see anybody, he would pretend that nobody could see him. And so it was again. Pretending the guards couldn't see him was as good a way of staying alive as any.

He owed Wernecke another apology, which could not be made. He shouldn't have asked about Wernecke's sickness. It was bad luck to talk about such things. Wernecke had told him that when he, Bruckman, had first come to the barracks. If it weren't for Wernecke, who had shared his rations with Bruckman, he might well have become a *Musselmänn* himself. Or dead, which was the same thing.

The day turned blisteringly hot, and prisoners as well as guards were coughing. The air was foul, the sun a smear in the heavy yellow sky. The colors were all wrong: the ash from the ovens changed the light, and they were all slowly choking on the ashes of dead friends, wives, and parents. The guards stood together quietly, talking in low voices, watching the prisoners, and there was the sense of a perverse freedom—as if both guards and prisoners had fallen out of time, as if they were all parts of the same fleshy machine.

At dusk, the guards broke the hypnosis of lifting and grunting and sweating and formed the prisoners into ranks. They marched back to the camp through the fields, beside the railroad tracks, the electrified wire, conical towers, and into the main gate of the camp.

Bruckman tried to block out a dangerous stray thought of his wife. He remembered her as if he were hallucinating: she was in his arms. The boxcar stank of sweat and feces and urine, but he had been inside it for so long that he was used to the smells. Miriam had been sleeping. Suddenly he discovered that she was dead. As he screamed, the smells of the car overpowered him, the smells of death.

Wernecke touched his arm, as if he knew, as if he could see through Bruckman's eyes. And Bruckman knew what Wernecke's eyes were saying: "Another day. We're alive. Against all the odds. We conquered death." Josef walked beside them, but he kept stumbling, as he was once again slipping back into death, becoming a *Musselmänn*. Wernecke helped him walk, pushed him along. "We should let this man become dead," Wernecke said to Bruckman.

Bruckman only nodded, but he felt a chill sweep over his sweating back. He was seeing Wernecke's face again as it was for that instant in the morning. Smeared with blood.

Yes, Bruckman thought, we should let the *Musselmänn* become dead. We should all be dead. . . .

Wernecke served up the lukewarm water with bits of spoiled turnip floating on the top, what passed as soup for the prisoners. Everyone sat or kneeled on the rough-planked floor, as there were no chairs.

226 Bruckman ate his portion, counting the sips and the bites, forcing

himself to take his time. Later, he would take a very small bite of the bread he had in his pocket. He always saved a small morsel of food for later—in the endless world of the camp, he had learned to give himself things to look forward to. Better to dream of bread than to get lost in the present. That was the fate of the *Musselmänner.*

But he always dreamed of food. Hunger was with him every moment of the day and night. Those times when he actually ate were in a way the most difficult, for there was never enough to satisfy him. There was the taste of softness in his mouth, and then in an instant it was gone. The emptiness took the form of pain—it *hurt* to eat. For bread, he thought, he would have killed his father, or his wife. God forgive me, and he watched Wernecke—Wernecke, who had shared his bread with him, who had died a little so he could live. He's a better man than me, Bruckman thought.

It was dim inside the barracks. A bare lightbulb hung from the ceiling and cast sharp shadows across the cavernous room. Two tiers of five-foot-deep shelves ran around the room on three sides, bare wooden shelves where the men slept without blankets or mattresses. Set high in the northern wall was a slatted window, which let in the stark white light of the kliegs. Outside, the lights turned the ground into a deathly imitation of day; only inside the barracks was it night.

"Do you know what tonight is, my friends?" Wernecke asked. He sat in the far corner of the room with Josef, who, hour by hour, was reverting back into a *Musselmänn.* Wernecke's face looked hollow and drawn in the light from the window and the lightbulb; his eyes were deep-set and his face was long with deep creases running from his nose to the corners of his thin mouth. His hair was black, and even since Bruckman had known him, quite a bit of it had fallen out. He was a very tall man, almost six foot four, and that made him stand out in a crowd, which was dangerous in a death camp. But Wernecke had his own secret ways of blending with the crowd, of making himself invisible.

"No, tell us what tonight is," crazy old Bohme said. That men such as Bohme could survive was a miracle—or, as Bruckman thought—a testament to men such as Wernecke who somehow found the strength to help the others live.

"It's Passover," Wernecke said.

"How does he know that?" someone mumbled, but it didn't matter how Wernecke knew because he *knew*—even if it really wasn't Passover by the calendar. In this dimly lit barrack, it *was* Passover, the feast of freedom, the time of thanksgiving.

"But how can we have Passover without a *seder?*" asked Bohme. "We don't even have any *matzoh,*" he whined.

"Nor do we have candles, or a silver cup for Elijah, or the shank-bone, or *haroset*—nor would I make a *seder* over the *traif* the Nazis are so generous in giving us," replied Wernecke with a smile. "But we can pray, can't we? And when we all get out of here, when we're in our own homes in the coming year with God's help, then we'll have twice as much food—two *afikomens,* a bottle of wine for Elijah, and the *haggadahs* that our fathers and our fathers' fathers used."

It *was* Passover.

"Isadore, do you remember the four questions?" Wernecke asked Bruckman.

And Bruckman heard himself speaking. He was twelve years old again at the long table beside his father, who sat in the seat of honor. To sit next to him was itself an honor. "How does this night differ from all other nights? On all other nights we eat bread and *matzoh*; why on this night do we eat only *matzoh?*"

"*M'a nisht'ana halylah hazeah. . . .*"

Sleep would not come to Bruckman that night, although he was so tired that he felt as if the marrow of his bones had been sucked away and replaced with lead.

He lay there in the semi-darkness, feeling his muscles ache, feeling the acid biting of his hunger. Usually he was numb enough with exhaustion that he could empty his mind, close himself down, and fall rapidly into oblivion, but not tonight. Tonight he was noticing things again, his surroundings were getting through to him again, in a way that they had not since he had been new in the camp. It was smotheringly hot, and the air was filled with the stinks of death and sweat and fever, of stale urine and drying blood. The sleepers thrashed and turned, as though they fought with sleep, and as they slept, many of them talked or muttered or screamed aloud; they lived other lives in their dreams, intensely compressed lives dreamed quickly, for soon it would be dawn, and once more they would be thrust into hell. Cramped in the midst of them, sleepers squeezed in all around him, it suddenly seemed to Bruckman that these pallid white bodies were already dead, that he was sleeping in a graveyard. Suddenly it was the boxcar again. And his wife Miriam was dead again, dead and rotting unburied. . . .

Resolutely, Bruckman emptied his mind. He felt feverish and shaky, and wondered if the typhus were coming back, but he couldn't afford to worry about it. Those who couldn't sleep couldn't survive. Regulate your breathing, force your muscles to relax, don't think. Don't think.

For some reason, after he had managed to banish even the memory of his dead wife, he couldn't shake the image of the blood on Wernecke's mouth.

There were other images mixed in with it, Wernecke's uplifted arms and upturned face as he lead them in prayer, the pale strained face of the stumbling *Musselmänn*, Wernecke looking up, startled, as he crouched over Josef . . . but it was the blood to which Bruckman's feverish thoughts returned, and he pictured it again and again as he lay in the rustling, fart-smelling darkness: the watery sheen of blood over Wernecke's lips, the tarry trickle of blood in the corner of his mouth, like a tiny scarlet worm. . . .

Just then a shadow crossed in front of the window, silhouetted blackly for an instant against the harsh white glare, and Bruckman knew from the shadow's height and its curious forward stoop that it was Wernecke.

Where could he be going? Sometimes a prisoner would be unable to wait until morning, when the Germans would let them out to visit the slit-trench latrine again, and would slink shamefacedly into a far corner to piss against a wall, but surely Wernecke was too much of an old hand for that. . . . Most of the prisoners slept on the sleeping platforms, especially during the cold nights when they would huddle together for warmth, but sometimes during the hot weather, people would drift away and sleep on the floor instead; Bruckman himself had been thinking of doing that, as the jostling bodies of the sleepers around him helped to keep him from sleep. Perhaps Wernecke, who always had trouble fitting into the cramped sleeping nitches, was merely looking for a place where he could lie down and stretch his legs. . . .

Then Bruckman remembered that Josef had fallen asleep in the corner of the room where Wernecke had sat and prayed, and that they had left him there alone.

Without knowing why, Bruckman found himself on his feet. As silently as the ghost he sometimes felt he was becoming, he walked across the room in the direction Wernecke had gone, not understanding what he was doing nor why he was doing it. The face of the *Musselmänn*, Josef, seemed to float behind his eyes. Bruckman's feet hurt, and he knew, without looking, that they were bleeding, leaving faint tracks behind him. It was dimmer here in the far corner, away from the window, but Bruckman knew that he must be near the wall by now, and he stopped to let his eyes re-adjust.

When his eyes had adapted to the dimmer light, he saw Josef sitting on the floor, propped up against the wall. Wernecke was hunched over the *Musselmänn*. Kissing him. One of Josef's hands was tangled in Wernecke's thinning hair.

Before Bruckman could react—such things had been known to happen once or twice before, although it shocked him deeply that *Wernecke* would be involved in such filth—Josef released his grip on Wernecke's hair. Josef's upraised arm fell limply to the side, his hand hitting the floor with a muffled but solid impact that should have been painful—but Josef made no sound.

Wernecke straightened up and turned around. Stronger light from the high window caught him as he straightened to his full height, momentarily illuminating his face.

Wernecke's mouth was smeared with blood.

"My God!" Bruckman cried.

Startled, Wernecke flinched, then took two quick steps forward and seized Bruckman by the arm. "Quiet!" Wernecke hissed. His fingers were cold and hard.

At that moment, as though Wernecke's sudden movement were a cue, Josef began to slip down sideways along the wall. As Wernecke and Bruckman watched, both momentarily riveted by the sight, Josef toppled over to the floor, his head striking against the floorboards with a sound such as a dropped melon might make. He had made no attempt to break his fall or cushion his head, and lay now unmoving.

"My *God*," Bruckman said again.

"Quiet, I'll explain," Wernecke said, his lips still glazed with the *Musselmänn's* blood. "Do you want to ruin us all? For the love of God, be *quiet*."

But Bruckman had shaken free of Wernecke's grip and crossed to kneel by Josef, leaning over him as Wernecke had done, placing a hand flat on Josef's chest for a moment, then touching the side of Josef's neck. Bruckman looked slowly up at Wernecke. "He's dead," Bruckman said, more quietly.

Wernecke squatted on the other side of Josef's body, and the rest of their conversation was carried out in whispers over Josef's chest, like friends conversing at the sickbed of another friend who has finally fallen into a fitful doze.

"Yes, he's dead," Wernecke said. "He was dead yesterday, wasn't he? Today he has just stopped walking." His eyes were hidden here,

230

in the deeper shadow nearer to the floor, but there was still enough light for Bruckman to see that Wernecke had wiped his lips clean. Or licked them clean, Bruckman thought, and felt a spasm of nausea go through him.

"But *you*," Bruckman said, haltingly. "You were. . . ."

"Drinking his blood?" Wernecke said. "Yes, I was drinking his blood."

Bruckman's mind was numb. He couldn't deal with this, he couldn't understand it at all. "But *why*, Eduard? Why?"

"To live, of course. Why do any of us do anything here? If I am to live, I must have blood. Without it, I'd face a death even more certain than that doled out by the Nazis."

Bruckman opened and closed his mouth, but no sound came out, as if the words he wished to speak were too jagged to fit through his throat. At last he managed to croak, "A vampire? You're a vampire? Like in the old stories?"

Wernecke said calmly, "Men would call me that." He paused, then nodded. "Yes, that's what men would call me. . . . As though they can understand something simply by giving it a name."

"But Eduard," Bruckman said weakly, almost petulantly. "The *Musselmänn*. . . ."

"Remember that he *was* a *Musselmänn*," Wernecke said, leaning forward and speaking more fiercely. "His strength was going, he was sinking. He would have been dead by morning, anyway. I took from him something that he no longer needed, but that I needed in order to live. Does it matter? Starving men in lifeboats have eaten the bodies of their dead companions in order to live. Is what I've done any worse than that?"

"But he didn't just die. You *killed* him. . . ."

Wernecke was silent for a moment, and then said, quietly, "What better thing could I have done for him? I won't apologize for what I do, Isadore; I do what I have to do to live. Usually I take only a little blood from a number of men, just enough to survive. And that's fair, isn't it? Haven't I given food to others, to help them survive? To *you*, Isadore? Only very rarely do I take more than a minimum from any one man, although I'm weak and hungry all the time, believe me. And never have I drained the life from someone who wished to live. Instead I've helped them fight for survival in every way I can, you know that."

He reached out as though to touch Bruckman, then thought better of it and put his hand back on his own knee. He shook his head. "But these *Musselmänner*, the ones who have given up on life, the walking dead—it is a favor to them to take them, to give them the solace of death. Can you honestly say that it is not, *here?* That it is better for them to walk around while they are dead, being beaten and abused by the Nazis until their bodies cannot go on, and then to be thrown into the ovens and burned like trash? Can you say that? Would *they* say that, if they knew what was going on? Or would they thank me?"

Wernecke suddenly stood up, and Bruckman stood up with him. As Wernecke's face came again into the stronger light, Bruckman could see that his eyes had filled with tears. "You have lived under the Nazis," Wernecke said. "Can you really call *me* a monster? Aren't I still a Jew, whatever else I might be? Aren't I *here*, in a death camp? Aren't I being persecuted too, as much as any other? Aren't I in as much danger as anyone else? If I'm not a Jew, then tell the Nazis—they seem to think so." He paused for a moment, and then smiled wryly. "And forget your superstitious bogey-tales. I'm no night-spirit. If I could turn myself into a bat and fly away from here, I would have done it long before now, believe me."

Bruckman smiled reflexively, then grimaced. The two men avoided each other's eyes, Bruckman looking at the floor, and there was an uneasy silence, punctuated only by the sighing and moaning of the sleepers on the other side of the cabin. Then, without looking up, in tacit surrender, Bruckman said, "What about *him?* The Nazis will find the body and cause trouble. . . ."

"Don't worry," Wernecke said. "There are no obvious marks. And nobody performs autopsies in a death camp. To the Nazis, he'll be just another Jew who has died of the heat, or from starvation or sickness, or from a broken heart."

Bruckman raised his head then and they stared eye to eye for a moment. Even knowing what he knew, Bruckman found it hard to see Wernecke as anything other than what he appeared to be: an aging, balding Jew, stooping and thin, with sad eyes and a tired, compassionate face.

"Well, then, Isadore," Wernecke said at last, matter-of-factly. "My life is in your hands. I will not be indelicate enough to remind you of how many times your life has been in mine."

Then he was gone, walking back toward the sleeping platforms, a shadow soon lost among other shadows.

Bruckman stood by himself in the gloom for a long time, and then followed him. It took all of his will not to look back over his shoulder at the corner where Josef lay, and even so Bruckman imagined that he could feel Josef's dead eyes watching him, watching him reproachfully as he walked away, abandoning Josef to the cold and isolate company of the dead.

Bruckman got no more sleep that night, and in the morning, when the Nazis shattered the gray pre-dawn stillness by bursting into the shack with shouts and shrilling whistles and barking police dogs, he felt as if he were a thousand years old.

They were formed into two lines, shivering in the raw morning air, and marched off to the quarry. The clammy dawn mist had yet to burn off, and, marching through it, through a white shadowless void, with only the back of the man in front of him dimly visible, Bruckman felt more than ever like a ghost, suspended bodiless in some limbo between Heaven and Earth. Only the bite of pebbles and cinders into his raw, bleeding feet kept him anchored to the world, and he clung to the pain as a lifeline, fighting to shake off a feeling of numbness and unreality. However strange, however outré, the events of the previous night had *happened*. To doubt it, to wonder now if it had all been a feverish dream brought on by starvation and exhaustion, was to take the first step on the road to becoming a *Musselmänn*.

Wernecke is a vampire, he told himself. That was the harsh, unyielding reality that, like the reality of the camp itself, must be faced. Was it any more surreal, any more impossible, than the nightmare around them? He must forget the tales his old grandmother had told him as a boy, "bogey-tales" as Wernecke himself had called them, half-remembered tales that turned his knees to water whenever he thought of the blood smeared on Wernecke's mouth, whenever he thought of Wernecke's eyes watching him in the dark. . . .

"Wake up, Jew!" the guard alongside him snarled, whacking him lightly on the arm with his rifle-butt. Bruckman stumbled, managed to stay upright and keep going. Yes, he thought, wake up. Wake up to the reality of this, just as you once had to wake up to the reality of the camp. It was just one more unpleasant fact he would have to adapt to, learn to deal with. . . .

Deal with how? he thought, and shivered.

By the time they reached the quarry, the mist had burned off, swirling past them in rags and tatters, and it was already beginning to get hot. There was Wernecke, his balding head gleaming dully in the harsh morning light. He didn't dissolve in the sunlight, there was one bogey-tale disproved. . . .

They set to work, like golems, like ragtag clockwork automatons. 233

Lack of sleep had drained what small reserves of strength Bruckman had, and the work was very hard for him that day. He had learned long ago all the tricks of timing and misdirection, the safe ways to snatch short moments of rest, the ways to do a minimum of work with the maximum display of effort, the ways to keep the guards from noticing you, to fade into the faceless crowd of prisoners and not be singled out, but today his head was muzzy and slow, and none of the tricks seemed to work.

His body felt like a sheet of glass, fragile, ready to shatter into dust, and the painful, arthritic slowness of his movements got him first shouted at, and then knocked down. The guard kicked him twice for good measure before he could get up.

When Bruckman had climbed back to his feet again, he saw that Wernecke was watching him, face blank, eyes expressionless, a look that could have meant anything at all.

Bruckman felt the blood trickling from the corner of his mouth and thought, *the blood . . . he's watching the blood . . .* and once again he shivered.

Somehow, Bruckman forced himself to work faster, and although his muscles blazed with pain, he wasn't hit again, and the day passed.

When they formed up to go back to the camp, Bruckman, almost unconsciously, made sure that he was in a different line from Wernecke.

That night in the cabin, Bruckman watched as Wernecke talked with the other men, here trying to help a new man named Melnick — no more than a boy — adjust to the dreadful reality of the camp, there exhorting someone who was slipping into despair to live and spite his tormentors, joking with old hands in the flat, black, bitter way that passed for humor among them, eliciting a wan smile or occasionally even a laugh from them, finally leading them all in prayer again, his strong, calm voice raised in the ancient words, giving meaning to those words again. . . .

He keeps us together, Bruckman thought, he keeps us going. Without him, we wouldn't last a week. Surely that's worth a little blood, a bit from each man, not even enough to hurt. . . . Surely they wouldn't even begrudge him it, if they knew and really understood. . . . No, he *is* a good man, better than the rest of us, in spite of his terrible affliction.

Bruckman had been avoiding Wernecke's eyes, hadn't spoken to him at all that day, and suddenly felt a wave of shame go through him at the thought of how shabbily he had been treating his friend. Yes, his friend, regardless, the man who had saved his life. . . .

Deliberately, he caught Wernecke's eyes, and nodded, and then somewhat sheepishly, smiled. After a moment, Wernecke smiled back, and Bruckman felt a spreading warmth and relief uncoil his guts. Everything was going to be all right, as all right as it could be, here. . . .

Nevertheless, as soon as the inside lights clicked off that night, and Bruckman found himself lying alone in the darkness, his flesh began to crawl.

He had been unable to keep his eyes open a moment before, but now, in the sudden darkness, he found himself tensely and tickingly awake. Where was Wernecke? What was he doing, who was he visiting tonight? Was he out there in the darkness even now, creeping closer, creeping nearer . . . ? Stop it, Bruckman told himself uneasily, forget the bogey-tales. This is your friend, a good man, not a monster. . . . But he couldn't control the fear that made the small hairs on his arms stand bristlingly erect, couldn't stop the grisly images from coming. . . .

Wernecke's eyes, gleaming in the darkness. . . . Was the blood already glistening on Wernecke's lips, as he drank . . . ? The thought of the blood staining Wernecke's yellowing teeth made Bruckman cold and nauseous, but the image that he couldn't get out of his mind tonight was an image of Josef toppling over in that sinisterly boneless way, striking his head against the floor. . . . Bruckman had seen people die in many more gruesome ways during his time at the camp, seen people shot, beaten to death, seen them die in convulsions from high fevers or cough their lungs up in bloody tatters from pneumonia, seen them hanging like charred-black scarecrows from the electrified fences, seen them torn apart by dogs . . . but somehow it was Josef's soft, passive, almost restful slumping into death that bothered him. That, and the obscene limpness of Josef's limbs as he sprawled there like a discarded rag doll, his pale and haggard face gleaming reproachfully in the dark. . . .

When Bruckman could stand it no longer, he got shakily to his feet and moved off through the shadows, once again not knowing where he was going or what he was going to do, but drawn forward by some obscure instinct he himself did not understand. This time he went cautiously, feeling his way and trying to be silent, expecting every second to see Wernecke's coal-black shadow rise up before him.

He paused, a faint noise scratching at his ears, then went on again, even more cautiously, crouching low, almost crawling across the grimy floor.

Whatever instinct had guided him — sounds heard and interpreted subliminally, perhaps?—it had timed his arrival well. Wernecke had someone down on the floor there, perhaps someone he had seized and dragged away from the huddled mass of sleepers on one of the sleeping platforms, someone from the outer edge of bodies whose presence would not be missed, or perhaps someone who had gone to sleep on the floor, seeking solitude or greater comfort.

Whoever he was, he struggled in Wernecke's grip, but Wernecke handled him easily, almost negligently, in a manner that spoke of great physical power. Bruckman could hear the man trying to scream, but Wernecke had one hand on his throat, half-throttling him, and all that would come out was a sort of whistling gasp. The man thrashed in Wernecke's hands like a kite in a child's hands flapping in the wind, and, moving deliberately, Wernecke smoothed him out like a kite, pressing him slowly flat on the floor.

Then Wernecke bent over him, and lowered his mouth to his throat.

Bruckman watched in horror, knowing that he should shout, scream, try to rouse the other prisoners, but somehow unable to move, unable to make his mouth open, his lungs pump. He was paralyzed by fear, like a rabbit in the presence of a predator, a terror sharper and more intense than any he'd ever known.

The man's struggles were growing weaker, and Wernecke must have eased up some on the throttling pressure of his hand, because the man moaned "Don't . . . please don't . . ." in a weak, slurred voice. The man had been drumming his fists against Wernecke's back and sides, but now the tempo of the drumming slowed, slowed, and then stopped, the man's arms falling laxly to the floor. "Don't . . ." the man whispered; he groaned and muttered incomprehensibly for a moment or two longer, then became silent. The silence stretched out for a minute, two, three, and Wernecke still crouched over his victim, who was now not moving at all. . . .

Wernecke stirred, a kind of shudder going through him, like a cat stretching. He stood up. His face became visible as he straightened up into the full light from the window, and there was blood on it, glistening black under the harsh glare of the kliegs. As Bruckman watched, Wernecke began to lick his lips clean, his tongue, also black in this light, sliding like some sort of sinuous ebony snake around the rim of his mouth, darting and probing for the last lingering drops. . . .

How smug he looks, Bruckman thought, like a cat who has found the cream, and the anger that flashed through him at the thought enabled him to move and speak again. "Wernecke," he said harshly.

Wernecke glanced casually in his direction. "You again, Isadore?" Wernecke said. "Don't you ever sleep?" Wernecke spoke lazily, quizzically, without surprise, and Bruckman wondered if Wernecke had know all along that he was there. "Or do you just enjoy watching me?"

"Lies," Bruckman said. "You told me nothing but lies. Why did you bother?"

"You were excited," Wernecke said. "You had surprised me. It seemed best to tell you what you wanted to hear. If it satisfied you, then that was an easy solution to the problem."

" 'Never have I drained the life from someone who wanted to live,'" Bruckman said bitterly, mimicking Wernecke. " 'Only a little from each man.' My God—and I believed you! I even felt sorry for you!"

Wernecke shrugged. "Most of it *was* true. Usually I only take a little from each man, softly and carefully, so that they never know, so that in the morning they are only a little weaker than they would have been anyway. . . ."

"Like Josef?" Bruckman said angrily. "Like the poor devil you killed tonight?"

Wernecke shrugged again. "I have been careless the last few nights, I admit. But I need to build up my strength again." His eyes gleamed in the darkness. "Events are coming to a head here. Can't you feel it, Isadore, can't you sense it? Soon the war will be over, everyone knows that. Before then, this camp will be shut down, and the Nazis will move us back into the interior—either that, or kill us. I have grown weak here, and I will soon need all my strength to survive, to take whatever opportunity presents itself to escape. I *must* be ready. And so I have let myself drink deeply again, drink my fill for the first time in months. . . ." Wernecke licked his lips again, perhaps unconsciously, then smiled bleakly at Bruckman. "You don't appreciate my restraint, Isadore. You don't understand how hard it has been for me to hold back, to take only a little each night. You don't understand how much that restraint has cost me. . . ."

"You are gracious," Bruckman sneered.

Wernecke laughed. "No, but I am a rational man; I pride myself on that. You other prisoners were my only source of food, and I have had to be very careful to make sure that you would last. I have no access to the Nazis, after all. I *am* trapped here, a prisoner just like you, whatever else you may believe—and I have not only had to find ways to survive here in the camp, I have had to procure my own food as well! No shepherd has ever watched over his flock more tenderly than I."

"Is that all we are to you—sheep? Animals to be slaughtered?" Wernecke smiled. "Precisely."

When he could control his voice enough to speak, Bruckman said, "You're worse than the Nazis."

"I hardly think so," Wernecke said quietly, and for a moment he looked tired, as though something unimaginably old and unutterably weary had looked out through his eyes. "This camp was built by the Nazis—it wasn't *my* doing. The Nazis sent you here—not I. The Nazis have tried to kill you every day since, in one way or another—and I have tried to keep you alive, even at some risk to myself. No one has more of a vested interest in the survival of his livestock than the farmer, after all, even if he does occasionally slaughter an inferior animal. I have given you food—"

"Food you had no use for yourself! You sacrificed nothing!"

"That's true, of course. But *you* needed it, remember that. Whatever my motives, I have helped you to survive here—you and many others. By doing so I also acted in my own self-interest, of course, but can you have experienced this camp and still believe in things like altruism? What difference does it make what my reason for helping was—I still helped you, didn't I?"

"Sophistries!" Bruckman said. "Rationalizations! You twist words to justify yourself, but you can't disguise what you really are—a monster!"

Wernecke smiled gently, as though Bruckman's words amused him, and made as if to pass by, but Bruckman raised an arm to bar his way. They did not touch each other, but Wernecke stopped short, and a new and quivering kind of tension sprang into existence in the air between them.

"I'll stop you," Bruckman said. "Somehow I'll stop you, I'll keep you from doing this terrible thing—"

"You'll do nothing," Wernecke said. His voice was hard and cold and flat, like a rock speaking. "What can you do? Tell the other prisoners? Who would believe you? They'd think you'd gone insane. Tell the *Nazis*, then?" Wernecke laughed harshly. "They'd think you'd gone crazy too, and they'd take you to the hospital—and I don't have to tell you what your chances of getting out of there alive are, do I? No, you'll do *nothing*."

Wernecke took a step forward; his eyes were shiny and blank and hard, like ice, like the pitiless eyes of a predatory bird, and Bruckman felt a sick rush of fear cut through his anger. Bruckman gave way, stepping backward involuntarily, and Wernecke pushed past him, seeming to brush him aside without touching him.

Once past, Wernecke turned to stare at Bruckman, and Bruckman had to summon up all the defiance that remained in him not to look uneasily away from Wernecke's agate-hard eyes. "You are the strongest and cleverest of all the other animals, Isadore," Wernecke said in a calm, conversational, almost ruminative voice. "You have been useful to me. Every shepherd needs a good sheepdog. I still need you, to help me manage the others, and to help me keep them going long enough to serve my needs. This is the reason why I have taken so much time with you, instead of just killing you outright." He shrugged. "So let us both be rational about this—you leave me alone, Isadore, and I will leave you alone also. We will stay away from each other and look after our own affairs. Yes?"

"The others. . . ." Bruckman said weakly.

"They must look after themselves," Wernecke said. He smiled, a thin and almost invisible motion of his lips. "What did I teach you, Isadore? Here everyone must look after themselves. What difference does it make what happens to the others? In a few weeks almost all of them will be dead anyway."

"You *are* a monster," Bruckman said.

"I'm not much different from you, Isadore. The strong survive, whatever the cost."

"I am *nothing* like you," Bruckman said, with loathing.

"No?" Wernecke asked, ironically, and moved away; within a few paces he was hobbling and stooping, vanishing into the shadows, once more the harmless old Jew.

Bruckman stood motionless for a moment, and then, moving slowly and reluctantly, he stepped across to where Wernecke's victim lay.

It was one of the new men Wernecke had been talking to earlier in the evening, and, of course, he was quite dead.

Shame and guilt took Bruckman then, emotions he thought he had forgotten—black and strong and bitter, they shook him by the throat the way Wernecke had shaken the new man.

Bruckman couldn't remember returning across the room to his sleeping platform, but suddenly he was there, lying on his back and staring into the stifling darkness, surrounded by the moaning, thrashing, stinking mass of sleepers. His hand were clasped protectively over his throat, although he couldn't remember putting them there, and he was shivering convulsively. How many mornings had he awoken with a dull ache in his neck, thinking it no more than the habitual body-aches and strained muscles they had all learned to take for granted? How many nights had Wernecke fed on *him?*

Every time Bruckman closed his eyes he would see Wernecke's

face floating there in the luminous darkness behind his eyelids . . . Wernecke with his eyes half-closed, his face vulpine and cruel and satiated . . . Wernecke's face moving closer and closer to him, his eyes opening like black pits, his lips smiling back from his teeth . . . Wernecke's lips, sticky and red with blood . . . and then Bruckman would seem to feel the wet touch of Wernecke's lips on *his* throat, feel Wernecke's teeth biting into *his* flesh, and Bruckman's eyes would fly open again. Staring into the darkness. Nothing there. Nothing there *yet*. . . .

Dawn was a dirty gray imminence against the cabin window before Bruckman could force himself to lower his shielding arms from his throat, and once again he had not slept at all.

That day's work was a nightmare of pain and exhaustion for Bruckman, harder than anything he had known since his first few days at the camp. Somehow he forced himself to get up, somehow he stumbled outside and up the path to the quarry, seeming to float along high off the ground, his head a bloated balloon, his feet a thousand miles away at the end of boneless beanstalk legs he could barely control at all. Twice he fell, and was kicked several times before he could drag himself back to his feet and lurch forward again. The sun was coming up in front of them, a hard red disk in a sickly yellow sky, and to Bruckman it seemed to be a glazed and lidless eye staring dispassionately into the world to watch them flail and struggle and die, like the eye of a scientist peering into a laboratory maze.

He watched the disk of the sun as he stumbled toward it; it seemed to bob and shimmer with every painful step, expanding, swelling and bloating until it swallowed the sky. . . .

Then he was picking up a rock, moaning with the effort, feeling the rough stone tear his hands. . . .

Reality began to slide away from Bruckman. There were long periods when the world was blank, and he would come slowly back to himself as if from a great distance, and hear his own voice speaking words that he could not understand, or keening mindlessly, or grunting in a hoarse, animalistic way, and he would find that his body was working mechanically, stooping and lifting and carrying, all without volition. . . .

A *Musselmänn*, Bruckman thought, I'm becoming a *Musselmänn* . . . and felt a chill of fear sweep through him. He fought to hold onto the world, afraid that the next time he slipped away from himself he would not come back, deliberately banging his hands into the rocks, cutting himself, clearing his head with pain.

The world steadied around him. A guard shouted a hoarse admonishment at him and slapped his rifle-butt, and Bruckman forced himself to work faster, although he could not keep himself from weeping silently with the pain his movements cost him.

He discovered that Wernecke was watching him, and stared back defiantly, the bitter tears still runneling his dirty cheeks, thinking, *I won't become a* Musselmänn *for you, I won't make it easy for you, I won't provide another helpless victim for you.* . . . Wernecke met Bruckman's gaze for a moment, and then shrugged and turned away.

Bruckman bent for another stone, feeling the muscles in his back crack and the pain drive in like knives. What had Wernecke been thinking, behind the blankness of his expressionless face? Had Wernecke, sensing weakness, marked Bruckman for his next victim? Had Wernecke been disappointed or dismayed by the strength of Bruckman's will to survive? Would Wernecke now settle upon someone else?

The morning passed, and Bruckman grew feverish again. He could feel the fever in his face, making his eyes feel sandy and hot, pulling the skin taut over his cheekbones, and he wondered how long he could manage to stay on his feet. To falter, to grow weak and insensible, was certain death; if the Nazis didn't kill him, Wernecke would. . . . Wernecke was out of sight now, on the other side of the quarry, but it seemed to Bruckman that Wernecke's hard and flinty eyes were everywhere, floating in the air around him, looking out momentarily from the back of a Nazi soldier's head, watching him from the dulled iron side of a quarry cart, peering at him from a dozen different angles. He bent ponderously for another rock, and when he had pried it up from the earth he found Wernecke's eyes beneath it, staring unblinkingly up at him from the damp and pallid soil. . . .

That afternoon there were great flashes of light on the eastern horizon, out across the endless flat expanse of the steppe, flares in rapid sequence that lit up the sullen gray sky, all without sound. The Nazi guards had gathered together in a group, looking to the east and talking in subdued voices, ignoring the prisoners for the moment. For the first time Bruckman noticed how disheveled and unshaven the guards had become in the last few days, as though they had given up, as though they no longer cared. Their faces were strained and tight, and more than one of them seemed to be fascinated by the leaping fires on the distant edge of the world.

Melnick said that it was only a thunderstorm, but old Bohme said that it was an artillery battle being fought, and that that meant that the Russians were coming, that soon they would all be liberated.

Bohme grew so excited at the thought that he began shouting, "The Russians! It's the Russians! The Russians are coming to free us!" Dichstein and Melnick tried to hush him, but Bohme continued to caper and shout—doing a grotesque kind of jig while he yelled and flapped his arms—until he had attracted the attention of the guards. Infuriated, two of the guards fell upon Bohme and beat him severely, striking him with their rifle-butts with more than usual force, knocking him to the ground, continuing to flail at him and kick him while he was down, Bohme writhing like an injured worm under their stamping boots. They probably would have beaten Bohme to death on the spot, but Wernecke organized a distraction among some of the other prisoners, and when the guards moved away to deal with it, Wernecke helped Bohme to stand up and hobble away to the other side of the quarry, where the rest of the prisoners shielded him from sight with their bodies as best they could for the rest of the afternoon.

Something about the way Wernecke urged Bohme to his feet and helped him to limp and lurch away, something about the protective, possessive curve of Wernecke's arm around Bohme's shoulders, told Bruckman that Wernecke had selected his next victim.

That night Bruckman vomited up the meager and rancid meal that they were allowed, his stomach convulsing uncontrollably after the first few bites. Trembling with hunger and exhaustion and fever, he leaned against the wall and watched as Wernecke fussed over Bohme, nursing him as a man might nurse a sick child, talking gently to him, wiping away some of the blood that still oozed from the corner of Bohme's mouth, coaxing Bohme to drink a few sips of soup, finally arranging that Bohme should stretch out on the floor away from the sleeping platforms, where he would not be jostled by the others. . . .

As soon as the interior lights went out that night, Bruckman got up, crossed the floor quickly and unhesitantly, and lay down in the shadows near the spot where Bohme muttered and twitched and groaned.

Shivering, Bruckman lay in the darkness, the strong smell of earth in his nostrils, waiting for Wernecke to come. . . .

In Bruckman's hand, held close to his chest, was a spoon that had been sharpened to a jagged needle point, a spoon he had stolen and begun to sharpen while he was still in a civilian prison in

Cologne, so long ago that he almost couldn't remember, scraping it back and forth against the stone wall of his cell every night for hours, managing to keep it hidden on his person during the nightmarish ride in the sweltering boxcar, the first few terrible days at the camp, telling no one about it, not even Wernecke during the months when he'd thought of Wernecke as a kind of saint, keeping it hidden long after the possibility of escape had become too remote even to fantasize about, retaining it then more as a tangible link with the daydream country of his past than as a tool he ever actually hoped to employ, cherishing it almost as a holy relic, as a remnant of a vanished world that he otherwise might almost believe had never existed at all. . . .

And now that it was time to use it at last, he was almost reluctant to do so, to soil it with another man's blood. . . .

He fingered the spoon compulsively, turning it over and over; it was hard and smooth and cold, and he clenched it as tightly as he could, trying to ignore the fine tremoring of his hands.

He had to kill Wernecke. . . .

Nausea and an odd feeling of panic flashed through Bruckman at the thought, but there was no other choice, there was no other way. . . . He couldn't go on like this, his strength was failing; Wernecke was killing him, as surely as he had killed the others, just by keeping him from sleeping. . . . And as long as Wernecke lived, he would never be safe, always there would be the chance that Wernecke would come for *him*, that Wernecke would strike as soon as his guard was down. . . . Would Wernecke scruple for a second to kill *him*, after all, if he thought that he could do it safely . . . ? No, of course not. . . . Given the chance, Wernecke would kill him without a moment's further thought. . . . No, he must strike *first*. . . .

Bruckman licked his lips uneasily. Tonight. He had to kill Wernecke tonight. . . .

There was a stirring, a rustling: someone was getting up, working his way free from the mass of sleepers on one of the platforms. A shadowy figure crossed the room toward Bruckman, and Bruckman tensed, reflexively running his thumb along the jagged end of the spoon, readying himself to rise, to strike — but at the last second, the figure veered aside and stumbled toward another corner. There was a sound like rain drumming on cloth; the man swayed there for a moment, mumbling, and then slowly returned to his pallet, dragging his feet, as if he had pissed his very life away against the wall. It was not Wernecke.

Bruckman eased himself back down to the floor, his heart seeming

243

to shake his wasted body back and forth with the force of its beating. His hand was damp with sweat. He wiped it against his tattered pants, and then clutched the spoon again. . . .

Time seemed to stop. Bruckman waited, stretched out along the hard floorboards, the raw wood rasping his skin, dust clogging his mouth and nose, feeling as though he were already dead, a corpse laid out in a rough pine coffin, feeling eternity pile up on his chest like heavy clots of wet black earth. . . . Outside the hut, the kliegs blazed, banishing night, abolishing it, but here inside the hut it was night, here night survived, perhaps the only pocket of night remaining on a klieg-lit planet, the shafts of light that came in through the slatted window only serving to accentuate the surrounding darkness, to make it greater and more puissant by comparison. . . . Here in the darkness, nothing ever changed . . . there was only the smothering heat, and the weight of eternal darkness, and the changeless moments that could not pass because there was nothing to differentiate them one from the other. . . .

Many times as he waited Bruckman's eyes would grow heavy and slowly close, but each time his eyes would spring open again at once, and he would find himself staring into the shadows for Wernecke. Sleep would no longer have him, it was a kingdom closed to him now; it spat him out each time he tried to enter it, just as his stomach now spat out the food he placed in it. . . .

The thought of food brought Bruckman to a sharper awareness, and there in the darkness he huddled around his hunger, momentarily forgetting everything else. Never had he been so hungry. . . . He thought of the food he had wasted earlier in the evening, and only the last few shreds of his self-control kept him from moaning aloud.

Bohme did moan aloud then, as though unease were contagious. As Bruckman glanced at him, Bohme said "Anya," in a clear calm voice; he mumbled a little, and then, a bit more loudly, said, "Tseitel, have you set the table yet?" and Bruckman realized that Bohme was no longer in the camp, that Bohme was back in Düsseldorf in the tiny apartment with his fat wife and his four healthy children, and Bruckman felt a pang of envy go through him, for Bohme, who had escaped.

It was at that moment that Bruckman realized that Wernecke was standing there, just beyond Bohme.

There had been no movement that Bruckman had seen. Wernecke had seemed to slowly materialize from the darkness, atom by atom, bit by incremental bit, until at some point he had been solid enough for his presence to register on Bruckman's consciousness, so that what had been only a shadow a moment before was now suddenly and unmistakably Wernecke as well, however much a shadow it remained.

Bruckman's mouth went dry with terror, and it almost seemed that he could hear the voice of his dead grandmother whispering in his ears. Bogey-tales. . . . Wernecke had said *I'm no night-spirit*. Remember that he had said that. . . .

Wernecke was almost close enough to touch. He was staring down at Bohme; his face, lit by a dusty shaft of light from the window, was cold and remote, only the total lack of expression hinting at the passion that strained and quivered behind the mask. Slowly, lingeringly, Wernecke stooped over Bohme. "Anya," Bohme said again, caressingly, and then Wernecke's mouth was on his throat.

Let him feed, said a cold remorseless voice in Bruckman's mind. It will be easier to take him when he's nearly sated, when he's fully preoccupied and growing lethargic and logy. . . . Growing *full*. . . .

Slowly, with infinite caution, Bruckman gathered himself to spring, watching in horror and fascination as Wernecke fed. He could hear Wernecke sucking the juice out of Bohme, as if there was not enough blood in the foolish old man to satiate him, as if there was not enough blood in the whole camp. . . . Or perhaps the whole world. . . . And now Bohme was ceasing his feeble struggling, was becoming still. . . .

Bruckman flung himself upon Wernecke, stabbing him twice in the back before his weight bowled them both over. There was a moment of confusion as they rolled and struggled together, all without sound, and then Bruckman found himself sitting atop Wernecke, Wernecke's white face turned up to him. Bruckman drove his weapon into Wernecke again, the shock of the blow jarring Bruckman's arm to the shoulder. Wernecke made no outcry; his eyes were already glazing, but they looked at Bruckman with recognition, with cold anger, with bitter irony, and, oddly, with what might have been resignation or relief, with what might almost have been pity. . . . Bruckman stabbed again and again, driving the blows home with hysterical strength, panting, rocking atop his victim, feeling Wernecke's blood splatter against his face, wrapped in the heat and steam that rose from Wernecke's torn-open body like a smothering black cloud, coughing and choking on it for a moment, feeling the steam seep in through his pores and sink deep into the marrow of his bones, feeling the world seem to pulse and shimmer and change around him, as though he were suddenly seeing through new eyes, as though something had been born anew inside him, and then abruptly he was *smelling* Wernecke's blood, the hot organic reek of it, leaning closer to drink in that sudden overpowering smell, better than the smell of freshly-baked bread, better than anything he could remember, rich and heady and strong beyond imagining.

There was a moment of revulsion and horror, and he had time to wonder how long the ancient contamination had been passing from man to man to man, how far into the past the chain of lives stretched, how Wernecke himself had been trapped, and then his parched lips touched wetness, and he was drinking, drinking deeply and greedily, and his mouth was filled with the strong clean taste of copper.

DOWN AMONG THE DEAD MEN

I don't remember the exact genesis of this idea. I do know that at some time during the '70s, probably the later '70s, I jotted the following sentence down in my story-idea notebook: "vampire in death camp, during Second World War."

And there it stayed, for years, until one night when Jack was down in Philadelphia for a visit—my calendar shows that it was March 6, 1981—and we were sitting around brainstorming in my rundown old apartment on Quince Street.

If you've thumbed through the book of photographs called *The Faces of Science Fiction,* you've seen that apartment. There I am, sitting on the sofa, looking bloated and glaze-eyed and stuffed, like an exhibit in some diorama in a museum case in the future, labeled SQUALID TWENTIETH-CENTURY URBAN DWELLER, and around me in all its cluttered glory spreads the living room of my Quince Street place. It was a cramped and uncomfortable apartment in many ways, but some good memories attach to it as well—it was there (or on the surrounding stoops and stairs of the neighborhood, when it got too hot inside) that I wrote all of the stories in this book (or, at least, worked on *my* parts of them), and we came up with the ideas for almost all of them right there in that rundown living room, too.

On this occasion, Jack and I were sitting in the living room with a bottle of wine, kicking around potential ideas for collaborative stories. I got my notebook out and started throwing ideas from it out at Jack; one of them was the vampire sentence I mentioned above. Jack took fire with that idea at once. We talked about the overall plot for a half hour or so, brainstorming, kicking it back and forth, and then Jack got up, sat down behind my ancient, massive

Remington office-model standup manual typewriter, which lived on one side of my somewhat-unsteady kitchen table—if you pounded the keys hard, as I'd learned to do as an old-style newspaperman before the days of computer terminals, the table actually swayed slightly with the rhythm of your typing, and the keys clacked and *ratatattatted* in a loud and gratifying way—and started writing the story.

Jack wrote like a madman for several hours, steam practically coming out of his ears, and by the time he stood up again, he had finished a rough draft of about the first nine manuscript pages, carrying the story through the brilliant Passover scene, which was entirely of his own devising.

Then he left for Binghamton, and the ball was in my court. I worked extensively on the story for a week or so, and then worked on it off and on for the next couple of months, with one hurried story conference with Jack at that year's Nebula Banquet to hammer out a plot problem, and the passing back and forth by mail of several different drafts of one particularly difficult scene—the final encounter between Wernecke and Bruckman—toward the story's end. It was finished on May 9, 1981.

The question of identity, it seems to me, is at the core of the story. Wernecke is perceived by the Nazis as a Jew, in spite of being a supernatural monster, and so that's the way they treat him, no better or worse than the other prisoners. We are what other people think we are, to some extent, whether we want to be or not. The real meat of the story for me is in the two long conversations between Wernecke and Bruckman, and those were the most difficult scenes to write in many ways.

We decided to call the story "Down Among The Dead Men," a line from an old English folksong that I'd always wanted to use as a title; it certainly seemed to fit the story well enough. The story bounced around for quite a while, longer than any of the other collaborations. It finally sold to *Oui*, and was later reprinted in *The Magazine of Fantasy and Science Fiction*, where its appearance prompted a major horror writer—one whose own work is pretty gore-splattered—to remark that it was the most morally offensive story he'd ever read. We were quietly proud.

This was probably the most controversial of the collaborations, and has drawn the most extreme responses—people seem either to *really* like it, or to loathe it utterly. It has been reprinted a fair number of times since, most recently in Ellen Datlow's vampire anthology *Blood Is Not Enough*.

AFTERWORD

GARDNER DOZOIS

After the beginning of 1985, there were no more collaborations. "The world is too much with us, night and noon," Wordsworth said, and, as 1985 progressed, we all became increasingly busy folk. I became editor of *Isaac Asimov's Science Fiction Magazine,* and for quite some while thereafter was too busy learning to stay afloat in the sea of paper the editor of a monthly magazine must swim through to have much time for *anything* else. (It's sadly indicative of the demands on such an editor's time that I've only been able to produce two short stories since taking the job, five years ago; neither of them happened to be a collaborative project.) Jack too became involved in a job that ate increasing amounts of his time; what writing time he did have left he devoted first to completing his brilliant mainstream novel *Counting Coup* (shamefully as yet unsold —wake up, publishers!) and then to the writing of a 1,000-page-plus historical fantasy about Leonardo Da Vinci (which, I'm glad to say, *has* been sold). Michael and his wife Marianne Porter became the parents of a young son, Sean, and what energies Michael could thereafter spare from the demands of parenting (itself a full-time job, as any parent can attest!) went into the creation of his novel *Vacuum Flowers,* and then into his new novel *Stations of the Tide.* Susan too was busy writing a novel, a big horror novel called *The Red Carnival,* finally finished last year (and still unsold as yet, too— what's the *matter* with you book publishers out there?).

What got squeezed *out* was the time needed to do these collaborations.

There are still some collaborative projects in the pipeline, in one stage or another of completion. Michael and I have been working on and off (more off than on, alas) for years on a collaborative novella 249 called "Blind Forces"; we have about 70 pages of it competed now. Jack and I have a partial first draft of a story called "The Wall" sitting in our files, and for years now we have been taking notes for a collaborative novel, and talking about writing the "man growing young" story and "the Elvis story": we *still* discuss these projects from time to time. (Jack and I are still regularly producing co-edited *anthologies,* but that's not quite the same thing.) Every so often, Susan and I talk about doing another collaboration, and one time Susan, Jack, and I even spent an evening talking about a novel-length expansion of "The Clowns." A children's book written by Jack, Michael, and me exists, and has been sporadically making the rounds for a while now, so far with no takers. I have about 80 pages of a collaborative novel with George R.R. Martin, called *Shadow Twin,* sitting in my files; not only did we go so far as to outline the book, we even drew a fucking *map* of the planet it takes place on! Jeez.

But, so far, the world is still too much with us all, and there those projects sit, gathering dust in the files.

Some of these projects may eventually be finished, if the gods spare us for long enough. I suspect that others of them will never be finished, and will be being poked at and pored over by students in search of obscure material for offbeat doctoral dissertations long after all of us are dead.

Whatever happens, our first cycle of fiction collaborations is clearly at an end—the last story to appear was a collaboration with Susan, written long before, that appeared in *The Twilight Zone Magazine* in 1987—and this book is its record and its memorial.

Looking back at the collaborations, I don't at all regret the time we spent on them, even leaving considerations of money and exposure aside. We managed to all remain friends *and* produce worthwhile collaborative work, even while doing three-way collaborations with various changes in cast. It seems to me that all of these stories are at the least competent entertainment, stories that helped to convince the reader of whatever magazine or anthology they appeared in that it had been worth spending the money to buy it in the first place; a few of them may be more than that, and last longer—but that's not for me to say.

I do think that in almost all the collaborations we managed to combine our strengths as writers rather than our weaknesses, and produced stories that *none* of us would have been able to write—or would have written—on our own.

And that, surely, is the point of collaborating in the first place.

OTHER
COLLABORATIONS

"The Apotheosis of Isaac Rosen," by Jack Dann and
  Jeanne Van Buren Dann.
    Omni, June 1987.
"Blues and the Abstract Truth," by Jack Dann and Barry N. Malzberg.
    Lord John 10.
"Bringing It Home" by Jack Dann and Barry N. Malzberg.
    Twilight Zone Magazine,, February 1987.
"Dogfight," by Michael Swanwick and William Gibson.
    Burning Chrome.
"The Funny Trick They Played on Old McBundy's Son,"
  by George Alec Effinger and Jack C. Haldeman II.
    Night Cry, Summer 1986.
"High Steel," Jack Dann and Jack C. Haldeman II.
    Magazine of Fantasy and Science Fiction, February 1982.
"Limits," Jack Dann and Jack C. Haldeman II.
    Fantastic, May 1976.
Nightmare Blue, by Gardner Dozois and George Alec Effinger,
    Berkley, 1975.
"Parables of Art," by Jack Dann and Barry N. Malzberg.
    New Dimensions 12.
"Sentry," Jack Dann and Jack C. Haldeman II.
    Twilight Zone Magazine, February 1987.

■
■
■
■
■

252

SLOW DANCING THROUGH TIME

by Gardner Dozois,
in collaboration with
Jack Dann, Michael Swanwick, Susan Casper, and Jack C. Haldeman II.

The text type for the stories and the story afterwords is Elante, Agfa Compugraphic's version of W. A. Dwiggins classic typeface Electra, originally designed for the Mergenthaler Linotype Company, and first made available in 1935. Electra cannot be classified as either "modern" or "old-style." It is not based on any historical model, and therefore does not echo any particular period or style of type design. It avoids the extreme contrast between thick and thin elements that marks most modern faces, and is without eccentricities that interfere with reading. In general, Electra is a simple, readable typeface that attempts to give a feeling of fluidity, power, and speed.

The text type for the introductory material, and the individual author's commentaries is Univers Medium, first released in 1956 by designer Adrian Frutiger. The titles for all the pieces are all set in different weights of the Univers family.

The type was set by Jeff Levin of Pendragon Graphics in Beaverton, Oregon, on a Compugraphic MCS/8400 digital typesetting system.

Slow Dancing through Time is printed on 60# Acid-Free Natural stock and is fully-sewn & clothbound for durability and longevity.

Jacket and jacket typography design are by Arnie Fenner. Interior book design by Jim Loehr.